THE MECHANICS' IN
ISSUE 11 AUTUMN 2

G000144226

The first Mechanics' Institute in London was founded in 1823 by George Birkbeck. "Mechanics" then meant skilled artisans, and the purpose of the Institute was to instruct them in the principles behind their craft. The Institute became Birkbeck College, part of London University, in 1920 but still maintains one foot in the academy and one in the outside world.

**The
Mechanics'
Institute
REVIEW**

The Mechanics' Institute Review
Issue 11 Autumn 2014

The Mechanics' Institute Review is published by MA Creative
Writing, Department of English and Humanities, School
of Arts, Birkbeck, University of London, Malet Street,
Bloomsbury, London WC1E 7HX

ISBN 978-0-9575833-2-0

Project Director: Julia Bell

Editorial Team: Erica Duggan, Kate Smalley Ellis,
Kieran Falconer, Alison Hitchcock, Heidi Midtun Larsen,
Rebekah Lin, Luke Terry

The Editorial Team would like to thank Russell Celyn Jones,
Sue Tyley, Julia Bell, and Anne-Marie Taylor for making
this project possible.

For further copies or information, please contact Anne-Marie
Taylor, MA Creative Writing, Department of English and
Humanities, School of Arts, Birkbeck, University of
London, Malet Street, Bloomsbury, London, WC1E 7HX.
Tel: 020 3073 8372. Email: a.taylor@english.bbk.ac.uk

Website: http://www.writershub.co.uk/mir.php

Printed and bound by Berforts Limited, 17 Burgess Road,
Hastings TN35 4NR

Cover design, quotations design and typesetting by
Raffaele Teo

The Mechanics' Institute Review is typeset in Book Antiqua

TABLE OF CONTENTS

Introduction: Wild Stories

JULIA BELL

The short story, that troublesome sliver of prose, is a difficult form to define. It allegedly makes no money for publishers, and yet it can create literary reputations – think of Raymond Carver, Lydia Davis, Kevin Barry, George Saunders, Katherine Mansfield, Anton Chekhov, Amy Hempel, Jorge Luis Borges. But no sooner have you defined it – a short story should be all show not tell, it should have a lyrical ending – than someone comes along and contradicts your newly minted orthodoxy with a piece that is only two lines long or that tells the events backwards or that crams a whole life story into four pages.

In Lydia Davis's most recent collection, *Can't and Won't*, there is a piece called "Housekeeping Observation" which is one sentence long:

> Under all this dirt
> the floor is really very clean.

Is this really a short story, we ask ourselves, or more of a wry observation? A short story should offer more than this, say the purists who want neat endings and epiphanies, and perhaps yes, Lydia Davis is a horrible example to give students as it can sometimes just generate fatuous and belligerent art-school imitations of the "I don't have to try harder so there" variety.

For me the joy of the short story lies in its wildness, in its licence to be anything. We pretend to say the same of the novel, but in reality the novel is more like a huge container ship: it goes slowly in the direction of travel, it needs plenty of open ocean around it, overload it with too many ideas and it sinks. The short story, however, because of its brevity, is light and quick to manoeuvre and, if it capsizes, easy to right with an edit or a new sheet of blank paper and nothing much is lost.

Perhaps it's because, as a prose form, it belongs more to the poem than the novel. William Carlos Williams said of the difference between prose and poetry: "Prose may carry a load of ill-defined matters like a ship. But poetry is the machine which drives it, pruned to a perfect economy. As in all machines its movement is intrinsic, undulant, a physical more than a literary character." This physical machine that drives a poem drives all good short stories, too – they can be moments of thought, ideas, all character, no character, in a space out of time, in a moment of time – and all the best ones are driven by a linguistic engine. The exact right words in the exact right order, and in an age where novels are increasingly driven by plot and are in competition with films, box sets and the infinite distractions of the Internet, a short story can offer a moment of pure literary pleasure. It doesn't have to meet the need for high concept, or generic structure; it can be about a short walk across an empty room if the writing is interesting and alive enough.

It might be useful here to consider what I mean by literary pleasure. In her essay *Writing Short Stories*, Flannery O'Connor talks about writers having the gift to "create life with words". This is essentially what a good story needs to do, however wild in its structure or subject or language: it needs to communicate lived existence to the reader, to offer up something that is an explicable version of life. The biggest lesson any writer can learn is that a piece of work, whether prose or poetry, is an *experience*. And should be for both the writer and the reader. O'Connor again, this time in her essay *The Nature and Aim of Fiction*: "Some people have the notion that you read the story and then climb out of it into the meaning, but for the fiction writer himself the whole story is the meaning, because it is an experience, not an abstraction."

The experiential nature of a good short story is easy to show by encouraging the writer to read, but hard to effect in the writing. Levers that might work for one writer – a good twist, robust characterisation, telling detail – might be lost on another kind of writer who much prefers more gauzy, poetic, Modernist stories or one-liners like Lydia Davis's, or minimalist stories, or stories like Borges's which are driven by a philosophical idea rather than by character. But the question for the writer always remains, How do I affect my reader? What effects can I employ? What sentences, scenes, lines of dialogue, descriptions will best transmit the sensibility I have in my head? How can I be seductive and get the reader to pay attention?

Raymond Carver says a short story should move us "off the peg just a little" from where we were before we started reading. It's the kind of experience one might have in front of a great painting or with a piece of music. We are stirred, perhaps challenged, confused, angry even, or moved to sympathy, empathy, pity, envy, greed – add your own abstract nouns as appropriate. Perhaps the biggest mistake a writer can commit is to inspire no response at all – to be boring.

Literature is often taught as something that must be interpreted rather than felt, and for creative writing students who are good literature students a great deal of unlearning may need to go on before they can start to write freely. To them, "literary" means achieving a certain kind of style or tone in the work. Their writing is often emulated rather than embodied. A good piece of writing remembers that words are a way of conjuring life, of delivering for a reader something that closely resembles an experience of lived life in the best and most appropriate words available to the writer. And in the same way that there can be no agreement about what constitutes a subjective experience of lived life, there are as many stories as there are writers to write them.

The short story, then, is one of the most innovative of all the prose forms. It sits between the density of the poetic and the expanse of the novel and has the most freedom to try different styles and structures. In the age of short attention spans and overwhelming digital media, the short story is undergoing something of a renaissance with more platforms, competitions and publications than ever. In the brave new digital world the clamour for the place of the short story as the torch-bearer for literary prose gets louder and louder. As novels lose their cultural capital, the short story gives us adrenalin shots of new thinking. Here is where literary prose writing is both preserved and reborn.

The Mechanics' Institute Review has been a key part of that renaissance for the past eleven years, offering a window into the work we do at Birkbeck in teaching the short story as a form. These pieces are a selection of the best writing by current students and alumni from across our MA and BA courses. They have earned their place in the anthology having been chosen by this year's editorial team from a large pool of submissions, and selected because each one in its own way offers up to the reader the sense of an encounter. There is no orthodoxy here, only the imperative to be interesting. However the writer wants to approach their storytelling is fine by us. All we ask is that they are alert to the experience of being alive, however strange, however wild.

This guy woke up to find his arm had turned into a mushroom overnight. What happened next will amaze you.

JENNIFER WHITEHEAD

The first thing that irritated Alan when he woke up on this particular Saturday morning was not that his left arm had turned into some kind of a mushroom overnight, but that he'd forgotten to unset his alarm. It went off at 6.37 a.m. when he should've been sleeping. As he stretched out what had previously been his left arm to switch the alarm off (thinking he should swap to the other side of the bed now that he no longer shared it with his girlfriend), he heard the bedside lamp clatter over and found he was unable to hit the Off button on the clock.

It took him a while to work out what was going on. He sweated in the chocolate-brown polycotton bedsheets his mother had bought him, listening to the beeps growing louder by four-beep intervals.

"I'm dreaming. I should write it down."

His fat tabby cat, Mingus, worried that Alan might drift back to sleep, jumped on his chest. Alan went to scratch the spot just above the M on Mingus's forehead where he usually loved being scratched. But on this morning Mingus drew back, narrowed his eyes and tentatively sniffed what had previously been Alan's left hand. Then he went and sat at the bottom of the bed, far from Alan's reach.

Alan looked at his left arm properly. He no longer thought he was hovering on the edge of a dream. Instead of his usual arm flesh,

5

with its fine dark hair, he saw a very pale, moleless, poreless but porous-looking substance. It wasn't quite white and it wasn't quite grey. The colour reminded him of a paint swatch his girlfriend had brought home when they'd been planning to repaint the kitchen. It was called Clunch by Farrow & Ball and it had made Alan laugh, firstly because it was called Clunch and secondly because it cost four times as much as the paint he'd suggested they use. A fortnight later his girlfriend had left him. He hadn't yet repainted the kitchen.

Where his hand used to be was a long, cap-like structure. It was darker than the rest of his former arm, and although it was fully attached, it seemed to be a separate entity. "Oh God. It looks like a glans."

Alan closed his eyes and held his breath and as lightly as he could he touched what he still thought of as his arm with the fingertips of his right hand. It felt slightly spongy. He squeezed it, gently at first, then more firmly. He couldn't feel anything that should've been there – no bones, no phalanges, no carpals, no radius. Not even a hint of ulna. He dared to open one eye, his left, and look again at the arm, running his fingertips up to the cap. It felt smoother. He snatched his right hand back in disgust.

"Double-u tee aye eff?" he said out loud, a habit he'd gotten into after his boss had introduced a swear box at the office. In a panic, Alan jumped out of bed and quickly pulled down his beige flannel pyjama pants to make sure none of his other appendages was affected. They seemed to be regular human flesh and skin. Mingus, too, jumped from the bed, and stopping only to lick his bottom vigorously, eyeing Alan as he did so, left the room.

Using his right hand, Alan hoicked his pyjama pants back up and decided that as he had no idea what to do next, he would have a cup of tea. In the kitchen he found that all his mugs were dirty. He picked up his favourite, tipped out the leftover tea, put it in the sink under the tap and turned the tap on hard, letting the water overflow before emptying it out. Ignoring the tannin-ring stain left behind, he wedged his tin of tea bags between his mushroom arm and chest, prised it open with his right hand and dropped a tea bag into the mug. Thankful that the kettle was just full enough – he could see through the limescale-coated water-level window – he switched it on, then, having filled the mug, he went back to bed while the tea steeped.

He opened his laptop and with the index finger of his right hand typed into Google arm turned.

> arm turned **black**
> arm turned **blue**
> arm turned **purple**

He looked at his arm. Not black, not blue and definitely not purple. He typed arm turned in.

> **mole on** arm turned in**to scab**
> **lump on** arm turned in**to bruise**

"Does my arm even have blood in it any more?" he said. He typed arm turned into a mushroom and pressed Enter.

One result came up. He clicked the link and was taken to a site called Landfall, which said it was a magazine published by Otago University Press, New Zealand. The page contained a précis of a story called "This guy woke up to find his arm had turned into a mushroom overnight. What happened next will amaze you." by Jennifer Whitehead. The précis read:

> Read Jennifer Whitehead's story about a man who wakes up one morning to find that his arm has turned into a mushroom.
>
> 🔒 THIS CONTENT IS FOR SUBSCRIBERS ONLY. READ THE FULL VERSION BY LOGGING IN. TO FIND OUT MORE ABOUT SUBSCRIBING CLICK HERE.

He clicked through to the subscription page.

> International subscription – 1 year rest of the world 4 issues airmail $62.

Alan was not familiar with the exchange rate for the New Zealand dollar. Even if it wasn't that high, he didn't think he wanted four issues of a New Zealand literary journal landing on his front doormat over the coming year. He clicked the Back button twice and kept searching.

He found many results about mushroom clouds but nothing further about human limbs metamorphosing into mushrooms. NHS Direct was unforthcoming on the subject. It did talk about fungal nail infections but even the worst cases of that, Alan concluded after a Google image search, seemed rather less encompassing than his condition.

So he took drastic action. He phoned the local GP surgery he had registered with four years ago but never visited. A message told him to call back later.

Alan had the feeling he wasn't doing everything he could to deal with the situation. His girlfriend would've known what to do.

He sank back against the pillows he'd propped up against the wall and nodded off. He woke again during a nightmare that his landline was ringing, and then realised it was real.

"Hello?" he said, as if it were a question, even though he knew it would be his parents.

"Did we wake you?" his father shouted.

"You've fixed your speakerphone," Alan said with a cheerfulness he did not feel.

He remembered his cup of tea and went into the kitchen, took a bottle of milk from the fridge and clamped it between his knees, using his right hand to unscrew the cap, all the while squeezing the phone between his ear and his shoulder.

"I gave your father a voucher for his birthday and he bought a new one," shouted his mother.

Alan wondered what it was his otherwise penny-pinching parents did during their weekly phone calls that made them so reluctant to embrace Skype. He suspected they didn't want him to know they were playing computer bridge at the same time as talking to him. For fun he would occasionally imagine they were concealing the fact that they phoned him while dressed in full fetish wear.

"We've just been aerating the compost heap," shouted his mother. "It was starting to get terribly whiffy."

Alan gripped his mug of tea. In spite of it retaining only a vague memory of warmth and being more red-mahogany-coloured than the antique pine he insisted upon when his colleagues did tea runs at work, he sipped it.

"How are things with you?" his mother shouted.

"Fine, thanks."

"Work OK?"

"Yes Mum. Quite busy though."

"You been putting in lots of hours, son?"

"Yes Dad."

"That's the way to avoid all this redundancy that's going around. Turn up every day, rain or shine, poorly or not."

Alan felt cross. "I might have to take Monday off, actually."

"What?"

"I'm not feeling one hundred per cent."

"Nonsense. What's wrong with you?"

"Ah, well." Alan paused. "It seems that my arm's turned into a mushroom."

"That's funny, we found some mushrooms growing in the compost heap. What did you do to make that happen?" his mother shouted.

"I don't know. I mean, nothing. I didn't do anything, it was just that way when I woke up this morning."

"Well it's never happened to your father and I."

"Your father and me," corrected his father.

"Did you bleach the shower curtain? It was very mouldy last time we were there."

"Sophie bought a new one."

"And then she left you."

Alan swigged a mouthful of brackish, almost cold tea.

"Maybe you caught it from her."

"I haven't seen her for weeks."

"Do you wash your hands after you've used the toilet?"

"Yes!" Alan answered, although he sometimes didn't bother if he'd only had a wee and the toilet seat had already been up.

"Did you eat at an Indian restaurant recently?"

"No. But they've found that's quite safe. Millions of Indians, none of them has mushroom arms."

"No need for sarcasm, I'm just trying to help," said his mother. "Maybe it was when you went on holiday to Thailand."

"That was three years ago."

"Well, it must be something you've done. No one in my family or your father's family has ever had their arm or any other limb turn into a mushroom, a toadstool or any other kind of fungus."

"OK, good to know."

Alan finished his tea in one big, unpleasant gulp.

"I'm going to go now."

"Don't take the day off work unless you're really, really sick," shouted his father.

"Thanks for calling. Bye."

Alan enjoyed the absence of his parents' voices for a few seconds, and then remembered his arm situation. It was 8.04 a.m. so he tried calling the GP again. He waited on hold for an era. Then he got through to a receptionist.

"Hello! I'd like to see a doctor."

"When did you want to come in?"

"Today, if possible."

"Is it an emergency?" the stern voice demanded.

"I'm not really sure."

"There are no appointments today but we're accepting walk-ins for emergencies between 9.15 a.m. and 9.30 a.m. Is it an emergency?"

"Well, I don't know if it's an emergency in the strict sense of the word. I can't find anything about it on Google."

"Walk-ins are for emergencies only."

Alan remembered that the government now told people they mustn't bother busy hospital A&E departments with minor broken bones or high temperatures, so he supposed his mushroom arm – which he had to admit was causing him no pain – might not be considered an emergency.

"Can I make an appointment for Monday?"

"You'll have to phone on Monday morning at 8 a.m."

"Can't I make an appointment now and cancel it if I don't need it?"

"If you want an appointment on Monday you'll need to phone on Monday morning at 8 a.m."

"But –"

"Or if it's an emergency you can come in this morning between

9.15 a.m and 9.30 a.m."

"OK. I don't think it's an emergency. But it's very strange. It's not on Google."

The line went dead. Alan put his phone down and turned to his laptop and the Landfall website. "The most important and long-lasting journal in New Zealand literature," it said. He wondered what New Zealand literature's second most important journal was.

"Maybe if I explain my situation," he thought, "they'll let me see the story for free."

He looked at the contact details. Under Editorial there were two email addresses – one for a Harry Ricketts and one for a Jane Westaway. It wasn't obvious whom he should address so he decided to try them both.

> dear Jane and Harry
> Sorry, it's not easy for me to type this, quite literally, bwcause

He deleted wcause.

> ecause I have woken up to find my left arm has turned into a mushroom overnight. The only thing I can find on the web about this is in your magazine buy

He deleted the y.

> t I don't have a subscription to Landfill and not sure it's worth signing up just for this.

He deleted the full stop.

> ! Im more a fan of Jo Nesbo and so on, so . . .
> Any assistance much appreciated.
> Best wishes
> Alan Kolas

He looked at the empty subject box at the top of the email. He typed unusual request.

He checked his email one more time and then before the

sentence Any assistance much appreciated. he added the line

> I don't suppose theres any chance I could just see the story for
> free?

and pressed Send. Then he picked up his phone and held down the Home button and said into the microphone, "What time is it in New Zealand?"

"In Wellington New Zealand it is 9.22 p.m.," the phone answered. On the screen it said:

> In Wellington New Zealand it is 9.22 p.m. Wellington Tonight,
> 13 hours ahead.

"So," thought Alan, counting on the fingers of his right hand, "it would likely be at least 10.22" – index finger – "11.22" – middle finger – "12.22" – ring finger – "1.22" – pinkie – "2.22" – thumb – "3.22" – unthinkingly turning to what was formerly his left hand and feeling a phantom digit somewhere in the Clunch-y, glans-y mess attempting to help out with the counting – ". . . it will be some hours or maybe even a day before I hear an answer."

He did not have to wait as long as he expected. Two hours later he received a reply.

> NICE TRY "ALAN". WELL, I SAY NICE TRY BUT TO BE HONEST
> YOU COULD'VE TRIED A BIT HARDER: KOLAS/SOKAL? TOOK
> ME ALL OF TEN SECONDS TO CRACK YOUR "CODE" AND
> ANYWAY YOU REALLY GAVE YOURSELF AWAY WITH YOUR
> HILARIOUS LANDFILL GAG HAHAHA CAN'T HEAR THAT
> OFTEN ENOUGH, VERY ORIGINAL. I AM SO SICK OF THESE
> ATTEMPTS TO HOAX US AND I THINK YOU REALLY NEED TO
> TAKE A GOOD HARD LOOK AT YOURSELF AND WHY YOU'RE
> HELLBENT ON MAKING ME LOOK LIKE A FOOL. AS SOON
> AS I'VE REPLIED I'M DELETING YOUR EMAIL AND DON'T
> EVER CONTACT ME OR ANYONE ELSE AT LANDFALL AGAIN
> BECAUSE WE WON'T ANSWER. AND DON'T PUBLISH THIS
> EMAIL ANYWHERE AS IT IS PROTECTED BY COPYRIGHT AND
> I DO NOT GIVE YOU PERMISSION TO REPRODUCE IT. HARRY

Alan felt annoyed. Anyone who knew him knew that practical jokes were not his style. Although, he wondered, did a literary hoax count as a practical joke?

He really felt it couldn't hurt Harry just to give him a bit of information. On the other hand, which he gloomily remembered was now a mushroom cap, he was scared of angry people. Harry seemed angry. Alan decided to risk replying anyway. New Zealand, after all, was a long way away.

> can you at least tell me the name of the character whose arm turns into a mushroom?

Then he looked back at the message and added the line

> I am very sorry if people keep hoaxing you but I am serious, I don't even like practical jokes!

He pressed Send. Fifty-seven seconds later he had an answer.

> AS IF YOU DON'T KNOW WHAT THE CHARACTER IN THE STORY IS CALLED, SEEING AS YOU'VE SET UP AN EMAIL ACCOUNT IN HIS NAME. NOW DO RACK OFF, I DON'T HAVE TIME FOR THIS.
> PS LITERARY HOAXES AND PRACTICAL JOKES ARE NOT THE SAME THING!!!1!
> PPS YOU ALSO DO NOT HAVE PERMISSION TO REPRODUCE THIS EMAIL ELSEWHERE AS I RETAIN COPYRIGHT.

It wasn't going as well as Alan hoped. He decided as he was poorly and wasn't sure how he was going to change out of his pyjamas, he ought to try having another nap and see if his arm would be back to normal when he woke up.

When he woke, Alan looked again at the Landfall website and the name of the story's author: Jennifer Whitehead. He Googled the name and amid the results for a flute teacher and a computer science professor he found a blog dedicated to new writers, which featured an interview with her.

> I meet up-and-coming author Jennifer Whitehead in a trendy Shoreditch café, one where the staff all look like lumberjacks and half the floor space is given over to a coffee-bean-roasting operation.
>
> Whitehead tosses her long, naturally wavy chestnut locks in a totally unaffected way and smiles winsomely as she greets me. "The coffee here is divine," she says. "What's your poison? No, wait. Let me guess. You're a . . ." She pauses momentarily, narrows her compellingly green eyes, and sizes me up. "You're definitely a black americano kind of a guy."
>
> Without waiting for an answer, she's ordered and paid for my drink. She's right, though, that is my coffee order. Is this a sign of incredible perspicacity, part of her unique talent for making her characters zing right off the page and into the room with you?

Alan snorted derisively. "Yeah, right," he said to himself.

> Whitehead is briefly distracted, but I'm not sure why, so I ask her about the origins of her story "This guy woke up to find his arm had turned into a mushroom overnight. What happened next will amaze you."
>
> "Funny story," she answers, biting with gusto into a thickly buttered slice of sourdough toast. "I eat like a horse, by the way," she laughs, which surprises me as she looks like she'd need to shop in the children's department.
>
> "I probably shouldn't admit this, but I'd never even read Kafka when I started writing the story. I don't know where the idea came from. Divine inspiration, maybe?"

"No, I'm pretty sure it came from Kafka," Alan said aloud.

> Whitehead suddenly shakes her pretty head, her nose wrinkled in slight irritation. "Excuse me for a moment, will you? I've just got a little problem to deal with." She smiles graciously and turns away from me.
>
> "Do you have some sort of problem you'd like to share with

me? Yeah, I mean you, Alan, you fucking loser. Why are you looking over your shoulder? You're the one reading this and there's no one else in the room with you, of course I'm talking to you."

Alan felt nervous. "Sorry, I just . . . started reading this interview because of a problem I'm having that I thought it could help me with," he said. "But I don't think it's very realistic."

"Realistic. You're telling me about realism. Oh, this should be great."

Alan said nothing.

"Do you know why you didn't say anything in that sentence above? Cos I didn't give you anything to say. How d'you like that? Is that real enough for you?"

Alan started to worry that having a mushroom for an arm might not be the worst of his problems.

"Too right, mate. Look at that conversation you had with your parents. They don't even like you! And your girlfriend left you, ostensibly over paint colours. Although I think we all suspect it's because you're terrible in bed."

He felt like crying, but he couldn't.

"Haha, sorry about that, but I'm not emotionally equipped to deal with criers."

Alan felt furious. "But you made me. You made me this way. Didn't you?" he shouted. "You could've made my parents like me. You could've turned my arm into something useful, like a Swiss Army knife. But you gave me a stupid mushroom arm and parents with a stupid speakerphone. I had to drink cold, oversteeped tea while you swan around drinking posh coffee. Not fair."

"Hey, I was very careful not to say that the tea was fully cold. And it could be so much worse. You could be in a Vonnegut story. Do you know what he said about writing?"

Alan shook his head.

"He said you have to be a sadist to your characters. You're lucky you got me. Someone else would make your balls slip down the leg of those vile pyjama pants you're wearing and land on the floor, and then make you watch as your cat picked one up between its teeth and proceeded to bat it about the room with its paws like a dead mouse."

Alan tentatively moved his right hand towards his crotch.

"Oh relax would you, you big baby. It's a joke."

"I don't even want to be in your story," Alan said sulkily.

"That's not your fucking choice to make, Alan. If you're not in this story, you don't exist. This isn't fanfic."

"Whatever. Can you just tell me if I ever get this stupid mushroom arm sorted out?"

"Nope. Sorry, man. I don't want some crybaby reader getting all huffy about spoilerzzzz when they've still got 500-odd words of the story left to read. Shame you're too much of a cheapskate to buy a subscription to Landfill and find out for yourself."

"Landfall."

"Oh do fuck off."

"I feel like there isn't any reasoning with you."

"There isn't."

"So I'm going to close this browser tab and get on with the rest of my life," said Alan.

Before Jennifer Whitehead could answer back, he had clicked on the little grey cross at the top of the tab and the page was gone. Straightaway he felt more positive.

"I just have to work this out," he said. "Then I can save myself."

But he felt he'd reached a dead end. If Google didn't have an answer, surely that meant an answer didn't exist. There was one more thing to try.

He picked up his phone and took a photo of his former hand and then opened the Twitter app. Am I the only person who's had one of their limbs turn into a mushroom? Any ideas what I should do about it? He attached the photo he'd taken and sent the tweet. Minutes later, his Mentions column was ticking over rapidly.

Roy Hyde @roy_hyde
Can anyone help my chum @alankolas1 out? His arm has turned into a mushroom. Can he turn it back somehow?

Joker Man @comedywriter76
@roy_hyde @alankolas1 Sounds like a real fungi!

Sandy Barstow @SandyBarstow1
@comedywriter76 @roy_hyde @alankolas1 It looks like a penis.

Landfall Editor @harrynricketts
@roy_hyde @alankolas1 JUST STOP IT NOW. IT'S NOT FUNNY ANY MORE.

Roy Hyde @roy_hyde
@harrynricketts @alankolas1 Er, was it ever funny? Do I know you?

Landfall Editor @harrynricketts
@roy_hyde @alankolas1 *BLOCKED*

Jennifer Whitehead @jenniferw
@roy_hyde @alankolas1 YES! It's really easy. Just paint it with

this stuff called Curanail Lacquer. Works fast too – overnight.

Jennifer Whitehead @jenniferw
@roy_hyde @alankolas1 I know the PR for the brand. Can ask her
to bike you a sample on Monday morning if you would like??? Let
me know x

Alan Kolas @alankolas1
@jenniferesque @roy_hyde Wow, thanks! Shall I DM
you my address?

Jennifer Whitehead @jenniferw
@alankolas1 @roy_hyde It's OK, I know where you
live.

Sophie Morrell @sophie_m
@alankolas1 Oh my God, what's happened? Are you OK?

The next morning Alan woke up at 6.37 a.m. again, even though
his alarm clock hadn't gone off. He was disappointed to find that
his arm was still a mushroom, but at least tomorrow held the
promise of a remedy and Mingus seemed to have adjusted to him
now being part fungus.

Alan reached for his laptop – a day of binge-watching
Scandinavian crime drama in bed was, he felt, the only way to get
through Sunday. He opened his email and saw a message from
Jane Westaway, subject heading Re: unusual request.

Dear Alan
So sorry to hear you've not been well and I do hope you make a speedy
recovery. Attached is a PDF of the story from Landfall (not Landfill! You're
not the first to make that mistake though) that you were hoping to read.
Best wishes
Jane
Jane Westaway
Publisher, Landfall

He opened the PDF and started to read.

This guy woke up to find his arm had turned into a mushroom overnight. What happened next will amaze you.

JENNIFER WHITEHEAD

The first thing that irritated Alan when he woke up on this particular Saturday morning was not that his left arm had turned into some kind of a mushroom overnight, but that he'd forgotten to unset his alarm. It went off at 6.37 a.m. when he should've been sleeping.

"There is a crack in everything. That's how the light gets in."

Leonard Cohen

Foreign Territory

SARA KEENE

"Damn fool question," thought Virginia, turning the radio off. "How would *he* feel if he'd just lost his whole family? Where are the facts and the analysis? I despair."

"Despair, despair," came the echo from the ancient grey parrot in the corner, but Virginia didn't notice that she had spoken aloud. She heaved herself out of the floral armchair, made her way slowly over to the perch in the corner of the living room and tickled the bird under its chin with the end of her stick.

"Pretty Birdie," she said. "Does Birdie love Ginny? Does he?"

"Pretty Birdie," said the parrot, rubbing its beak along the ribbed sleeve of her dressing gown.

Virginia was satisfied with his reply. She looked at the four clocks above the gas fireplace, set for London, New York, Tokyo and Sydney. It was 8.00 a.m. in London and time to put the kettle on for her second cup of tea. She negotiated herself out of the small, square room, past the only other armchair and into the equally bare kitchen. She couldn't straighten her back and neck these days, and as she moved she studied her feet in their scuffed maroon leather slippers, shuffling across the cheap laminate. "If I'm going to have to look at my feet for the rest of my life," she thought, "I could treat myself to some better slippers."

She had been up for an hour but she had a strict rule about how many cups of tea she was allowed and when. If she didn't regulate them, all her little pleasures would be over before you could say "Godammit" and then there was only Social Services to look forward to. And it was a sorry world in which a visit from one of those harassed and uneducated women was a highlight.

While she waited for the kettle to boil she gazed sideways out of the window onto her small balcony. The two geraniums in a plastic trough, a birthday present from Jane, had died a while ago. She had been meaning to throw them away and sweep up the dead leaves for some time now and she couldn't think why she still hadn't got around to it, but then she remembered, again, that she had misplaced the door key. She couldn't recall which birthday it had been. Perhaps it was her seventieth, although, even by Jane's standards, a couple of geraniums didn't seem much of a gift for such a landmark date.

The kettle switched itself off too quickly and she saw that she had forgotten to put any water in it. Waiting again for it to boil, she sat down carefully at the small pine table, its surface marked with coffee rings and biro strikes, the varnish long gone. She put her hands out in front of her and studied her swollen knuckles. She needed to remove the rings on her right hand but she would have to ask Jane to help her when she arrived later that morning.

When she looked up, there was a young Indian doctor sitting opposite her.

"There is no mistake, Miss Johnson," he was saying, over the throb of the Kensington High Street traffic through his surgery window. "You are definitely pregnant and my guess is you are about sixteen weeks. Had you not noticed that your periods had stopped?"

She stared at him. She didn't have time for periods and kept no track of the few occasions when they happened. You couldn't buy sanitary towels in most of the war zones from which she reported, so she had been thankful when her body adjusted itself accordingly.

"But I'm forty-nine," she said. "I can't be pregnant."

"It's unusual but not impossible," replied the doctor. "And we can look after you, whatever you decide to do. I recommend an amniocentesis, as your age creates a higher risk of Down's Syndrome. I also recommend . . ."

But she wasn't listening to him. What on earth did she want with a baby? She didn't have time and she didn't have a partner. She knew who the father was – that photographer from Agence France-Presse. She thought his name had been Alain but she wasn't sure. It hadn't seemed important to remember it. At least the sex had been good, she did remember that. They had been drinking in one of those makeshift back-room bars in Beirut, just a few of them, the Frenchman, an Italian TV journalist, a man from the BBC World Service and a German called Heinz. She recalled the incomprehension when she had cracked a joke about his name.

Nobody was saying much, just smoking and drinking in exhausted concentration. It was hot and damp in the windowless room and she could feel the sweat trickling between her breasts. Condensation dripped down the cracked plaster walls and collected in small pools on the concrete floor. A couple of wooden crates with a plastic tablecloth draped over them formed a bar and the drinkers sat on boxes or on the floor or leaned against any dry wall space they could find. The air was acrid with smoke, stale bodies and the unspoken fear of missing a story. The Frenchman was staring at her. He was tall, well over six feet, and his cameras had made him a little lopsided. His shoulder-length hair was glued back from his face with grease and sweat. She held his gaze.

"You are Virginia Johnson?" he said, offering her a cigarette without taking his eyes off her. "I am a fan of your work. We met one time in Kabul."

"And did I find you attractive then too?" she asked, with a smile. She usually wasted no time on preliminaries. Even at forty-nine, she was still handsome and she knew it. Her legs were long and her figure was good. She wore her blonde hair pulled high into a ponytail and her T-shirts cut low at the front. Just because she was operating in a man's world, there was no need to look like one. She had a taste for casual sex and it was easy to find.

She took him back to her hotel room and fucked him three times before falling asleep across his chest. In the morning he was gone. He had left a note: *"Merci et au revoir. Ton ami français."* A week later she received two photographs from him, sent to the hotel. He had snapped her striding across a Beirut street, a baseball cap pulled down over her eyes, her jaw set. In the other shot, she was asleep across the bed, naked and tousled. A few days after that, she heard that he had been killed in sniper fire.

The kettle came to the boil with a loud click and she struggled to her feet, leaning heavily on the table. Two teaspoons of Assam in the pot for the 8.00 a.m. cup, milk, no sugar. At 10.30 a.m. she would take the jar of coffee beans from the fridge, grind a small portion, brew it and drink it with milk, one sugar and one digestive biscuit. At 12.00, a second cup of coffee, reheated from the earlier pot, no biscuit. At 4.00 p.m. it would be Earl Grey, no milk, no sugar. She would have a cigarette with the first coffee and then one roughly every forty-five minutes until 9.00 p.m., fifteen in all. At 6.00 p.m. she would start on the whisky, taken with a little water, no ice, and by 10.30 p.m. she would have fallen asleep during the news. She would wake in the small hours with Birdie and the television both hissing at her, and manoeuvre herself painfully to bed where she would sleep fitfully till 6.30, when the counting would begin again. She grazed all day on fruit, raw vegetables, nuts, which she shared with Birdie, and tins of beans, eaten cold. For several days after one of Jane's visits, she would eat ready-made meals until the freezer was empty again. She was happy with her diet. On assignments she had survived for days on Pringles and chocolate. And adrenalin.

She was both outraged and grateful that after a stroke two years ago, when she had lost the use of her right arm and a lot of her mobility, Social Services started sending someone in twice a day to help her to dress and undress and to make sure she was still functioning.

They want to check that I'm putting food in one end and that it's still coming out the other. As long as I eat and shit and don't set fire to myself, they think I'm fine, she wrote in one of her weekly emails to Jane. She typed painstakingly, with her left hand, taking pleasure in assembling a bulletin from the tiny details of her life. Jane was too busy to write much in return but sometimes she sent amusing postcards that she found, *Punch* cartoons or original saucy seaside jokes for which Virginia had an inexplicable fondness. She would just write *Hi Mum, love Jane*. But it was something.

Virginia had liked the kindly Jamaican woman that Social Services had sent for a while and who had fussed over her and insisted on washing and drying her hair once a week. She couldn't remember her name but it didn't matter because she had stopped coming after three months and now they never sent the same person twice or, if they did, she didn't recognise them. And as they had to do everything in just thirty minutes, she was sometimes left without any knickers on or without her socks. She was usually dressed for bed by 4.30 in the afternoon. Since the loss of the Jamaican, she had arranged for a hairdresser to come in once a fortnight. She also had a cleaning lady once a week, a Polish woman who never smiled and who spoke almost no English, to Virginia's relief, but who changed the linen and made up the bed neatly and whose cleaning was thorough – except that she would not go into Birdie's corner, whose tray was cleaned only once a month, when Jane visited.

The tea was ready but she couldn't carry it into the next room without spilling it, so she sat back down at the table to drink it and let her thoughts wander.

The doctor had said that, given her age, it would not be difficult to obtain a termination and he sent her away to think about it, but over the following couple of days, at home in her large, sparsely furnished, Kensington mansion flat, she found herself putting her hand on her belly, trying to feel something, anything.

She paced up and down her living room, her shoes squeaking on the bare parquet. She hated being back in London, between assignments. She had never been good at friendships and since she had started travelling so much, she had lost touch with nearly everyone apart from work colleagues. She felt more at home in the company of other war correspondents, drinking themselves stupid in one bar after another, in half-bombed hotels and basement drinking dens in which she could persuade herself that the short-lived bonds and sudden intimacies were as good as, if not better than, the long, slow burn of real relationships with friends, partners or family.

My mother would have liked a grandchild, she thought, in a flash of understanding. But there was no family now to care whether she reproduced or not. She had been grateful when her mother had endured her aggressive cancer quietly and without fuss. She took the call from the Boston hospice on her satellite phone in the remains of a school building in Tehran and hung up dry-eyed. An Iraqi Scud missile had landed there just half an hour earlier and she was looking at dead and dying children scattered across and under the rubble. Clouds of dust hung in the air over the sudden graveyard. Rescue workers were on the scene, hampered by parents, hysterical and vocal in their fear and grief, scrabbling through bricks and plaster, toys and body parts. At her feet, an intact lunch box, decorated with lions and giraffes, balanced on its side against a pink trainer laced around a small severed foot. It was the worst civilian tragedy she had ever seen, and nothing later would come close. On the day of her mother's funeral she was still in Tehran, writing her first Pulitzer Prize-winning story.

Trying to comprehend the news about her pregnancy, she felt as if there were no ground beneath her in London, nothing into which she could send any roots. She didn't really exist here. If she dropped dead in her flat, her body might lie undiscovered for weeks. To her own surprise, and later regret, she decided to keep the baby. It would earth her and, in some way that she could not articulate, it might make up for the way she had treated her mother at the end. Perhaps it would even force her to give up smoking. She called the doctor.

Staring now at her feet, Virginia could see out of the corner of her eye the packet of Silk Cut in the fruit bowl. Still two and a half hours until the first cigarette. Social Services were disapproving but they hadn't tried to confiscate her stash, which was replenished regularly by Kalim from the newsagent down the street, who would deliver a carton every ten days or so, whenever she called him.

Twisting and lifting her head with difficulty, she looked at the small collection of framed photographs on the wall above the kitchen table in which she was pictured meeting Idi Amin (an overwhelming cologne), Gaddafi (confused and erratic), Mugabe (surprisingly tall, short-sighted), even Saddam Hussein (a poisonous charm). She supposed that the cohorts of carers who now supervised her life didn't recognise any of these titans. Still, a little respect for her achievements would not go amiss.

She had had to take a desk job when she could no longer hide the pregnancy. Her colleagues at the London office of the *Boston Times* learned to keep their distance as her frustration at being away from the heart of the news made her short-tempered and often unkind. She endeared herself only to the correspondents out in the field whom she managed with skill and tolerance because she understood them.

The baby, however, she didn't understand at all. It was immediately alien. Five weeks passed before she named her and within three months of the birth she had installed a live-in nanny and was back at her desk, making herself indispensable and returning home later and later every evening. She lost count of the number of middle-European nannies whose relatives were suddenly taken so ill that they had to return home without delay. She spent a miserable five years shackled to London. She formed arm's-length friendships with some of the other mothers at Jane's nursery and, by working hard at it, created a network of contacts, other mothers who would look after Jane when the nanny was sick or she was between help. But she was just marking time and, finally, when she had managed to keep one girl for nearly six months and Jane was settled at school, she begged for an assignment.

"I'm going out of my mind with boredom," she told her editor on the phone. "I'm ready to get back out there. Jane will be fine for a couple of weeks – send me to Iraq. I want to write about what Saddam Hussein is doing to the Kurds."

As she drank her tea, she heard the front door shutting. It was Jane letting herself in. She must have taken an unusually early plane from Edinburgh and no doubt she would leave very early too. Virginia often caught her checking her watch during these visits. How is it possible both to look forward to seeing her and dread it at the same time? she wondered, already anticipating their too bright, brittle conversation fading into silence.

She couldn't muster any interest in Jane's work or imagine what got her out of bed in the morning. It was so unlike the addiction of her own calling, the need to see it for herself, the obligation to bear witness, the double rush of the excitement and the fear, the sharpening of the senses, the feeling of being so comprehensively *alive* when you knew that the very next minute you could be blown to pieces by a shell or shot through the head by a sniper. She recalled a line that had summed it all up for her: "the addiction to the poison elixir of battle". Who wrote that? She hoped that she had. There were no such fine phrases to be turned about Jane's work.

"I'm working on a new clause in the Bank of Scotland's

employee contracts."

"That sounds interesting."

"Yes. It's about preventing staff sharing inappropriate information via social media."

"Why would they do that?"

"Oh, you know, silly photos and idle, unthinking gossip."

"Can't they do that round the water cooler or in the pub?"

"The ether is alive with chatter these days."

"Oh, the ether . . . Doesn't sound like much fun."

She had once put out feelers about Jane's personal life but had been firmly rebuffed, and thereafter no attempt at intimacy was made on either side. One Christmas, Jane had brought her friend Christine to lunch at the restaurant. Virginia thought they were probably lovers. She didn't care.

But it wasn't Jane at the door. She must have misunderstood the date again. It was today's carer, hurrying into the living room where Virginia was surprised to find herself in her armchair. She couldn't remember having had her coffee and biscuit yet. She ran her tongue around her teeth. No, there was no sugar coating.

"Hello, dear. It's Maggie, remember me? Sorry I'm late," said the short, stout woman who was rolling towards her, taking off her coat as she moved and throwing it over the chair. "Right, let's get you dressed. I haven't got long today." And she heaved Virginia to her feet and half carried her towards the bedroom. "Have you had your shower? No, I thought not. Well it will have to wait till tomorrow now. I haven't got time to do everything and I need to clear up that mess in your kitchen before I go. I didn't have time to do it yesterday."

Virginia was surprised to hear this and looked through the kitchen door as she was hustled past. There were dirty plates and cups all over the small table, and piled in the sink she could see empty aluminium food trays.

The tussle in the bedroom was brief but not mean, and fifteen minutes later she found herself alone again, in her nightclothes, in her chair, in the living room. Her head hurt where her long, grey hair had been tied back too tightly. The TV had been turned on and she could see a tennis game in progress but the sound had been muted and she couldn't find the control anywhere.

She tried to lever herself to her feet to look for it but fell back exhausted. She hadn't the strength and she wasn't sure that she had the will either. She looked at her legs. They were thin and blotchy and she didn't recognise them. On her feet she was wearing new sheepskin slippers.

"What is happening, Birdie?" she said, turning towards the parrot's corner. But there was no parrot there and no perch. Virginia felt her eyes begin to fill, but as she fumbled in her pocket for a handkerchief she had already forgotten why she was upset.

Anyway she was nearly there now, the seat-belt signs were on and the plane was starting its descent. She had been commissioned by *Vanity Fair* to try to get into Kosovo following the failure of the NATO peace talks and she already knew that her starting point would be the mass grave of Kosovo Albanians recently discovered. Some of the hundreds of women and children in it had been mutilated and decapitated. Her pulse quickened at the idea of being back in the field and with another opportunity to open the world's eyes. No doubt the magazine hoped she would win her second Pulitzer.

Jane was now eighteen and away at university and Virginia could travel as often as she liked. She had officially retired two years before. There had been a stiff little get-together in the office after which she had never heard from any of her colleagues again. She and Jane had scratched along together in the mansion flat for two years while Jane completed her schooling. For one year, Virginia taught a course at the London School of Journalism but she was irritated by the ignorance of her students and didn't renew her contract. She spent the next year writing a memoir but abandoned it when her editor asked her to personalise it more.

"It's impressive history but it's terribly dry," he had said over lunch at Joe Allen's. "What about something more personal – the relationships that suffered, the one-night stands, the orphaned children you met, the birth of your daughter?" Virginia had nodded, eaten her burger and made the decision to abandon the book. She put out the word that she was available to write, for the best publications only. The *Vanity Fair* commission came quickly.

"How do you feel?" said the businessman sitting next to her on the plane.

"I feel desperately sad for these people," she answered. "I used to be able to remain objective. But it's getting so much harder as I get older. What about you? What will you be doing in Albania?"

"I'm just doing a few little tests," he replied. "We want to make sure everything is working the way it should. Have you emptied your bowels today?"

She turned her head in surprise to look at him, wondering how he could be so impertinent, and saw that he was much younger than she had first thought. And he had changed into a white coat. In fact everything was very white – white room, white bedcover, white hospital gown, white blinds. Even the woman sitting on the other side of the bed was wearing a white summer dress. After a moment, she realised it was Jane. The young man was holding Virginia's wrist.

"Is it all white?" she said to no one in particular, closing her eyes against the dazzle.

"You're going to be fine," said Jane, putting aside her phone. "You had a little fall and you were unconscious for a while. The hospital just wants to check you over and then you can go back to the nursing home. I expect you'd like to be back in your own bed."

What Virginia really wanted was her lunch. She was pretty sure now that she had had neither coffee nor lunch yet today. And if she was in hospital, who would be taking care of Birdie?

"Birdie died years ago, Mum."

She must have dozed off for a little while because when she opened her eyes, it was dark outside the windows and there was a stranger on the sofa on the other side of the unfamiliar room. She had short blonde hair, greying at the temples, was smartly dressed in a grey linen trouser suit and was reading through a document, pen in hand, frowning in concentration. On the table beside her was a red geranium in a pot, and two pink balloons floated above the end of the bed, with numbers on them that meant nothing to Virginia. She wanted to be alone and thought that if she pretended to be asleep the visitor might get bored and leave, but she must have made a sound because the woman looked up from her work and smiled at her, brightly.

Son of an Honest Man

WALTER JONES

"I 'll give you ten for the day, but no lunch," she says. You nod. "Yes ma'am."

She unlocks the gate and you follow her down the path through the garden, to the garage with the door wide open. Inside, it takes a few minutes for your eyes to adjust, and when they do, you notice the back wall is covered with hundreds of tools. Most are still wrapped in their original packaging, lined up and waiting for the day they'll be chosen to do the work they were made for.

"Do you have an overall?"

"No ma'am," you say, standing there in a long-sleeve shirt and your father's suit trousers. Your mother buried your father without his suit so you could have it to come here to find work because, she said, "Those people need all the help that God can send them. And you know how things work so you can show them how to fix their things."

The small dog under the woman's arm snarls and barks at you, like a miniature lion. She has to raise her voice so you can hear what she's saying over the growling and yapping and every one of her sentences is punctuated with a reprimand.

"Stop it! Flossie! Stop it!"

She hands you the overall. "Here," she says. "Come to the house when you've changed and I'll tell you what to do. And hurry up. My husband will be back soon and I want everything done by the time he gets home."

She turns to leave and the smell of floor polish reminds you of the tall buildings in town, a dull sweet perfume covering something more basic.

You hear a phone ringing inside the house, like a bird calling, cold and urgent. A chill runs up your spine, an icy-fingered warning. These things matter in the place you are from, but not here.

You take off your shirt and trousers and fold them neatly on a large paint drum by the garage door. You put on the overall, leg by leg, lifting one of the sleeves up behind you to meet your arm, but you can already feel they are too short and the top of the overall is too narrow to fit around your shoulders. You try the other sleeve, pulling it around behind you, stretching your arm to meet the opening, but it is too tight, like the shed skin of a smaller man, so you tie the top half around your waist and tuck your vest in behind the sleeves. You take off your shoes and roll your socks inside one of them.

You walk out to the front of the house and up to the door. You see her peering through the lace curtains at the window she's opening. You hear her say: "Hold on, the boy is here."

And then she tells you no, not here, while she cradles the phone receiver on her shoulder. You must go to the back of the house and she will talk to you there. So you walk past the garage and around the house to the back door. A lawnmower is propped up against the wall, by the steps. You wait there.

A key turns in the back door and you stand up straight and smile at her as the top half opens, and you notice her young skin is smooth, like butter, as she slides her arms over the bottom half of the door and hands you a slither of white power cable.

"There, take it," she says. "It's already turned on. When you've finished, come back here and ask me to turn it off for you."

You take the cable and she tells you to mow the lawn in the front. The back garden is bare ground but she wants you to sweep it before you go. And the edges of the garden beds should be lifted, with the big spade, when you're finished weeding and raking the path.

You nod and say, "Yes ma'am," wondering how far the power cable will reach, but it is surprisingly long. It pulls and twists and curls around the side of the house, as you wheel the lawnmower to the front yard, as far as the gate.

When half the lawn is cut the lawnmower stops, so you go back to the back door to ask if she's unplugged the power cable or switched off the wall plug, but she hasn't, she says, and she tells you to try the plug in the garage and to be careful not to break anything else.

But it doesn't work when you plug in the cable and try starting the engine again, so you go back to the back door and tell her you know something about how engines work and that you would like to see if you can fix it.

She says that's fine but not to expect any more money if you do and to expect nothing if you don't.

"And don't work in the garage," she says. "My husband likes to keep things clean."

It's already past noon and the day is like fire. You ask her for water and she gives you an old cup and says you can use the tap by the back door. So you drink from the cup and pour water over your face and your head and neck and your arms and feet, and you feel refreshed and alive and thankful for the gift of being able to fix things. This matters here, but not in the place you are from.

You sit on the driveway in front of the garage and start taking the lawnmower apart, carefully feeling, cleaning and putting every piece right in front of you. You make a mental note of the order of each piece as you remove it – first the blade nut, then the square washer, then the insulator, then the blade – laying them all in an ordered line, like metal soldiers, only powerless lying apart from the engine.

A round man, with a red face and good shoes, pushes open the gate and walks purposefully up the driveway.

"Boy, it's hot out here," he says, smiling as he stops and looks at the front door and then down at what you're doing.

"What are you doing?"

"It's broken. Your wife said I could fix it."

"Oh, she's not my wife," he says, looking surprised, and then says something about coming to fix something else. He laughs but it sounds forced, like an engine that hasn't worked well for a long time, and you see the woman standing at the window with the dog under her arm before the door opens and he pushes himself inside.

You carry on taking the engine apart. The grass looks uneven now with one side shorter than the other, and you tilt your head as if to balance your perspective, but it doesn't make a difference.

You hear ringing again but it's the tiny bell around the dog's neck. It barks furiously at the small gate that's blocking the bottom half of the open door. The red-faced man is at the door holding a cup and saucer and the woman is on the phone, again, peering at you through the lace curtains.

You lift the cutting disc and eye the garden through the hole in the middle. A van, the colour of margarine, slides in through the gate. Two men climb out of the front and the red-faced man goes to meet them.

They're both in uniform, the same blue as yours but with short sleeves and big brass buttons. One man is shorter than the other.

You tilt your head again and close one eye to block out half the sun.

The three men come up and stand around you, watching what you're doing for a minute, and then the red-faced man says: "You see" – pointing at the line of engine parts – "military precision."

They ask you your name.

You say nothing.

They ask you why you are here.

You say nothing.

They ask where you are from.

You say nothing.

"He won't talk. Typical terrorist tactics," the taller man says.

The woman is outside now but she's left the dog inside and closed the front door.

"What are you going to do with him?" she asks, folding her arms.

"We'll take him to town. He'll talk to us there."

She nods. "Yes. Good, good."

"Will he come back?" asks the round man with the red face, looking anxious.

The shorter man replies, "This one? Probably not, but another one like him will. Eventually. Probably."

"This is fucked up!" shouts the round red-faced man, kicking the engine parts across the lawn as they lead you to the van.

"Don't worry, we can get another one," she says.

"There are plenty in town," says the taller man.

They open the back of the van and there are two men inside.

"A thief and a murderer," says the tall one.

"He's in good company now," says the short one, patting the roof.

You close your eyes and as the engine starts you can smell the honeysuckle choking the gate, and you smile to yourself.

"We have to continually be jumping off cliffs and developing our wings on the way down."

Kurt Vonnegut

Sowing Seeds

MELANIE JONES

I drain the cup and split in two.

At first I don't notice. I enjoy the warmth of my head. I squint across the lounge and see Jack stumble. His laughter dances around the room and I try to smile as the fuzz in my stomach spreads out to the rest of my body, through my hair and up, up and away. It hovers above me and I watch it twinkle like rainbow dust, animated by a light that is long gone.

I close my eyes too soon. When I open them the world is bright, the sofa and Jack are gone. My pupils refuse to constrict and all I see is whiteness. I reach for something to hold onto but my fingers just flail in the air. It occurs to me that I am standing up. I feel different, shorter and a bit slimmer. The hairs on my arms are raised and there is a breeze. I wrap my arms around my body looking for something real and my fingers brush against stiff cotton. I am wearing a dress, perhaps floral, perhaps polka dot. The wind catches it and the spinning pattern makes me dizzy. I look up before I'm sick.

I am being held up. When I look to the side I see that I'm leaning against a slim spiral of metal, painted white. Shapes are starting to form and I see that this pillar and three others hold up the copper awning that is shading me from the sun. I am on my own front porch but in startling daylight. Morning has come too soon.

His voice cuts through the glare. He comes closer and I

smile. Jack will know. He always has a grip on things. But as the figure approaches I see that it isn't Jack at all. This man is broad-shouldered with a whisper of frailty. I don't place his age until he steps into the shade. He's thirty, maybe, younger than I thought. Brown eyes, sandy-coloured hair, a clumsy smile. He takes hold of my hands and a stiffness passes from him to me; it travels up my arms and rests in my shoulders. I want to snatch my hands from his and run inside. Perhaps Jack is still sprawled out in his favourite chair or perhaps he's awake and cooking bacon. I try to remember coming out onto the lawn but there is nothing. My hands stay wrapped in the stranger's and I don't pull away. My limbs are frozen. I wait for him to break the moment.

I've lived in this house for as long as I've lived in London. In a section of it, anyway. It used to be one house for one family but people can't afford to live in whole houses any more so it was chopped up and plasterboard walls were erected to section it off into flats. We rent the bottom right-hand corner. We've got half of the original kitchen and a new-build bathroom at the back; the old living room has been split to give us one bedroom and a small lounge. Three other couples occupy the rest of the building.

We were flat-hunting for months before we found it. On the day of the viewing we arrived early and stood on the other side of the road waiting for the estate agent. Jack leaned over and whispered in my ear, "That is the ugliest house I have ever seen." I frowned at him. He'd already dismissed half a dozen Victorian conversions. He was right, though. Rose bushes tangled with jasmine and passion flowers in the front garden. Bindweed crawled around the iron railings that marked the perimeter. Trees grew at forty-five-degree angles.

"What a mess," Jack said.

Attached to the side was a lean-to greenhouse that ran the whole length of the house and on into the back garden. The plants inside it were pushing at the glass. A copper awning, covered in patination, protected a large front porch. Wooden bunting hung from it and it was supported by struts that looked like twisted candy canes. The house belonged on a colonial homestead, not in London, not in Peckham.

But once we were inside, we forgot about the exterior. The space had been modernised. There was parquet flooring. The walls were a uniform white. Glass patio doors led onto a massive communal back garden that was in much better shape than the one at the front. It was bigger than anything else we'd seen and the rent was lower, so we took it. Perfect for a couple not quite ready to buy.

It didn't take long for the house to become normal. When I was sitting inside on my IKEA sofa, I forgot about how it looked from the outside. Three years later, when Jack started saying things like, "We could always buy a Victorian house and just completely gut it," I realised I had come to love it.

We were sitting on the bed scrolling through property search sites. Jack was excited about beautiful attic rooms and he bookmarked a flat with polished-concrete floors.

"If we won the lottery, I would buy this whole building and do a *Grand Designs* on it," I said.

"Really?" said Jack.

"Well, no. But if that flat by Solomon's Passage that looks like the Jetsons live in it is unavailable, then definitely this one."

"What about Harefield Lodge?"

The detached Georgian villa overlooking Peckham Rye was on the market for 1.6 million.

"Well I guess it depends on how much we win. We'd need a rollover to get Harefield Lodge."

A few weeks later we were waiting for the night bus when Jack kicked a stone into the road and announced, "I've decided that all of our friends are boring."

He was always a decisive drunk.

"They aren't all boring," I said.

"They are grey and dull and boring. Every single one of them."

"That's not what I meant. I meant they aren't totally boring – they all have boring and non-boring qualities."

Jack screwed his face up.

"If they are grey, then what colour are we?" I said.

"We're silver and red and laser green!"

We were on our way home from Rachel and Henry's engagement party. Everyone had been pretending to be grown-ups. They talked about mortgages, they talked about their kids, they talked about their jobs. Rachel asked us about our weekend plans. Jack doesn't like me to talk about it but I was bored so I told them. Rachel broke the silence that followed.

"But it's opium," she said. "It's basically heroin."

"There are opiates in diarrhoea medicine," I told her. "There are opiates in codeine and cough medicine. You are taking opiates all the time. It's no stronger than weed – it's not even as bad as drinking lager. It grows in the garden. It's just a really really good herbal tea."

"It's not addictive?" Henry said.

"Not really. I mean, you might get a bit sniffly a few days later but it doesn't last long. Not like a coffee addiction." Or a breeding addiction, or a pay-cheque addiction, I thought.

They laughed. We were back on common ground. The conversation moved on and Jack decided it was time for us to go home.

"They were all smoking pot at Rachel's birthday party," I said as he checked the bus timetable on his phone. "Amanda brings a bottle of absinthe out at the end of the night whenever she's had a bit too much and I know that all of them have taken speed. People just have this paranoia about opium."

Jack rolled his eyes. The bus was coming and we don't talk on buses.

As we walked up the hill towards the house, Jack bit a hole in the bottom of the plastic bag and rained seeds in the borders of all the front gardens. They were easy to plant. There was no need to dig down in the soil so he just peppered the surface. He chose sheltered areas so they wouldn't get blown away by the wind or waterlogged before they took root. They took a long time to flower. The shoots developed into thick stalks and then buds appeared with heads pointed down towards the ground. They hung there for weeks until, just before the end, they turned their faces up to the sky and opened. We had bags and bags of seeds. Enough to fill every one of our flowerpots, enough to waste liberally in cakes. Enough to populate the neighbourhood. Jack rolled them into slices of bread and catapulted them onto the wasteland behind our building. There were already field poppies growing everywhere so he didn't think anyone would notice if a few more interesting varieties cropped up. The tangled mess of our own front garden has germinated hundreds.

The garden is just lawn now, the only plant is grass. My stomach rolls as I bring myself out of heavy memory and into the bright sunlight. The stranger is still gripping my hands. I want to cry. He starts to speak.

"I'll cut the turf out along the front for rose bushes. We can plant an apple tree on each side to give us a bit of shelter from the road. Plenty of space for a greenhouse. Cucumbers love a greenhouse."

The greenhouse hasn't been built. There is no Jack waiting for me inside with a bacon sandwich. The man is grinning and pulling me away from the safety of my leaning post. I want to tell him that I am not who he thinks but my voice has dried up in the back of my throat, my tongue is pasted down. I peel my lips apart and suck in the air. He hears the intake of breath and turns with an expectant, indulgent smile.

"Poppies," I say.

My voice sounds like a croak and he tilts his head, confused.

"Plant poppies in the borders." Softer now.

He looks back at me for a moment and then grins.

"Yes. Lovely," he says, before leading me into the house.

Inside there are no plasterboard walls and no parquet floors. Instead there is carpet, navy blue with flourishes in green. I feel like I'm standing on a damp towel, like I've just stepped out of the shower onto a dirty bath mat. I want to flick this carpet off my feet like a cat flicks water off her paws. The man drags me into the undivided living room. He leaves me standing there while he polishes the mantelpiece with his handkerchief, showing me the colour hidden under the dust. He's eager for approval, but it isn't me he wants it from. I think about running but I don't know where to go.

I follow him into the kitchen, enormous now that there is no separating wall. There's a tiny window over the sink that looks out onto the back garden. I think about our beautiful patio doors and the light that streams from them into the whole flat. One day someone will realise how much better this room would be if the bricks were replaced with a wall of glass.

"You can look out while you do the dishes," he says, beaming.

I want to turn away from him but my feet are sinking into the floor, it's tugging on my ankles. My face feels like it's smiling. I am slipping into his world.

Jack bought some dry pods from a florist. They were huge, rattling with seeds and on long stalks like maracas. But they'd been washed. Lost their potency. The tea left me aggravated and whiny.

"It's not working. I feel noooooormal."

They always worked on Jack. He floated away from me, sending fluffy platitudes my way until I shook him awake and demanded popcorn. He didn't mind, he let me flit around him until he fell asleep and I watched the polar bear show again and again until four in the morning. Home-grown were always better.

It was clear that we needed to restock. A few nights later, we set out to harvest the neighbourhood pods. We took a rucksack and some carrier bags along with two pairs of kitchen scissors. We waded through the wildflower meadow on The Rye but none of those plants were ready. There was too much competition; greedy coltsfoot had sucked up all the nutrients.

There were plants growing in our own front garden but I was reluctant to harvest them. The tenants from one of the other flats had seen us sowing seeds in the borders and asked us if we had permission from the landlord. I was worried that they might suspect what we were up to. But it was gone midnight when we returned and no light was coming from any of the windows.

"Everyone's asleep," Jack whispered. "We'll be fine."

A few of the seed pods still had petals clinging to them but most had fattened up, dark green and swollen. Jack scored the edge of one with the scissors and latex bubbled to the surface.

We were cutting stalks and dropping them into the carrier bag when I saw the curtains twitch. I gestured to Jack but he shrugged it off. I stopped what I was doing and folded my carrier bag over, ready to run.

"We're just picking flowers that *we* planted," he whispered.

A light came on in an upstairs window. Always the scaredy-cat, I gasped and scuttled to the corner of the street. Jack stayed where he was, finger on his lips, trying not to laugh. After a few minutes the light flicked off. Jack gestured for me to return and we crept through the shared entrance. I turned the key slowly while Jack shook his head in mock despair.

I helped him tie the stalks in bunches with the seed heads hanging down. I could feel them pulsing, the juices rushing away from the rawness of the cut. I've never managed to get my head around the magic of gardening. It's a mystery to me that tomatoes spring from tiny white flowers. How do wispy roots that blow and break in the wind during repotting transform into carrots? It seems impossible that from the tiniest of seeds, drunkenly discarded, come bulging beauties, full of poison, full of dizzy calm, full of the memories of soil.

Jack checked the pods once a week. When they had dried out to his satisfaction he cut them down the middle and emptied the seeds into a jar. On the next available Friday, I left him in charge of preparation while I went for a run with Amanda. We were only on day four of the Couch to 5K, still too unfit to talk during the running sections. During the walking parts we compared date nights. She was on her way back to steak and a bottle of wine. The kids were with her sister. I told her I was heading back for meatballs and poppy tea.

"What does it feel like?"

She'd never asked me this before.

"It's relaxing. We have such stressful jobs, you know?" I paused because I was still catching my breath. "I get home on Friday and I'm thinking about work and the meetings I have on Monday and the endless shitty phone calls I've had all day."

She nodded. She'd known all about it before she had the girls.

"And that can last all the way till Sunday night. It's just great to turn that off. Right away, on a Friday. Our jobs make us miserable, you know? We deserve to be happy on the weekend."

She nodded again, infinitely supportive. I wondered if I could convince her to try some. She probably would have said yes a few years ago.

When I got back from the run, Jack was already making dinner. I went for a shower while he chopped onions and boiled the kettle. I could hear the metallic whir of the herb grinder above the running water and it set my teeth on edge. He was waiting for me in the bedroom. Tomato sauce was simmering. Meatballs were resting. Tea was brewing. We had twenty minutes. He peeled me out of the towel.

Alone on the counter, opium seeped into water turning it dark and bitter. But that wasn't all that escaped. Things that had been deep and buried swirled in the water. The roots of older plants had tangled with the roots from ours. The ground remembered all the feet that had trodden it, the spades that had cut it away. It had listened to every conversation on the lawn and reached back to places older than I could imagine. The soil knew everyone that had ever lived here. It knew the forests that had grown before the house was built and the animals that had made their dens under watchful trees. It remembered the axes that had chopped those trees down and the hands of every young gardener growing older and older. It had tasted spilled champagne, spilled lemonade, spilled milk. The soil gave all of this knowledge to the plants and as they faded on the counter they gave it all to the water. It all added to the flavour, it all deepened the colour.

The taste of that batch was better than any we'd had for a while. It usually took me a few gulps to finish it, sipping Ribena in between to suppress the gag reflex. But that batch was sweeter, it barely needed sugar and there was far less grit. I drained the cup and . . .

There is nothing else to remember. The man pulls me towards the apex of the house. I've never been upstairs and I don't want to go now. He walks ahead of me, holding my hand so I can't drop back. The landing seems long but there's only one door left. I try to drag my heels but my feet just keep walking, heel, toe, heel, toe. I want to dig my fingernails into the cracks in the wall where the paper meets but my hand lies against my side. I'm shouting, "No, I don't want to go, this isn't me," but that's in my head and in reality I'm smiling and compliant. Somewhere inside is a girl who can't wait to see what's behind the final door. I notice a skip in my step. I'm losing control.

I want to see the kitchen again and the view of the garden. I want to do the dishes and look out at all the plants he's going to grow. I want to put my feet on the squishy, newly planted lawn. But on we go. He's opening the door and light is jumping around the landing. Here are the dust shafts again, but there's no rainbow. It's just light. I follow him into it.

There's a large window in this room. He raises the sash and a breeze lifts the skirt of my dress. I shriek and the man smiles widely.

"Isn't this a beautiful room for a nursery?" he says, not waiting for a reply. "You can have a rocking chair up here for feeding, and that beautiful old cot from your mother's house. And you can see right down into the street and watch everyone come and go."

I look down through the window; the breeze is quelling the dizziness. Below me I see the lawn, uncut. Then I see the borders and the rose bushes, the lawn chairs and the garden parties, the children running across the grass through the sprinklers, screaming and laughing. I see it stretching on for ever in this place where the walls hold you down and the only reds are the field poppies dancing in the wind.

"You can never cross the ocean unless you have the courage to lose sight of the shore."

Christopher Columbus

Switzerland

DAVE WAKELY

Outside, snow mounts on frozen sills, each window thickly underlined in white. Inside, Judy and I huddle in the kitchen's warmth as teenagers swarm and disperse, soggy sockprints leaving animal trails across the quarry tiles. Their conversations roar through the open doors like runaway fires. Occasionally we catch a spark and fizzle in their orbit for a few seconds before the flame moves on and we settle back into calmer chatter.

As composed as her greying hair is tousled, Judy leans against the cool slate of the old counter, life's contradictions rounded up for now like wayward ewes. She's always been the axis that the vortex swirls around, the still eye of the cyclone. She's no more ruffled by the world now than she was when we met thirty years ago, her serene amid the chaos of the art-school disco and me the anxious penny-plain craftsman in a sea of peacocks. "*You* look different," she said. "Need a drink?" We've been friends ever since.

Around us, T-shirts and leggings hang on chair-backs, shucked snake skins left to desiccate in the heat of the wood-burning stove. On the windowsill, an old glass jar has slowly filled with the badges and lapel pins of forsaken bands and abandoned causes, forgotten grace notes in whatever tune the household dances to now. If a volcano struck tonight, future generations of anthropologists would uncover us with shrieks of glee.

Her phone throbs into life every few minutes in her cardigan

47

pocket as the flock check in, sending updates with the vowels left out and casual kisses thrown in at the end. She stopped keeping tally of who was or wasn't in the house when the eldest two left for college. Now three remain, dragging a random combination in on their tide: schoolfriends, neighbours, girl- or boyfriends. She leaves food in the larder, assumes that those who miss the meals she makes will somehow fend for themselves, teaches subtle lessons in self-sufficiency as she carves out time to audition stepfathers.

"Gary, you're never going to make it up the hill in this. Why don't you text Tony and let him know you're staying over? I can easily find you blankets and a pillow, and you know you're always welcome."

I look out of the window as she rests a hand on my shoulder for a moment and fresh tea arrives unbidden in a huge blue mug. The snow is several inches deep now, blowing in horizontally on the wind. Porlock Hill will be closed soon if it's not already, and we're sealed in as tight as an Alpine village after an avalanche. Our own little Switzerland.

"Well, if you're sure it's OK, that'd be great." And then I remember my manners. "If I'm not just passing through, do you know if Drew's in or out? I've not seen his portfolio yet and I reckon that art-school place at Falmouth deserves some praise, yeah?"

"Probably still upstairs, investigating the contents of Zoe's jumper. Still young enough for the mystery to be enchanting. But he could show his godfather some respect, eh? I'll find him."

Picking her way through cat bowls and discarded shoulder bags, she makes her way to the stairs, rubber clogs clacking across old floorboards. I hear her calling up to him.

"Drew? You still in, sweetheart? Gary's going to stay over as he's stuck in the snow. Why don't you come and join us in the kitchen for a bit, maybe bring down your portfolio?"

Clandestine as a crocodile sliding into a river, she lowers the hint into the current. Barely a ripple, no call for alarm. Drew's always been bashful. To look at him, you'd never guess at a talent for art. Tractor-driving, maybe, or bricklaying. He's thickset and lumbering, wholesome and rustic as the Somerset burr that still clings to him like bum-fluff.

He'll pick up on her suggestion, though. Nothing gets past him.

Those green eyes have always moved faster than his tongue. He was the one who asked why I stopped being Uncle Gary a few years ago, became just Gary. And now that he's old enough for the joke, sometimes his Fairy Godfather. Even if it's mostly me cracking it.

He was the one who wondered why he *was* a godson, when his mother's a Buddhist and the only time his father's ever prayed is when he's still three miles from the Dog and Duck ten minutes before closing. Tradition must have struck him as being as mad an answer as it did me, but Judy's mother had insisted: baptisms and godparents. So between them, her brood have got me, a yoga teacher, a white witch, a Hindu and a Druid. Judy's never said we were chosen to spite the matriarch, tweak the vulture's beak a bit, but then I've never asked. We've known each other long enough not to dwell on the awkward stuff.

Overhead, I can hear Drew's heavy tread and the scrape of cupboard doors. I can hear Zoe's voice, too, although I can't make out the words, just the abstracted tone of petulance at having her sleepy afternoon disturbed. After the bedroom door has creaked open and shut, I can hear the music grow louder as she finds another way to pass the time.

His younger sister, Ella, clatters into the kitchen like a steam train, sparking with a thirteen-year-old's energy and an appetite for answers.

"Uncle Gary? How fast exactly does the earth spin?" she demands.

"Round here, Ella, or generally?"

I sip my tea and look up at her, glad I've remembered not to suggest asking her father. Beyond the lingering heritage of genes, there's no trace of Jay now. A hundred miles east, he'll be sounding off about media and representation theory at a room full of kids Drew's age, earning as much attention from them as he ever got here and probably giving as much as he ever gave. The ties were always loose, and then the knot finally unravelled. Now he's merely absent, like a tea chest they left behind during a house move. Anything that anyone needed has been quietly replaced, and the rest slowly forgotten.

Ella has already turned on her heel, ready to interrogate someone else.

"Boys," she spits as she leaves. "Bloody useless, all of them."

I'll dare say she'll find a use for some of us one day, even if she's not sure quite what it might be just yet. For now, she'll content herself with a gaggle of girlfriends in the living room, whispering and shrieking about whatever it is thirteen-year-old girls find so endlessly fascinating. Swapping film-star gossip and daydreams, I suppose, or tips on faking adulthood. I'm hardly the man to ask. But a girl who's so set against the opposite sex would surely fasten one more button?

And then, without fanfare, the gelled straw-heap of Drew's hair leans around the doorframe, his shy grin following a second later.

"Gary . . . Hi! I . . . er, I should have come to say hello. I was . . . er, I . . ."

"You were being seventeen, Drew. It's OK. I mean, you *are*."

Even though I've tried to make light, to be just an older friend, his freckles fade as a blush softens the contrasts of his face. I'm trying to picture him at art school, among all those radical hairstyles and statement clothes. The only thing his old checked shirt is saying is "I'm not very good at being spoken to. Please just look at the pictures."

He's always thought he's slow and yet he's straight into a Fine Art degree at seventeen. And a pretty girlfriend, too. I was nineteen before I got my hands up anybody's jumper, and here he is with the world at his feet. Maybe that's why he can barely look any of us in the face. I tell myself a better godfather would find some way to give him a thicker skin, one he can swagger in a little. Behind me, Judy wordlessly gathers armfuls of flotsam from the old oak table, making space for him to show me his work without actually mentioning the idea.

"Anyway," he says, "I need to thank you."

"What for? I'm just some old stonemason. What did *I* ever do? Chisel a load of old Latin cobblers into lumps of stone? I can't even read it, let alone believe it."

"Well," he says, taking a breath like someone preparing to read a long list, "you gave me your old camera, the birdwatching binoculars. That set of really good French pastels . . ."

As he reels off presents I've given him, some of them years

ago, his enormous hands unfasten the portfolio's black ribbon ties with unexpected grace. Peering through the narrow opening, his long fingers riffle through its contents and pull one picture free.

". . . and you inspired this. It's what got me into Falmouth."

If it was an image snatched on a phone, it would just be a happenstance – the kind of thing you'd text to a friend but never look at twice. It had been the day after Drew's birthday, the year we gave him the pastels, a few months before Jay finally moved out. Tony and I had been sat on a floor cushion in the next room, watching a film about Frida Kahlo. Jay had talked the whole way through it and Tony had nodded off on my shoulder, one arm draped round me and the other across my chest.

I still remember how I tried to catch Judy's eye, hoped my eyebrows could clearly signal "Is this OK? Us, I mean? In front of Drew?" How she brought us an old blanket and tucked it over us, whispered to me about the cute little hamster noises Tony makes when he's asleep.

I can recollect how Drew had been crouched in the corner, sketching away in silence, keeping quiet to avoid getting sent to bed. How he'd finally relented of his own accord, tiptoeing off upstairs with his pad clutched to the front of his jumper. Fifteen and furtive.

And now I see what he'd been hiding. In front of me is the same evening replayed, lamp-lit and nocturnal. The iron stove's soft glow in a warm room, late on an autumn evening after too much Rioja. Just looking at it, I can almost smell the wood smoke and the brie ripening by the fire.

"I know it's my best piece," he tells me, bold as I've ever heard him. "School wouldn't have liked it if I'd handed in something called 'My Godfather and his Husband', so I kept it back. You know, wow them at art school with it. Show them I can do more than just the set pieces."

My camera bag is hooked over my chair, but he stops me as I reach for it to capture the image, promises me a proper digital print for our anniversary. I try not to blink in shock that he remembers the date. Before he can close the folder and scuttle back upstairs, I ask him to show me more.

His tongue might not be the swiftest, but the folder shows

a photographer's eye. A paparazzo's shutter finger too. There are photos of osprey chicks taken with long lenses from distant hides, caught in the days before their first flight, of otters playing on the banks at Watersmeet. Charcoals of the cliffs at Hurlstone Point and coloured pencil drawings of the wild flowers on Lundy, places where he's captured the beauty and the silence. There are flashes of memories of the places we've taken him when we've been passing through: the abbey ruins at Glastonbury, a gargoyle at Wells Cathedral that reminded him of his grandfather. Snatches of my world through his more observant, more detached eyes.

But Tony and I are the only people. Are we the only ones who stayed still long enough for him to capture? The only ones he wanted to? Or maybe just the only ones he was brave enough to draw. I wonder if he'll find the courage to venture more. Eyes as clear as his would make for probing portraits if someone could encourage him to make them.

"Have you ever tried to draw Zoe?" I ask him. "I'm sure she'd be flattered."

He hesitates, and then shows me an incomplete pencil sketch. Just a few lines, like Chinese brushwork, more a suggestion than a presence, but beautiful nonetheless.

"She won't sit still," he mumbles, diffident about discussing her.

I lean across and whisper like a conspirator. "Wait till she's asleep." His blush rises again, fingers scrabbling at the sheets in the folder to find a new subject.

"So did *you* have a good godfather too?" he asks me suddenly. "I mean, you must have had lessons, right?"

"You mean Danny?"

I'm asking myself the question as much as Drew is. I can picture Danny already: my dad's brother, dapper and suave. Drier than an old-school Martini but always the first with the latest gadgets and the newest fashions. The diplomat, we called him. "Trust me, I'm a diplomat from the future," he'd told Mum once, dropping hints about how she should modernise her kitchen. After that, it just stuck.

"He was just kind of *there*, really. Always came for Sunday lunch. He was always really classy, I guess – a masterclass in just being yourself. And very kind, too – insisted on it. Unless there was a really bitchy quip that was funnier."

Even with his head down as he looks back through his artwork, I see Drew raise an eyebrow.

"Oh, yeah. Danny was gay too. I mean no one ever actually said so. We just . . . well, *knew*. He was just . . . hell, he was just *Danny*."

"Just Danny?" As the eyebrow lowers, the eye looks more sombre. "Never anyone else?"

"Oh no, there were boyfriends too. Partners."

I try to picture some of the men Danny arrived with over the years. Always well-groomed and on their best behaviour, being introduced. Not that there were *that* many. Dimitri, the handsome Greek. Saif, the nervously grinning Lebanese guy. And Australian Mike, who always brought me presents. Mike was my favourite. Danny's too, I think. We didn't see him for a long time after Mike was killed in a car crash. I was too young to ask questions back then. Too young to know what to ask.

"He sounds great. I'm glad he wasn't lonely," Drew says. And then, more seriously, "So why did he never mention it, then?"

"Oh, he almost admitted it once. What was it he said? 'Don't mention the g-word, Claude, people will clutch their pearls.' But it was like knowing the Queen's posh. It didn't need spelling out. And no one ever behaved as if it mattered anyway. Hey, it's not like I've ever actually told *you*, is it?"

Drew was still half smiling, half smirking from the joke when the question pulled him up straight.

"Yeah, but it's like you know that I know. I've known since I was old enough to realise there was anything *to* know. And pretty soon after that, I figured it wasn't actually important. You're just Gary and Tony, aren't you? What's not to like?"

He's smiling up at me now, while I silently realise that something can go from unspeakable to insignificant in the space of a generation. From a gasp to a shrug. The world always spins faster than we notice.

"So, what did *you* mean to *him*?"

The question catches me unawares, leaves me playing with a teaspoon and stroking my chin. I can see Judy watching me too, intrigued. How can I know? Even if I'd asked him, he'd never have been so indiscreet as to actually answer. Maybe Drew just wants to know that godsons matter to somebody.

"Someone to spoil, maybe, or to encourage. Someone you could treat without needing to have a reason. Without them having to do anything special. That's a nice feeling, you know?"

I've not meant to, but I've embarrassed him now. Like a cat that's had too much attention and needs to stir, he's carefully shuffling his work back into order and shifting to his feet, asking Judy if he can make Zoe more tea. I let him go, retreat upstairs to recover from the unexpected flattery.

Before dinner arrives, I text Tony and grab a few things from the car, high-stepping through the snowdrifts like a disgruntled dog being walked through puddles. He rings me back, sends love to everyone and commiserations. "There are worst places to be stranded," he tells me. "Remember West Virginia?"

How could I forget? A metre of snow in a few hours, and we slept under gaudy plaster Jesuses in separate freezing motel rooms, too scared to ask the owner if we could share. No, this was definitely better, even if Tony wasn't here. And at least he knows how fast we're all spinning. 1,038 miles per hour at the equator, he tells me, my little know-all. Even faster than Ella's tongue, he says. I hope she'll be impressed.

The dinner table is crowded, ten of us altogether, everyone talking and reaching across each other without apology. Ella and her friends are lost in their own conversations, arguments cresting and crashing like surf. The rotational speed of the planet has their attention for a few seconds before I'm ignored again. Too old, too male. Too alien. At the far end, Drew's older sister Gemma ignores us all. Swathed in black jersey, her attention fixed on a textbook about probate law, she's absorbed in rehearsals for a thousand funerals, a vulture perched on a wheel-backed chair. "Very much her grandmother's girl," Judy whispers to me.

Drew and Zoe are squeezed together on one end of a bench, looking shy to be eating together with us but glad to be there, accepted. She asks me where I get the inspiration for the gargoyles, and giggles when I name a few actors and politicians. I tell her that she really means grotesques, that we carve the ogres and the ugly faces for entertainment more than anything else.

I explain how gargoyles are practical things, part of the guttering. There to protect more than scare, to stop the rainwater damaging the stonework. That even masons don't think they're all beautiful.

As the plates are cleared and the coffee mugs handed along, she leans across the table.

"Drew and I can sleep in the attic, so you can have his bed if you like? You'd be more comfortable. And" – her blushes are almost as deep as his – "he wants to finish a picture of me he's started."

I half expect Judy to protest, but she simply smiles and thanks Zoe for being so thoughtful.

The scented candle that Zoe's lit for me flutters in the draught from the old sash window and I pull the blankets up to my nose. The drifting sandalwood smoke merges with something earthier, the whole room pungent with late adolescence – hair gels, skin creams, other smells it would feel intrusive to contemplate. Judy taps at the door, brings me a mulled-wine nightcap and lingers for a moment.

"Thanks for today, my love. It's been hard for Drew without Jay. Poor lamb's drowning in girls, and he doesn't get a lot of encouragement. I can't any more – I'm his mum, aren't I? I'm just an embarrassment at his age."

She's not heartbroken, just wondering how to still be helpful, trying to be useful. I laugh, not so much to agree as to show her that I understand, allow her to josh with me.

"And hey, stonemasons are good for *one* thing, aren't they?" she teases.

"They are?" I'm not getting the reference, missing the joke.

"Oh yes. Patiently chipping away," she says with a cheeky grin before she closes the door behind her.

I sip the hot wine and think about Danny, try to imagine what I meant to him. He was always a blessing to me. All those sly lessons in life that went a little beyond my parents' curriculum. Nothing boldly labelled, just left for me to absorb. Little nuggets of wisdom along with the gifts and the treats, tucked in pockets ready for when their time came.

They say seeing is believing, but it's not the same as understanding. Sometimes it's just seeing. And there he was, Sunday lunchtimes. Uncle Danny, bold as brass and brassy with it, pouring gravy over his roast potatoes and a different kind of sauce into the conversation. No one said it was unusual, so it wasn't. Just my godfather and a handsome man giggling along to *Round the Horne* and teasing Mum as she tried to get everything on the table on time so we'd finish eating before Dad's football started on the telly.

There he was, as far back as I can remember, casually dispensing a cocktail of hard spirits and blithe remarks. Sometimes holding hands under the tablecloth with Dimitri or Raoul or Graham or Mike. It stands out in hindsight, but at the time it was just what happened on Sundays. An education supplied in jigsaw pieces, one by one. That was the first lesson, I guess. Style over substance isn't a victory, just an overlay. A neatly embroidered surface with all the stitchwork hidden underneath.

There was never a big reveal, a clear view of the picture on the puzzle-box lid. A steady stream of evidence, but no actual crime. Dad had known him all his life, Mum half of hers: Danny had been acquitted from the start. Not that anyone would quite have chosen the word innocent. Not even him. He'd have just glided round the whole issue like an ice-skater coming to a sharp bend.

Maybe that was what drew him back. Godless and childless, more secular angel than plaster saint, and adored all the more for it. We were a safe republic, well-ordered and neutral, no visa required. No interrogation on arrival, no contemptuous rummage through personal baggage. Just a comfortable vantage point above the fray. His own little Switzerland.

Did I ever get a clue what I meant to him in all that? Maybe, right at the end. When I'd have been about six, Mike and him had brought me a toy koala from Australia, soft and tactile with velvety fur. When I was older, we'd joke about the way Dad had said how beautiful he was and asked Danny where he found him. Mike had misunderstood and started to say, "Well, I was in this waterfront bar in Sydney . . ." before Danny kicked him under the table and rescued the story. Everyone kept that laugh in for thirty years. And at the time I'd been unaware, hugging the bear and singing a hit song of the day.

> *You're there every night when I whisper my prayers,*
> *My pillow share, my teddy bear;*
> *When I brush my fingers through your fur*
> *Whatever I hope for, you concur.*
> *Though others may think I'm a curious fish,*
> *I just close my eyes and make my wish . . .*

On summer days over the next couple of years, apparently I always sang it when Danny and Mike took me out for day trips, bought me all the sweets Mum disapproved of.

Danny stopped visiting when he got ill, when all those elegantly smoked cigarettes caught up with him. I was in my thirties by then, long since moved away, but I knew somehow. The postcards from exotic cities stopped coming, their absence like a sign. Mum told me he was in hospital and refusing visitors. Undeterred, I made up a tape of his favourite songs and found an old spare Walkman, went to visit him. I told myself I could leave them with the nurses if he wouldn't see me.

He'd been asleep when I got there, resplendent in his silk pyjamas in a private room. The bedside table was covered with vases of flowers from men whose names I didn't recognise. I slipped the headphones gently over his ears, and played the first song very softly.

> *You're there every night when I whisper my prayers . . .*

He opened his eyes groggily and I waited till he could focus. He just smiled and took my hand in his.

"You remembered," he said. "How lovely."

"Here's to the crazy ones. The misfits. The rebels. The troublemakers. The round pegs in square holes. The ones who see things differently."

Steve Jobs

Love with Impediments

HARI KUNZRU

You walk across the stunning oak-laminate flooring and little animated hammers dance around your feet, indicating toughness and durability. Your kitchen has flipped into its clinical mode, a thousand-watt wipe-clean temple of hygiene, so you smile and twirl, showers of tiny sparkles cascading from the shoulders of your linen tunic, your tunic so deep-down clean and optically bright, and for a brief moment your eyes are rimmed with silver and some kind of headset snakes its way around your perfect jaw. Then you laugh and the light dims and colour blooms in the kitchen and you put your finger to your lips because you're a woman with a secret. All women have secrets, particularly beautiful women like you; they have sexual secrets and homecare secrets and secret hair and make-up tricks they use to get ahead of their rivals, secrets they paradoxically love to share, to spread far and wide until they're no longer secrets at all, but it never matters, because there's always a new one to share, a new secret for a beautiful woman like you.

Now you pull a face, a cute scrunched-up little-girl face, because though you're a beautiful woman, and quite grown-up, it's attractive to act like a child, and (despite your beauty, your radiant beauty) you've just realised you're looking a fright! What's the problem, pretty girl? It's your hair, dummy! You're being humorously reprimanded by a talking shampoo bottle which is perched on your shoulder like a demented parrot. Now you look shocked – not frightened, just surprised – because this nannying little bottle is upending and dumping a gem-like cascade of capsules and atoms and spinning scientific whatnots onto your hair, which magnifies and simplifies, scaling down to a single follicle that acquires a protective green force field and a bouncy sheen men love to touch. As you twirl once again (you're always twirling) your silken carpet of tinted red-blonde brunetteness whips around the axis of your swan-like neck and the kitchen lets off a great fart of light and the *1812 Overture* plays and a pile of bright pine-fresh self-ironing clothes explodes upwards like a flower trumpeting pollen. White net curtains billow out of the window onto an electric-blue sky, because it's summertime here in the kitchen and all's very well indeed, which is why you can hear your favourite summer song as you sashay through into the living area to see your Man.

Here he is. Not any man. Not the Man of Your Dreams, who usually appears against a backdrop of coconut palms, his smooth chest lightly oiled, his ribs a precise architectural sand-dune ripple. No, not him, but your Real Man, the one who has a football shirt and a cute little tummy which you pat as you switch his regular cereal for a low-sugar alternative. He's sitting at his laptop, smart casual in pastel cottons, choosing between an array of tailored financial products, his head literally spinning with the difficulty of the task. You put a perfectly French-manicured hand on his shoulder and smile your beautiful bright smile. His head stops whirling and you exchange a mutually complicit glance as the laptop flares into transparency, revealing the complex electronics inside. Hand in hand, you take a dark-ride through the digital tunnels and alleys of its superfast processor, your holiday photos and music collection whizzing around you as you accelerate towards the light, towards a bright cosmic disk which sucks you into the unimaginable total future of technology – and pops you back out into the primary-coloured world of stress-free financial planning.

As you stand with your Man, mouths agape in wonderment, your house disassembles itself around you like a piece of flat-pack furniture, then reassembles into a much larger house, more appropriate to your age and station, then just as suddenly shrinks into a delightful country cottage, with a thatched roof and a rose garden in which the two of you, white-haired now, exchange a tender kiss freighted with a lifetime of happy memories. Your secure retirement fades into a golden glow, a cruise ship vanishing over the horizon as smiling people in business suits usher you back into your fast-paced contemporary lifestyle, with all its challenges and excitements, but you have no fear of the unforeseeable, because you're safely in possession of a flexible policy, adapted just for you. The policy warps its shiny body, smiling and waving its little arms, snapping itself like naughty knicker elastic. The street where you live is drenched in euphoria, personified by a white woman who leads a vast gospel choir, a choir as endless as the Red Army marching across the steppe, marching through thousands of other streets just like yours, streets exactly the same as yours, streets that could be clones of your street, because you are absolutely one hundred per cent typical. You are safe because you're typical and things are organised just for you by people just like you who know what you want which is to be free and normal and safe. You are one hundred per cent safely normal and people just like you are marching through all the streets of this great land, thousands of voices raised in praise of that greatest of virtues: *flexibility*. Hallelujah!

You skip up to the bedroom and flop down again and again and again on a series of beds, on beds in all their infinite variety, with all their many covers and bedsteads and throw cushions and optional storage drawers. Then, because you're naughty and enjoy a night out with the girls, you wipe a fleck of crumbly chocolate away from your beautiful lips and dance a few steps in an instantaneous disco pub, rubbing like a cat against the Man of Your Dreams, who toasts you with a bottle of some sophisticated bright-green drink. The Man's sculptural pecs are half exposed by his tight shirt. His teeth are like glossy bathroom tiles under the shifting light of the glitterball. This is the pub, but it's also the bedroom, and the lights are low and you're at the edge of your comfort zone, because darkness is here. Darkness is always lurking somewhere in the bedroom, in this place where naughtiness shades into something you can't talk about, the creeping nagging sense that perhaps you're not just naughty, you're actually bad. Perhaps you're a bad beautiful woman, because you have doubts. You have guilty doubts, secrets that you don't like to share, and you find yourself wondering, *What does he do when I'm not there?*

You creep to the keyhole and look through. There he is, your Man, his cute tummy hidden under a pair of striped pyjamas. He has a cold. His face is a contorted mask and little icicles hang from his enormous distended nose, which glows red as he tries to blow it on an absurdly undersized handkerchief. Luckily he has a fail-safe remedy, which leaps down his throat, suffusing him with green-tinted relief and reducing his nose to its ordinary manageable size. He looks like himself again, ready to earn money and impress the boss, who's swivelling round to face him on his graphite-grey chair.

There is a scream behind you. It is Little Ethan, in his nappy. Little Ethan points his finger. "You are a guilty woman," he snarls. "You are wrong. You are unattractive."

"No, Little Ethan," you beg. "Say it's not so."

In answer, his beautiful soft baby face goes slack and a torrent of blue liquid gushes down his legs, spurting from the waistband of his nappy and pooling on the floor. The nappy flies away, folding and unfolding itself in fantastic origami designs. You are left with the gushing flow, which must be wiped up. You get down on your knees and give thanks that there is such a quality as super-absorbency in this mean world, that there are tiny cavities and pockets and sacs to soak up moisture, even the bright-blue gushing kind which is the most unmentionable kind of all.

"Naughty Ethan," you say. Little Ethan lies on the floor, kicking his legs. His eyes are bright. He is surrounded by a dancing entourage of animated bears and rabbits. "Little Ethan," you croon. "You are so beautiful. What will you be when you grow up?" Little Ethan morphs and changes, for he is a creature of infinite potential, worthy of the love you lavish on him. Little Ethan is a racing driver, a teacher, a doctor saving lives in a remote African village. Little Ethan is potential incarnate and you must defer to him. He is hope. He can make up for all the things you lack. "Tell Mummy, Little Ethan," you coo. "Tell her what you want to be, what you want to do."

"I want to preside over an administration that produces record levels of growth and prosperity for this country. Get me one of those!"

He points to a monstrous truck, the size of a twenty-storey building. The truck is clad in lurid yellow and green panels. It spits fire from the muzzle of a front-mounted cannon.

"Yes, Little Ethan," you promise, chucking him under the chin.

"I will run a tight ship," screams Little Ethan. "I will reinstate traditional values."

You know he is right. Though you are a beautiful woman, you sometimes suspect you are not normal. The mean world is so unstable, so filled with risky choices. You know you lack values. You wish you could believe in things like they did in the olden days, when Men were Men and Beautiful Women were either in the kitchen or lying in alluring yet demure poses in their traditionally furnished bedrooms. Sometimes you secretly wish all this choice were taken away from you.

As you think this guilty thought, blue liquid starts gushing from between your legs. You plaster yourself in super-absorbent pads, stuffing them into your enormous unflattering underwear as you look wildly around to see if all the other Beautiful Women, who are playing sports and wearing white clothing in a variety of social settings, have noticed the horrible thing happening to you. "I need puréed organic vegetables!" screams Little Ethan, and you open tub after tub, spooning it into his mouth faster than the eye can see. As you spoon you can feel the blue liquid filling the absorbent pads, but you don't have time to check because you have to spoon purée into Little Ethan, and though you try as hard as you can, you don't spoon fast enough, and things turn bad, bad down there in the unmentionable place, bad in the gaping red mouth of Little Ethan, bad all around you in the kitchen. The light is getting worse. Your products are less attractive and work less well. Things are moving downscale, helter-skeltering down from bespoke to luxury to quality to economy to supersaver to product recall and your body, your beautiful body, is changing, unwelcome sections of it expanding and magnifying, revealing the true horror of you – a suppurating mass of head lice and embarrassing itching and smell and hair. "No!" you whimper. "Little Ethan, help!"

Little Ethan is gigantic now, his nappy bulging with nastiness that oozes over the waistband, green animated germs and parasites and fuzzy creatures which are perhaps anxieties or sleeplessness or ailments that could have been easily cured if only they'd been diagnosed in time. To your horror Little Ethan grabs the Velcro tabs of his nappy and yanks it open and with a sound like rolling thunder all the nastiness falls on you and you tumble backwards, flailing your beautiful arms and screaming because you are falling down into hell.

You reach out amidst the darkness and unmentionable substances, groping around, pleading for help. Then someone takes your hand in his. It is your Man! Hallelujah! At least he's here too, even in hell. But when you take a look at him, you realise he's not the Man of Your Dreams, or even your Real Man, but a drawn and rather pathetic bespectacled figure, an invalid of some kind, his woollen dressing gown tied tightly around his concave chest, a ratty tartan blanket spread across his knees. You're holding hands with him, shackled by bonds too tight to break. Of all the horrible things that could happen, this is the worst. You're sharing your life with the worst kind of Man, the Man Who Made the Wrong Choice. His product let him down. It didn't do what it said on the tin. You're sitting together outside an old-fashioned convalescent home. Evidently his Wrong Choice has brought on some kind of mental and physical collapse. It's possible his legs are missing. It's very possible he doesn't function in other unmentionable ways.

A terrible thought crosses your mind. This Man is a bad chooser *and he chose you*. What can that mean? As you agonise, you see your neighbour, that smug woman who has always been less beautiful than you, who has always been jealous of the ease and elegance of your choices. She is reclining in a bubble of beach-hued yellow, raising a smugly plucked eyebrow at the bulging packet of a passing surfer. No, it can't be! She's draped over the smooth oiled chest of a Man, and not just any Man but the Man of Your Dreams. She's rooting around, digging deep into the unmentionable recesses of his shorts. The horror!

Minute by minute your world grows greyer. You've been badly injured and had to stay in hospital and the helpline couldn't help you and the bills were overwhelming and you didn't win your claim but still somehow had to pay a fee and it's possible you won't ever get better, because you and your Man, your sad pathetic Man, are now entangled in coils of red tape, like the tentacles of a Japanese sea monster. You're sinking down into murky depths filled with shipwrecks and hollow yawning sounds, the air escaping from your lungs as you reach the place where Men and Women go to suffer. They are all around you, faceless suffering people outlined in red, discs of pain bulging and pulsing at their elbows, their foreheads, in the small of their backs. They are lifting heavy things, performing easy tasks that have suddenly become hard. Elsewhere lithe twenty-somethings are thwacking tennis balls and adopting yoga poses without the least sign of strain, but here in hell it is orange and red. You are no longer yourself, just an orange silhouette with discs pulsing at your joints, no longer an individual but a nameless member of the oppressed masses of pain. Little Ethan stares at you from a watchtower. The braid on his uniform glints in the sickly light.

"You are not alone!" screams Little Ethan. "If you want, you can feel like a person again!" And in great anguish you get down on your knees and bow your head and listen to the inspirational words of Little Ethan, who has a sun tan and a lemon-yellow sports shirt, who combines faith in a higher power with motivational linguistic checkpoints that will help you achieve your goals and exist in harmony with a balanced planet. And you think to yourself, *If I cut the head off, would it die? How will I ever find the head?*

"If you only read the books that everyone else is reading, you can only think what everyone else is thinking."

Haruki Murakami

Grand Theft

ANGELA SHOOSMITH

I pull up to the kerb opposite the jeweller's. It's easy to park in Miami again. The college kids and rich families that annex South Beach all March have gone back to their woollen winter up north. I cross the empty street, enjoying being left alone in my quiet corner of the city.

There's a handwritten sign taped inside the door of the shop: *Back in 20*, it says. Face to the glass, I cup my hands round my eyes to read the clock on the wall. 12.40. Must be at lunch. It'd be a pain to come back; our new conductor has us in rehearsals for the Mahler the rest of the week and Nathan really wants his watch working again. He says the kids get restless if he stays on one topic for longer than five minutes. At that rate, I told him, he must be able to cover the whole of American history in a week.

The car is a cool refuge from the afternoon heat. I watch the shop door a few minutes for signs of activity. What's taking them so long? If I'm late getting back again I'll lose the solo – the other flute players already have their eyes on my chair. But Nathan promised to cook tonight if I did this for him. Tit for tat, the rhythm of marriage.

I change the station on the radio from NPR to BIG 105.9, "Miami's home for classic rock". As the announcer segues into the opening notes of *Sweet Child o' Mine*, I tilt my head back and close my eyes. I used to wear black leather to concerts; now it's a black gown. The sundress I put on this morning feels tight across my chest and the air conditioning chills the skin where it gapes. Resting my hands in the dents between my hips and the swell of my belly, I feel for any percussion.

A loud knock at my window makes me snap forward. I grasp the steering wheel to steady myself then look up. There's a young man with his fist to the glass. He's no older than one of Nathan's students, black, with thick cornrows striped along his scalp.

"Hey lady," he says, looking over each shoulder, "can I talk to you?"

Is he in trouble? Am I? He's staring at me now, his palm pressed to the window. I search his face for some sort of clue, but find none.

He purses his lips and cocks his head to one side. "Hablo inglaze? Look, I just need to talk to you."

It's so quiet on the street I can hear the old man's keys jangle as he does up the locks, top, middle, bottom. Krazy told me the locks wouldn't matter, that the sledgehammer would do the trick. I asked him how I was supposed to get the sledgehammer on two buses. He told me figure it out. That's part of the process, brother. I found one with a shorter handle on a construction site and put it in Raymond's gym bag. Raymond yelled at me, said he'd tell Mama, but I told him I needed his bag for a special mission. Told him he could carry his stuff to school in a grocery sack for one day. He asked me when I was coming back to school. I told him I didn't know.

I watch the old man shuffle off down the sidewalk. He's got white hair that sticks out above his ears and his bald spot is shiny with sweat. It's hot. My sweatshirt's getting damp where the bag rests against my back. I shift the bag to my other shoulder and the sledgehammer knocks against my spine. I know I don't have much time, that the old man will come back with his sandwich in twenty minutes. But it's enough. Just smash and grab, Krazy said. Show us you can do it. You got to prove yourself.

I pull my hood up as I start across the street. A car comes round the corner. It's nothing special, not like Krazy's black Range Rover. I duck behind a dumpster in the alley and try to make myself small.

The sledgehammer clanks against the metal. I hold my breath.

The car door slams. I wait a couple of seconds then look around the wall. A lady's at the shop door with her face squashed against the glass. *It's closed lady. Go away.* Her dress is short and it looks like whatever she's got up in her belly's about to fall out the bottom. *Come back tomorrow. I got shit to do.*

She gets back in her car and I can hear the engine start. I wait for the crunch of tyres on the road, but nothing happens. I look around the wall again, my hood still up, shading my eyes. The white lady's just sitting there in her car. I can see she's got her eyes closed, but her lips are moving, like she's singing.

My phone vibrates in my pocket and I jump back, knocking into the dumpster again. I check the number. Home.

"What?" I try to whisper.

"Where are you?" It's my little sister. She's screaming and crying something fierce. "You gotta come home right now."

"What's going on? Why ain't you at school, Jayla?"

"I was sick so Raymond took me home an' then we found a gun in your room and . . ."

"Shit, Jay, what happened?"

"We were just playing. He said it wouldn't shoot. His leg's bleeding so hard. There's blood all over. I started to call nine-one-one but he said no, call you. You'd know what to do."

I tell her to find some towels and wrap his leg tight. I tell her to get some water and make Raymond drink it. I tell her not to call nine-one-one, that it's going to be OK. I don't tell her it's Krazy's gun, the shit I'd be in if he found out, if the cops came. I tell her sit tight, I'll be home quick.

I remember the two buses, the million and one stops it took to get here from Pork 'n' Beans. I look round the wall again and the white lady's still there, singing away. I pull my hood back and smooth my hands over my cornrows. I gotta look straight or she's just gonna take off.

I go up to her window and knock on the glass. She jumps up off her seat. "Hey lady," I say. I look over each shoulder to check if anyone's around. Street's empty. "Can I talk to you?"

She doesn't move. She's frozen, like some mannequin at the mall. She's just staring at me. I stare straight back, trying to figure out what to say next. Maybe she doesn't speak English. "Hablo inglaze?" I try. "Look, I just need to talk to you."

There is something about this boy that makes me want to help him. Something in the way his voice broke when he said it was an emergency. It's hard to turn down an opportunity to give someone a hand. "You're always paying it forward," Nathan says. It's not like the boy gave me much of a choice. When I offered to call the police he shouted at me. "Don't you fucking call the cops!" he yelled, and slapped my window with the palm of his hand. But when I started to open the door he slammed it back shut. "This ain't no carjacking," he said. "You drive," and then he got into the back seat as if this were a cab. He won't tell me where we're going.

"So which way now?" I look at the reflection of the boy in my rear-view mirror. He's wound tight.

"Straight here. I'll let you know when to turn."

"You want me to get on the freeway?"

"I said straight, didn't I? Just do what I say, got it?"

I drive on, my hands at ten and two on the wheel. I try to keep an eye on him in the back seat while also trying not to appear obvious when I check the mirrors for police cars, in case things get out of hand. Maybe I should keep it casual. He's looking out of the window with one hand on the door handle and the other on the red nylon bag next to him. The bag appears empty except for something large and T-shaped.

"What's in the bag?" I ask. "Were you on your way to school?"

"Just drive and mind your own business."

We're now miles from the jewellery store and I wonder what he was doing on that street.

Rehearsal will be starting again in a minute. They'll be warming up. I imagine them gazing at my empty chair and the tune from *Jaws* pops into my head.

"You sure you don't want me to get on the freeway? It'll be fast this time of day."

The boy doesn't look up.

There's a somersault in my tummy. I've nicknamed the baby Flipper but I haven't told Nathan that. He's still worried something might happen. Like last time.

"Look. I want to help you. But I'm going to need a little bit more to go on. What's your name? I'm –"

"Lady, I don't care if you're the Queen Empress of Dixie. I just need you to get me from A to B."

I exhale and focus on the road. Nathan always says no one can do everything, but everyone can do something. I'm always up for lending a hand, but this has got to take the cake.

"Fine," I say, glancing back again. "You know, I can help you better if you tell me where we're actually going. If this is a real emergency, then why are we going past every fricking Sedano's in Miami?"

This gets his attention. He looks at me in the mirror. His mouth is tight and he looks young. Too young. He can't be more than fifteen. Probably never even driven before.

"Christ," I say. "We're not going the bus route, are we?"

"You got a problem with that?"

"I don't have a problem with it, but the bus has got to be the slowest way around this city. I will take you wherever you want to get to, but you need to do us both a favour and tell me where that is."

The boy is looking out the window again. He doesn't answer straightaway. After a few moments he draws the hood of his sweatshirt up, obscuring his face.

I try not to think about Raymond. I think that if I can pause my brain the action will stop like in a video game, but the lady keeps asking me questions. What's in the bag? What's your name? Where are we going? The less she knows the better. I don't tell her in case she decides to flag one of the cop cars we pass. Instead I count the Sedano's. I notice them because Mama says they have chicken real cheap. We just went by number four.

"Christ," she says. "We're not going the bus route, are we?"

"You got a problem with that?" I say, but maybe she's right. It took me an hour and a half to get there. In an hour and a half Raymond could be in real bad shape. I can't think like that, though. I pull up my hood to keep my negative brainwaves from escaping my head.

"Liberty City," I tell her.

I never thought a white lady would drive like this. I guess I never thought about it at all, but when she takes the corner I'm pressed up against the door. My bag slides off the seat and the hammer lands on my foot.

"Fuck, lady. Where'd you learn to drive? *Grand Theft Auto*?"

"Close. Minnesota."

I pick the bag up off the floor and put it back on the seat. Krazy will want to know where I've stashed it. It's supposed to be filled with jewellery. I look at the lady in the front seat, driving like it's the Indy 500. She's got a real nice diamond ring on. Krazy wanted a new Rolex. I check my phone but no one's called. I should call Jayla. I don't even want to begin to think what I'm going to tell Mama.

"So, are you going to tell me what this big emergency is?"

This lady is getting pushy. Now I *know* that if I tell her someone's been shot all hell will break loose. She'll be on her phone faster than the ladies at Stunna's Hair when they've got some new dirt, and then there will be ambulances. And cops. I definitely don't want no cops. I can't have her calling no cops.

"Why you ask me so many questions?" I smooth my hand over the hard shape in my bag, making sure it's there if I need it.

"I can stop this car any time, you know."

"Yeah, and I got a sledgehammer says you won't." As soon as I say it I wish I hadn't. I want to catch the words and wrestle them back into my mouth.

I've gone this way enough times to drive it on autopilot. Nathan teaches near here. Is teaching now, I realise. Without his watch. He's always forgetting stuff and asking me to bring it to him at school. It's an emergency, he tells me, though it never is. I wonder if this emergency qualifies as genuine.

"So, are you going to tell me what this big emergency is?" I ask the boy.

"Why you ask me so many questions?"

I see him reach for his bag and rest his hand on the T-shaped item. It looks like it could be a hammer.

"I can stop this car any time, you know," I tell him.

"Yeah, and I got a sledgehammer says you won't."

What a little bastard. I've tried to be nice and now he's threatening me?

"Good luck getting back home once you've bashed my skull in. Is that what you're going to do? Is that the plan? Do you even have a plan?"

I don't know why I'm hassling him like this. He could hit me any time he wanted. I think I'm more outraged by his ungratefulness than I am by being threatened. Threats I can take. Ingratitude, though, that's something entirely different.

Maybe I shouldn't mess with this lady. I think she's a little crazy. Before the Puerto Rican chica next door popped her kid out she was always going all mama bear, throwing empty yoghurt cups at me even if I just walked by. Moms love to protect kids, especially their own.

"My plan is to get home to my little brother, got it? That's it."

"Why? Is he home on his own? How old is he?"

There she goes again with the questions. Seems like she's used to being in charge. Maybe I should tell her everything, come clean. She'd probably know what to do.

"He's home with my little sister. There's been a . . ." I find the sentence hard to finish. A shooting? A gun went off? "An accident," I decide. An accident. And it's because of me.

"Is he hurt? Is that it?"

She's looking at me in that mirror again. I wish she'd just look at the road. Her eyes are green. I've never seen anyone in real life with green eyes. Just on TV. I wonder what it's like to look into them.

"So what's his name, then? Your little brother," she asks.

"Ray. Raymond," I tell her. "My little brother's name is Raymond."

When he tells me his little brother's name it's like the balloon has burst and he can stop blowing. He puts his hood back and slides down a bit in his seat.

"Raymond's a nice name," I say.

"Mama used to call him Ray the Runt."

"How old is he?" I ask.

"He's nine. Smallest in his class but he don't act like he even notices."

I keep my eyes on the road but can hear the worry in his voice.

"Sounds like a brave kid."

"Stupid, more like. Talks to anyone. If Krazy comes round, he asks him question after question: How big your rims, Krazy? What kind of stereo you got in your ride, Krazy? How much can you lift, Krazy? He's like that yappy dog from *Bugs Bunny*."

"Who's Crazy?" I ask.

"Why you wanna know?" His voice is angry again.

"No reason. It's fine."

The boy goes quiet again and I exit onto Martin Luther King Boulevard.

"Krazy's just around, you know?" he says. "He likes to go out, right before dinner time, when he knows folks 's out on their porches. Doing the rounds, he calls it. So Raymond sees him when he's out cruising the neighbourhood in that big-ass Land Rover he's got. Ray calls him Mr Bling Bling, but if Krazy heard that he'd swat that boy like a fly."

"Isn't he afraid of him?"

"Nah, Ray's not afraid. If he knew what was good for him he would be. But he just thinks of Krazy like some kind of Santa Claus just cuz every time he comes round he brings Ray a Snickers."

"That seems like a nice thing to do."

"It ain't nice. It's recruiting. He gives candy to all the kids on the block."

"Are you in Crazy's gang?" I ask. The question hangs there, unanswered. "Does Raymond know about . . ." The words get left on the road behind. "Does he know what you've been up to?"

"What do you mean, 'been up to'? It ain't like I've been planning a surprise party exactly, now is it?"

"Does he respect you for it?"

"What do you know about *respect*, lady?" He says it like he's spitting. "I got plenty of respect."

I think about him approaching my car, each of us alone on that street by the jewellery store. Him with his red nylon bag.

"Then why are you the one across town robbing a jewellery store with a hammer?"

*

Sometimes I think being in Krazy's gang *is* like throwing a surprise party. You know you shouldn't talk about it, but when you finally own up, all you want to do is yap about the food and the games and the music. Now we're back in the neighbourhood I can't seem to keep my mouth shut. Shit.

Keep it casual, I remind myself. I tell the boy I've never properly been in Liberty City, that Nathan's a bit north of here, at Miami Central.

"I know some kids who go there." He points to a row of houses on our left. "This is it. Pull up here."

I'm surprised at the houses' tropical pinks and blues and greens. It looks cheerful here, not at all like I expected. What did I expect? A war zone? Gangs of backwards-capped youths roving the streets armed with baseball bats? Instead it's quiet. I wonder if I should stay in the car or follow him in. I still don't know if it's actually serious or if this boy just didn't have bus fare. The sun is shining. There are two mothers pushing their baby strollers down the street.

Of all the things to be sweating when we get home – how the front porch looks. Having a white lady here makes me want to hide the broken lawn chairs and plastic toys. I didn't ask her to, but she's following me in. She didn't even lock her car. She's clutching her belly like LeBron after tip-off.

"Jayla!" I call. The curtains are closed and the only light is from the TV. *Judge Judy*'s blaring. There are dirty dishes everywhere and it smells like cheese.

"Marcus! In here!" I follow Jayla's voice to the bedroom. It's a disaster. There's blood everywhere and Raymond's on his back with his leg wrapped up in towels, like I told Jayla. The gun is on the floor and I kick it under my bed, where Jayla's sitting. "You did good, Jay," I tell her. "I'm here now. We're here now."

I let the boy go ahead before I follow him into the bedroom. The house is small but well-kept. The afghan on the back of the sofa looks hand-knitted. I take a deep breath and prepare to see anything. When I enter the bedroom, the younger boy – Raymond, presumably – is lying on the bed, his leg covered with bloody towels. He's small, his face ashen. His eyes are closed and his chest is rising and falling in a staccato rhythm. My hands go straight to my belly.

"I haven't told nobody. Like you said, Marcus," the little girl, Jayla, says. She is crying on the bed opposite.

"What happened here? We have to call an ambulance. Raymond needs to get to a hospital." I open my purse and pat around for my phone.

"No. Look, lady, I got this under control. No ambulance."

"Under control? Raymond is hurt. Seriously hurt. How did this happen?" I turn to the little girl who is staring at me in bewilderment. "Sweetheart, you need to tell me how this happened so I can help."

She rises from the bed and stands next to the boy, Marcus. Her head reaches only just above his elbow. "We were playing with Marcus's gun. Didn't think it'd go off." She starts crying again and buries her head in the crook of his arm.

"Jesus."

I've always thought that if I tried hard enough, if I always did the right thing, one day a million small acts of generosity might be repaid with one big act of grace. I'm not religious, or even superstitious, but I can always see the logic in karma. The bigger the sacrifice, the greater the inconvenience, the more I should get back, as if Life keeps score.

It isn't just any good deed that has brought me here, but a touchdown, a full house, a maximum-points-scoring deed that will overshadow all the others. *One time I took a gang kid to the projects just because he asked.*

"It's Marcus, right? Marcus, listen to me. Raymond is going to bleed to death if we don't get him some help right now." But seeing Raymond here, bleeding, his life flowing out onto the light-blue blanket on the bed, staining the cartoon trains with blood, at this moment I would trade all of those banked good deeds for my moment of grace to come now. And I'd give it to him. But karma is not currency and this boy is going to die.

Dad Is Not Equal To $81,750

MARTYN BRYANT

I nstead of being twenty-three years old, having a dad, $43.94, and no car, Anthony is twenty-four, drives his dead dad's Volkswagen Jetta and has $81,790.94 in his bank account.

Anthony has $81,788.37 and his mom passes him a photo of his dad in his twenties, when she loved him. Anthony looks like his dad in the photo; they both have the same dark-brown bangs brushed across their foreheads and hair that mostly covers their large ears.

Anthony has $81,735.34 and instead of living with his mom, in his bedroom covered with his favourites of the 100 Sexiest Women in the World 2008 posters, he drives to his dad's old apartment in the west side of Toronto.

He pushes the door through his dad's mail (bank, utilities, etc.), which he has yet to cancel, sits on the couch beside the indentation where his dad used to sit, closes his eyes and listens to himself breathing.

Anthony has $81,452.28 and rotates the apartment out of its death orientation: the dining room becomes the lounge, lounge the bedroom, bedroom the dining room; the kitchen remains the kitchen.

He flips the mattress so his dad's sunken bodyprint (which

was on the right when his parents were together and seems to have been on the right ever since) is on the underside.

He takes down his father's inkjet prints of spiral galaxies and puts up the chaotic canvases he dripped, poured and splatted when he was sixteen.

The only things he buys are a 64-inch flatscreen to replace his dad's old cathode-ray-tube TV and a gym membership.

Anthony has $79,967.89 and a man from the bank says, "We notice you have a large sum of money in your current account."

Anthony says, "Stop calling me."

The man says, "Please be polite, I'm just doing my job."

Anthony says, "I am being polite. Don't tell me to be polite. I could find a new bank."

Anthony has $79,956.21 and finds a new bank. A way better bank.

Anthony has $79,230.45 and gets a room-service job at the airport Holiday Inn and expects to get big tips from the business travellers who'll order late-night champagne and oysters.

Anthony has $79,567.13 and teaches himself to assemble a medium-risk portfolio. He questions his morality as he adds a few high-risk Filipino shares.

Anthony has $82,300.98 and a lady opens Room 912 wearing a silky black nightgown. He gives her the onion rings and mayonnaise she ordered. She gives him one onion ring and a $5 tip.

Anthony has $84,327.27 and stops drinking alcohol and, if he has to go up or down fewer than eight flights of stairs, stops taking the elevator.

Anthony has $84,339.97 and his supervisor says, "Please don't talk to me with that tone."

Anthony says, "This is my normal tone."

Anthony has $81,984.32 and changes his cell-phone number so his supervisor cannot contact him.

Anthony has $81,980.87 and the Jetta spins one-and-a-half times and the passenger side hits a row of trees.

Anthony has $81,825.08 and buys a two-year-old BMW. He puts his dad's golf driver in the trunk.

He tells his mom the cost of insurance and she looks at the car and nods but won't get in and sit on the lovely heated leather seats.

Anthony has $59,983.21 and joins a new gym because the first gym was too expensive. On the way home he gets a whole-milk latte for the protein.

Anthony has $59,768.29 and his body conditioning is on schedule for him to enter the Mississauga Classic in six months.

Anthony has $59,238.70 and changes his profile picture to one of his developing abs. A friend comments within two minutes, "Anthony, It's called *Face*book for a reason." Another friend comments seven minutes later, "shit, you're jacked!!" and Anthony clicks Like.

Anthony has $59,108.11 and realises the first anniversary of his father's death was yesterday. He was in the gym yesterday, busy trying to change his life.

Anthony has $58,835.72 and burns his mouth on the trapped steam from a dim sum shrimp dumpling. He cools it with Sprite.

Anthony has $58,620.20 and is basically running the gym – this includes using it for free. Today he isolates his upper body because his quadriceps are in agony.

Anthony has $58,459.02 and wakes with a dead arm from sleeping on his side. He massages it for twenty minutes to get the feeling back.

Anthony has $58,459.02 and buys an XL T-shirt with a coiled python on the front.

Anthony has $58,502.98 and it's Chantel's first day at the front desk of the gym.

Anthony leaves at 10.38 a.m. for twenty-three minutes to get them each a whole-milk latte.

Anthony has $58,602.98 and the trunk of his BMW contains some of the gym owner's possessions: three Samurai swords and a large box of pirated Chinese pornography.

Anthony has $58,902.98 and the dim sum server shakes Anthony's hand and says, "Hello Anthony."

Anthony and Chantel sit by the window so he's able to see anyone touch his car.

She burns her mouth on the trapped steam from a pork dumpling and he laughs and then offers her a sip of his Sprite.

Anthony has $56,034.34 and his calves are almost cramping as he gallop-runs out of Starbucks and says, "What the fuck are you doing?" to an old man who just opened his car door onto Anthony's BMW.

Anthony has $53,540.07 and the gym owner says, "There seems to be some money missing from the cash."

Anthony has $53,345.65 and Chantel wants sex. She always wants sex. He obliges so she doesn't get moody.

He holds himself above her by putting tension into his triceps, anterior deltoids and pectorals. She touches his obliques. He tries not to fall on her.

Anthony has $51,493.94 and Chantel says, "You are lucky to have this opportunity with all that money."

Anthony says, "I would rather have my dad."

Anthony has $48,023.29 and isn't present when the police raid the gym.

Anthony has $43,380.77 and sells his flatscreen to the Pakistani guy who owns his new gym.

Anthony has $43,480.77 and the drive-thru server at Starbucks doesn't fill his coffee to the top. He drives back to the drive-thru intercom and says, "Can you fill it to the top?"

She says, "Please don't speak to me with that tone."

Anthony has $38,451.62 and his body conditioning is almost on schedule for him to enter the Montreal Classic in six months.

Anthony has $32,989.65 and sells his Filipino shares and ups the growth hormones.

Anthony has $29,001.02 and is hitting golf balls over the fence at the end of the driving range. An old man who works there says, "Can you put your T-shirt back on, sir?"

Anthony has $27,891.19 and drives Chantel to the mall to pick up application forms.

Anthony has $25,667.66 and whilst drinking a GroTech™/ AbHalo™ Chocolate Powder Shake realises that the third anniversary of his father's death was yesterday. Anthony is pleased with the coincidence that yesterday was a rest day from the gym and he was sitting at home alone for most of the day, in peace, looking at the art he made ten years ago.

Anthony has $22,215.29 and buys four chicken kievs – three for him, one for Chantel.

Anthony has $22,214.04 and his body conditioning is almost on schedule for him to enter the Mississauga Classic in six months.

Anthony has $17,000.00 and reclines in the bath and Chantel injects him in the left deltoid.

Anthony has $12,998.03 and his mom asks, "How much have you got left?"

He says, "65, 70k, something like that."

Anthony has $6,006.88 and calculates that in addition to her house he will inherit $200k+ when his mom dies.

Anthony has $5,888.76 and quits the gym because the owner just made another racist comment towards him.

Anthony has $609.07 and he sits in his car for the last time. Chantel says, "How much did you get when your dad died?"
Anthony says, "A lot."

Anthony has $6,009.07 and finds someone to rent his apartment from the first of the month.

Anthony has $5,146.39 and he proposes to Chantel and she says, "Yes."
In the evening he says to her, "I'm moving back home and I want you to come with me."

Anthony has $4,040.50 and remembers that the fourth anniversary of his father's death was last month. He can't remember what he was doing that day.

Anthony has $3,003.95 and when his mother opens the front door it takes her a moment to recognise him. He no longer looks like his dad in his twenties.

Anthony has $1,609.53 and is too tired to fill in the Travelodge application form and too tired to take down the 100 Sexiest Women in the World 2008 posters – he'll do them both in the morning. He gets into his single bed for the first time in five years. Chantel joins him and she holds him as they fall asleep. His muscles begin to reduce and water stops retaining on his face and neck.

Ça Plane Pour Moi

LEN LUKOWSKI

"And where do you see yourself in five years' time?"

"Either dead, a medical drugs zombie or in a mental hospital," I reply flatly and without hesitation, fixing my gaze on the off-white floor. I can't look up at the nurse, not because what I'm saying is awful – the future can't be worse than what already is – it's just that my brain has detached itself from my body so I can't make my head lift. Or maybe I can with some effort, but why bother?

"Well," she begins in her relentlessly upbeat way, almost with a wink, "I'm not going to put you in a mental hospital!"

I didn't think it would come to this. I thought I could hold it back for ever. I still felt that way a few months ago when I met Mika.

Mika was travelling around Europe. She was from Seattle – well, Tokyo originally, but she'd moved to the States with her family when she was a kid. Her accent sounded Californian to me – "We moved around a lot," she explained. When I say Mika was travelling around Europe, what I mean is, that had been her plan; she didn't actually see a lot of Europe because she spent two months living in my bedroom.

I met her at a gay indie night in King's Cross, which I went to a lot because they still played music from the mid-nineties. I was dancing overenthusiastically to Pulp when I clocked her. Not only was she hot but she too was dancing overenthusiastically to Pulp and singing along with all the words, and it wasn't *Common People* or *Disco 2000*, which everyone knows, it was *Pink Glove*, which although well known amongst true Pulp fans, had never been released as a single.

I looked at Mika when she wasn't looking at me and when I turned back to my friends she did the same. Soon it became obvious what we were doing so we gave up the pretence. After Mika and I had kissed for a long time I propositioned her: "Do you wanna come back to my place and have really terrible drunk sex?"

In the morning we lay tangled up in bed together and Mika told me she'd be leaving London in a couple of days. Her time at the hostel would be up and the city was too expensive. I told her a week wasn't long enough to not hate London and she should stay with me until she had mixed feelings about it.

"I don't hate London," she protested.

"You will. Then you'll have mixed feelings about it."

"How long did it take you to stop hating London?"

"I still do sometimes, I'm ambivalent."

"Well how long did that take?"

"About seven years."

"I am *not* staying here for seven years! Maybe just a little longer."

"Really? You'll stay?"

"For a bit."

I am not usually the move-in-after-one-shag type, but Mika and I were immediately drawn to each other, which almost never happens, not in my experience anyway. I also knew she had to go back to the States in a couple of months, so I didn't feel the usual crushing claustrophobia I get when someone likes me. My flatmate was always on tour with her band or at her boyfriend's, so before Mika came along I'd been coming home to an empty flat most nights. I loved Mika being there; she distracted me from myself. Just before I met her the thoughts had been increasing in volume and getting harder to ignore, but when I was with her I almost forgot anything was wrong.

"How many units of alcohol a week do you drink?"

"Erm . . ."

"So if you think about it, a pint of beer or a glass of wine are about two units. How many units?"

Jesus. "I don't know. It varies."

"Roughly."

"Fifteen?"

We got drunk every night, typically beginning with shots in some dimly lit pub and ending with cans of cider as we got home. We went to gigs in grimy basements, bars in Soho, squat parties; one night after my payday we went to a strip club. Mika wasn't jaded about London like everyone else I knew and when I was out with her things I'd long since gotten over felt exciting again.

We spent hung-over days in bed getting to know each other's sexual preferences; suggesting role plays whilst looking away in case our desires were a cause for horror, alarm or disgust. One of the first times we fucked I shyly pressed my hand down on her shoulder as she lay under me. She grabbed it and moved it to her neck and I pushed down, hardly believing I was allowed to. Thrilled.

I wasn't keeping track of time because I didn't want to think about Mika leaving. She sprung it on me one morning as I groggily dressed for work. She was lying on the bed in one of my T-shirts, laptop in front of her.

"I have to go back in three weeks and *I haven't even been to France!*" she told me, frantically clicking on Ryanair's website.

"France is rubbish," I said and climbed on top of her. "You'll have a terrible time."

"You're a jerk. Come to Paris with me!"

I always found Paris to be an overrated and unfriendly city, but I would have gone there with her in a heartbeat had I not been so skint. I'd spent all my money going out places with her and working at the gallery barely paid enough to live on. I resigned myself to never seeing her again.

"So you're going?" I rolled off her and lay beside her on the bed.

"I booked a flight for tomorrow."

"Tomorrow?"

She climbed on top of me. "You should come. You can totally stay with me at the hostel, I've got my own room. You just need to get a flight!"

I said I couldn't. I was a little hurt she'd given me no warning. Still, I called in sick that day and spent it with her.

"So can you tell me a bit about why you've come here today? I can see you're *very* distressed."

"I have all these thoughts. All these bad thoughts and they take over my head and I'm scared they'll make me hurt people. I try to stop them but recently it's been like . . ."

A memory flashes in my mind of being in my bedroom aged twelve, suddenly struck by the fear that if I lost my temper it would put everyone I loved in danger. That's how it began. Back then my sense of right and wrong was developing at terrifying speed and I realised so much of what was in my head was toxic. And if I could think toxic things they must be a part of me and I must always be on guard to stop them taking over. The bad thoughts.

I collect myself enough to speak to the nurse. "It's like they took over my head, like there's nothing else in my head, there's just the thoughts and that proves it."

The nurse tilts her head and tries to catch my eyes, which are still fixed on the floor. "What was that, darling?"

The day Mika left I was hung-over and exhausted. I was also a little sad. Whilst bored at the airport she sent me pornographic messages which I received at work. In my break I went to the disabled toilet, locked the door and started masturbating. I know that might make me sound weird, but I had this feeling like there was so much in me that needed releasing and if I didn't do something maybe it would just come out its own way. I was getting to climax when I heard an energetic and insistent knocking on the door from outside and the voice of a young child. "Mum! This one's locked, this one's locked Mum." I came. If I came whilst hearing a kid's voice did that mean I was . . . ? Ridiculous, I told myself. Why are you even thinking that? But why was I so worried if there was nothing to it? No. Get a grip.

I got home intending to go straight to bed but then accidentally ended up on Facebook for five hours. I took a break only to buy a can of cider to try and make myself feel better but it made me feel lower. I wrote on Mika's wall, *Happy travels! xx* and posted a video of Plastic Bertrand singing *Ça Plane Pour Moi* because she was in France. I couldn't think of anything else to say so I turned out the lights and crawled into bed. In the darkness I saw an enormous malevolent mass hovering above me and when I closed my eyes it was still there. I could rationalise that it's normal to see shapes when we close our eyes, but that wasn't much comfort when the thing was looking right at me. As ever, my flatmate was at her boyfriend's and I was alone. I switched on the light so I could sleep.

"You say the thoughts are taking over your head and that just 'proves it'?"

I'm scared the nurse will lock me away if I tell her too much. Like why I try to avoid the news. Every time some atrocity happens – a rape, a gruesome murder, a paedophile scandal, ethnic cleansing – I am convinced for days, weeks, longer sometimes that I could do those things as well if I don't keep a grip on my head. All the ruminating is done alone. I've never been able to tell anyone my fears because I can't risk letting them know the thoughts are part of me.

"Proves what?"

But nothing can be worse than this feeling, this moment, now. What do I have left to lose? "Proves I'm all the things in my thoughts. Sometimes I think I'm a murderer or a rapist or I'll become a neo-Nazi."

"Why?"

"Because I can think about it."

"But people think all sorts of things. It doesn't mean they're going to do them."

"I wish I could think like everyone else. I feel like it's different for me. I can't ignore any of my thoughts."

The morning after Mika had gone my alarm sounded its painful notes. The first thing I did was check Facebook. Mika had replied to my *Ça Plane Pour Moi* post with *He's not French! He's Belgian! Come to Paris!*

I went to the bathroom to brush my teeth and ended up in the shower, then put on a record and stumbled around my room getting dressed. I heard the sound of an instant message which I was preparing to ignore, when I saw it was Mika asking how I was. I wished she hadn't because that morning I'd almost forgotten how I was. I told her I was good.

It was quiet at the gallery. I sat at the ticket desk in the cold white entrance hall, flicking between my personal emails, Facebook and my work emails, which I pretended to read whenever my manager came near. It was sunny so I had my lunch break outside with Roberto on a bench in the staff garden. I ate, he chain-smoked. Roberto was a cute, faggy, forty-five-year-old Spanish gay boy. It might sound patronising to refer to a forty-five-year-old as a boy, but Roberto still looked like he could star in twink porn. Besides, he was always complaining about how old and terrible he looked, so he'd probably take it as a compliment.

"So has the Japanese girl gone?" he asked.

"Mika?" I said, as though she was one of many. "Yeah, she's gone to Paris then she's going back to Seattle. *Then* she's going to move to Mexico City to be a teacher."

"She's going places!"

"Yeah. Not like us." I glanced at the grey walls of the gallery. "We'll be here till we drop dead, won't we?"

"So this is it? You're not going to see her? Aren't you sad?"

"Sort of. I liked her, she was really hot. But . . . I think I care less with each" – I put on a comedy-melodrama voice – "with each new disappointment and heartbreak." I fake laughed but then started to cough.

"Are you OK? Is it my cigarette?"

I shook my head. I told Roberto I needed to go inside then practically ran to the toilet where I had masturbated the day before and vomited. Half an hour later I was back behind the ticket desk and whenever customers came over images flashed in my mind of my hands around their throats, particularly if they were very old or young or disabled. Then I got images of my hands around Mika's throat like when we fucked, but this time pushing down relentlessly until she stopped breathing and died. I tried to forget we'd ever had sex like that or that I'd enjoyed it. I tried to make all the images stop but they just took up more and more space. Alarm sprang through me. I ducked off the counter to throw up again, shouting, "Sorry, just be one minute!" at Rochelle who was on shift with me. She barely looked up from Facebook.

I splashed cold water on my face from the sink, trying to reset myself. I tried to cancel out the strangling thoughts with other thoughts, but I felt like an animal struggling in a net that kept getting tighter. By my afternoon break I was hungry. I tried to eat an apple but every time I bit into it I gagged.

Just before I left work I got an email from Mika. *Do you like long coach journeys?* was all it said. I liked being in confined spaces with no responsibility except listening to music. I also found them uncomfortable, but then I spent my entire life feeling uncomfortable and I'd already guessed she'd gotten me a ticket to Paris. I answered *yes*, resisting the urge to write *Cheap sod! Haven't you heard of Eurostar?* in case she didn't get that I was joking. She emailed me a return ticket, apologising it wasn't for a flight. I told her, *Shut up! It's amazing* and smiled as I left work.

All that positive-thinking bullshit about how smiling makes you feel better is true: I forgot about feeling crazy as I walked to my bus stop full of thoughts of Paris and Mika. In my excitement I began to run without noticing I was running until Roberto saw me and shouted, "Hey! Off in a hurry?"

"Oh . . . no." I stopped, embarrassed.

"Oh. Well you look happier than at lunch. Are you OK?"

"Yeah yeah, I'm great. Guess what? I'm going to see Mika in Paris!"

"That's wonderful."

"Don't tell anyone yet though, in case I have to call in sick."

"My lips are sealed." Roberto lit a cigarette. "I was worried about you earlier. What happened?"

"I felt sick."

"Sick in the body?"

"Body. Head."

"The body and the head are really connected. Look after yourself, I want you to be OK." He took a drag on his cigarette.

I raised my eyebrows. "That's really good for your body, isn't it?"

He blew smoke out. "They're menthol."

"Have you spoken to your friends or family about this?"

"No. No I haven't told them."

"This seems like a lot to carry alone. How long have you felt like this?"

"Since I was twelve!" I shout quickly, trying to get it all out at once. Then, more quietly, I tell her, "But it started getting really really bad in the last week."

"Do you have a partner? Does your partner know?"

I shake my head. I think about Mika, but she's back in Seattle now. Or maybe she's gone to Mexico already. Anyway, I never told her anything.

"I'm sure you have some friends?"

"I do but I can't tell them because they might think I'm all the things I'm scared of. Sometimes I get thoughts about hurting them." I picture looks of horror on the faces of my friends, or on Mika's, who had trusted me so much.

The hostel where Mika was staying in central Paris was awful. It was dirty and garishly painted, with an all-night bar full of xenophobic tourists desperate to have, or look like they were having, fun. I got there earlier than expected; Mika was still out so I sat in the bar, next to a table of Australians, who were guzzling pints and brightly coloured shooters and complaining loudly about how no one in Slovenia spoke English.

"I'm sorry it's so horrible," was the first thing Mika said to me.

"Are you joking? It's great!" I hugged her.

"Are *you* joking?" She gestured to everything around us.

"Aww, we just need somewhere to stay, right?" I nodded at the Australians. "At least we don't have to share a room with them." We stood in silence for a moment, feeling awkward. "Errr, shall we go up to your room?"

We wrestled on the bed and in a couple of hours we were both bruised and sore. Our friendly hostel neighbours banged on the thin wall and yelled at us, "*You're fucking disgusting!*" We ignored them. In the morning I went to use the showers and some charmer had left a big shit right in the middle of the shower-room floor.

The shit haunted my dreams but it was better than what I usually dreamt about.

Everything we did in Paris was a cliché. We walked along the banks of the Seine and drank red wine. We went to Montmartre and drank red wine. We went to Père Lachaise cemetery and drank red wine and I got excited counting all the dead celebrities, photographing every grave with a famous corpse. I said I was going to start reading Proust. "You're so pretentious!" Mika told me and I took it as a compliment.

"Do you ever take drugs?" the nurse addresses me with her winning talk-to-loonies-as-children smile.

"Drugs?"

"Yes. Don't worry, it's *completely* confidential here. I'm not going to tell anyone."

"Errr, occasionally I take speed and MDMA. And sometimes mushrooms. Actually I took mushrooms a few weeks ago."

"And how did that affect you?"

"I enjoyed it."

"Oh good! I love mushrooms but sometimes they can give you the horrors."

"Sometimes, yes."

I think about me and Mika lying in bed together, making out, rubbing our bloody chests against each other after we'd taken mushrooms. That was a good feeling. I will never feel anything good again. I begin to weep.

"Oh dear, is it all feeling like a bit too much, sweetheart?"

I nod. *Yes. Oh God, make it end.*

"I think you need something to chill you out." And she passes me a blue pill like she's giving a child a sweetie. "Go on." She nudges me. "Why don't you take one *right now*?"

On the last day in Paris we decided to pierce each other for sexual play. Mika had some needles she'd somehow sneaked through airport security; she bought them at an S/M workshop she'd gone to in London. I'd had some experience of piercing but it had always been very controlled. Hardcore S/M people are obsessed with health and safety. Not us. We were wasted. Worse still we'd met some generous French boys in one of the gay bars earlier that night who'd shared their magic mushrooms with us, and before we got back to the hostel we'd ordered large shots of absinthe. The absinthe was so strong we couldn't drink more than a few mouthfuls and poured the rest into a plastic bottle to take back with us.

I am amazed I did not kill Mika that night, or vice versa, and sometimes it terrifies me thinking about it, but at the time it was wonderful. I climbed on top of her and pinched some of the skin on her left breast so I could push the needle through. She sighed and we fixed eye contact for a moment, both breathing heavily. "Now you do me," I said once I'd pushed more needles through her and she was grinning and stoned on endorphins. I sat up opposite her. When she did it she put the needles in slowly and hard so they bruised.

When Mika had finally finished, I reached for the plastic bottle of absinthe and took another sip. "OK," I said. "Let's pull them out."

Slowly we started pulling the needles out of each other's chests and the blood trickled. That's when the mushrooms began to kick in and I started laughing because I saw our blood floating in the air above us as it coagulated. Mika began laughing as well. I don't know whether she could see what I could but I pointed up at the floating blood and she seemed to understand. When we'd pulled out all the needles we just kissed because neither of us knew where to begin having sex in the state we were in.

I closed my eyes and dreamt hallucinogenic dreams. I was seeing Paris from a bird's eye view as though from Montmartre, but when I looked down at the city, the buildings and avenues weren't straight lines and cubes and rectangles, instead everything was squiggly and doused in red.

When I woke the next morning I screamed. I thought I'd killed her. We were both lying naked, dried blood on our chests. She opened her eyes and sat up, startled. "What's wrong?"

"Oh fuck . . . I thought . . . fuck, I thought I'd killed you . . ."

"No no . . ." she said sleepily.

"Wow. I mean, how are we even still alive?"

"We only did four piercings each. You should have seen the

demonstration woman in the workshop. I swear to God she was like a pincushion."

My head was pounding, my heart too. I pulled Mika close and closed my eyes again, thinking, It's OK, everything's all right.

I was happy for a few days after Paris – or at least I was OK, but then it got worse again. The bad thoughts became constant and it felt like they would burst out of me. I couldn't sleep and the vomiting returned, but this time it didn't stop after a day like it had before. I tried to be healthy. I bought salads but threw them all up – threw everything up. I stopped drinking but it was too late.

I managed to sleep one night for a few hours but dreamt vividly about corpses hanging. When I woke I had my own hands around my neck and was trying to strangle myself.

This morning I burst into tears on shift with Roberto. "You need to go home right now," he commanded. "I'll cover for you. You can't be here like this."

I got on the bus intending to go home but got off at A&E.

"And how's your sleeping?"

"I can't sleep."

"Not at all?"

"Not in the last week. Hardly at all. But when I do sleep I have nightmares."

I often dream I'm on the run from the police, dragging around the corpse of someone I've murdered. I can't find anywhere to hide it. Or I'll be back at my parents' house, having a family dinner when we're all well aware a time bomb is about to go off and destroy us. Despite our terror we are all trying to ignore it. Or I dream of falling in slow motion from a great grey tower, which is the only structure that exists in a world of darkness. I wake up with a sick feeling and a dry mouth, wet with sweat, jaw aching from grinding my teeth, exhausted, infected.

"Oh sweetheart. Not very nice, bad dreams, are they?"

The most tragic thing about this whole event is that there's no language adequate to convey how bad this feeling is. Everything is black and white. All the horror in the mind has taken over the body because the brain can't contain it any more. Every molecule of serotonin has been sucked from my being and I will never feel all right again.

The nurse asks me if I'm suicidal and I say it doesn't matter, I don't need to kill myself, there's no life after this feeling. She makes a confused face.

She leads me to a room in another part of the building, a room with a grey hospital bed. She helps me onto it and I sit up on the sterile paper that will protect it from my sweat. She gives me another blue pill and a cup of water. I look back at her. I swallow it. I think. Mika. And before long I am sleeping without nightmares, without any dreams at all.

Polynya

TALIM ARAB

Only yards from the seal, Inna heard a groan from beneath his feet then a creaking that grew louder. It was too late. The sea ice cracked, parted, and swallowed him whole.

Walls of blue-white ice surrounded him. He kicked his legs and thrashed his arms to reach the surface but it did nothing. He saw a distorted disc of light above him which shrank as his clothes and boots became lead weights pulling him down. His lungs burned, his limbs grew tired, and his movements slowed until he became limp. He closed his eyes and sank into the freezing abyss.

Inna heard the crackling, spitting of a fire and a muted clang of metal. His nostrils flared, picking up a waft of smoked bacon. It was a heavy, greasy smell that made his stomach growl.

He felt the brush of fur against his arm as he lifted it to wipe the sleep out of his eyes, blinking several times before his vision cleared. His elbow clicked as he sat up and he massaged the back of his head to ease the dull pain. Candlelight lit the room, casting flickering shadows on the wooden walls around him.

Inna rose from the floor, lured by the curiosities of the many cupboards and precarious shelves before him. The floorboards creaked on his first step and he stopped. He took another step, lifting his foot carefully this time and lowering it on the floor without making a sound. He gazed at the cupboards, which stored slender vessels, Codd-neck bottles, Bocksbeutel bottles, bottles with glazed decorations. Some bottles were empty and some were full with maroon liquids and burnt-orange oils. The jars on the shelves were filled with a cobalt powder, dried insects, and a large one contained a pig foetus. The glass magnified the piglet's white eyelashes and wrinkled body suspended in an amber gel.

"I thought the bacon might wake you."

Inna turned sharply. An old woman, wearing a grease-stained smock, with grey hair peeking out from her red headscarf, sat by the fireplace. She had doll-size feet, and Inna wondered how they supported a body the shape of a wine barrel. She ladled soup from a huge iron pot into dented metal bowls. She placed the soup on the wooden table between them.

"Men are always hungry. Sit. Eat."

Inna opened his mouth to say, "Thank you."

Nothing.

He tried again.

Nothing.

He held his throat, feeling his hand press against his Adam's apple. The squeeze box of his chest expanded as he inhaled and bellowed.

Nothing but silence.

He ran to the door of the hut, opened it, and shielded his eyes. As he opened them again cautiously he was confronted by a landscape pure white with snow, where the land and sky were indistinguishable.

"Close the door! The heat will escape," the old woman snapped.

Inna stormed in and grabbed the old woman's neck. Her feet dangled as he held her. She made choking, gurgling sounds. Inna could snap her windpipe with ease but he let her go abruptly and she fell to the floor.

She picked herself up, sat at the table and cleared her throat. "This is gratitude for saving your life! As for your voice, it's in a vial somewhere safe."

Inna looked at the cupboards and shelves.

"Not there, you idiot," said the old woman.

He slammed his fist on the table and soup splashed out from

the bowls. The old woman grinned; her front teeth were black as rot.

"Stay for the winter. I will return your voice at the start of spring if you help my son, Herring, with chores."

Inna frowned. The old woman rose and picked up a wooden spoon from the table. Beside the fire was a bed with a mound of blankets on it. Thwack! She hit the blankets and out sprang an ethereal-looking boy: his hair was crow black reflecting blue, his lips reminded Inna of the vermilion silk curtains at the theatre he once visited. He wondered how a hag could produce such an enchanting child.

"I fucked his father for three tins of herring, hence the name. The boy is dumb and not yet nineteen. He fell from his cot when he was a babe and has never been right since. But he knows the forest the way you know the sea. Are we agreed?"

Inna's mother and father were accustomed to him spending months at sea; they would not search for him. He looked at the soup. Chunks of potato and cubes of bacon bobbed on the oily surface, and curling fingers of steam rose from the bowl. He was starving. He nodded his acceptance and ate.

The next morning, the old woman gave Inna an axe and ordered him to collect kindling. Inna pointed to a small pyramid of logs beside the fireplace.

"The fire is gluttonous. Shut the door, Herring." Her eyes narrowed as she smiled. "Looking for your coat?"

Inna raised an eyebrow. Herring closed the door.

"I cut up your coat to make more blankets. It had to be done. Fine fur, that was. Don't panic."

Inna cursed inside his head.

The old woman walked to a drawer, removed a pair of large iron shears. She pinched the fire with her hand, and cut off a piece; there came a sound like gas escaping from a bottle. The flame wriggled between her fingers the way a worm would when cut in two.

This isn't real. I am dead, Inna thought, as Herring tugged at his sleeve. Inna stood in disbelief, transfixed by the old woman as she removed a chain with a silver locket on it from her apron pocket. She opened the locket, placed the flame inside and snapped it shut. She approached Inna but he stepped back. The old woman grabbed his shirt and pulled him towards her. She stood on tiptoe to place the locket around Inna's neck and he flinched. He felt no burn but a deep heat flooded his entire body. He then felt his arms tugged by an impatient Herring who pulled him out of the door and into the white wilderness.

It was so cold, if Inna pissed it would freeze mid-arc. He and Herring had walked for miles. He wore only his shirt and trousers, held up by braces, but the locket kept him impervious to the chill. There was a gentle crunch each time his boots sank into the snow. He saw how the snow revealed the bone structure of the landscape: the land was a clavicle that rose and fell in soft gradients. The hills before him were a series of undulating white lines. *If high tide were a solid surface*, he thought, *the contours would be similar.* Inna longed for the sea.

Herring scampered ahead; his lithe body made light work of travelling across the snow. Occasionally, he turned to see Inna struggle and would run back to help him, though Inna would push Herring away.

They passed isolated trees, then a few more dotted here and there, until they stood at the beginning of hundreds of fir trees. Inna noticed how the snow weighed heavily on the trees, bending and contorting them into grotesque shapes, while sunlight razored through their branches. The snow brought camouflage to the creatures living there, for they could be heard but not seen. The distant cawing of a crow. A dull scuttling noise, perhaps a vole burrowing beneath them. Inna knew the wolf and tiger roamed these woods. Such beasts had the advantage, for they hunted by stealth, and if he saw one, it would be too late to run. He worked quickly.

Hack! Hack! Inna swung powerful blows with his axe and felled a tree within minutes. He chopped the tree into logs but each time his axe rose Herring would interrupt him, showing him a leaf crippled by ice crystals or an oblong-shaped stone. Inna pointed to the ground, where Herring was supposed to find twigs and fallen branches. How he wished he could shout at the stupid boy.

The hours of light were lessening, and Inna decided on one

more tree. He chose a sturdy-looking fir and held his axe high but Herring pulled him back before he could deliver the blow. *Blasted boy!* Inna mouthed, feeling the veins in his neck pulse. Before Inna could strike Herring, he was already climbing the tree. He moved with speed, nimble of foot, his body a weasel weaving through the branches. He grabbed something and climbed down. Herring held a nest in his hands and showed it to Inna. An owlet sat inside, clad with down, moving its head from side to side. *Must be the last chick of the season*, Inna thought, and took it from Herring. Inna placed it in a nearby tree, knowing the parents would hear the chick's call and come to it.

Inna and Herring, carrying the bundles of logs, journeyed home in silence. Halfway, Inna placed his arm around Herring's bony shoulder.

Inna awoke the next morning to the sound of oil spitting and a stodgy smell. He saw the old woman by the fire with a pan of fish fillets and potatoes. Thick granules of salt lay on the sliced potatoes as they sizzled to a crisp and the fish whitened, flaking when the old woman nudged it with her wooden spoon. He licked his lips and moved towards the pan. The old woman raised her hand. "Herring wants you." Inna felt a sting in his shoulders and he massaged his temples; he was in no mood for games. "A little longer for the potatoes. Go to him. And close the door!"

Herring sprang to Inna when he stepped outside, grabbing his sleeve and pointing to the sky. Herring managed to utter the word, "Look." Inna shrugged in reply.

Slowly, Inna understood. The cinereous sky pressed upon him with a cloud deck so dense it would not sieve a single beam of light. Inna had never seen a sky like it. He thought it was desperate to speak but silenced by the isolation around them. The two stared up at the sky, captivated by the strangeness. They startled at the old woman's call. "Hurry inside! A storm is coming."

Sure enough, a snowstorm appeared. All three spent the day inside. After breakfast, the old woman began to sew. Inna taught Herring how to play cards. Herring taught Inna how to cheat. They heard the wind cry its loss, and from a window above Herring's bed, watched the snow. It was as if the flakes were falling onto

Herring's pillow. Inna drank his coffee, feeling the locket grow warmer against his skin, and he thought of his family. He wondered if they missed him.

The storm cleared the next morning. The old woman presented Inna with four fish. He held all four by the tail. They hung waist-high. Though the fish were frozen, Inna could see the eyes were intact and the skin had faint colour. They were caught recently.

"Don't look at me with bulging eyes," said the old woman. "I have my ways of finding things. Go and scale and gut them."

Inna sat on a tree stump outside the hut, and placed the fish between his legs. They were heavy as silver bullion. Inna deliberated over how the old woman might have dragged them inside. Herring came running out of the hut and sat beside him with dog-like obedience. Inna allowed him to watch as he slid the knife's edge from the tail up towards the gills and scales, like teardrops, fell to the ground. Inna noticed Herring wince when he cut off the dorsal and pectoral fins. The underside of the body did not open easily and Inna began to sweat, sawing downwards then removing the innards. The organs were off-white, except the red-tinged liver. Inna cut out the stomach and the intestines that were no more than a single pipe, coiled tightly. He pulled out the air bladder with his bare hands, scooped up the other organs and threw them on the floor. Using the tip of the knife, Inna carefully scraped out the eggs – they were delicious shallow-fried. He left the tail and the eyes, for they added the most flavour. Inna remembered when he watched his father catch and clean fish. He looked at Herring and smiled.

Inna entered the cabin and slammed the gutted fish on the table as if they were his own catch. The old woman looked up from her sewing; her pince-nez eyeglasses balanced on her stubby nose.

"Thank you," she said, with little enthusiasm.

Inna tried to mouth a question.

"My name?" The old woman looked surprised. "I had one. It's so long ago since I used it. Besides, names are for people with friends. I've no use for such people." Inna saw her face darken. She was a woman who ordered, not answered. "Herring learns from you. Perhaps I'll keep you until summer. There is much to do in summer. That would suit us well."

Inna grabbed the only porcelain plate on the table and threw it across the room. The plate smashed against the wall and Inna stood breathing heavily. The old woman did not flinch. She looked at it with a moment's regret and continued sewing.

That night, the sickle moon cut open the sky. Inna awoke, and there was enough moonlight to see by. He rose from the floor. By the fire, the old woman slept in a chair. Her head was tilted back and her mouth agape. Inna picked up a knife from the table. He made no sound as he walked to the old woman. He held the knife inches away from her throat. He stood there for minutes. The fire snarled. He pulled back. He placed the knife on the table and lay down on his bedroll. He stared at the darkness above him, wondering if he would ever taste his mother's honey cake again. It took hours for him to find sleep.

Winter descended, plunging the land into darkness for the morning was only as light as twilight. The old woman told Inna and Herring to collect cowberries. Inna stood in the forest, before a small bush, surprised the leaves remained green. His hands were too large to pluck berries from inside the bush. Herring pestered him to look at a stone and Inna caught his wrist on a thorn. He'd had enough.

Inna began to walk away. Herring hurried after him, tapping him on the shoulder. Inna turned and Herring handed him a caterpillar as if it were a trophy. Inna snatched the insect, squashed it between his fingers and threw it away.

Inna saw Herring's top lip quiver, then Herring clenched his teeth and swung a punch to Inna's stomach. Inna lurched then threw Herring to the ground. Soon they were wrestling in the snow. Inna had strength but Herring had speed. Herring bit Inna on the shoulder. Inna pinned Herring, sat on top of him and pulled down his trousers. Inna took his cock out, spat on it, and shoved it inside Herring. A flock of birds burst out of the forest at the sound of Herring's scream. As Inna continued thrusting, he felt the tightness, the warmth. And as his rage towards the old woman faded, a strange desire filled his head. He lay on top of Herring and began to kiss his neck. His cold skin smelt of damp flowers.

When Inna finished, he rolled over and lay on the ground beside Herring for a time. He turned onto his side and pushed himself up from the ground. He walked away but stopped after some yards. He turned and returned. Herring had not moved, though his body shivered. Inna scooped Herring up and started the long journey back to the hut.

As Inna trudged through the snow, he noticed the sky was cloudless. There were faint patches of green light against a procession of stars. Gradually, the light gathered into an emerald curtain that hung in the sky. The light was ghost-like and wavered. It was as if the sky were sending out a warning. And though Inna's arms grew tired of carrying Herring, he began to hurry.

Inna entered the hut and the fire growled at him. The old woman sat snoring in a chair in front it. He placed Herring on his bed. On the opposite side of the room, Inna rested on his bedroll, though he didn't sleep. The locket felt cold.

After a long night, Inna sat at the table. Herring's seat was empty, and the old woman served him breakfast. She sat and watched him eat. The coffee was weak as water. Inna ate his fish. He felt a jab on his soft palate. He removed a bone from his mouth. He took another mouthful and felt a prick inside his cheek. When he had finished, his plate was covered with thin sharp bones.

"Next time, kill me instead," said the old woman, as she cleared the table.

Inna hung his head. She knew everything.

Being inside the hut made Inna restless. He needed to walk. The old woman sat at the table crushing dried berries to a fine powder. As he rose to leave, the old woman rested her pestle in the mortar.

"Don't wander too far. You don't have Herring to guide you."

Even if Inna could have spoken, he had nothing to say.

Though the sunlight was weak, it was enough to shine the snow. The blanket of glittering crystals refreshed the landscape but blurred the route of any pathway. Inna was not sure in which direction to travel. He used the hut as a compass point. Inna and Herring never explored the land behind the hut, so Inna travelled in that direction. Inna remembered how carefully Herring had held the chick and how roughly he had held Herring down. He thought of the times when Herring had shown him wonders. His hands made fists as he walked on, angered by his guilt. He thought of Herring's selflessness. And he thought of love.

When the hut was nothing more than a brown dot in the distance, Inna stopped walking. He felt the snow flattened underfoot, giving way to a large sheet of ice before him. He approached until he reached the edge. The hut was built by a lake and Inna visualised a summer of splendour, as the water would be home to sea birds, fish and surrounded by lush trees, bearing fruit. He looked down at the frozen surface, a harsh grey and white colour, and covered in scratches and clumps of snow. Inna knew that only a few feet below the solidity of ice was a warmer place. *The water is jailed*, Inna thought.

As Inna returned to the hut, he glimpsed footprints. They were small, narrow and as light as the snow that captured them. He saw Herring's black hair in the distance. Inna ran towards him but Herring sprinted away. It was impossible to catch up, Herring's long, light limbs travelling at speed that allowed him to move like a winter hare. He darted this way and that as Inna fumbled in the snow, feeling the locket bounce against his chest. Soon enough, Inna tired and stopped. Though out of breath, he called Herring's name. No sound left his lips. Stillness cloaked the landscape.

Months passed, and winter began to weaken its grip on the land. Herring became a disappearing creature. Though one morning, as Inna sat outside the hut with a piece of wood that was soft as soap, carving it with a paring knife, he heard a rustling. He looked up but saw nothing. He ignored it, and began gouging, shaving and sweeping over the wood, never breaking his rhythm, until it transformed into a creature. He heard a rustling again, raised his head and caught a glimpse of Herring.

Inna dropped his knife and ran after him. Herring ran to the back of the hut and squatted with his back towards Inna. Inna knelt beside him and held out the object. The way a timid animal slowly realises they are in no danger, Herring eventually turned to Inna. In Inna's palm was a carving of an owlet, similar to the one Herring had saved from the tree before Inna cut it down. Herring's cheeks rose and his eyes smiled. He took Inna's hand and ran.

They ran until they reached the forest. But it was a different part, where the dense trees locked out the light. In near darkness they walked, until they came to a clearing and stood by the edge of a lake. Its current kept it open all year like a polynya. Inna wondered why Herring had brought him here. Herring wore a wicked grin. He pushed Inna into the lake.

Panic filled Inna, as the dark water cut off any sense of direction. Before he made for the surface, the locket free-floated and pulsated violently. It became luminous and lit up the water. It pulled downwards and that was when Inna saw what Herring had meant him to see.

He swam to the bottom of the lake, passing creatures with holographic bodies, hideous fish with disproportioned fins. Some had telescopic eyes that moved independently; some had slender antennae with incandescent bulbs at the end, while others had needle-like teeth so large their jaws could not close. There were even prawns, with translucent bodies. Inna continued downwards, where on the lakebed was a vial containing a green iridescent liquid. Mottled fish were inspecting it with gulping mouths. He snatched the vial and the fish darted away, leaving a cloud of sand behind, and raced to the surface.

Inna climbed out of the lake and hugged Herring, spinning him around. He tried to pull out the stopper but it would not give. He tried again. And again. But the vial remained sealed. This was the old woman's work. Again.

Inna arrived at the hut and paused at the door. He tried to think of a way of outsmarting the old woman but nothing came to mind. He opened the door enough to glance at her sitting by the fire. "You might as well come in," said the old woman, startling him. He walked to her and saw her comforted by the purring, spontaneous clicks of the fire. The gold and deep oranges of the flames moved with a frenzied energy – so different to the stillness outside.

Inna shoved the vial in her face. She sighed. "I cannot open it."

With an iron poker, the old woman nudged logs in the fire to stir it. Inna glared at her.

"So Herring revealed my hiding place. No matter the hurt, his heart remains open. His heart is a polynya. The boy has no malice in him whatsoever, I don't know where I went wrong. Herring is the only one who can open the vial." The old woman turned her head to Inna. "But if you let him drink from that vial, he'll be fixed."

Inna went outside the hut where Herring was busy playing with the wooden owlet. He watched Herring running in circles, rolling in the snow, flapping his arms and pretending to be a bird travelling the light of summer that would soon be upon them. Inna felt his stomach tighten as he wanted to hold Herring, protect him. The boy was as simple as sunlight.

When he saw Inna, Herring ran to him. In one hand, Inna held the vial. With his other hand, he touched Herring's check. Inna closed his eyes and kissed Herring on the forehead.

"every sentence
is a step
along the
rope, and you
can so easily
misplace your
step and break
your neck"

Kevin Barry

Mule Variations

DAVE McGOWAN

I'm dozing off in my mezzanine bed, home from the pub and well-contented. The shipping forecast soothes me into a fluffy slumber then I'm jolted back awake by our dismal national anthem. I reach blindly behind me and turn down the volume on the radio and as the preposterous dirge fades out, the World Service steps in to coax me into a dreamy sleep. I nuzzle into my bedding, tuck my hands between my knees and treat myself to a few self-satisfied grunts. I'm just approaching the Land of Nod, when my head is flooded with a horrible certainty. I sit myself bolt upright, slap my head with both hands and think, Oh shit, the tone of her recent messages. She sounded so together whilst she was inside, but she's out and back at it, isn't she?

What have I done?

I take my seat on the plane next to a bonehead Norwegian guy; he's got black metal tattoos on his neck and self-harming scars on his forearms. We appraise each other and exchange perfunctory nods. I look at the dislodged wall panel to my right and at the cracked fold-down table in front of me and then I look sideways back at the Norwegian guy.

"That's a bit shit, innit?"

"What do you expect from a cheap flight?"

I'm thinking, If £745 is cheap to you, son, I want what you're having. I buzz for a flight attendant and point at the ragged fittings.

"I'm sorry but I don't want to look at that broken stuff for the next eleven hours. It's just too depressing."

I'm ushered to another seat.

To my left, there's some bird with a screeching baby in a cot on a hook. I give her a dirty look: "Nice one, lady. You could've FedExed the brat."

She returns an even dirtier, sanctimonious look.

I consider showing her a photo of my adult daughter. "See, you're not the only one in the world with working reproductive organs, señora. You're nothing special and neither is your ugly, noisy kid." But I don't. This is a long-haul flight and I don't fancy a long-haul fight, so I just raise my eyebrows and give her my best sarcastic smile (which involves screwing my eyes up a bit). Sensing a potential ding-dong, the nice, hirsute cabin-staff lady moves me once again, to an even better seat. I say "hirsute cabin-staff lady" as if this might distinguish her from her colleagues, but this is Iberia and the Spaniards employ people on their ability to do their job, not their beauty. So hairy is cool. All the female staff members are hirsute. The token male attendant is plump but firm, pointedly hairless and cavalier with the free beer; his skin is notably un-orange for a man of his profession. It would take a brave soul to match a High Street spray tan with the orange blazers of Air Iberia.

"Would señor like pollo or pasta?"

I ask for pollo; I get pasta. Nice one. I order an extra beer, some nuts and a whisky and ginger. I swallow two 5 mg of valium and a zopiclone and read some Bukowski. Eight hours later, I wake up smiling beatifically at my neighbour, my head ensconced in his armpit. I've dribbled onto his pullover and my right nostril is encrusted with dried snot. Some people are frowning at me. Maybe I do snore, after all. I order two beers, a whisky and two bags of nuts. I nudge my neighbour and proffer him one of my bags of nuts; he appears inordinately pleased and flashes me his warm fatherly eyes.

We descend from the skies over Montevideo and cross the Rio de la Plata, then bank into Buenos Aires. My neighbour is a healthy-looking, handsome man in his early seventies. He says in faltering English, "English?"

"London," I say.

"First time Argentina?"

"*Si.*"

"Please, you sit here by window. I have seen many times. You can look."

We change places.

"We are circle now." He waves his arm in a circle. "We must wait permission land. Is good opportunity for you look city." He points down. "See, this field wheat, rye, cow. Many swimming pools. Rich people area. I have skiing. Europe is good for ski. I go much."

"Where do you go in Europe?" I ask.

"Everywhere. Austria, Switzerland, France, Italy."

"Turkey?"

"Turkey yes. Uludağ very good."

"How about Scotland?"

"Huh?"

"Scotland."

He slaps his thigh. "Scotland. No."

The plane tilts to the right. I look down at the city and try to guess where she lives. I wonder if she's checking the sky and blowing kisses at me. I blow one down and give a little wave just in case she is.

The seat-belt light bongs on, and a stewardess buckles herself into the seat opposite me. We get chatting. It turns out she used to live in Brixton and drink in the Albert, my old local. "If you like Brixton, if you are a London man, you will love Buenos Aires." I tell her I am a London man. She smiles, I smile. I raise a can of Colombian lager and sit back and admire the hair on her capable, trans-Atlantic arms.

Autumn has arrived and the temperature has plummeted to a frosty 27°C. The powers-that-be at Ezeiza International Airport have taken this as their cue to turn off the air conditioning. It takes ninety minutes to get through passport control and I am the only person standing in a pool of sweat and not wearing an overcoat. To the inhabitants of this immigrant city, 81°F is a bit on the chilly side. Looking around: doubled-over old ladies brazenly jump the queue; moustachioed husbands shoot the breeze whilst small children use them as climbing frames; fat women, short women, plain women, balding women, sporty women and mad-eyed women stand self-assuredly. No one bats an eyelid about the long wait. I suppose when you grow up in a country where people were routinely disappeared for such heinous crimes as joining unions or being gay, a bit of a wait at the airport is no great shakes. There is a pulsating singularity that radiates from these people, the Porteños.

When my turn comes, I hand over my passport, and my retina and thumbprint are electronically checked and recorded. Why don't you get a charcoal rubbing of my balls, while you're at it, I think. The immigration officer has the warm, friendly face of a torturer. He smiles.

"¿Cuál es el propósito de su viaje?"

"Ah, perdón, soy Inglés."

"What is the purpose of your visit, Mr MookGoowaine, business or pleasure?"

"Pleasure. I'm here on holiday, visiting a friend."

"Where will you be staying? You must provide me with the address."

There's a beat; my insides do a flip. I feel sick. This is the first time the enormity of what she's done hits home and I use all my powers not to let anything show. I'm not doing anything wrong, after all; I'm visiting a friend in need, bringing her laptops and camera. I'm a tourist with nothing to worry about. And I'm almost ninety-five per cent sure that I probably haven't got any traces of any drugs on me. I'm hoping his inscrutable gaze can't detect associated guilt as I hand him my friend's details. I'm also hoping that his computer terminal doesn't ask him to ask me why I've come to visit someone who's awaiting trial for attempting to smuggle two and a half kilos of cocaine out of Argentina on a Lufthansa flight to Berlin.

Nobody wants to walk around with a head full of hope. Momentary hope, yeah, I can dig that. Like, I hope the bus comes in a minute. But fuck hope. It is not on your side. Hope will stroke your hair and clutch your hand and gently walk you to the grave. It wasn't hope that put an end to the concentration camps. It was soldiers. When hope is all you've got, you're in a seriously fucked-up situation.

No hope is preferable to hope; at least you know where you stand. I've come to see someone who's relying on hope so much, she hasn't got a hope in hell. She can't meet me at the airport because the conditions of her bail don't permit it. I jump in a cab and show the driver her address.

I peer into the gloom through the wrought iron and broken glass and see her come skipping down the stairs. She pulls open the big old wooden door. Six months on remand haven't done her much damage, a few more lines around her mouth, maybe. Her eyes light up a luminous, lantern green, she breaks into a toothy, gummy smile and throws her arms around me. I lift her off the ground a bit. I put her down, pick up my bag and we go inside.

She shares her apartment with a bunch of gay guys and lesbians, all less than half her age. I'm introduced to a cute lad with a pierced eyebrow; he's smoking a Marlboro Light.

"Alé, meet my good friend, Dave. Dave, this is Alé."

He's heard so much about me.

She grabs his chubby arm. "Ah, he's like the son I never had. I'm like his mother."

In her room she tells me she's booked a hotel so we can get fucked up uninterrupted for a few nights.

"You'll love this," she says. "The rooms are massive with great big balconies over the Avenida 9 de Julio. I stayed here at Christmas."

I ask her how she can afford it. She tells me she can't, really. She's spent all of her money on our three nights here but she's got some more money coming from her flat in Brixton.

She swipes the card through the security lock and opens the door. The room isn't massive, just a bit big. There is no balcony, no view of Avenida 9 de Julio. The windows look out onto the grim backsides of the surrounding buildings.

I hang out of the window to have a good look, my belly resting on the windowsill. There is a seven-storey drop. I envisage plummeting past our neighbours' windows, bouncing on the washing lines below and hitting the concrete with a splat. It's not an overpowering urge or a latent death wish. It's no different from daydreaming about mundanely plunging your hand into a jug blender or thinking you can step off of a clifftop and join the cackling seagulls. Normal stuff; it's the Imp of the Perverse sitting on my shoulder. I pull back into the room.

"This isn't the same room I booked last time."

"Really? Shit. Let's have a word with that bird at reception. Did you ask for the same one?"

"No."

"Oh."

We do all the perfunctory hotel-room stuff: we turn on the telly and run through the channels, jump up and down on the bed and try to touch the ceiling, check for mosquitoes and blood splats, open all the drawers and doors, turn the shower full on to test the water pressure, laugh at the prices for the minibar, rub our faces in the towels.

"This'll do," I say. "Shall we go for a wander?"

We kiss and clutch hands as we wait for the open-fronted lift in the majolica-tiled stairway.

In the Chinese shop (all the neighbourhood shops are Chinese), I'm all wide-eyed at the foreign beers and choose eight different types to see which one fits most snugly in my hand. We add to the basket crunchy things, chocolate and cured meats. I feel a frisson of sexual excitement as we select a few soft fruits. I don't forget to buy some rum.

Back in the room, she opens her bag and pulls out a little velvet pouch that contains some fragrant Patagonian weed, a glistening, flaky chunk of coke and a large rock of crack.

"Good girl," I say. "I knew you wouldn't let me down."

I make good use of the weed, the coke and the booze whilst she fashions a crack pipe out of a miniature whisky bottle. We take our clothes off.

"Oh God, I've just realised. You're not going to conk out on me with jetlag, are you?"

"I don't think so, darling. There's no difference between jetlag and staying up all night, is there, when you think about it, except you're 37,000 feet above the Earth in a free bar. I don't know what all the fuss is about. Jetlag, lightweight, tosser, cunts." I smile.

She bends forward and rummages in her handbag. Her vertebrae pop up like a range of hills. Her ribs are bony terraces. She looks up and proffers me two pegs: a blue wooden one and a red plastic one.

"Which one do you want where?" I ask.

"Oh, you choose." Her eyes are fucking mental and her nipples are fat and rubbery.

I apply the pegs and I take out my camera. Click.

I wake up around 10 a.m. She is snoring like a thousand walruses. I'd forgotten about that. I get up, draw the blinds, drink a slug of juice from the carton and take a shower. When I return, the blinds are closed.

"Do you fancy a bit of a stroll?"

"I'm really tired. A bit later."

"Oh, OK. I'm going to get out in the sunshine. Are you sure you don't want to join me?"

She's sure.

I get dressed and grab my camera and notebook, pound out a line and take a slug of rum. I kiss her goodbye and pick up the key. In the open-fronted lift, I try to get my nose as close to the wall as I can.

The city is all spirit. There's a march going on to remember all the shit they've had to go through. There are women wearing T-shirts that say "We would rather die on our feet than live on our knees"; they carry wooden clubs and fan out across the street. Dope smoke fills the air, kids are hanging off of the buildings, security guards hang out and smoke cigarettes, fireworks explode underfoot. I get in amongst them and take photos. While this is going on, high above the widest street in the world, the latest Pope waves his holy Argentine hand on giant digital screens. He is everywhere, on tea towels, posters, beer mats and flags, emblazoned with the legend: "*Gracias* Francisco", which I think means, "Cheers Frank!" According to the bookies, it's currently 8/1 on the next Pope coming from the USA.

At 5 p.m. I let myself into a darkened room. She stirs under the bedclothes and I grab a beer from the fridge and sit down next to her.

"You OK?"

"Mmm, I'm really woozy. How was your day?"

I tell her. "Have you got that coke?"

"Oh, I'm sorry, it's all gone."

"But there was loads. I thought you've been sleeping."

"I've still got quite a bit of that rock."

She hands me the pipe.

We've been back at her place for a few days. I've been out to rooftop clubs, parks and art galleries. I've doubled my money on the blue market. Life is sweet. Then things start to get creaky. Every time she goes off to try to score me some pot she comes back with a lump of crack, claiming that they'll have some pot later. When she's not on the pipe, she's snoring. Really fucking snoring. When she's not snoring, she's slathering herself in moisturiser and squirting cheap perfume everywhere. I've made a few playlists but whenever I stick the stick on she changes the music when I leave the room and puts on the same techno podcast; I've never been a fan of techno. She gyrates and moisturises.

Conversation is limited. She tells me about her time in prison: the cockroaches, the fleas and the violence. Everyone in there was a mule or a prostitute. You had to work the sewing machines to buy food you could cook in the communal kitchen, because the official stuff they served would put you in the ground.

She says "I miss Sid" several times a day. Sid is her mentally ill springer spaniel.

"I hate Andy," she says.

Andy is looking after Sid. He once gave Sid some ketamine.

"I wish my mum was dead," she says.

"I'm sure you don't," I say.

"Yes I do and I wish my dad was still alive in her place. I miss my dad."

I ask her about her crack habit.

"I haven't got a habit. I take it to relax. It's no different to you having a drink," she says.

I wake up in the middle of the night and she's scraping the

rebate off the back of the gauze from the pipe.

"It's the best bit," she says.

"How are the cakes?"

"They're all right, thanks," I say.

"This coffee's a bit weak," she says.

"That's because you've used a coarse grind in a cafetière."

She spits a mouthful of chewed-up custard slice into her hand and throws it onto the other cakes.

"I CAN'T FUCKING DO ANYTHING RIGHT, CAN I? I FUCKING KNOW IT'S THE WRONG COFFEE!"

"Well why did you say what you just said, then?"

"YOU CUNT. THAT PIZZA YESTERDAY WASN'T GOOD ENOUGH FOR YOU! YOU DIDN'T LIKE THE ART GALLERY! YOU DIDN'T LIKE THE SHOPS!"

"Hey, none of that is true. Well, the pizza was a bit shit but . . . WHAT THE FUCK! I'VE COME ALL THIS WAY TO BE SHOUTED AT? THANK YOU VERY FUCKING MUCH. AH FUCK, FUCK, NOW YOU'VE GOT ME SHOUTING!"

"Hah, the language of the wife beater. It's all coming out now."

"You fucking what?"

"I made you shout, did I? That's what the wife beaters say."

I want to explode. I tell her she's a lying crackhead cunt, and that, all things considered, had she been honest about her habit, I wouldn't have crossed the Atlantic fucking Ocean to see her.

I go for a long walk around the block, and when I come back we hug and I stroke her hair. We're going for a four-day trip down the coast tomorrow.

While we're packing, I fish my envelope full of cash from under the mattress and sit down to count it. It's well short. I count it again. I go through every pocket in every item of clothing, check every drawer, twice. I count the money again. I lift things up and throw them about. I grab a pen and some paper and account for every penny I've spent since leaving London. I'm about £400 short.

She walks into the room.

"Have you found it?"

"Does it look like I've fucking found it?" I say. "Do you know anything about this?"

"I'm going to pretend you didn't say that."

"Well, you are a crackhead." I glare at her.

"I'm going to have to go out for a minute."

"Oh yeah, where?"

"I would never steal from you," she says.

"Well you already owe me £200, how are you going to pay that back? Where's this rent money? How come you can afford crack when you've got no money?"

She goes out and bangs the door. I count the money once more, for luck. It's the right amount.

The coach is two hours late; there's been flooding down south of the city. The drive to Mar de las Pampas takes five and a half hours and we'll still be in Buenos Aires Province. It's flat all the way, flat and featureless and grey. Our driver seems reluctant to exceed 30 m.p.h., giving us plenty of time to enjoy the boredom. We've come to a soft impasse. I'm not going to apologise for falsely accusing her of stealing if she doesn't apologise for not telling me that she's a crack addict. We swig beer, read and look out of the window. I want to have holiday-coach sex, but not with her. I think about having a wank in the bog but the moulded plastic and the smell put me off.

We pull into the bus station at Villa Gesell, the nearest town to the resort. We have to get the connecting *collectivo* to Mar de las Pampas. By the end of the bumpy fifteen-minute ride, we aren't talking. She wanted me to dig out my notebook to show the driver the address of our apartment. I had trouble finding it and questioned whether it is normal to ask a bus driver to take you to an exact address. This small exchange developed into a clench-jawed row.

"Everyone was laughing at you," she says as we alight at the terminus.

"I think they were laughing at the whole situation."

"No, they were laughing at you. They were calling you '*gringo loco*'."

I look around. Only about one in ten of the shops and restaurants are open. She told me this is a big weekend for the

Porteños but there's nobody around.

"Let's get a taxi to the apartment," she says.

"I don't think that's down to you," I say. "I fancy walking."

"You're a cunt, Dave."

The streets are made of sand and it's been raining. I set off dragging our large wheely bag and muttering putrid hatred. She hangs back, stopping to take a closer look at the occasional tree or shrub. Every now and then she hollers an insult at me. I think I'm going mad.

Mar de las Pampas is a manufactured resort that sits in a manufactured pine forest next to a white sandy beach by the Atlantic Ocean; everywhere looks the same.

By the time we find the apartment – near a building site on a side street named after an Argentine general and made of wet sand – I'm dripping with sweat and too knackered to be angry. I present myself to the proprietor and hand him my passport. She hands him a photocopy of her impounded passport and whispers to me that she's broken the terms of her bail. Sweat pisses through my eyebrows and stings my eyes. The man asks me if I'll be paying in US dollars and flinches a little when I say no, Argentine pesos. They like their dollars here.

Our wooden apartment overlooks a tiny swimming pool. Every television channel is reporting on the upstate floods, thirty-five dead and rising. We go down to reception and act like we haven't been fighting. We decide it'll be nice to walk to the local shops via the beach. We can hear the waves as we climb to the top of a ridge. When the ocean comes into view she drops to her knees and sobs so violently it looks like she's being punched in the guts by a ghost. There's nothing in the way of comfort you can offer to someone who's in a place like that. But you can't really walk off, either. She looks at me and I look at her and the tip of Cornwall is only, what, four inches away on the map? Her eyes are the green of young leaves and full of water and despair and all my eyes can say is, "I'll be going soon."

She wants to get back to the apartment but I decide to stay on, so I can be on my own. I have a wander round but there's not much of interest apart from a few tethered horses and a large dead rodent with its guts hanging out. On the road adjacent to ours she's written "DAVE I LOVE U AND I'M SORRY" in the sand and scattered it with flowers. When I get back and she hints at it, I pretend that I haven't seen it.

I stock the cupboard and the fridge with booze and food and take a shower. When I come downstairs, she's rearranged all the lighting and furniture and closed the curtains. I pull them open.

"I really don't want to sit in the dark, honey."

"Oh, don't start, Dave."

She lights a cigarette, steps out of her dress and whacks on that fucking techno compilation, then she slathers herself in body lotion and starts dancing at me. I go upstairs to get dressed and when I return the room is in darkness again. I open the curtains.

"You fucking cunt, you have to ruin it, don't you?"

"It's fucking light outside. I don't want to sit in the dark. DO YOU FUCKING UNDERSTAND!"

I throw the spare key down on the table and peel off a 100-peso note.

"Get yourself some fags or something. I'm off out."

She screams all kinds of barrel-scraping abuse at me and snatches up the money as I close the front door.

When I return from my hilarious dinner, she's retired to the main bedroom. I can hear her humming tunelessly. She's doing it on purpose. I turn on the TV, put my feet up, roll a joint and crack open a beer. About an hour into a film I'm watching, she comes steaming down the stairs.

"How long are you going to keep this up?"

"Keep what up?"

"We're meant to be having a nice time."

"Yeah, we might be if you weren't coming down off crack."

"WILL YOU STOP CALLING ME A CRACKHEAD!"

"That's not exactly what I said, but funnily enough you are actually a crackhead. Why don't you just admit it and we can both move on."

"I'VE TOLD YOU, I JUST TAKE IT TO RELAX!"

"Sure you do. Look, I can't be doing with this any more, really. Let's just stay out of each other's way for the next few days. Pretend

I'm not here, and just enjoy your time by the sea. Can you do that? I'll give you some wedge. Stop wasting your time trying to get a rise out of me. I'm not angry, I'm just fucking done with you."

She says, "I get it, you're a fucking queer, aren't you, Dave? You could be fucking me but you'd rather ignore me. Why won't you fuck me? Are you queer, Dave? You must be queer, Dave. Is that why you always want to fuck me up the arse?"

She bursts into song: "Sing if you're glad to be Dave, Sing if you're happy that way, hey!"

She breaks off from goading me to ask for a cigarette and some money for some nail varnish. Meanwhile, on the TV, Dustin Hoffman is doing his thing as Raymond Babbitt.

I'm strolling down the beach photographing dead things: a gull, a bird of prey, a half-eaten fish. I want to go in for a swim but the shoreline is littered with huge jellyfish. I head towards a city that juts out in the haze, miles down the coast, and come to Villa Gesell along the way. I'm the only person on the streets, there's nowhere to go and nothing to do, so I catch the *collectivo* back to the apartment. I use the laptop in reception to book a room in a hostel for the rest of my stay in BA and feel glad to be free of her.

On the table in the kitchen she's left a note, begging forgiveness and promising to behave and to repay her debts and please will I stay with her for my last few days. I can stay in the spare room, if I like. I go to reception and cancel my hostel room. When I return, she's waiting for me in a floral dress. We decide to go for a walk on the beach before dinner and are joined by a young man who wants to talk to me about his boyfriend. She storms off saying, "Fuck off with your new friend, then. I thought we were going for a romantic walk."

It turns out that he means girlfriend when he says boyfriend and that he's a nasty little homophobe.

I'm glad to get back to BA. I feel at home in a city, even if I don't know anyone. There is no spare room at hers, there never was, so I sleep on the edge of her bed, my arms folded. A woman who looked after her during her first five nights in prison gets released and comes to visit her for a crack-fest; she gets shouted at and thrown out in the middle of the night. Everywhere we go together, she takes me the wrong way on purpose. She walks slowly on purpose. One night I let her have a go on me for old times' sake while I read a book. And she snores and snores and I can't sleep. I go out on my own. I eat steak on my own. We visit a forty-foot animatronic Jesus. We go down the delta and she screams in a restaurant. We go to San Telmo. She's always got to get home soon. Now and then she talks about escaping across the Iguazu Falls to Brazil on a false passport, but we both know she ain't going any further than the end of her dealer's street.

I'm leaving for the airport so we hug in the street outside her door and I tell her to hang on in there, gorgeous, stay strong, you'll be OK. I look into her eyes and tell her that I love her. She cries like a baby, so I give her arms a squeeze and look into her eyes again. The taxi driver loads my bags into the boot of his car and I slide into the back seat. He's got swags of religious tat dangling off his rear-view mirror; it starts swinging from side to side as he pulls out onto the main road. I twist around to look out of the back window and she's standing there on the pavement with her arms hanging by her sides. I wave at her; she coughs into her hand and waves back.

Genre Confusion

PAUL FLACK

"Do you know what you're looking for?" she said.

I didn't see her approach. I had put a Graham Greene back on the shelf and probably appeared indecisive as to what I would do next. With an empty weekend ahead I wanted to buy something I could learn from.

"Just browsing," I replied. I knew exactly what I was searching for.

She wore glasses and smiled gently. "Well let us know," she said.

It was nearly six and I presumed she wanted to clear the shop of customers. I glanced around. I was the only customer. She moved a few feet away and looked at the shelves. A small stud or stone was set in her nose. There were five or six years between us, I guessed. In profile, her frame seemed unhealthily slim. She repositioned a book. I had taken in every author from A and H was next. I had to choose whether to move closer or move round her. The Greene would have to do if nothing else appealed, but I preferred a more modern author.

I slipped around her and faced the Ks. She went down on one knee and shuffled up to J. She had brown, straight hair, simple and neat, shoulder-length. If she was trying to intimidate me by her close proximity then she was failing. It wasn't because my determination to find a novel in the next two minutes was stronger than anything off-putting about her presence. It was because of the softness of what I could only term the aura she had about her.

I was scanning L when she rose. She was an inch or so shorter than me. I've become more conscious of my marginally sub-average height lately. Women seemed very fussy about it. Even more fussy than I was about what I read.

She must have thought I was about to say something but had chickened out.

"Do you need a suggestion?" she said.

"No. No thank you."

"Is it an author you can't find here?"

"No. Just browsing."

"Or a title you don't know the author of?"

In a way she was right. Though I didn't know the title, either.

"A particular genre?" she asked. Still the gentle smile. Even teeth. Eyes the tone of her hair.

"I don't think so," I said.

"What is it about it, then?"

I wasn't expecting a conversation. I didn't want to keep her if the shop was about to close, so I offered something token. The Graham Greene would be my choice.

"Contemporary," I said.

"Well that hardly makes it easier." Her narrow-lipped smile expanded.

"And dramatic."

"And?"

"Realism. Has to be credible."

She folded her arms and nodded and blinked in a way that suggested she knew what I was about.

"Crime," she said.

She definitely didn't know. I shook my head. "Not cops and robbers. Not a genre and all its rules."

"Why not?"

"Too many predictable elements. The same old furniture."

"So you know about Crime? You've read lots of Crime?" Her folded arms tensed. She had probably read lots of Crime.

"Not much," I said. "Raymond Chandler was good."

"He's not contemporary. But I can find something like that."

"No, no, no."

"What sort of drama, then?"

"I don't know. The sort in everyday lives."

"Your sort of life?"

"I guess so."

"Why not try a ghost story?"

Did she mean I was lifeless?

"Not genre," I replied.

"Even Humour?"

"Not as the main purpose. It can occur. Be part of it. But it still has to be a story with weight."

Her head angled back a little, her smile maintained. I was providing humour for her, I assumed, but it was a harmless humour. She raised one forearm to rest her chin on her palm. I was being studied as a curious specimen.

"So what interests you?" she said.

This must have been beyond the scope of what she was trained to say. I wondered if it was a form of market research she would tell her management about.

"Drama. Intriguing characters. Dilemmas." I'd better stop there, I thought.

"Mystery?"

"Definitely."

"Atmosphere."

"Essential."

"Attraction and conflict."

She knew my list. She knew what I liked. That meant she knew about me, or at least important parts of how my mind worked. There were other items on the list but that would be giving away too much.

She lifted her chin from her palm. "Nature," she said.

I took a step back. It wasn't on my list. It should have been. It was now.

"Do I get to suggest something for you?" she said.

Still astounded, I nodded.

She changed pose, opening her arms. On her chest was a badge I had deliberately not studied before. "Can I Help You?" was above her name: Simone.

"Drama, nature, mystery, a bit of suspense," she said. "Gothic?"

"Possibly. I don't know much about it. Not the usual stereotypes, though."

"The blood and fangs?"

"Or any Frankenstein monsters. It still has to be contemporary."

"Ghost story." She said it slowly and conclusively. "You do believe in ghosts?"

"I've no reason to."

That smile of hers widened again. "Very well."

"But please suggest more. I'm not taking up your time, am I?" I should invite her for a drink and find out what else we had in common. "Do you have to close the shop?"

A slight shake of her head as she continued her examination of me.

"War," she said.

"No, no, no. Not in fiction."

A fractional narrowing of her eyes.

"Too serious to make entertainment from," I said. "Not unless you were there, really experienced it. Or did vast amounts of research in trying to be realistic. But it's still not the same. Just not my thing to read about. Not now."

We faced each other square on. We hadn't engineered it, but our bodies were close. They were the right sizes to fit together easily.

"So what would you like to research?" she said.

She must have known what I was thinking. She hadn't stepped back or flinched at all. I wasn't used to such bold behaviour.

"I don't currently have anything to research," I replied. "How about you?"

"Not in terms of what you read?"

"That's why I'm here."

"Then I'll have to make the right suggestions."

I opened my hand in a gesture that she should continue. Instead, her gaze hardened.

"But what else?" she said. "What makes the difference in your choice?"

"Beauty," I said. The word slipped out before I could stop it.

"Of sorts," I added swiftly. I had made a strategic mistake.

"In the natural world? Or in personality? Some sadness is required. But you're into realism."

"Maybe the sort you have to look really hard for."

Her eyes scrunched a little.

"Charm, then," I said. "Not chat-up charm. Well, it could be. I mean uplifting things. People's mannerisms, little examples of care. Wit and humour are part of it. I'm not there in defining it yet."

"Whimsical?"

"Amongst the drama. More than whimsical. Humour that comes out of the struggle."

"Class struggle?"

"No. I've got myself to struggle against first."

"It's still imprinted on you. Part of how you think about yourself."

"Class as a sub-genre? You have a book in mind?"

"Possibly. How many suggestions do I get?"

"You must be on commission."

"Make it just the one, then. You don't have to buy it."

Of course I would buy it, whatever she suggested. But I didn't want the conversation to end too soon. I didn't want it ever to end. Not that I didn't have the chance of conversation at work, but I wouldn't be able to talk as freely as this, or on a topic as important to me.

"You're too choosy," she said. "Read widely. Lots of blockbusters have war as a backdrop. It's about characters being tested."

"You don't need a war to be tested. Every day is a test if you don't want to squander your life."

She leaned back, as if my statement took up too much space. Without her saying anything, my words and their implied relevance to myself were deflected back at me. I had to close the gap in the conversation.

"What about style?" I said. "It's as much about how it's written as what it's about."

There were no rings on her fingers, her chin now resting on her other palm as if swapping over helped her consider my question from a different angle.

"I'm guessing you mean straightforward. Economical."

"Direct. But I know pace has to vary."

"Not stylised?"

"Everything is stylised. Direct is stylised."

"You mean not too clever? For you."

"That's right. Story first. We're not in the Poetry section."

"You know exactly what you want."

I wanted her. Exactly as she was. Whatever realities surfaced later. If she had a medieval map of the world tattooed on her back I'd still want her.

"You're pretty straight," she said. "In what you read."

"Not too many semicolons, please."

The grammatical reference seemed to miscue what she was planning to say. Her lower lip sagged as she mulled a possibility.

"Technical stuff," she said. "Strange. So you must be into the making of fiction."

I looked around in case anyone heard.

"Certainly not," I said.

"Oh yes you are," she said.

"Well, possibly."

"Definitely you are. Definitely definitely."

I closed my eyes briefly and nodded.

"So is your work already on these shelves?"

"Not yet."

"Rate yourself, do you?"

"If I don't no one else will."

"And all these criteria about what you'll read. That's to copy the style, isn't it?"

"Learn from. Imitate in places, hopefully. 'Copy' doesn't sound right."

"Can't you devise one of your own?"

"I'm thinking that happens anyway. Being publishable comes first right now."

Her eyes blinked but there was no reaction to my words.

"So what other limiting parameters do we have in making your choice?" she said. "You might as well make it totally impossible for me."

"I'll read anything you advise. I can see my approach was pointless."

"I can tell there's more."

"Subtlety, for instance. Surprise. Sophistication. In places. Still story first. Nothing depraved. Well, not too much. No explicit violence."

"Something your mother could read."

"Ideally. It is the women who buy the books. That's a fact about fiction."

With her thumb and the knuckle of her forefinger she touched her chin as if she hadn't finally decided yet. I sensed a sizing-up check as her eyes swept me up and down. I believe I passed.

"I have something for you," she said. "I'm sure."

"I'm open to that."

I would ask her out, suggest a drink. I would have to decide the words and how to deliver them.

"Oh, you'll have to be open to this," she said.

"You've chosen something?"

"A while ago."

"I'll be inspired?"

"In a different world, I promise."

"I might have read it already."

"I'd be impressed if you had."

I wanted to impress her. She had impressed me. I had never felt so in tune with someone.

"Just one little snag," she said. "Though not insurmountable."

"Then it's not a problem." There would never be any problems. Not if I shared my life with her.

"We don't stock the book."

If this was a code, then I couldn't decipher it immediately. I would confirm my interest in her. It could be a test.

"I can wait for the order. I'm prepared to wait."

"This one could take a while. A long while."

"But it's your choice. I'm fascinated. Can we order it now?"

"You won't have to. It's in my bag. I've just finished reading it."

"I can borrow it?"

"Sure. Then we can discuss it."

That's as good as sex, I thought. I'd better not say it.

I was about to utter my selected words, but it was her who

said, "Shall we go for a drink now?"

I nodded and smiled. I couldn't do any more. I was so struck by how lucky I had been.

"I'll just get my coat," she said.

"And the book. It had better have a good first page."

Her smile was lit by glee rather than the professional one she started with. Perhaps she wanted this meeting even more than me. We were destined.

I watched her turn and stride towards what I presumed was an office-cum-storeroom. About to disappear, she looked back as if to check I was really there. Another grin from her.

Part of her presence was in my being now, a chromosome switched on that would direct my fate for ever. Our coming together was more than obeying instinct. At its centre was a truth that this was our only option for happiness. There was also an unreality about it, like the essence of a dream that dwindled each time I awoke, its details escaping definition no matter how hard I tried.

The Graham Greene occurred to me. I went to the shelf and took the book. It would make an interesting comparison with her novel. How it could take me to "a different world" intrigued me. A ghost story, perhaps. Knowing my luck, she was probably a ghost herself. Or maybe it wasn't a novel or any form of fiction at all. Neither of us would ever need fiction in the same way again.

I looked at my watch. I was surprised at the time. She must have kept the shop open for me. For us. My life would change now. No more weekends alone, no more wandering around town for hours – café to café, bookshops, museums – though I did enjoy my walkabouts, in a way.

She would have an opinion on my stories. She was welcome to read them. Not too critical an opinion, I hoped. My confidence is easily crushed. As if I'd have time to write anyway.

I wondered what her suggested book was. It must have been out of print if this nationwide bookstore didn't stock it. It had better not be religious or classified under Self-Help. I didn't need that sort of guidance. Not from anyone.

I returned the Graham Greene to its shelf. It was still a candidate, but before I made a purchase I needed to think again about her genre suggestions, which would require another visit.

Another look at my watch. I thought she'd be back within a minute. I knew I would rush to return to her. Yet she presumed I would wait, as I would.

A movement took my attention back to the office-cum-cupboard. A second bookseller appeared. He began walking towards me.

"Can I help you, sir?"

"No thanks. Just waiting for someone."

He was checking me over, I thought, after Simone had told him about me.

It also occurred to me then that there was a hint of suffocating righteousness about her, an unquestionable assurance about herself, despite her being so thin, almost too thin.

The bookseller pulled the first of a pair of glass doors into its closed position. He took a key from his shirt pocket and twisted it in a lock above head height. A bolt clicked into the ceiling. He bent down. A second key. A bolt clunked into the floor.

I would be easy to control. That was my failing before. I back down, make it easy for them. I bet she sensed that. She was obviously the sort that trawled the bottom of the aquarium. Her choices would be limited, too.

The bookseller unhooked the other door from a clip outside.

"I'll wait out there," I called.

He looked back at the office and then at me.

"You sure?" he said.

"Just need some air."

I edged past him. Instead of closing the second door, he began striding towards the office.

I could leave. I could wait. I should stay. There was a second or two to choose.

I ran.

"Sweet, crazy
conversations full
of half sentences,
daydreams and
misunderstandings
more thrilling
than understanding
could ever be."

Toni Morrison

North Bull

DESMOND BYRNE

It had rained during the night and everything was still wet, the blocks of flats and the road and the path and there was a sandy, metally taste in the air like putting the end of your tongue on a stone. Hatto was saying things like 'it'll be grand' and 'y'know yourself' and barrelling along and not looking at Jem; him not looking at Jem and Jem not wanting to look at him but having to, hoping he'd look back and they'd be looking at each other for a second and that might make it easier to say something like 'what about Alan Roach?' or 'maybe the Bradys'd be better?' and all the time thinking it's only fuckin' Hatto and I should just say whatever I like. Hatto wasn't even glancing to see where Jem was and that he hadn't left him behind or something and Jem was having to run nearly to keep up with him, disgusted with himself; he didn't even like people seeing him with Hatto and now here he was having to chase after him down the road. He hadn't liked the way Hatto hadn't said 'how'ye Jem' or anything when he opened his door and hadn't brought him in, just came out and hoofed off and Jem having to hoof off after him. It wasn't like Jem wanted to be brought into Hatto's flat, Hatto's mental flat, with all the ornaments and mirrors and the pink carpet in the jacks, and he definitely didn't want to see Anita Hatterley, but not getting brought in together with the walking quickly and the not getting looked at and the not being able to say anything was making him feel like he couldn't breathe, that he was having to hold his breath or something, and that he even felt like he was going to fucking cry for fuck sake.

"Marcantonio's," Hatto'd said when Jem asked where they were going and Jem'd said: "Okay," but not in a way that meant *okay* but meant 'are you sure like?' and Hatto not paying the blindest bit of notice anyways and Jem really wanting to say 'no fucking way' because it would royally fuck things up with Marcantonio, going round there with Hatto and it looking like he'd gone to Hatto to get Hatto to get Marcantonio to sort him out. He felt like the biggest prick going, afraid that he might annoy Hatto if he said anything else and all worried that he was annoyed already because he'd gone to him asking to get sorted out (even though he hadn't asked to get sorted out, he'd asked for a sub and Hatto'd said: "Are you needin' to score?" and that he'd get someone to sort him out so it was as if he had asked now and you were never supposed to do that but go to Marcantonio or Doyle or Johnno or Alan Roach or the Bradys).

Jem had last been round Marcantonio's the day before, potless, having put every penny he had into his arm over the two days before that. That he had done this at Marcantonio's and with Marcantonio (not that he had actually shared the gear he bought from Marcantonio with Marcantonio but had taken it in her company while she took some of her own) and that he had been round there every other night for the previous month, hanging around after he'd scored, watching telly, having a laugh with Marco and that, meant that Marcantonio felt uncomfortable enough with Jem being sick and potless to give him a generous hit followed later by a less generous but equally warmly appreciated other hit. By Jem's estimation, though this had been a gift and not a lay-on, he was now into Marcantonio for about twelve pound fifty, which Marcantonio, even though she wouldn't ask for it back, would round up to twenty quid. The giving of gear for nothing would never be forgotten of course, but it could be all niced out again by him offering her a hit or two the next time he scored off her. He'd go over there when he got paid for doing the door for Hatto next Saturday night, buy loads more gear and offer Marcantonio some, all easy-going, in a we're-all-mates-together-my-gear-is-your-gear sort of way. Marcantonio would say no because she'd be stoned on her own gear (which wasn't stepped on with shit like the gear she sold) but him offering would keep her sweet and mean that he could continue to enjoy certain privileges, such as going round there late at night to score, getting given the odd temazepam or the odd Special Brew, getting given lay-ons and all the other bits and pieces that came with being 'in' with Marcantonio. Marcantonio definitely liked Jem (as much as she was capable of liking anything other than gear or benzos or temazis or Special Brew or whatever) and Jem (though he couldn't exactly be said to *like* Marcantonio, and would never again set foot in her flat should she ever cease to deal gear) had certainly grown to enjoy his evenings there with her and Marco (in spite of the occasional presence of Sally Marcantonio, whose wordless visits and equally wordless assumption of his entitlement to gargantuan quantities of his sister's gear would put Marcantonio into a royal snot). Jem was spared (most of the time) the treatment she gave the rest of the heads who scored off her, such as doorbell-ignoring, gouching out in her bedroom while you waited to get sorted out, gouching out on the couch in front of you while you waited to get sorted out, having hits in her groin or between her deformed toes in front of you before sorting you out or refusing to sort you out at all for no reason. She was easily browned off though and Jem had seen other favourites given the cold shoulder over the years for pissing her off. Turning up potless and sick and preying on whatever sympathy a holding junkie might have for a sick, potless junkie would definitely be seen as acting the ballicks if he didn't iron it out sharpish.

But that morning after banging up the two tamazis he found in a coat pocket and doing the manky heroin-free filter that was in the press in the kitchen twice and sucking heroin-free smoke off the blackened bit of foil that had been on the locker beside his bed since forever, there was just no getting away from the fact that he was dog, dog sick and it was Monday and he had no money coming in until Saturday. Doyle had gone awol, Johnno had nothing and Roach or the Bradys would never do him a lay-on. The only thing he could do was to ask Hatto for a sub.

Fucking Hatto. Whatever happened to Hatto the tubby little knacker with his burst runners in December and no schoolbag just a plastic bag and clothes that were never washed and too small or too big where they'd been given to him, his big roundy, dopey face and his haircuts his ma did for him and no lunch and never knowing the answer and him just being a joke really for the whole time they were in school? Even when it was Hatto then throwing shapes in his baggies and his George Webbs and winning a few scraps and everyone on about his dead oul' fella who was supposed to have been some hard-man republican or whatever and it was like Hatto this and Hatto that, you'd still be thinking, are we talking about the same fuckin' Hatto? And now here he was, for some mental reason, the big man around town, one of Fintan's lads, Jack the fucking lad, doing the doors, giving hidin's, with his maroon suit and his white socks and his loafers, his God-awful long-at-the-back footballer haircut and his stupid-lookin' bit of a ronnie and him the main wholesaler now so every fucker, even Doyle, even Marcantonio was beholdin' to him. When he'd asked Jem to come and do the doors for him he'd been all like 'y'know yourself Jem, you'll be well able for it, sort out any bother and that' like they were oul' mates but then once Jem'd started, bit by bit getting snottier and snottier so it was like now he'd hardly talk to him at all, nice as pie to all the other heads on the job, with their shit suits and their shit hair and them all ignoring Jem as well mostly and Jem knowing that if he had to deal with any *real* bother he'd be on his own, that not one of them would put themselves out for him. And hating it, really hating it but needing the few quid so just swallowing it and now here he was sick as anything and the only thing between him and getting even sicker was fucking Hatto.

So Jem had gone to the phone box at the end of his road that morning, snotting and shaking, carrying half a batch loaf and a piece of cheese wrapped in cling film that Mrs Hinch next door had insisted on giving him when he'd borrowed a handful of fivepences off her. Someone had pissed in the phone box and he pushed his back against the door to hold it open while he dialled the number and the phone-wire thing not long enough for him to stand outside away from the stink and the receiver warm near his mouth and the warm coins in his hand and the coins reminding him of Sean.

"Look at his little micky," he'd said and him and Jem had laughed at the little bull on the brand-new, new fivepence when the new fivepences had just come out and Jem shut his eyes tight against the thought of Sean and thinking about Sean made him think about talking to Niamh about Sean, how sad she'd been about it, properly sad, not just trottin' out all the usual shite you were supposed to trot out when someone told you that someone was dead. He pulled his fingers together across his eyes like he was pinching them shut even tighter. He listened to the bubbly ringing sound, praying Hatto was in, that he'd answer the phone, that he'd be okay about the sub and he opened his eyes and there was the cheese next to the bread on top of the metal box under the phone where he'd put it, looking not-right there on the black metal box with the black worn away and little holes and grey metal showing through with spots of rust and there was air under the cling film on the cheese making a shape like a little worm or something and a massive retch started like his stomach was making a fist really quickly and then the big heave, feeling it right down between his balls and his arsehole and up it came and he made an 'mmmh' sound then an 'oh oh' like if he made the right sound it would stop and nothing coming out of course and then Hatto answering the phone.

"Wha'," he'd said and Jem'd said: "How'ye Hatto it's Jem," and asked for the sub and Hatto knowing that he was needin' to score and Jem not pretending he wasn't, even though you weren't supposed to say you were doing gear or ever talk about doing gear or being stoned or not stoned but Hatto not seeming to mind and saying to come over to his and he'd get someone to sort him out.

They went through the courtyard of Marcantonio's flats and up the stairs and it was good to be out of the bright, and the cool of the stairwell made Jem notice how wet he was with sweat, that it was cold on him and another big shudder went through him and he folded his arms and held his leather closed at the throat and Hatto in front of him, his loafers making a chick chick sound on the stairs, his tippy-toed way of running up them like a girl nearly and Jem said to himself, fuck him if he was after annoying him and fuck Marcantonio as well as long as he got sorted out. A really old oul' one was coming down the stairs and Jem remembered the bread and the cheese, that he'd left them there in the phone box and that Mrs Hinch might go and use the phone and see them. There was nothing he could do now and he wished he'd kept them and just thrown them in a bin as soon as he saw one and he thought about Mrs Hinch's little bowl of fivepences and twopences for the phone and her Sacred Heart and her picture of Mr Hinch and her little knotty hands and he had pains starting in his legs now like he was jacked from running or something and didn't he say loads of times that he was grand that he only needed fivepences for the phone? When they got to Marcantonio's door Hatto rang the bell three or four times and knocked the knocker as well and Jem thought she won't like that, at the same time still thinking about Mrs Hinch and her big long yellow horse's teeth when she smiled and the smile withering when she'd see the bread and cheese if she went to use the phone box and thinking why should he give a fuck about this either that it was her fault the stupid oul' bitch he never asked her for any bread and cheese in the first place.

"Keep an eye out for Sally," said Hatto.

"Wha'?" said Jem and his stomach heaved and the heave going downwards like he was going to shit.

"Keep an eye out for Sally like." Hatto looked around and on the ground and rang the bell again.

"Fuckin' Sally?" said Jem. He pushed the hair back off his forehead and held it on top of his head and squinted at Hatto, knowing suddenly what a royal prick he'd been to think that Hatto gave a fuck about him needin' to score. He could hear sound behind the door and he thought what's he fucking doing and he thought about Sally Marcantonio and Marcantonio opened the door a little bit and as soon as she did Hatto shoved it open wide and grabbed her by the front of her shirt, bunching it up into her face with his fist and pushed her backwards into the hall and said: "There y'are Maria c'mon an' we have a little chat."

"Ah Jaysus Hatto for fuck sake," said Marcantonio.

"Close the fuckin' door," Hatto shouted over his shoulder to Jem and Jem thought ballicks, I'm just going to fuck off and then Marco came out of the living room into the hall with just a jumper and a nappy on him and food round his mouth and screaming crying looking at his ma getting reefed by Hatto and Jem went in and pulled the door behind him and picked Marco up and carried him into the living room. He was much heavier than Jem remembered and he started kicking his legs like he was riding a bike or running and Jem nearly dropped him, barely holding on to him with his hands in his armpits and Marco lifting his arms making it even harder to hold on to him. Jem could hear that Hatto had pushed Marcantonio into the kitchen and heard him say: "Good girl yourself have you got the water on for a nice cup e' tea," and Marcantonio screaming: "Jaysus Hatto for fuck sake Hatto fuckin' don't," and Marco screaming at Jem: "Jo wan jo. Jo wan jo," and Jem saying: "It's all right baba, you're all right, good man," having to get a better hold on him, hitching him up, getting his arm under his arse and then the smell of stale milk off his breath and the nappy that Jem could tell now was full and Marco's face nearly touching his own and the snot shining on his upper lip. Jem felt the flutter in his throat and another big retch starting; he held Marco at arm's length and carried him to the armchair furthest from the door and dropped him into it and as he did he went down on his knees, retching and coughing, the strain of it making it feel like something was tearing between his legs.

From the kitchen Marcantonio screamed, a long high-pitched scream that went even higher and then wailing and sobbing and the clatter of a pot on the kitchen floor. Marco, who'd landed on his back in the armchair, struggled to his feet and went to go for the door. Jem grabbed him by the front of the jumper and pushed him back into the chair and said: "It's all right baba, you stay there, there's a good man, it's all right baba."

"All of it. Every fuckin' thing," Jem could hear Hatto saying and Marcantonio's voice small and quiet: "Please Hatto. Please. For fuck sake," and Hatto roarin': "Fuckin' all of it. Now, you fuckin' stupid bitch," and Marco going red in the face, screaming: "Jo wan jo. Jo wan jo. Jo wan jo. Nah wammy." And he got up from the armchair again and Jem, still on his knees, having to grab him again and being rougher with him, shoving him back and trying to keep a soft voice but starting to shout.

"Stay there now there's a good boy, stay there will ye." And hearing Marcantonio and Hatto going down the hall to the bedroom, hearing bumps and thuds knowing it was Marcantonio getting reefed and shoved.

Jem looked at the beige carpet with the round brown and orange shapes on it and the shiny grey patch next to the armchair where drink and ash had been spilled and watery saliva ran down from his upper lip and he thought about Sally Marcantonio who would, whatever this was about, definitely, definitely kill him and at the same time he thought about the gear Hatto was now taking off Marcantonio and that he'd be getting sorted out and he heard Hatto and Marcantonio in the hall again and Marcantonio crying and screaming.

"Please Hatto. Please."

Marco got up off the armchair again and Jem held him by the front of the jumper and slapped him hard across the face and threw him back on the chair and shouted: "Sit down ye cunt ye," and Marco landed sitting up making little gasps with his mouth open and then started crying loudly holding his face and pulling his shoulders in like he was trying to make himself smaller and Jem leant over to him and starting to cry now himself saying: "Jesus Marco I'm sorry. Oh fuckin' Jesus Marco please I'm sorry. Marco look at me, Jesus, oh fuck sake Marco please I'm sorry." And trying to stroke him and see if he was hurt and wanting to pick him up but not being able to with the smell and thinking it'd probably make him worse and Hatto came into the living room and said: "Are ye right, c'mon," and Marcantonio behind him, her hair all sticking up and her eyes red with make-up running and the front of her shirt torn and she looked at Marco and looked at Jem and she made a high, quiet sound, making a face like you'd make if you were coddin', pretending to be mental so she looked really, really mental like she didn't care or didn't even think what her face looked like and in the same high, quiet way as the sound she was making she said: "Marco Marco Marco Marco," and went over and went to pick him up but stopped and stood there with her hands out, the right one red raw all over and up the arm from the boiling water and her head to one side looking at him and Marco crying with his mouth wide open and his arms up to her wanting to be picked up and Jem, looking up at her saying: "He's all right Maria. He's all right. He's grand," and Hatto said: "Will you for fuck sake come on."

Jem got up on his feet but stayed hunched over with a hand out to Marco and a hand out to Marcantonio with the palms down like it would help to calm them down, looking from one to the other and wanting Marcantonio to pick Marco up and saying: "He's grand Maria. He's grand," and Hatto roared at him: "Fuckin' come on," and went out into the hallway and Jem followed him but walking backwards slowly and still looking at Marcantonio and Marco with his hands out and he heard Hatto fling the front door open and it rattling against the wall and he went out after him.

Hatto stopped in one of the half-landings and said: "Here," over his shoulder, glancing down at the hand he offered back to Jem. Jem took what was in it, a big seal bag with smaller bags inside it, and stuffed it down inside his underpants behind his balls. He could feel the folded corner of the plastic scratch against the top of his leg as he went down the stairs. In the courtyard he zipped up his leather and pushed his hands down into his jeans pockets and hurried to come alongside Hatto. Without slowing his pace Hatto took out twenty Major and made an upside-down V with two of them at Jem for him to take one; he struck two matches and Jem took the light and the fingers of one of Hatto's cupped hands touched his chin and Jem winced.

"Tell any of them that went to her to go to you from now on," said Hatto. "I need you up in Leeson Street on Thursday and Friday night as well now an' if you sell an'in' at the clubs be careful. Y'know yourself, use your loaf." He tipped his head in Jem's direction and did a big twitch with his shoulders and stretched his neck.

She won't have given him everything, Jem thought. No matter how much the boiling water hurt or no matter how scared of Hatto she was or worried about Marco she was she'll have kept something. She won't be there with Marco screaming and a scalded hand and no gear. He thought about Marco's face and about Marcantonio's red-raw hand and that it would be scarred and he thought about Sally, and the aches in his legs were there again and spreading up his arse and into his back, and his neck was going stiff. Sally would come after him; it wouldn't be like a row or a scrap with a few digs or him taking a hidin', Sally would come after him with a knife or probably a shooter to kill him. He'd know soon, in the next couple of hours, by the end of the day definitely. He'd know that him and Hatto had gone to Marcantonio's and scalded her and slapped Marco and taken all her gear off her and Jem knew that now was the moment to tell Hatto to fuck off, that he was a slithery little cunt, that all he'd wanted was a fucking sub so he could score, not to get into some mad fucking aggro with Sally Marcantonio and start dealing and he said: "Yeah, listen Hatto," and Hatto before he could finish glanced down at Jem's crotch and said: "Fifty fifty on that an' I'll do you a lay-on when it's finished," and Jem said: "Right yeah, grand," and they were outside Hatto's flats then and he stopped and watched Hatto walk inside into the courtyard and Hatto called over his shoulder: "Thursday up at Miranda's. Nine yeah."

Jem didn't say anything. He watched Hatto cross the courtyard and go into his block, his legs looking really short in the baggy trousers with the really narrow ends and his feet looking really small bet into the tight loafers, his barrelly walk like a cartoon or a puppet or something. Jem raked the damp strands of hair off his forehead again and held them in a fist on top of his head; he was having to take big breaths and sniff back runny snot from the junk sickness, made worse now from having been crying and walking quickly alongside Hatto. He stood there like that, like he was holding himself up by the hair, and stared into the courtyard. The sun was out and everything was starting to dry but there were puddles still, with green and yellow and yellowy-orange leaves in them turning to mush. He felt the coldness of the damp tee shirt under his leather and shivered and felt the aches in his legs and his arse and up his back. He put his hands back into his jeans pockets and shifted the position of the bag between his legs and started home down Summerhill towards North Strand.

From Redview

VANESSA MacDONALD

The girl didn't look like an everyday drifter. Jed was sitting in his usual spot, on the empty side of Redview Street, and had only just finished propping up his signs. The mail truck drove past, honking twice as it always did during the morning mail run. Jed waved, and glanced to his right, and there she was, trotting down the sidewalk in a long fur coat, orange silk peeking out from the bottom, and muddy boots.

It wasn't the fact that she was walking, though no one ever walked in this town. It wasn't even the clothes that made him stare. Nothing about clothes these days surprised him; jeans that would have been thrown away when he was young, ones with three-inch holes in the knees and frayed cuffs, were being sold in every store he passed in the mall. It was the look on her face: blank and at the same time, concentrated. It was as if she had been hypnotised.

He watched her walk past the hospital, and then the bus stop, bouncing on the back of her heel with every step. She neared the driveway to the hospital's parking lot, and suddenly turned left, jaywalking to his side of the street. He tensed as a car shot out of the parking lot, moments before she reached the sidewalk. Her pace didn't change as the driver leaned on his horn, and she continued walking straight until she reached the end of Redview, turning left onto Palo Verde Road, out of his sight line.

Jed was twisted around in his chair; he couldn't see her, but remained leaning forward, his back scrunched in an uncomfortable position, until a blue Ford drove by and honked. Jed turned and arched his back, waving and reaching for the small laminated sign he kept by the side of his folding chair. The car was down the street by the time he picked up the sign, but he kept it out anyway; it would soon be 8.30, and mothers would be making their school runs. He settled into his chair, resting his elbows on the armrests with the sign pinched between his fingers. He was starting to sweat already.

Jed smiled as Roger hopped from the steps of his truck. It was close to noon now, and the heat was rising off the asphalt in three-foot waves.

"I don't know how you manage out here during the summer."

Jed tapped the pole of a large umbrella stuffed into the ground next to him.

"Not so bad with this. I've got the fan, too."

"Supposed to go up to a hundred and fifteen later this week. You should think about skipping a few days."

Jed shook his head.

"Well, you're tougher than me. How's Lisa?"

Jed flexed his leg out in front of him, and winced when he heard a pop. *Mad as hell*, he thought.

"She's fine."

"I haven't seen her out here in a while." Roger looked down at a freshly painted piece of plywood, large blue letters written neatly on white. "And today . . . I mean, today being –"

"She wanted to stay home today. She doesn't come out here much after May anyway. She says the dust gets worse."

"She still helping out with the ankle biters?"

Jed forced a smile.

"Yeah. She loves it."

Roger nodded and wiped his forehead. He pointed to the hospital across the street.

"Think this will be the day?"

A silver BMW drove out of the parking lot, and Jed raised the sign, Roger jabbing his finger at it. The driver didn't react. Jed lowered the sign, and rubbed his lips. *Chapped*.

"You would think the bastards could at least wave at you."

They were quiet for a moment, and Jed watched the dust rise and settle into the gravel in front of him. Roger sighed before clapping Jed on the shoulder.

"Well, tell Lisa hi for me. And about the . . ." He gestured to the white plywood. "Well, it's a good sign."

Jed nodded, and watched Roger back his truck into the weeds before pulling out. A green Dodge gave three quick honks, and Jed raised his hand, saying loudly, though he knew he couldn't hear him, "Hey Frank."

It was 1 p.m. when she came walking back. He didn't see her turn the corner from Palo Verde. He was coughing up handfuls of dry crackers, groping for the water bottle stored under his chair, when he looked up and saw her coming towards him. She was sopping wet – he could see the matted fur of the coat dripping down onto her boots, the orange dress clinging to her ankles.

"Hiya."

She continued to stare straight ahead, and Jed looked to his right, but there was nothing to see except the empty rising street. He looked back towards her; her gaze didn't falter, but it was unfixed, like she was seeing things that he couldn't see. She was almost in front of him now, a few feet away. Her dark hair was curling at the ends, little drops of water falling from the curls onto her shoulders.

"You OK? Are you . . . lost?"

She didn't answer, but he could see her mouth moving. She walked past, bouncing on her heels a little less than before; her boots, as wet as the rest of her, were weighing her down, and she left two damp trails in the dirt. Jed shook his head. *Damn drugs. Or not enough of the right drugs.* He watched her continue up the hill until a red van honked and pulled in next to him. *Jesus, of all days. Mrs Garrett.*

"Hello, Jed."

She cocked her head and gave a half smile, opening the back door to let her son out.

"How've you been, Mrs Garrett?"

"Oh, fine, fine. Busy with this one. He's seven now – such a handful at that age, aren't they?"

She chuckled, then looked at Jed and grew quiet. She frowned, and said, "Well . . . I drove past this morning and saw the new sign. I just wanted to ask . . . well, how is Lisa? She still working at the pre-school?"

More like living there.

"Mmhm."

"Full time?"

Jed looked at her. She made a humming sound, then said, "Of course, I admire her, I really do. To go from the shock to having to . . . I mean, to working. Such a change."

Jed felt his face flush. *Damn.*

"Still, it keeps her busy, doesn't it?"

"She could go down to part time if she wanted. She loves those kids."

Jed was watching the boy throw gravel onto the plywood sign. Mrs Garrett fanned herself with one hand. *She'll ask about church next.*

"We sure miss you at Sunrise. You don't think . . . I mean, you don't think it might help – well, this day especially – you don't think it might help to come and . . ."

She trailed off and stared at him. Jed scratched his elbow.

"Has Lisa said anything about coming in? He helps all of us, especially those who . . . who are troubled."

She looked down at the white sign. Her son was squinting at it and running his finger along the blue letters.

"'TODAY . . . IS . . . HER . . . BI- . . . BI- . . . BIR-' –"

Kid couldn't read himself out of a paper bag.

"Adam, please –"

"'BIRCH-' –"

"Adam, it says 'birthday', and what did we say about shouting –"

"'TODAY . . . IS . . . HER . . . BIRTHDAY'!"

Adam smiled up at his mother. Mrs Garrett turned pink and looked at Jed. He was suddenly aware of the large sweat stains around his neck. He pulled at the front of his shirt. Adam picked up a stick and screamed as he swung it through the air.

"Jed, I'm sorry –"

"Nah, it's all right. What he lacks in phonetic skills, he makes up for in enthusiasm."

Mrs Garrett's pink cheeks turned red.

"His phonetic . . . No, I didn't mean that. I meant I'm sorry. About Emily. Her birthday. How old would she . . . ?"

She looked down at the sign again, then stood silently. Jed watched the boy stab a tuft of blond weeds with the stick.

"Thirty. She would have been thirty today."

Mrs Garrett made the humming sound again. *Woman sounds like she's circling a hive.*

"Did I hear something about a company buying this field? Are you going to . . . Does that mean you'll –"

"I'll stay here as long as I can."

"Well, if you don't mind me asking, wouldn't it make sense to pack up now? I just worry about you out here in this heat, and if they're going to make you leave anyway . . . And the hospital has never recognised the . . . the incident. Even if it was their fault . . ."

Jed clenched his teeth.

". . . they won't admit to it. And He says . . . well, He speaks of forgiveness, and after four years –"

"He can forgive them if He wants to, Mrs Garrett."

She raised her eyebrows at his sharp reply. Jed forced the corners of his mouth up.

"I'll tell Lisa you said hello."

Mrs Garrett nodded, said, "God bless," and motioned to her son. He could hear her through the open window telling the kid to sit still as they pulled away. Jed looked down at his shirt. *Should have brought the fan out earlier.*

By 3 p.m. it was 107 degrees. Roger shouted out the temperature from his window, then came back fifteen minutes later with an energy drink. *What a God-awful colour.* Jed put the chilled bottle against his forehead, then rolled it under one of the signs as Roger's truck pulled away. He felt drained by the steady heat; his chin drooped down onto his chest. He dozed for several minutes until a car honked. He jerked his head up, and raised his arm to wave, instinctively. And the girl was there again.

She was dragging her feet now, and limping slightly. Her

face was bright red. Her hair still looked wet, but he guessed it was now from sweat. She looked like she might pass out at any moment. *No wonder, a fur coat in the middle of June.* He sighed and pushed himself off the chair, groaning at the ache in his lower back, then leaned down slowly to grab the bottle from under the sign.

"'Scuse me."

She was walking towards him but she didn't respond. He didn't expect her to.

"Are you all right?"

The coat was perched on her shoulders. It was dry now, except where her left hand was clenching a fistful of fur. Her stomach stuck out under the thin orange silk. *Looks just like a squirrel in summer*, he thought: *belly plastered to an oak branch, tongue sprawled out, panting like a dog.* He felt queasy; he didn't want to be disgusted. *Poor crazy thing.* He looked down at his hands.

"'Scuse me for saying so, but you're not looking so good."

She was directly in front of him now. She stopped walking, and he looked back at her face: where before her eyes had been suspended, steady, they suddenly began to roam. He held out the bottle, but she started walking again, moving around him so that he had to turn in place to face her.

"It's none of my business, but you might want to think about taking off the coat."

She continued on. He shook his head and uncapped the bottle. He took a short swig, curling his lip at the sweet taste, and a moment later heard a thump to his right. She had shrugged off the coat; like road kill, it lay in a grubby heap, the dust puffing around it.

"I didn't mean leave it with me!"

She didn't turn. He clicked his tongue, and shuffled the few feet to pick it up. As he was leaning down, he heard a burst of honking in front of him. He straightened up, holding the collar of the coat in one hand, ready to wave with the other.

"You going to prom?"

A white Honda was edging along the sidewalk. He could see a group of them piled inside. A shirtless teen was leaning out the window towards the girl.

"You going to be prom queen?"

She continued on, slowly, seemingly oblivious to their

laughter. The teen pushed himself further out of the window.

"Hey. HEY." He waved his hand a few inches from her face.

"She's stoned, man."

"No, no it's even better. She's nuts."

"Get out, she won't even notice if you . . . Just move over, I'll do it."

The teen was pulled from the window. Jed could see them switching places, three or four of them writhing around on the back seat to let a skinny boy through. The door opened and he flung himself out, stumbling over the kerb and landing on his knees. The laughter turned hysterical. Jed frowned, and moved towards them. The skinny boy crawled a few inches and then stood up behind the girl, who was now babbling loudly.

". . . because they're still trapped in there, but I can disappear. I can leave. And you won't see me, I'll sink right under . . ."

The boy plucked at the back of her dress.

"Oh God, she's wet."

The car was shuddering beside the girl, its door slightly swinging each time the driver braked. Jed quickened his pace. He was a few feet away when he heard one of them shriek, "Loony, when's the last time you were kissed?"

A hand shot from the open door of the car, pushing the skinny boy into the back of her. He stepped on her dress, pulling it tight around her neck, and stumbled until they were folded in half, one buckled under the other. He rolled sideways into the street and cussed at her before wiping off his shirt. She let out a low, guttural scream, and hugged her arms around her body.

Jed stood still for one moment, stunned, then yelled, "Get away! You little bastards, get away!"

He jogged the last few feet to the car, the uncapped drink splashing out of the top, the sleeve of her fur coat hitting his face. The boy jumped into the car and it sped through the stop sign, laughter still spewing from the open door. The girl was running now, a pathetic limping gait that seemed to drag her down as much as it moved her forward.

"No, no! You can't see me! You . . ."

"Get away, you bastards! You idiots! Damn ugly ignorant . . ."

". . . can't take me back! I can disappear! You won't find me there . . ."

Jed slowed his pace as he reached the corner of Redview. He was wheezing and he bent over to catch his breath, clutching at the cramp in his side. Blue liquid trickled down his wrist. *Jesus, I look as crazy as her.* He straightened up and leaned around the corner. She was limping down Palo Verde, her arms still wrapped around her. He hesitated for a moment, then followed after her, keeping an eye on the bright orange in case she collapsed.

After a few minutes, the road changed from cracked asphalt and power lines to packed dirt and a hash of trees bordering the edges. That was normal here; though the central streets looked like any other mid-town grid, they branched off to quiet roads obscured by curves and buckbrush. Most of them were, in effect, private driveways that ran a few hundred feet and stopped at neglected houses. Palo Verde stretched on and on, all the way to the water tower. Jed couldn't remember how far it went – *a mile? two miles?* – but there were no houses out here.

They walked for fifteen minutes, Jed keeping twenty feet behind her, trying to match her pace. She slowed only when she reached the small bridge. It hung over Salt Creek, simple and rusted and just large enough to let one car pass at a time. She let her arms drop to her sides; she had stopped shouting, or even mumbling. Jed could see her chest lifting and dropping in exaggerated breaths. He wiped the sweat out of his eyes and stopped where he was, worried he would scare her if he came too close. She stepped out of her boots and pushed them behind her. She wasn't wearing socks; he could see blood on the back of her heels. She closed her eyes and placed her hands on the rail of the bridge, bending her legs lower and lower until she was almost squatting on the dirty metal, her sweat-stained dress gathering in crumpled layers around her. Then suddenly she sprang into the air. Her arms straightened as she pulled herself up onto the rail. Jed's eyes widened. She gripped the rail with one hand as she moved from her knees to her feet, then slowly, fluidly, she stood, her arms flexing out to the sides for balance. Jed started to call out, then stopped himself, placing one hand over his mouth. He inched closer to the bridge and watched as she opened her eyes and looked down into the water. She stayed there for a few moments, long enough for Jed to creep only a few feet away. Her mouth moved and he leaned forward.

"They can't see through you."

She seemed to be talking to the water rolling below her. Jed glanced down. The creek was half-full, rising maybe three feet from the bed. He saw her make a sudden movement and jerked his head up. She was looking at him.

"You trapped too?"

Jed opened his mouth and a rasping breath escaped. She smiled, showing a broken tooth. She pointed down to the water.

"They can't find you there."

The top half of her body was still twisted towards him, her face still searching his. He didn't even see her bend her knees. She was there. And then he blinked, and she was not.

Jesus Christ.

He didn't feel himself move; he only heard the coat drop behind him, heard the empty roll of the plastic bottle on metal. He found himself at the rail. He gasped for air and felt a trickle of spit lodge in his throat. He coughed then heard a dense splash below, like planks hitting water. He bent over the rail, squinting his eyes against the blaze of reflected light. For a moment, all he could see was the orange dress waving in the current, and then he heard it.

She was laughing.

He wiped his eyes, and saw her crouching in the creek, poking at the wet fabric ballooning around her. She lay back and let herself float. He leaned further over the rail, the hot metal pressing into his stomach, as the water carried her under the bridge. He stumbled over her boots and moved to the other side in time to see her hair, streaming ahead of her body, drift into view. Like a paper boat, the rest of her slowly appeared. Jed pressed his forearms into the rail, letting it hold him up. She flung her hair away from her shoulders and let out a high-pitched, squealing laugh as she sat up, sinking slightly before her feet found the creek bed. Jed patted his chest to slow his heart. She stood laughing for several minutes, twisting back and forth to make the dress, now floating near her waist, wave with the current. When the water began pushing against her, she moved to the edge of the creek where it was shallow, only a foot high. She got down on her knees and stuck her head close to the ground. She very carefully picked something up; he thought it was a small pile of stones and twigs, until he noticed the feathers. She was still talking to it, whispering into her cupped hands, when Jed heard the car.

White and chunky, it approached the bridge slowly and parked in front of him. He recognised it as one of the medical vans they used at the hospital. A woman in a navy suit opened the passenger door, frowning; a man jumped out of the driver's side. They started to come towards him until the girl laughed. Jed looked down; she was crawling over the small rocks to get to the bank, where the water just barely lapped. She held the dead bird with one hand, and pushed the other in and out of the mud, laughing at the sucking noise. The driver, a large man in green scrubs, peered at her over the edge of the slope.

"She's here, Sue."

The woman pursed her lips and let out a long breath, moving towards the rail of the bridge. She motioned to the man and he started down the hill. She turned towards Jed.

"Is this your property? Did she do any damage?"

Jed pointed to the man.

"What's he doing?"

"We're from Unity Hospital. I just want to make it clear that this is very unusual – we haven't had a patient slip away in years. If this is your property –"

"It's not."

The woman gave a nod and rubbed her eyes. Jed looked below. The girl was standing up, violently shaking her head back and forth.

"No, no. You can't speak to me here."

The man went towards her and gently took her arm. Her eyes flitted back and forth from his face to the sky to the copper-coloured creek. He reached towards the hand still clutching the bird, and she raised it above her head, wrenching backwards away from him. He let go and she twisted around to set the animal on a rock in the shallow water. She started whispering again – at the water or at the muddy remains, Jed wasn't sure. The man moved closer, murmuring reassurances. She whimpered and seemed to draw into herself, making her chest concave, but she didn't resist as he led her to the slope. She slipped once, landing hard on her knees, and wouldn't move again; the man had to pick her up, lifting her by the elbow with one arm and using the other to steady himself. Jed gripped the woman's sleeve.

"He shouldn't do that."

"It's all right, he knows what he's –"

"No, she'll break. She'll break!"

The girl let out a weak howl.

The woman slid her arm away from Jed, and took a step towards the van.

"She's fine. She just slipped away. It never happens, you understand. We're very careful about that. It couldn't have been more than an hour. We make sure our nurses check on them throughout the day."

Jed didn't say anything. She didn't notice, and continued rambling about safety measures until the girl was safely in the back seat. The man locked the door and came towards them. He picked a soggy feather off his shirt and flung it to the ground, shaking his head at the woman.

"Another bird. God knows what it died of. Look at this." He lifted his hand. "Bacteria, maybe bird flu, all over me. And her. But she's not hurt." He looked at Jed. "She's harmless, of course. We were worried she would be unsettled, being outside of her normal environment. But she doesn't know where she is, or what's around her. She doesn't interact with anything. Nothing alive, anyway."

Jed stared at him.

"So I can't imagine she bothered you . . . ? If she's caused damage –"

"It's all right. It's not his property."

The woman motioned him away and picked up the boots. Jed could see the same glazed expression as before on the girl's face as they drove past. He could see her mouth moving rapidly, her chin quivering; she was staring into nothing again. He grimaced as they bumped over the fur coat. They sped away, and he stood there for a moment, listening to the water below. He picked up the trampled coat and shuffled back down the road. He turned from Palo Verde onto Redview, walked past the parking lot and the bus stop and finally the hospital. He didn't hear the blue Chevy honk as he neared his spot on the side of the street. He stood under the umbrella, staring at his signs.

A daughter died because of you.
Recognise your mistake.
She deserves to rest in peace.

The heat had soaked into him; his limbs felt both heavy and slack, as if he could drift away or sink into the ground. He lowered the umbrella, and threw the chair, small laminated sign and fur coat into the pale weeds behind him. He dragged the signs to the edge of the street and lined them up in a row. He looked towards the hospital; the sun was just starting to lower, casting shadows from the oaks onto the sides of the building. He went back to the weeds and picked up the coat, flicking off the chunks of dried dirt, pulling a star thistle from the sleeve. Carefully, he folded the coat and placed it on top of the new sign. He moved into the street, and a car slowed to let him cross. The driver shouted out to him. *Frank.* Jed moved towards his window.

"I couldn't hear you, Frank."

"I said, 'Happy birthday to Emily.'"

Frank drove past, leaving a brief burst of cold air from the open window. Jed smiled and backed away, slumping onto the uncovered bench at the bus stop. He looked over at the crooked row of signs; red dust was stamped into the base of the plywood, a loud underline to the blue-painted words. He nodded.

Happy birthday, honey.

Our First Lesbians

REBECCA ROUILLARD

Grace spotted the couple with the young child as they walked into church on Sunday morning. They were new – she would have to be friendly, introduce herself and make conversation. Grace found it tiring to initiate conversation, particularly with the weight of responsibility she bore. It wasn't easy being the pastor's wife, even in a fledgling congregation – they'd only started The Lighthouse six months ago and there were not usually more than fifty people at their Sunday meeting.

But as Grace prepared herself for the familiar ordeal, she noticed something interesting. The woman holding the toddler was wearing a dress (they were not the kind of church that required women to wear dresses but it was more comfortable in the dry heat of Joburg summer), but the other one, the taller, sturdier one with short hair, wearing a T-shirt and cargo shorts who Grace had taken for the husband, was in fact a woman as well. The child was black but the sight of a white couple with an adopted black baby was hardly unusual in their community. She wondered if the women were friends who'd decided to visit the church together. But this was Melville; it seemed much more likely that they were a couple.

Grace and Jacob had not realised before they moved that Melville was known locally as a "gay area". When they were looking at houses there seemed to be a lot of photos of naked men stuck on fridges, and bathrooms with no doors, but it was only after they relocated that it all began to make sense. There was even a Melville Mardi Gras – they should have worked it out.

Jacob had always dreamed of starting a church in downtown Joburg – of saving the city. But the city itself, despite continued efforts at urban renewal, was still rather frightening and definitely not a suitable place to raise a family. They had ended up in Melville – a slightly dilapidated area (the estate agent described it as "up-and-coming"), close enough to the city to be called "metropolitan" but much more family-friendly.

Jacob was at the front, going over his preparation notes for the meeting. Grace caught his eye, lifted her eyebrows and nodded in the direction of the door. He looked at the door, looked back at her and shrugged his shoulders.

Grace went up to him, leaned in and whispered, "Our first lesbians!"

Jacob looked towards the door again; he didn't seem very excited.

Several of the congregation members were already talking animatedly to the women – they didn't seem awkward or uncomfortable about it either. Grace thought about how members of their old congregation in Krugersdorp might have reacted to lesbians in church and felt slightly smug; people in the suburbs were so closed-minded.

When it had become obvious that they might expect gay visitors to the church, Jacob bought a book about the issue by a well-respected theologian. It was called *Connecting but Not Condoning: A Handbook for Integrating Homosexuals into the Body*. Grace hadn't actually read it herself but she was sure she'd got the gist from the title: love the sinner but not the sin – that kind of thing.

They'd had a gay man in the church before, but he was celibate so it hadn't really been a problem. And then he'd left anyway, to work on a contract in Saudi Arabia. He had thought that living in a place where there was a death penalty for homosexuality might be a good motivation for him to stay straight. They hadn't heard from him in a while.

"You should go and talk to them," Jacob said.

He didn't sound worried, Grace thought. He sounded resolute. He obviously had a strategy. Grace wasn't sure exactly what the strategy was supposed to be but the book title seemed to suggest that it was about connecting. She could do that, surely. She could be friendly. Jacob would know what to do about everything else.

Grace hauled her two-year-old, Hannah-Rose, from underneath a chair and headed towards the door to meet the new couple.

"Hi, I'm Grace. Welcome to The Lighthouse," she said, trying to smile in a welcoming way. She wasn't sure if handshaking was appropriate in this situation; she wasn't much of a hugger. It helped to have a two-year-old to carry – that usually required two hands.

"I'm Savannah," said the woman in the dress. "This is Marlene and Naledi."

Savannah looked in her early thirties. Up close she had a multitude of freckles on her arms and face, and she had fine lines around her eyes that showed when she smiled, but when she smiled she was radiant. Marlene was older.

"Hello, Naledi." Grace addressed the toddler directly; parents liked that. "This is Hannah-Rose. She's two. How old are you?"

"You're two as well, aren't you?" said Savannah, as the two little girls ignored each other.

"I love how you've done her hair." Grace put out a hand to touch Naledi's decorative bunches, plaited and laced with colourful ribbons. "I wouldn't know how to do that."

"We had to get someone to teach us. It was a nightmare at first – we had a one-year-old with dreadlocks," Savannah said.

"It's gorgeous. Are you new to the area?"

"We've been here a couple of months. We love Melville," said Marlene.

"Such a great sense of community," Grace said. "We have a toddler group on Tuesday afternoons if Naledi might be interested."

"That sounds good," said Savannah. "She goes to a playgroup in the mornings but we're always looking for things in the afternoon. Thanks."

"Where does she go to playgroup?"

"Little Rainbows, in Parktown."

"I think I know some people whose kids go there, you might even recognise someone here," Grace said. "Well, lovely to meet you, you're very welcome."

They moved in the direction of the circle of chairs and Grace went to find them a family-resources brochure with details of all the children's groups that the church offered. It had gone better than she had expected.

The meeting started with a drumming circle. They had about ten proper djembes and the rest of the congregation joined in on shakers or just clapped and stamped their feet. The kids ran around shrieking, rattling bells and maracas. Jacob shouted encouragements into the microphone over the noise of the drums.

When they'd finished the worship session they had a discussion about the true meaning of community, based on Acts 4:32–37. The congregation split up into groups, each with a flipchart to record their ideas. They chatted for twenty minutes and then came back together for feedback time. Jacob wrapped up and everyone went outside for coffee.

"That was unusual, but I enjoyed it," Savannah told Grace. "Are your meetings always like that?"

Grace had followed them out to make sure they got some cake. Savannah was breaking off bite-sized chunks of hers for Naledi and the little girl was jumping up and down with her mouth open.

"We didn't want to do church in the traditional way – people have got bored of that," said Grace.

Hannah-Rose was pulling on Grace's dress and pointing at the cake she was holding.

"I know what you mean." Savannah was nodding but Marlene frowned.

"Mommy," Hannah-Rose whined.

Grace tried to break off a piece of her cake but it disintegrated into crumbs. She gave up and handed Hannah-Rose the whole slice.

"We want The Lighthouse to be about *creativity* and *community* and *authenticity*." She wasn't sure she was explaining very well.

"It's good to do things differently," said Marlene.

"Yes, it is." Grace was relieved.

It was all on the website – their vision and values. She just wasn't very good at communicating it. It was a good website, most people really liked it. Jacob had designed it himself. He was good at that sort of thing. They made a good team, she often thought.

Jacob led the meetings and she did the catering.

Toddler Group was on a Tuesday afternoon in the community centre. Grace was looking out for Savannah and Naledi. She was hoping they would come but she was also worried about what she would say to Savannah. The difficulty would be to get the tone right – welcoming but not affirming. She imagined a conversation of omissions – awkward gaps to be papered over. They could always speak about Naledi, at least.

But when she saw Savannah it was easy to find something to say. "I'm so glad you came."

"Well, I wasn't keen but Naledi was just dying to see Hannah-Rose again."

Grace laughed as the two little girls sized each other up without a hint of friendliness. Hannah-Rose had recently taken to biting; Grace hoped she wouldn't bite Naledi.

"Have you had Naledi since she was a baby?" Grace asked as they walked into the community centre, lowering her voice in case Savannah minded her asking in front of Naledi.

"We got her when she was five months," Savannah replied, apparently not concerned about Naledi hearing.

"What does her name mean?"

"It means star – it's Sesoto."

"That's lovely."

"We thought it was important to give her an African name. We want her to know where she came from."

"That's so important."

The singing was about to start so Grace left Savannah and Naledi to sit down and went to fetch Hannah-Rose who was terrorising a small boy with a bell stick.

They sang the usual songs, including Hannah-Rose's favourite, *Five Little Ladybirds*, and then they made ladybirds with red paper plates, black stickers and pipe cleaners for antennae. Towards the end of the session Hannah-Rose scratched Grace on the cheek with the sharp end of a pipe cleaner and she had to take her for a timeout.

She looked for Savannah and Naledi when she came back. Naledi was digging in the sandpit and Savannah was sitting alone on the grass watching her; the sun was glinting off the highlights in her auburn hair. Grace wasn't sure if Savannah would be sick of her by now but no one else was talking to her so she walked over and sat down beside her. Hannah-Rose headed for the sandpit as well.

"Naledi must keep you busy, but do you work?" Grace asked Savannah.

"Yes, I'm an artist."

"That's amazing. I always thought there were loads of artists in Melville – it seems like such an arty area – but you're the first proper artist I've actually met."

"Have you met many improper artists?"

"You have no idea. There's Bill who paints really bad wildlife and Sheena who does scrapbooking. But no one who does proper art."

"How do you know I 'do proper art' – perhaps I paint bad wildlife, too?"

"You don't, do you? I'd love to see your work. I used to paint when I was younger, but I haven't done anything for years."

"You should come to my studio."

"I'd really like that."

"How old are you, Grace?" Savannah asked, after a pause.

"I'm twenty-six. Why?"

"You seem older, and younger."

Grace didn't really know what she meant; she was used to people telling her that she seemed older, that she was an "old soul". Sometime she wished she was thirty. People didn't take you seriously until you were thirty.

In the sandpit Grace saw Hannah-Rose empty a bucket of sand over Naledi's head.

"Oh no." She started to get up, expecting Naledi to cry, but the other little girl gave Hannah-Rose a shove and she fell backwards onto her bottom. Hannah-Rose was surprised but she didn't cry either. Then the two little girls began to laugh.

"I think they'll be all right," Savannah said.

Grace sat back down again.

When Grace waved Savannah off at the end of the afternoon she realised she had not thought about her being a lesbian once in the last few hours. Without Marlene there it had been easy to forget that Savannah wasn't just the same as any other mom.

"By the way," Jacob said to Grace the following night, as they were getting ready for bed, "the lesbians are coming round to see us on Saturday."

"Did you speak to Savannah? You didn't tell me." She felt annoyed, she wasn't sure why.

"No, the other one, Marlene. She phoned me yesterday."

"Do you know what for?"

"I imagine they want to join the church."

"But that's all right, isn't it?" she asked.

"Of course. They're welcome to *join* the church." He emphasised the word "join" as though they wouldn't qualify for anything more than entry-level membership. "The important thing right now is that we make them feel welcome." The way he said it didn't sound very welcoming, though.

"Savannah's really nice," Grace put in.

"I'm sure she is," he said. "That doesn't make a difference." He folded his clothes and put them on the chair in the corner of the room. "But everything else can come later when they know us better. We have to build a bridge of relationship strong enough to withstand the weight of hard truth."

She wasn't sure exactly what the "hard truth" was but it didn't sound pleasant.

"I'll make some banana bread," she suggested.

That night Grace dreamed about Savannah. They were sitting on the grass together, talking. Savannah threw back her head and laughed and her neck was like the stem of a calla lily – it seemed the most natural thing in the world to lean forward and kiss it.

"Grace, what are you doing?" Jacob asked her in the dream. His face was screwed up in repulsion.

"I don't know." She was confused, disorientated.

Savannah was gone; it was just Jacob, looking at her with accusing eyes.

Grace woke up with the feel of Savannah's skin still vividly present on her lips. It was 2 a.m. Jacob snored next to her.

When Grace was eleven she'd become aware of what it meant

to be gay, and that it was bad. And because she was eleven and had never kissed a boy, or had a boyfriend, or even held a boy's hand, she worried that *she* might be a lesbian. Boys were a foreign land – what if she never learned to interpret their signs and bridge the divide? What if she was trapped in the territory of women for ever? She had always felt that she was different; perhaps *this* was the thing that would finally mark her and separate her. She cried herself to sleep for many nights until she found other things to worry about. And then, over the next few years, she started to realise that the boys would find their way to her – she didn't need to go anywhere. She started dating Jacob when she was seventeen and they were married by the time she was twenty. By then she knew that relationships and marriage were about making a commitment to someone based on common values and shared beliefs – she knew that love was a decision, not just a feeling.

It was just a silly dream – it didn't mean anything, she decided.

Marlene, Savannah and Naledi arrived at 3 p.m. on Saturday afternoon.

"Hannah-Rose, why don't you show Naledi your toys?" Grace said.

She had put out some of Hannah-Rose's toys in the study in hope that the little girls would occupy themselves for a while – give the adults a chance to talk. Hannah-Rose took Naledi by the hand and pulled her away.

"We really like the church. Everyone's been really friendly and welcoming. We've tried a few churches in the area and that's not always the case," said Marlene.

They were sitting in the lounge, drinking their coffee. Grace had baked a banana loaf and they had been very complimentary about it. She was hoping that one of them would take another slice – she'd cut too many. She wondered if she should take the plate away.

"I'm sorry about that," Jacob said.

"You didn't go to The Ark, did you?" Grace couldn't resist asking.

The Ark was the local Pentecostal church; they were always preaching on street corners about hell and damnation. She wouldn't want anyone to associate them with that kind of judgementalism.

"We're not suckers for punishment," Savannah replied.

"The reason we came here today," Marlene continued, "is because, as I'm sure you know, the law has changed – it's been a huge milestone victory for our community."

For a moment Grace was confused; she thought Marlene was talking about the church community and she couldn't think of any recent milestone victories.

Savannah was looking down but Marlene looked straight at Jacob. "What we're actually looking for is someone to marry us."

And then Grace realised which community Marlene was talking about. Somehow they'd skipped a step in Jacob's strategic plan. Perhaps it was her fault. She'd got the tone wrong – she'd obviously been *too* welcoming. It was supposed to be "connecting but not condoning". But how can you be welcoming and disapproving at the same time? Was it even possible? She looked at Jacob. How would he handle this? *She* hadn't read the book, it was *his* book.

"I'm afraid we're going to have to disappoint you," Jacob said. "You are very welcome at our church but we won't marry you. We love you but we don't condone your lifestyle choice."

Grace cringed at the "we love you", shifted in her seat and braced herself for their anger. But they didn't say anything. Savannah studied one of the pictures on the wall with intense concentration.

"We looked on the website," Marlene said, "but there was nothing about it there. Perhaps you should put it on the website."

"Yes, you're right, we should put it on the website. Sorry," said Jacob.

Grace had nothing to do with the website; it was *his* website.

"Where are those girls?" she said. "They're very quiet – that usually means trouble."

She got up and walked towards the study and Savannah stood to follow her.

A sea of toys lay abandoned on the rug and the two-year-olds were standing on the far side of the room. As Grace came in they turned to face her, black permanent-marker pens grasped in their hands.

"Look, Mommy, it's you," Hannah-Rose said, indicating the wall.

Savannah gasped. The girls had drawn two giant faces; spiky hair sprouting on top, arms protruding from the sides of their heads, legs from their chins. The faces had toothy grins and huge protruding, bulbous eyes.

Hannah-Rose was beaming but Grace hardly saw her. Behind her, Savannah was apologising repeatedly, but Grace wasn't listening. All she was aware of was the eyes – those unblinking, accusing eyes.

Escaping Time

MARY BRACHT

He said he'd leave the door unlocked tonight. That he'd leave his shift five minutes early and walk down the road without turning his key in the deadbolt. Five whole minutes before another soldier would arrive to take his place, so that I could slip out and be free. He told me all this as he raped me, again. I was obliged to listen to his words, heavy in my ear, but I was not obliged to believe them. My thoughts were my own. No man could take that away from me, yet so many, like him, tried. He kissed me when he was done. Like a lover. A kiss that promised things. Like an unlocked door.

I closed my eyes as I waited for him to finish probing my mouth with his tongue. I saw him in my mind, going through the motions of his promise. *He glances at the clock on the kitchen wall. Passes through the empty dining room. His boots tread softly on the wooden floor. His shaded face, always hidden by his military cap, looks upwards at the staircase as he exits the house into the night. He walks down the road towards the soldiers' barracks. He smiles. The door is left unlocked.*

"I'll wait for you beneath the bridge," he said when he finally let me breathe. He rolled off and stood, towering above me.

I watched him dress. His starched uniform suited his clean-shaven face. His boots shone even though he'd been on duty for eight hours, four in the field, four here, guarding their women. He never failed to visit my room during his shift. He would wait until the queue of soldiers who required my body to service their needs had finished and gone home. Then he came to fulfil his own. Like them, he needed to invade my body. He needed to destroy me. Only then could he feel like a soldier again and return to the battlefield to fight the Emperor's world war. They called us comfort women.

As I sit here staring at my bedroom door, I know that his shift ends in ten minutes. In five he will leave, and the door will be left unlocked. That is what he promised.

He is Japanese, but when he whispers into my ear at night, it is my native Korean that assaults me. It is forbidden to speak in my tongue. The Emperor demands that all his conquered subjects assimilate the Japanese way of life, but he whispers the forbidden words to me, nevertheless. He wants to comfort me as he explores my flesh. He wants to remind me of home. He wants me to feel close to him. He wants too much. Feelings destroy women like me. Trapped women, forced to feed the never-ending lines of hungry soldiers.

Of them all, he is the hungriest. He fights each night against my flesh, desperate to feel like a man. Tonight, he must have won his battle. Like a conquering king, he has offered me terms: follow him through the unlocked door and into his arms so I can be free. The Emperor is losing the war, and he wants to flee to Mongolia before the troops retreat. I am to bear his children in the wilds of the mountainside. His terms are a second kind of death.

It is now two minutes before his shift ends. I can hear him move through the rooms below. I tiptoe to my door and slowly open it. Snores greet me in the hallway. Yes, women snore, especially these women, my sisters-in-captivity, used up each day and discarded like soiled rags. We have all become reflections of one another, pale, emaciated, bruised and broken. Each of us bares our enslavement on our flesh. Their snores fill my ears, my heart, the inner depths of my soul. I'm sure my own snores join theirs when I, too, finally fall asleep. Our minds escape our tired bodies each night only to relive our lives in our dreams, loud dreams, painful dreams, images of cruelties we've suffered, men we fear but must face over and over when they return to our rooms. It's always the ones who hurt us the most that queue up first.

Careful to edge my feet around the boards that creak, I make my way to the landing and listen for his boots on the polished wood. They head across the dining room and out of the back door. I hear the door hinges squeal shut, the doorknob as it is released, and my ears strain for the familiar slide of the key into the lock, the turning of the deadbolt as it shrieks into place, and the silence that follows. But there is nothing, except whistling. I listen to his song as it slowly fades away.

I have four minutes before the next soldier arrives to take his place. My mind is tormented with indecision. A girl found out of her room is punished with ten lashes and solitary confinement for three days. If she is caught trying to escape, they saw off one of her legs. There is no judge or jury, just a group of men to hold her down. My fear of getting caught does not outweigh the memories that plague me, memories of home. Do my parents miss me? Did they search for me?

My father was a fisherman. He navigated the Southern Sea with the other village men, far off the coast of Jeju Island. My mother and I were *haenyo*, women of the sea. On our island, diving is women's work. Our bodies suit the cold depths of the ocean better than men's. We can go deeper, hold our breaths longer, and keep our body temperature warmer, so for centuries Jejudo women have enjoyed the freedom to work and sell our bounty at market.

I followed my mother into the sea at an early age, just as all my female ancestors before me had done. I was eleven the first time she showed me how to cut an abalone from a rock on the ocean floor. In my excitement I lost my breath sooner than expected and had to race to the surface for air. I clutched my knife in one hand and the abalone in the other as I swam with all my might towards the light. My lungs burned for air. When I broke the surface, I breathed in more seawater than oxygen.

"Always look to the shore when you rise, or you can lose your way," my mother said and turned me to face the land. There on the sand my younger sister sat, protecting the day's catch. "Look for your sister after each dive. Never forget. If you see her, you are safe."

My sister was too young to dive. She sat on the beach and threw stones at gulls when they crept too close to the tubs of shellfish. Sometimes, when I surfaced, I would look to the shore to find her chasing after them, waving sticks wildly in the air. She was like a butterfly dancing across my sight line. As the years passed, I grew accustomed to seeing her in the distance, a miniature version of the girl who shared my bed at night, endlessly fighting with the birds. She was my anchor, as my mother had intended.

It was late in the afternoon, long after the other divers had gone home for the day, when I saw him. I had come up for air and looked first to the shore. My sister was squatting on the sand, shading her eyes to look out towards us. I had just found a large conch and was ready to shout at her to express my glee, when I noticed a man on the beach. Treading water so that I could lift myself higher to see him more clearly, I realised he was a Japanese soldier, and he was headed straight for my sister. A ridge of rocks shielded her from his view, but it wouldn't do so for long. He would stumble upon her if he stayed on his current path. He would take her away like the other young girls.

I dived under the waves and swam towards the shore. The current crushed against me as though desperate to push me back out to sea, to safety. Panicking, I breached the water's surface to take a deep breath and caught a glimpse of the soldier's progress. He was still headed towards the rocky ledge.

I started to swim above the waves, unable to bear staying too long beneath the water for fear of missing his advance. I was halfway to her, when I saw him stop. He dug in his pocket for something. I plunged my head back into the water to swim even faster. In my next breath, I saw him light a cigarette. With every breath, he moved just a little more. He blew out a puff of smoke, took a drag, breathed it out, again and again with each lift of my head, until the last breath, when he looked towards the sea and saw me.

I was only ten metres away from the shore. He couldn't see my sister from where he stood. She was still hidden by the rocks, but not for long. Her hands were on the sand, and she began to push herself up. I couldn't shout at her to stay down. He would have heard me above the lazy sea wind. I could only swim faster.

I pitched beneath the waves, pulling the water out of my way with each stroke, until my hands hit the beach. Then I shot to my feet and lunged at her, seizing her and knocking her to the ground.

He didn't hear her cry out in surprise. I had covered her

mouth with my hand as I fell upon her, and when she saw my face hovering above hers, she knew better than to cry. I gave her a look only a little sister would understand. There was no time to explain. I pushed her towards the base of the cold rock ledge.

"No matter what you hear, don't move," I mouthed more than whispered.

Her trembling body felt so small beneath my hands. Her fear was contagious, and I too began to tremble in my fingers and my knees.

"Where did you go?" the soldier called down to me. "Has the mermaid transformed into a girl?"

His boots crunched on the rocks above us. I took three huge steps away from where my sister lay, before I stood up. His eyes were sharp, and I felt them pierce as they crept over my body. I wasn't certain whether he had spotted my sister before I could hide her. I could only hope I had reached her in time.

"Not a girl, but a grown woman," he said and let out a low, grumbling laugh.

He wore a beige uniform and field boots, with a cap that shaded his face, and his eyes were black like the rocks beneath his feet – the rocks that hid my sister from him. I was still recovering from the swim to shore, and each time I gasped for breath, his eyes glanced at my chest. My shirt was thin and drenched with seawater. I hurriedly covered my breasts with my hair.

"Are you here with your husband?" he asked.

I shook my head.

"Ah, you are not married?"

I shook my head again. He took a step towards me.

I took a step away from him. Away from her. He followed me, taking two more steps to close the gap between us.

"Where is your family?" he asked, glancing around.

I looked over the water and saw my mother's head duck beneath a wave. My father's boat was far out to sea. My sister and I were alone with this soldier, and two more had just ventured onto the sand from the road. They were heading our way. I knew that nothing I said would save me, but I was not the only one at risk.

Tearing my eyes away from the rolling waves that beckoned me to dive in, to escape, I said, "They're dead."

"A tragic mermaid," he said, and smiled. "There *are* treasures to be found at sea."

The other two soldiers arrived, swiftly coming up behind me and grabbing my arms. They conferred with the first soldier, who never took his eyes off me until a decision was made. Then he turned and trudged back up the way he had come. The other two soldiers dragged me behind him.

I didn't scream. I couldn't risk alarming my sister. I couldn't risk her trying to help me. They would just take her, too. I went without a fight, without saying a word, but my legs wouldn't go as easily. They defended me in wordless opposition by refusing to work. They hung from my body like useless logs, weighing me down, but it didn't deter the soldiers. They gripped me harder and raised me off the ground so that only my toes dragged in the sand.

I never looked back. Not once. Not even to catch a last glimpse of my mother swimming in the sea as they carried me away from her. I couldn't risk it, not even to save one final beautiful moment in my mind, before they did to me what the village rumours said happened to every girl caught by the soldiers. I was fifteen and naïve, but like all the girls in my village, I had heard the rumours about the Emperor's soldiers. It happened as they foretold, all of it happened. They mounted me in turn as the other soldiers held me down on the hard earth, but he was first.

Afterwards, they threw me into the back of a truck with four other girls. Then we were driven to the port where a ferry took us to the mainland. It was the first time I had ever left my island. We travelled for two days without stopping, except for fuel, until we reached a railway station. Two of the girls were put on a train heading for northern Korea. The other two were sent with me to Manchuria. The youngest of our trio died on the way. The soldiers buried her beside the tracks in an unmarked grave. They said she died of an infection from a cut on her leg, but I knew the infection really began in her ravished womb. She was only twelve, too young for so many things, yet above all, for death. I think of her sometimes, late at night when I'm too tired to sleep. I think of how quickly she died, and I wonder whether she had found the better path.

"You're my secret mermaid," he often whispers into my ear as he climaxes. "My tragic, mermaid whore. I made you." His words echo in my head long after he has left my room, shutting the door behind him, closing me off from the world.

My feet are cold from standing so long on the landing, remembering. How much time has passed? A minute? Two? I leap back inside my room. Underneath my straw mat is everything valuable I have acquired in eighteen months, wrapped carefully in a square of cloth: coins tossed to me by grateful young men, a gold necklace left by a commander, a ring left by a homesick private, a silver hair comb left by another faceless, nameless soldier. These are the only things of worth I have, and yet they are not enough to get me very far on my own.

"I'll take you to a land of such beauty, you will forget this place," he said before he left me for the night. "On the sacred mountains of the Khangai, men hunt with falcons and camels roam free on the steppes below. We can make a life there. Far away from all of this."

"What about your family in Japan? You would leave them behind?" I didn't look at him when I spoke. I knew better than to meet his eyes.

"They don't know what I have suffered," he said quietly. "Only you can take away my pain."

His hands reached for me, and I went to him. He held me close. I listened to his chest as his heartbeat slowed to a steady, marching pace.

"Only you," he whispered into my hair.

Holding my meagre belongings, I know he is already out there, hiding in the shadows of the night and waiting for me to come to him. I stuff the cloth bundle into my knickers. Then I fly down the staircase two steps at a time and run through the house towards the back door.

Rushing to the kitchen, I am nearly there, and I fear someone will stop me, that there will be a deep voice behind me, followed by a rifle aimed at my back, or a hand ready to stab me with a knife, and my muscles seize. My steps falter and I fall to the floor. On my knees, I am prepared for the inevitable. My heart beats fast. But only gentle snores drift to my ears, and I want to turn back. If I leave, they will suffer. The soldiers will punish them for my escape. Is my freedom worth their torture?

The front door opens on the other side of the house. Heavy boots stamp on the wooden porch before entering. I have to cross the dining room to get back to the stairs. The night guard would see me. Will he accuse me of trying to escape? My legs burn at the thought of the saw against my skin. Or will he simply whip me and throw me into the hole? Will he beat me with his fists first? Or cut off my nose? I cannot stay, not even to spare my sleeping friends. I rise to my feet and hurry to the back door.

I turn the metal doorknob with sweaty fingers. It squeaks, and I cringe, holding my breath until it stops turning. I breathe out, and then I pull.

The door doesn't budge. It is locked. Heat prickles my cheeks. I pull again. It doesn't move. I am a fool. He is laughing at me. In my mind, I can see him as clearly as I saw him above me as he made his false promise. This is my punishment for believing him, and my punishment for being so selfish.

I lean my forehead on the door, resigned to my fate. Very slowly, it opens. *Push, not pull.* Footsteps march toward the dining room. I push the door just wide enough to slide out. The hinges squeal, but that is the only sound. I shut the door behind me and disappear into the night.

I know the way to the bridge where he is waiting for me. It is the same bridge I can see through the bars of the window in my room, a mile north down the road, just before the camp. I can picture him as he waits for me in the darkness, his smile as I approach and his relief that I am unharmed, that I am free. I can see him fold me into his arms and kiss my cheek, my neck, my forehead, before hurrying me along the river to the life that he has planned for us in Mongolia. I can see him, and I run.

The stars light my way, and I run as fast as my legs can carry me to the south, back to Korea, and the sea. My legs know it will not take him long to realise I am not coming to him, and they are swift. They will not stop until I can see the shore where my sister once stood, anchoring my life with hers. I keep her image in my mind as I race through the darkness, but sometimes the face doesn't belong to her. Sometimes it transforms, and she becomes my other sisters, the ones I've left behind. I see their horror when it dawns on them that I am gone, but I keep running, until my lungs burn and my chest aches. I push through the pain, as though it's the deepest dive of my life, and I am swimming out of the ocean's dark depths toward the light.

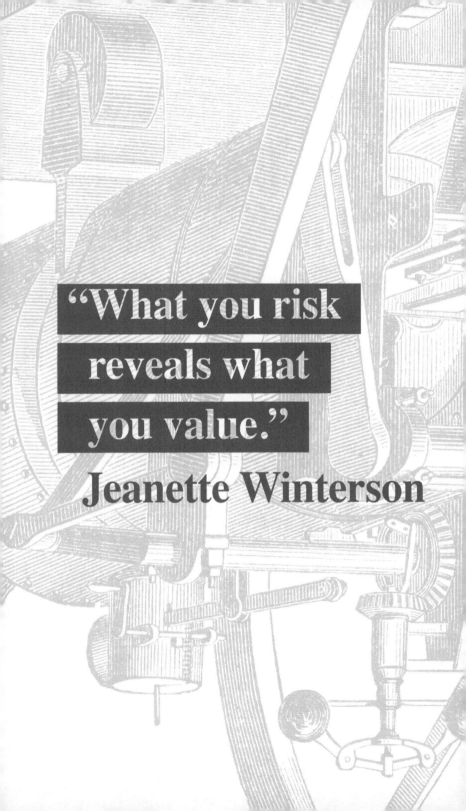

"What you risk reveals what you value."

Jeanette Winterson

People-Watching

JULIA GRAY

"Why do we say people-watching, rather than watching people?" asks Kajsa as they unfold their chairs. She has brought an artist's stool, her own: a rickety tripod and a scrap of sagging canvas built to hold only the lightest of occupants. Paul's chair, though not dissimilar, is a sturdier construction; his father used to take it shooting. They are set up side by side, between the Upper Crust and the cash machines, on the concourse of Paddington Station. It feels odd, thinks Paul, to be stationary here, when everyone else is in transit.

Kajsa hops into her chair. Sitting on one unshod foot like an origami fairy, she can hardly be comfortable, he thinks. Her shoe, an apricot-coloured ballet pump with stained, unravelling ribbons, is upended carelessly beside her. Before Paul sits down he makes a point of nudging it closer to the wall, where it will be out of sight.

"You don't like my clothes," says Kajsa.

"No, no, on the contrary. I do. They're most unique and interesting. I just don't want someone to see a spare shoe on the floor and chuck it away. They come round all the time with those bins on wheels."

"So you think my shoe looks like rubbish?" Kajsa pauses a moment before she smiles. "Anyway, Paul. You haven't answered my question. Why do we say people-watching?"

"I don't know," he says. "I suppose it's in the same vein as

173

trainspotting."

"Meaning what, exactly?"

"We don't say 'spotting trains'. If we did, it would sound like they were bleeding."

"Yes, or being covered in spots," says Kajsa, unwrapping a bagel. "By a giant brush."

A detuned, insouciant bing-bong; a platform revealed like a guarded secret; a tidal surge of rucksacks and wheeled suitcases. A man hurries on crutches towards the barriers, his ticket in his breast pocket. It always seems to Paul that they don't allow enough time for people to get to their trains. He turns to Kajsa, but she is fully engaged with her bagel. He notices that she eats with a birdlike intensity, both savage and dainty. In eight or nine bites the bagel is gone. She thumbs a smear of Philadelphia from the paper wrapper; she swallows fallen raisins. Paul does not like bread particularly. It has an unpleasant, cardboard bloat to it; he gets this feeling, sometimes, that he might choke. Kajsa, fearless crosser of roads, wearer of improbable coats and headscarves, would be unlikely to fall prey to such phobias.

Now she is pulling a manila sketchbook from her corduroy bag, and a pencil, and a bundle of waxy oil pastels. Her fringe is dip-dyed in mermaid green; her chipped front tooth gives her the look of an inquisitive child.

"I would like to paint a train," she says, opening the book. "I mean on its surface."

Paul shuffles backwards, hoping she won't want to talk incessantly.

He met Kajsa a couple of weeks ago, at the start of term. They had both chosen Introduction to Drawing at the Slade, a borrowed module. Paul's actual degree is Architecture; Kajsa's is French. Their instructor, a ferocious, frazzle-haired woman whose patchwork skirts and modest proportions reminded Paul of Mrs Pepperpot, insisted that they keep a sketchbook between classes, and draw directly from life.

"Become expert people-watchers," she said last Thursday, eyeing the room: two biochemists, a Philosophy student, three modern linguists and tall, laconic Paul, who had barely spoken other than to introduce himself.

"I expect to see some evidence of your progress next time," said Mrs Pepperpot. "Capture more than just visuals, if you like. Words – sounds – smells – absorb your experiences like *sponges!*"

Allowing himself to cringe very subtly at the cliché, he was surprised to feel the tap of Kajsa's fake-suede boot against his leg.

"You want to go with me?" she whispered, and he smiled politely back: *Sure, why not.*

And so it is eleven on a Monday morning, a time at which he would ordinarily be in the library, or working in the Russian Tea Rooms near the house he shares with three other undergraduates, or walking to Parliament Hill. But instead of doing any of those things he is sitting in Paddington Station with Kajsa the French student, who is not French, or English, but perhaps Swedish, although he is not sure. That he is not able to answer her question satisfactorily – why people-watching, not watching people – irritates him; he thinks it may be to do with predicates. Or inflected syllables. Or perhaps it's about putting the noun first? His sister, who suffered for many years from eating disorders, used to resort to an activity called water-drinking when it was time for her to be weighed by the nurses. (Her name was Jemima, but the family knew her as Turtle; something about the way she poked her head above the surface of the swimming pool, apparently.) At the age of seven, he hadn't understood why; later he realised that by drinking a litre of water Turtle could hope to register a kilogram more on the scales, and have her calorific intake adjusted accordingly. He would occasionally wonder, as Kajsa is wondering now, why his sister said water-drinking, not drinking water.

Water-drinking, trainspotting, fox-hunting. Actually, there's quite a lot of them, now he thinks about it. Stamp-collecting, sheep-worrying, soul-destroying. Wait, though: that last one doesn't work as a compound noun. It's more of an adjective. These things bother him: things he knows he may never understand. People-watching, regardless of its syntactical make-up, is not a practice that interests him, but he is doing it nonetheless – or, he is about to do it, when he finishes his coffee – for several reasons. First, it's a university assignment, and he would like his 80 per cent average to remain undisturbed at the end of the module. Second, Kajsa has invited him, and he finds her alluring. There's an otherworldliness about her that charms and unnerves him in equal measure.

As he watches her, she looks up, leans over and says, "Are you done with your coffee?"

"Yes, sure."

Kajsa has drawn a sketch of a woman with two bandy-legged children in tow, queuing for baguettes at Delice de France. She's drawn it quickly, in confident, linear scribbles, the tip of her pastel barely leaving the page. Now she dips the corner of her sleeve in his cup and wets the page with coffee, dragging a blur of moisture across the lines which results in a not-unpleasing sepia effect. With the tip of her finger she pushes the shading around, blowing on it until it's dry.

"What?" she says. "You never saw anyone paint with coffee?"

"Never," he replies. "But, now I think about it, water is so conservative."

His own page of heavyweight cartridge paper beckons blankly. Twisting to face the platforms, he blocks in the furthermost arch of the roof. Then he begins to pattern in the others, glorying in the business of geometry, his needlepoint pencil to-ing and fro-ing like a gramophone arm. Kajsa is silent. Perhaps she thought he was making fun of her, when he said "water is so conservative", when in fact he wasn't. Honestly: it's refreshing to see someone dip their sleeve in coffee and paint with it. But of course, he didn't say that. Maybe he should have.

There was a third reason for coming today. This is it: his ex-girlfriend, in one of a series of increasingly unhinged and accusatory emails that detailed his various shortcomings, recently used the word "myopic" to describe him. And despite the fact that she was in many ways illiterate – "they're" and "there" used interchangeably, sentences that drooped, verbless, like abandoned puppies – that one sharp jolt of *myopic* has remained with him, tailgating his everyday stream of consciousness. Is it possible that she is right? True: he didn't remember when her period was due, that she didn't take milk, preferring some kind of rice substitute that disintegrated like baby-sick, that she had a phobia of cats and Barbie dolls. He failed to notice her fringe, cut to look like Marianne Faithfull; he failed to compliment her on her newly whitened teeth.

Personally, he doesn't think that makes him *myopic*, but he has found himself thinking about it lately, all the same. What better practice, then, for the criminally unobservant, than to set up next to the Halifax machine and observe?

"Paul," says Kajsa. "You haven't drawn any people."

"I'm doing the background first."

"I thought this would be a nice place for people-watching," says Kajsa. "Which is why I chose it. So many different types and kinds."

Singing under her breath, she takes a cobalt-blue pastel and a purple one, and holding them closely together draws a pair of old women who are sitting in Caffè Nero. The twin lines create a hallucinatory doppelgänger effect: each old woman has a purple shadow, a hovering psychic field.

"Do you know this station well, Paul?"

"It's a good place to change from the Hammersmith and City Line," he answers blandly. Paddington Station isn't really a place he thinks about much. Then again, he remembers coming up to London with Mum and Turtle, looking for the exact spot where Paddington Bear might have been found, in his coat and hat – or perhaps the coat came later; he isn't sure. He remembers this station before there was a Yo! Sushi and a Monsoon, before there were quick-collection points and you had to queue for hours off to the side, sweating into your hair at the thought of missing the Plymouth train. He remembers looking with wonder at the domed ceiling, and thinking about the brain that had come up with something of such magnitude. He remembers saying goodbye to Turtle, when she'd finally kicked all her problems – for the time being, at least; there was always a sense, with Turtle, that another problem was lurking in the distance – and booked a flight to Thailand. In fact, he and Mum and Dad had stood not ten metres from where he is now, by the Heathrow Express, and watched as her train departed.

A man in a duffle coat approaches and asks for change, and Paul becomes absorbed in the contents of his pockets. But there's only a jangle of 1p and 2p pieces, so he gets out his wallet and gives the man a fiver.

"You know, your work is really accurate," says Kajsa. "I forgot you are studying Architecture."

She asks him then about buildings, and to distract himself from the sight of a girl with a tangle of foamy blonde hair, walking – with turned-out, ballerina feet – towards the turnstile, he tells her. He tells her about Nunney Castle, his favourite moated building, and about designing unmeltable igloos for the Young Architect of the Year Award. He tells her about Hardwick Hall and Chatsworth, Brunel and Zaha Hadid, and how he'd like to specialise in access arrangements when he graduates, because the best thing about buildings, really, is that you can use them to keep people safe.

"Aha!" says Kajsa. "So you *do* care about people."

"Of course I care about people," he says, his consonants rigid, like spilled beads.

"But you still haven't drawn any."

"I think I need another cup of coffee. Would you . . . ?"

She shakes her head; her mermaid fringe bubbles. He gets up, cracking his knees, and goes over to Nero. He stands in the queue, quelling a roiling of indignation that has started a reflux in his throat. Why would Kajsa imply he doesn't care about people just because he hasn't gotten around to putting them in his drawing? Did he not give a fiver to the man in the duffle coat? Unlike her, he is not slapdash; he needs time, he needs to get the proportions of things right, he needs to choose his subjects with thought and care.

He waits until he is calm before he returns to his chair.

Kajsa has covered six pages with watery, narrative sketches: a family of American sightseers (sightseeing; that's another one) clustered under the clock, a lone man with a springer spaniel at his feet, a boy and a girl both covered in webbed tattoos buying flowers outside WH Smith. Taking the instructions of Mrs Pepperpot seriously, she has inscribed loose threads of conversation in looping cursive underneath her drawings, embellishing her verbal hoardings with flowers and butterflies. *Call me*, she's written, in overwrought calligraphy, *when you're safely home*.

Something similar was said to Turtle on the platform of the Heathrow Express, thinks Paul. Those were the earlyish days of mobile phones. Reception was poor; the idea of *using it abroad* sent a bolt of terror down your dialling arm, and his sister's cracked Nokia was in any case unlikely to withstand the journey. Turtle had therefore been furnished with a BT code: a number she could dial from anywhere in the world to call Mum and Dad, reverse-charge.

"Call us when you get there, love," Mum had said. "Let us know you're all right."

But Turtle had not called.

Paul turns to a fresh page of his sketchbook, abandoning his picture of the roof, and looks about in search of a subject.

The homeless man is sitting on a bench near the departures board. He has bought, with Paul's fiver, perhaps, or else with another donation, a bagel. Paul decides to begin with the boots, and teases an outline onto the page. His pencil moves upwards, suggesting the crinkles in the man's cargo trousers. Now he draws the torso, the shoulders angled protectively towards the food, the down-bent head. People-watching, not myopic, Paul looks more closely.

Then he puts down his pencil.

"I can't do this," he says.

"Why not?" asks Kajsa, leaning over. "It's great! You should keep going!"

"I can't, I can't, I just can't. It's an invasion of privacy, what we're doing. Haven't you ever thought of that? Do you think that American family wanted you to write down every bloody thing they were saying? Do you think this guy wants me to fucking *draw* him while he's sitting there in peace?"

"Paul," says Kajsa quietly. "We are just people-watching. There really is no law against that."

"Yup. Yes, you're right. Sorry."

"Draw what you *see*," says Kajsa, parroting Mrs Pepperpot, her syllables long and didactic.

Silently, Paul imagines his deft riposte: "I see dead people," in – of course – the sepulchral rasp of the kid in *The Sixth Sense*. That would shut her up. And, besides, it's true: while he does, theoretically, think that it's an invasion of privacy to render in pastel and pencil and coffee the actions and aspects of people going about their own business in Paddington Station, it's more than that. When he looks at people closely – really studies them – he becomes aware of their mortality. He pictures them dead, stretched out in some cool mortuary, or angular open coffin.

"Paul? Are you all right? What do you see?"

It is not possible to people-watch with pleasure when each subject appears in the guise of an eventual corpse.

"I see things that aren't there, Kajsa. Sometimes."

How mad she must think I am, he thinks. But she says mad things all the time. Perhaps she won't judge.

He adds: "I'm perfectly all right, though. Thanks."

Was Turtle ever all right? There must have been a time when she was: he pictures her aged six, aged eight, dangling from low-slung branches, her hair studded with clip-on gems. Sewing Brownie badges – Agility, Booklover – onto her dress, stitching the sleeve closed by mistake. Playing a nun in *The Sound of Music*. Dancing with turned-out toes to *Carnival of the Animals*.

Yes: in those moments, surely, she was all right.

Another bing-bong; another eddy of travellers. Kajsa shifts restlessly in her chair, and he wonders what she's still doing here. She opens a packet of banana chips, offering him a handful; he declines.

"I, also, see things that aren't there," says Kajsa. "Often. Like yours, my imagination escapes sometimes. The boy and the girl with the tattoos – I imagined that inside the bouquet of roses, they had concealed a weapon, and they were going to open fire on the station. I imagined the man with the dog was a policeman and he was going to try and stop them, but he became distracted by the American woman because she was so strange and beautiful. I find it so hard to draw only what I see, and not what I imagine. Look – I have covered these sketches with butterflies and things – it's stupid!"

Laughing, she begins to tear the pages from her sketchbook, sending a patter of banana chips to the floor.

Alarmed, Paul says, "Don't do that. They're good. Really good."

Kajsa stops, and looks at him sideways, scrabbling for the last of the banana chips.

"So *draw* someone," she says.

He picks up his pencil again. The homeless man has gone. A

woman buys an armload of lilies; a child runs screaming away from its mother. The American family finally makes for its train, like a line of hastening ducklings. Kajsa starts on an Innocent smoothie. The roof of the station opens out like a magician's hat and a single eye peers in. The air is a suspension of Paddington Bears, each with a label pinned to their front: *Please look after this bear. Call me when you're safely home.*

Let us know you're all right, love.

Before she was taken out of school, Turtle would call from a pay phone outside the library. Sometimes he, Paul, would answer, and he would always know it was Turtle because he'd say "Hello?" and it would be quiet on the other end, so quiet that it sounded like no one was there. And then he'd hear the snuffle, the unworded choke that betokened a lost place, an unsafe place. And he'd go to find Mum and Dad, and he'd say, "I don't think Turtle is all right," and hold out the cordless phone.

Suddenly, when she was eighteen, Turtle rounded some hidden curve between not all right and all right. Her limestone skin turned rosy; the lustre returned to her hair. She finished her sentences; she saw her friends again. One of them was working in a bar in Thailand; Turtle, who had rarely been well enough to travel, decided to join her. Mum and Dad had said no, at first, because it might not be safe. Because anything could happen. But anything could happen anywhere, argued Turtle. So off she went, like Nellie the Elephant, with her travel-size guitar and the right malaria pills, the ones that don't make you think you're the devil. A week passed; there were no calls, but it was likely that she'd lost the phone card.

They did not worry, particularly.

With tremendous ocular flexion, Paul concentrates. His eyes become filmy and soft-focused; he allows his hand to move freely, sketching in a series of feathery, side-to-side motions. Sometimes he sips at his coffee. The station is an orchestra of unsynchronised sounds: the shriek and hiss of departing trains, the footfalls of travellers, the beeps and whistles of mobility vehicles. He allows these sounds to dissolve; he becomes unhearing.

Finally he breathes out. There's a heaviness in his lungs. He looks down at his work.

"Oh, Paul, well *done*," says Kajsa.

Paul says, "I'm just no good at drawing people. I'm better at bridges and stairs."

"Who is this?" asks Kajsa, tracing a curious fingertip over the page. "She is very pretty."

She casts delicate glances about the station, cross-checking the blonde heads and backpacks in the baguette queue, at the cashpoints, at the ticket machines. But she won't find anyone here, thinks Paul, with flared jeans, because no one wears them any more.

"Where is she?"

Ah, but there's no answer to that question. At last, when they were beginning to get anxious, when emails to Turtle's Hotmail had gone unanswered for a fortnight, the phone did ring. It was the consulate. The roof of the bar had collapsed; *why* was unclear. They'd had a hard time identifying her body, apparently. Turtle returned in a zinc-lined coffin. He'd wanted to read at her funeral, but had been too shy.

"I'm not really sure," he says. "But her name is . . ."

We would like to speak to someone regarding Jemima Grover.

". . . Turtle."

For a while Kajsa says nothing. Quietly, she gathers up her discarded pastels and makes a bundle of them, like rods of polychrome dynamite. Paul, for whom sympathy – from strangers, from friends, from in-between acquaintances – has always been the worst thing, stares down at the first portrait he's managed to draw for ten and a half years. It is, he decides, not a bad likeness.

"Turtle is an excellent name," says Kajsa suddenly.

And then: "I think we should go to the pub. The one upstairs, with the fruit machines. I am sick of people-watching, watching people – what does it matter? It would be nice to have a beer."

They put away their sketchbooks. They fold up their chairs. As he follows Kajsa to the escalators, Paul thinks about the people who cannot be kept safe, even in the safest of buildings. He wonders if there are people watching them: the girl with the mermaid fringe, the tall boy whose eyes betray the beginnings of tears. But he doesn't really care.

What Does Mother Know of Cormorants?

JOSH RAYMOND

I am sure my phone sounds different when Mother is calling, but it might just be because it's 7 a.m. She tells me my great-aunt Ruth has died. I am sharing a single tea bag drippily between two mugs because Louise has a thing about waste.

"Oh Jonathan," Mother says, "I can't believe I wasn't there."

The tea bag's soggy little corpse drops onto the overflowing mound in the compost bin. Auntie Ruthie was ninety-five. I point out that dying had, for some time, been what she was going to do next.

"I feel terribly alone now," Mother says.

The milk oversloshes and the tea lurches sickly pale. Louise hasn't been living here long, and my wrist is not yet calibrated for four-pint bottles.

"Are you . . . busy today?" The quaver in Mother's voice plucks a string between my lungs. She will never say directly that I haven't visited lately, but it's true; Louise says she finds her terrifying.

And Mother knows full well that I'm no more "busy" than she is. I've had auditions since finishing my Master's but been plagued by a kind of inverse anxiety; I play the right notes but can't seem to imbue them with any meaning. The old violinist I accompany at a hotel on Eversholt Street sounds like his instrument is strung with actual cats' intestines, and even that is only two nights a week.

I tell her I'll come for tea.

"What about coffee?" she says. "It's just . . . Ruthie . . ."

An ant makes its way cautiously from beneath the pile of plates around the sink. "Coffee" means the morning. It's the bridge, the beacon, the Hermesetas hitching post by which Mother navigates the hours between her breakfast boiled egg and the lettuce she eats for lunch. She does not even walk the dog any more; its strength has violently increased, or hers diminished. I suspect that Mother would be happier if she *did* a bit more, but my Yamaha is greyed with reproachful dust: doing is easier said than done.

In our bedroom, Louise props herself solidly up on her pillows and touches the rim of the mug with the tip of her tongue. "Grief is essentially selfish," she says.

Louise's sister died in a car accident the year before we met, and it left Louise very self-contained. She will drink tea in bed until exactly 7.15, shower, then eat cereal standing up and leave for her solicitors' firm. She says that when she feels like crying she goes to the gym.

"Jonathan," she says, "you need to clean the flat today. It smells like a landfill site. There's no way we can go on living like this."

I always get a seat at Brixton Tube; it's at the end of the line. The CD of death-appropriate songs I've compiled is wedged in the outer pocket of my satchel. Mother will refer to it as a "tape". I will fail to hide my irritation. She has been unable to buy any music for herself since the Hampstead Our Price closed down in 1998 but treats all classical suggestions with disdain. I therefore provide the high-end acoustic folk of her youth: Paul Simon, Van Morrison, Bob Dylan – the same thirty or forty songs in slightly varying combinations. No Leonard Cohen this time.

At Stockwell I change onto the Northern Line, and the doors have closed before I realise my mistake. This is, eventually, Mother's line, but it splits and dawdles through Central London. It would have been quicker just to stay where I was and make the transition at Euston.

These little wrong notes are becoming more common. I lose objects, then misplace others while searching for the first, and leaving the house is stressful. Someone on my Master's recommended mindfulness meditation. I tried it one morning while preparing to boil some eggs, concentrating on breathing and "inhabiting" my every action, but became so mindful of clattering the saucepan out of its drawer that I forgot about the eggs themselves, and one rolled off the worktop and smashed. There's something very sad about a broken egg.

At the top of its North London hill, my ancestral home clings to the Porsche-strewn gravel pavement, its chimneys teetering against the sky as if all five floors might topple backwards into Hampstead Heath. I still remember it as a ruin in 1983 – another of my Czech grandfather's speculations, like those against conversion bonds or Ian Smith's government in Rhodesia. He would point his mottled index finger and intone, "When the revolution comes, we will want to be on top of the hill." Predicting downfalls made him rich.

The road is called "The Grove" like it's the only one and, with the exception of a well-divorced schizophrenic whom she "looks after" sometimes, Mother is the only person here who isn't famous. She subsists on the dividends from pharmaceutical shares. They are defensive stocks; when financial markets founder, people seek refuge in drugs. Right now the European Union teeters, which means that Mother is doing quite well.

Ellie – a shaggy German Shepherd the size of a double bass – starts barking before I am halfway across the front garden and sneezes heavily onto my trousers the moment Mother opens the door. Mother has "made an effort": lipstick, earrings, hair "done", a blouse that looks like Armani, charity-shop 501s and a pair of black slip-on pumps that are annoyingly understated and cool. If she's been crying, it wasn't recently. Her impossible-to-track-down-at-Christmas perfume makes my own eyes water when we hug.

"Why didn't you come in the car?" She has to shout over the barking.

I half pat, half strike the dog a few times. Mother prefers it when I travel by car, whether due to inaccurate notions of its safety or simple snobbery I've never worked out. I haven't told her that renewing the insurance isn't even near the top of my list of undone administrative tasks.

"I'm sorry about Ruthie," I say.

"Last of the first generation." On the subject of our ancestors, Mother can sound a bit *Lord of the Rings*.

I follow her across the hall, which is an actual hall; five rooms leading off it with a tapestry above the staircase and no surface untroubled by ornament. Her current best friend Maria is in the drawing room, reclining on the floral George Smith sofa bought during the dot-com crash, smoking a cigarette through an ivory holder and wearing brown fur-and-suede boots. Mother believes removing shoes in the home to be middle class, and the carpet is marshy with dog drool anyway.

"Swedie!" Maria cries. "Jonathan, swedie, it's good to see you. So sad for your mother today."

Ellie's barking has subsided into high-pitched whines, invasive as microphone feedback. Maria calls everybody "swedie". She claims to be half Cherokee but her accent's Baltimore and B&H. She toured as a photographer with the Rolling Stones and, Mother insists, once had an affair with Ronnie Wood. She now lives in a houseboat just upstream of Hammersmith Bridge, and takes pictures of aquatic birds. She says that she can hear the tides like the river is breathing.

"How's your music going, swedie?" she asks.

This question. Everybody, always, this question. Lang Lang recited Chopin at the Beijing Concert Hall aged thirteen. A four-year-old girl called Mimi recently played the Royal Albert. I am twenty-six and I play on Eversholt Street.

"Shall I make some coffee?" Mother says.

We drink Nespresso from cups with impractical handles. Mother and Maria chain-smoke Dunhills from a box lidded with mother-of-pearl.

"When's the funeral?" I ask.

The women exchange a look.

"There's a lot to arrange," Mother says. "Where's Louise today?"

"At work."

Mother plinks another sweetener into her cup and drinks

without stirring. "She'll have *you* applying for an office job next."

I suppress the urge to say that steady work sounds quite appealing; Mother has had enough upsetting news for one day. Throughout the year I have been seeing Louise, it has been made subtly yet definitely apparent that Mother does not think her "special". By this she means "Jewish", or at least European of ancestor or psychologically unsound. Before Louise I dated musical girls: hysterically thin, damp-armpitted creatures whom Mother always seemed to want to adopt. Louise does too many spin classes to be fat, but she is covered, protected, underexposed – warm of body if not always of temperament.

"Have you got time to stay for lunch?" Mother says. "I went to L&D."

I pretend to think, then actually think. I should go home, practise, clean the flat, but there is no food in my fridge and L&D means the Semitic delicacies of childhood: fishballs, smoked-salmon bagels and houmous topped with pine nuts. Ellie tilts her head when we go into the kitchen but barks only once.

Laying the table is oddly difficult; the knives and forks are two differently sized sets jumbled up, no three glasses are alike and everything has to be arranged around a vast central garland of white flowers: a funeral pyre for an absent swan.

"Aren't the camellias lovely?" Mother says. "I saved them from the rain."

Maria smiles and exhales an obscene, implausible plume, as if she is composed entirely of lung.

We walk on the Heath in the afternoon, plodding round Kenwood House at mourners' pace. Ellie does not understand death, and her paws exult through the mud. The delay to Ruthie's funeral is clarified anyway – we Jews normally inter so quickly that the corpse isn't even cool, perhaps so things below will be *gemütlich*.

"She converted," Maria says. "She had a nurse who was a Christian and the nurse converted her. Filled her full of morphine and then converted her. She asked for a Christian burial. How about that?"

"So it won't be for a while, then?" I ask.

"No," says Mother. "No, it won't." She sounds relieved, but

Ellie has just spared the life of a lamb-like Bichon Frise that had made the mistake of an overture, so it might just be to do with that.

The crow-dotted hump of the far field swells into view. As a child I found a red-brick building in the trees above there – a disused hospital, it looked like. Mother didn't want to see it, in case she were reminded of boarding school in Kent, a place she did not attend of her free will but because my grandfather, that bursar of ruin, loved his only daughter just a little too much. "Not abuse, darling," Mother told me in a candid moment, "but getting close." My grandmother, already twice divorced, sent her daughter away instead of her husband, to cold dormitories, cold matrons and eventual expulsion one cold, cold night for stealing a horse from a neighbouring farm and trying to ride it back to London on the grassy verge of the A2, having knotted together a bridle from her dressing-gown cord.

Mother's spirits lift in the evenings. It's to do with the antidepressants. She suggests inviting Louise for dinner at the local Italian with what sounds like genuine enthusiasm.

"How was your day at work?" Mother asks. There is a tiny pause before the final, foreign word.

"We had a team-building day," Louise replies. "We made a model of the Taj Mahal."

I ask her, "Out of what?"

"Meccano," says Louise. "And yoghurt pots."

"Me and Keith went there once," Maria says. "Smoked hash and just looked at it for hours."

Louise stiffens. I excuse myself and go to the toilet, and when I get back Mother stops talking to Louise and returns her attention to the breadsticks. My girlfriend's pale skin looks too tight.

Maria's conversation flows on. "I saw the strangest thing," she says, "on the boat. This cormorant dove for a fish. It dove, but it never came up." She lifts an anchovy from her pizza with avian precision.

"Maybe you missed it," says Louise.

But Maria's ageless skin is the same strong-tea colour as the Thames; she understands her home. "It was a clear morning," she says. "In summertime. The water looked like velvet. That cormorant dove in and it didn't come up. I think it felt supported down there. Like it was safe on all its sides."

"It would die," I say. "If it stayed down there, it would drown."

"The water was smooth," Maria says. "Like velvet. That bird just felt secure."

Mother's head snaps up from her salad. "They look like seals!" she cries.

"What do?" asks Louise.

"The cormorants." Mother's hazel eyes are unfocused. "They're black and smooth and . . . when they dive, they're exactly the same shape as seals. The water is where they belong."

The waiter refills our glasses. We don't speak.

In bed, at my flat, I'm restless; something wasn't right about tonight. Mother is somebody people *go to see*. The orbit of her failing Jaguar is delimited east by Marks & Spencer, and west by the extent of the Heath. She never ventures south at all, and the farthest north she's ever been is Auntie Ruthie's house in Finchley. Nowhere in any of those places are there cormorants.

The next day, Thursday, when I have finally got around to practising, my phone rings. It isn't seven in the morning this time but the sound still has an altered quality, as if Mother somehow *emanates* across the ether and affects the very timbre of the bell.

She's crying. "I always visited Ruthie on Thursdays. Can you come?"

I can still feel the Schubert in my fingers; I don't want to go anywhere. The great Artur Schnabel said he handled the notes no better than many pianists, but that the art resided in the pauses between the notes. Every pause on my childhood Steinway – that black baby-grand beast that still lives in the garden room at The Grove – was suffused with sympathetic resonance, but South London walls are thinner; here I play in headphones and the pauses are electronic and dead.

It isn't natural for a grown man to spend too much time with his mother, but people prone to depression should not be left to grieve on their own.

The garden at The Grove is divided into sections, each a little smaller than the previous one. We deadhead daffodils, facing the house on the main lawn. At our backs, ivy-thickened arches lead to the impenetrable "wild garden", behind which is the pool, perennially under a dark-green winter cover because heating it to a temperature Mother can bear has proved impossible. Overlooking the pool is the conservatory, lost to bindweed, and behind the conservatory a woodlousy place of water butts, plant pots and the ash of pre-global-warming bonfires.

I snip high on the daffodils' stems. There is something soothing about the repeated use of scissors, and Mother tells me how much she liked the tape I made her, and that Maria sold a photograph of a crested grebe. She never mentions Auntie Ruthie at all.

Just after the sun has passed over the beech tree, the cordless telephone rings from the garden table. Mother stands quickly, but I have already picked it up.

"Hello?"

"Jonny?"

Only one person calls me that – Mother's brother, Uncle Max. Just as she could do no wrong in her father's eyes, poor Max could do no right. He came out as gay in a letter to the local newspaper and it was declared "for the best" that he leave home after his O levels. He qualified as an electrician and got back at his father in the only way he could – by turning down all the old man's money even after the bowel cancer had done its work and the mottled finger could point no more.

"How are you, Jonny?" he asks.

I tell him I'm all right, that it's sad about Auntie Ruthie dying. There's a pause, then, "What?"

"Ruthie. She had a stroke two nights ago."

"Jesus Christ!" says Max. "That's terrible! Why did no one tell me?"

Mother is making her "oops" face – shoulders hunched, teeth clenched. She often says that she can't imagine her brother poking around in fuse boxes all day. One Christmas Eve Max and I ended up in the pub and he said he thought she was fundamentally evil. They don't speak often.

She takes the phone from my hand and heads for the house. "Maxie, darling," she says. "Maxie, I'm so sorry . . ."

Ellie is becalmed on the grass, dinner-plate paws in the air. I snip the scissors open and closed, open and closed, then turn and look through the white French door of the garden room, at the Steinway's sleek black hull.

Louise brings an overnight bag. After dinner, Mother shows her something in the drawing room while I stay in the kitchen with Maria, who is making Irish coffee in a wine glass, pouring cream onto the back of a spoon. A little while later, Louise and I climb to my childhood attic bedroom, high in both altitude and the hierarchy of spare rooms Mother maintains for guests she never hosts, which means it has a double bed.

"It's weird here, Jonathan," Louise says. "How long are we going to stay?"

"I'm not sure," I tell her. "Mother's upset."

She bites her lip.

"What?"

"Don't take this the wrong way," she says, "but are you sure?"

"Her aunt died, Lou. They were close."

"I just . . ."

"She's depressed."

"She's not," says Louise. "Or . . . she doesn't *seem* to be. She . . ."

There's an edge in my voice. "She what?"

But Louise just shakes her head.

"It's not *so* bad here, is it?" I ask, and then I tell her about the Steinway, how one note's vibration sets off resonances in its neighbours so that the pauses between the notes sound rich, how even the quality of the instrument's silence – the way the air in the room passes over the strings, or the wood expands and contracts with temperature, just the sheer potential there is for sound – is marvellous.

Louise's vole-brown curls seem to scrunch even tighter, and her blue eyes are glistening full.

"What is it?"

She sniffs.

"Tell me."

"It's Ruthie," she says. "How silly is that? I'm sad about Auntie Ruthie."

"I thought you said grief was selfish," I say.

Louise smiles, blinks and replies, "It is," then moves closer, kisses my lips and makes love to me with quick, surprising intensity. I remain on my back and look at the wooden ducks on the ceiling cross-beam, imagining them hunting over the tidal Thames and diving, black, slick-winged and seal-like. By the time it occurs to me that Louise has never even met Auntie Ruthie, she is already asleep, crescented like a bass clef.

When I wake up in the morning, the other side of the bed is cold. Downstairs, my tea bag drips uncertainly onto the counter before falling, half-wasted, into the bin. There is no compost here; Mother gets muddled by recycling of any description.

"I'm going to see Dr Craven this morning," she says. "Will you pick up some bits from the village? We need flowers. A lot of flowers for the drawing room, and olives, and biscuits – whichever sort you like. And go to the bookshop. There's a new book about a girl who weaves baskets that everybody's raving about. Ask the man what it's called. And get washing-up liquid. A big bottle."

She stubs out her Dunhill in a heavy green-glass ashtray and counts out a wild, disproportionate quantity of cash. "And one more thing: if the phone rings during the day, don't pick it up. It's only people selling things and I'm trying to pretend there's no one living here."

Pond Square in Highgate Village is said to be haunted by the ghost of a chicken that once belonged to Sir Francis Bacon. I feel spectral, insubstantial myself as I walk up the narrow stone steps at its far side to where a woman in a quilted coat sells flowers.

"Need any help?" she asks.

I need help to clean my flat. To reinsure my car and be punctual for auditions. I force myself to look at the bucketed stems. "Which are nice?"

"They're all nice."

"This is the problem."

The woman smiles. "Who're they for?"

"My mother."

"Oh," she says. "Then tulips. Everybody's mother likes tulips."

I pay and take the flowers and cross the road to the corner shop, where old Raj recognises me. Raj sold me the first thing I ever bought, aged ten – a Curly Wurly bar for 24p – and abetted, five years later, my unsuccessful experiment with Camel Lights. His shelves are plentiful and neat, and my fellow customers elderly and quiet. By comparison, the Brixton Tesco is like shopping in a psychiatric ward.

I stroll on, adagio, to the bookshop, then back to The Grove, where my pleasure at the ease of things propels me into the kitchen and to pick up the ringing telephone before I remember my instructions not to.

"Hello?"

There's a pause. Mother was right; a pause means a call centre, a telemarketer.

I repeat myself. "*Hello?*"

A breath comes down the line, and then an ancient female voice rasps, "Who is this?"

I put the tulips down.

"Jonathan. Jonathan Atkins."

Another pause, another breath. "*Yonassan?* This is *you?*"

My mouth is dry, my palms just as suddenly wet. What was I told to say when I picked up this phone as a child? "Who's speaking, please?"

"*Yonassan!*" The voice is louder. "This is *Rroos!*"

"Ruth? Auntie Ruth?"

"Yes! Of course! There is *another* Rroos?"

The tulips look like they've fainted.

"I thought you were dead."

Auntie Ruth's laughter becomes a hacking tarry cough. "Chance would be a fine thing," she says. "God has no interest in your auntie Rroos. I have the tiniest *little* stroke, and they put me in the hospital. But I have discharged myself. Where is your mother? I want to speak with her."

My voice sounds like it's someone else's. "She's gone to see Dr Craven."

Ruth gets louder. "Craven? *Ach!* This fraud, this . . . this *penguin!* You do not need a psychiatrist if you are feeling depressed, you need fresh air and *exercise!* I will speak with her later."

And the line clicks, and she is gone. I stare at the plates on the wall, painted with galloping horses, and the nameless dried foliage above the Aga.

Mother knows what's happened as soon as she sees my face. Maria is at her back. "Oh, swedie," she says. "Oh, no."

"Ruth didn't even sound ill!"

"She was!" Mother says. "They said she had a matter of weeks!"

"*Weeks?*"

"I know, I know!" she cries. "It was terribly awful of me, but I just wanted us to have some time! That lovely piano sits in there and nobody ever plays on it!"

I feel the Steinway's undertow but snap myself free. "I'm going," I say, "I'm going now," and I stride past Mother and grab my jacket from the hook in the utility room. Ellie is flumped down on the doormat.

"Move."

She doesn't.

"Ellie! Get out of the way!"

I pull on her collar. She flattens her ears and whines. I prod her flank with my shoe, and the whine portamentos quickly into a growl.

"Stay for a coffee," Mother says. "Just one."

I ignore her. No more coffee, no more shopping, no more flowers. I am going home to my filthy flat and my uninsured car and my lovely, boring girlfriend. I march through the hall and out of the front entrance, across the crazy paving of the front garden and away under the towering lime trees.

The flat has been burgled, or at least it looks that way; it is purged, pristine, twice its previous size. The washing-up is done and the surfaces shine and the air smells brightly of Cif or Harpic or Cillit Bang. If any ants are still alive, they're hiding.

In the bedroom, the sheets are smoothed and the pillows plumped and all my clothes that were on the drying rack have been hung up in the wardrobe and Louise's clothes are gone. All Louise's clothes are gone and so are her toothbrush and her Swiss ball and her books.

Her phone goes straight to voicemail. I listen to the silence for a while and then hang up. It doesn't feel appropriate to telephone Mother immediately, but I don't know what else to do.

"Oh, darling," she says. "Some things just aren't meant to be."

"I think Louise was good for me," I say. "She cleaned the flat."

"Anybody can clean a flat," Mother says soothingly. "Louise was a lovely girl but . . ."

"But what?"

"Nothing. You're upset."

"Mother . . . What?"

A little sigh comes down the line. "She always reminded me of one of those English cakes," Mother says, "the sort one buys at church sales. Perfectly sweet, but somehow just a little bit stodgy."

My stomach clenches. Louise was not stodgy. Louise was honest and kind and sad and maybe the only person I have ever been out with who could read Mother as Mother truly is. Because Uncle Max was right that Christmas Eve; if his sister ever did go into a church, for the purposes of a bake sale or otherwise, she would probably burst into flames.

"Come and stay, darling," she says. "Just until you're feeling better."

I look around me at the living room that Louise has made so beautiful. It will not stay like this. I have to cook, wash up, renew my car insurance, shop for food, go to auditions, send emails, do laundry, and now do all of it on my own. How can anyone get Schnabel's pauses right with all of that nonsense to attend to? Would it be so bad just to give myself a break from the whole pointless lot of it? My Yamaha looks at me pleadingly, like a soon-to-be-abandoned dog. I will come back, I tell it. I promise that I will come back.

I remember to stick with the Victoria Line this time. When I get to The Grove, to the garden room, I spread the score for the first movement of Schubert's *Fünf Clavierstücke* on the Steinway's music rest and warm up with a few scales. My playing is good, the instrument magnificent, and as the tension leaves my wrists and shoulders I realise that it has been there for a long time. Musicians have patrons sometimes, don't they? People who help them while they find their feet? When Ellie detonates the calm, barking at an imagined enemy in the hall, I do not even jump, I just turn slowly on my piano stool to face the white French door to the garden.

The sun has passed over the beech tree. Made hazy by high ripples of cloud, it looks like it's shining down through water: smooth summer river water with the consistency of velvet. I am safe in this house, supported on all my sides. I think I will have just one quick cup of coffee with Mother before I start my practice, just until the dog quietens down.

Olivia in 4 Parts

JACQUELYN SHREEVES-LEE

Olivia 1

Olivia's first memory is of making mud pies in the back garden. The slimy worms squirming in the earth make her toes wriggle as she bores her T-bar shoes deep into the black, curdled soil.

Olivia is seven years old and her friend David a year older.

"Ride a cock horse to Banbury Cross . . . rings on her fingers, bells on her toes . . . music wherever she goes," Olivia sings. "I'm the best singer in the whole wide world," she says.

"No, you're not."

"I am."

"Not."

"Am."

"Not."

"Am."

Frowning with concentration, Olivia watches her small, clever hands gather the earth and pat it down firmly into the bucket. Tipping the soil out, she folds it into a newspaper.

"Half a crown," Olivia says to David. "That's half a crown, please sir."

Olivia receives a pretend coin in exchange for a bundle of newspaper and mud.

There's a rabbit hutch along from the kitchen door, near the corner where the brick wall bends. Uncle Tommy creeps outside with a few carrots clutched in one hand. Olivia looks at the man who has one ordinary leg and one extraordinary short leg weighed down by a heavy black boot.

"It's to keep him steady," her mother has explained, but Olivia doesn't get this thing about being weighed down and keeping steady. The boot reminds her of reins and being held back.

Uncle Tommy opens the rabbit hutch and forces a big hand inside, full of carrot and frilly green bits. The rabbit scurries towards the carrots and Olivia hears the insistent sound of biting and grinding. Uncle Tommy turns. He winks at Olivia and opens the fly to his trousers. The worm he holds is long and fat and pink.

Quickly Olivia looks away. She doesn't want to play any more. With his back to the kitchen door, David sings about London burning and when the children glance over at the rabbit hutch, Uncle Tommy has disappeared inside the house.

Dinner is fish, chips and sweet garden peas. It's Friday, fish day. Flo Shulver doesn't cook on Fridays, it's an evening off and down the Chippy. Olivia asks for the tomato ketchup and when she isn't looking, David steals a chip from the dark puddle of Sarson's vinegar on her plate. He always does.

Aunty Flo and Uncle Tommy are neighbours who take care of Olivia while her mother's at work. She works at Gestetner's, the local glue factory. It's a big red building near Tottenham Hale, Olivia remembers that, and knows the narrow kitchen cupboard where her mother hides the little glass bottles of adhesive that she brings home. They have enough glue to mend anything that breaks; teacups, doll's house furniture, vases, ornaments and her father's reading glasses. Her father needs his glasses to do the Pools, read the newspaper and the many letters that fall through the slot in the front door.

Uncle Tommy gobbles down his food and Aunty Flo murmurs, "Manners, Tom," but he continues eating like he's not seen food in a long while and eventually Olivia stops eating her supper altogether. She drops her spoon and doesn't want to bend down under the dinner table to pick it up, not wanting to look across in the dark and see the strange worm thing.

"Pick up your spoon, love," says Aunty Flo. "You'll need it for your pudding."

It's Jam Roly-Poly. Olivia likes the jam circles that go round and round and round. With sharp green eyes, Uncle Tommy watches her, one hand shovelling his chips, the other beneath the table.

Scratching at her elbow, Olivia looks across at David, willing him to read something in her face.

"It's all right, Ollie. I'll get it," and, sighing, David reaches down and brings the silver spoon up from the dark.

"Wash it off, David, there's a love," Aunty Flo says. With the help of her little finger, she picks at her long, narrow teeth. "That's the only problem with fish. The bloomin' bones." Olivia's dad says that Aunty Flo looks like a horse. Olivia likes horses.

David returns with the wet spoon and Olivia eats her portion of Jam Roly-Poly.

"You know what'll happen if you eat too much Jam Roly-Poly, don't you, Ollie?" Uncle Tommy asks, craning his head forward. "You'll turn into a Roly-Poly yourself! Ha!" and he laughs out loud, his mouth breaking open like a bread bin, showing a clatter of yellow and gold teeth.

Aunty Flo digs him in the side. "Give over, you silly bugger. Don't be telling the child that, she'll go off her food." Turning to Olivia, Aunty Flo says, "You eat up, Ollie. You need all that food inside you if you're going to be a big, strong girl."

"Ollie doesn't need to be big and strong. She's made of sugar and spice and all things nice, aren't you, Ollie?"

Olivia is suddenly full. Her stomach heaves as though she's been eating gravel and she vomits down the front of her pink dress, onto the carpet beneath her chair.

"Now look what you've gone and done," Aunty Flo scolds Uncle Tommy and rises from the table. "Not to worry, Ollie. Accidents happen. Come on, I'll clean you up," and Aunty Flo leads Olivia to the bathroom. Olivia's hand grasps Aunty Flo's large padded palm. Aunty Flo is a big woman and Olivia likes nothing better than sitting in the warm, safe valley that is Aunty Flo's lap.

When they return, David has fallen asleep on the sofa. He

purrs, his mouth open. Uncle Tommy is watching the television, guzzling crisps from a plastic bowl, and Olivia's mother is waiting, her brown eyes heavy and flecked with tiredness.

"She been all right, Flo?"

"Good as gold."

Olivia has a nightmare that night. She wets the bed and tells her mother about slimy worms. Missing school the following day, Olivia says that she's scared of the rabbit in the garden and doesn't want to return to the Shulvers'.

The Johnson family live at the corner of Harringay Road and Colina Mews, in a tall, terraced house. Mrs Johnson has strong, stout legs and rides a bike. Lynnie Johnson wears a neat bob and plays Hopscotch with Olivia at school playtimes. Lynnie can balance on one leg to a count of nine. At the end of each school day, Olivia goes home with Lynnie and Mrs Johnson until her mother collects her. In her mother's pockets wait packets of gobstoppers, fruit pastilles and the odd bottle of glue.

Mrs Johnson does not allow playing in the back garden or on the stairs. With thin, tight lips she says that she's the grown-up and she knows what's what. Olivia is given the house rules and told that hands must be washed before dinner and Grace said. The rooms with their high ceilings are draughty and the permanently drawn curtains shut out any light. Olivia suspects that Mrs Johnson thinks wicked things might creep in from outside under cover of daylight. She mutters about the bad things that go on at the Salisbury pub, the importance of keeping a clean mind and minding your Ps and Qs. In a quieter voice, Mrs Johnson also warns about loose women. Unsure of what this means, Olivia imagines the loose bodies of these women coming undone, the buttons and zips of their clothes unfastening, their skin peeling back and flesh falling apart, leaving behind mysterious puddles of snow-white bones. Sometimes the Johnsons' house feels like a church and Olivia finds herself talking in whispers. Her mother doesn't seem to notice her new stooping.

Over a cup of tea Mrs Johnson explains to Olivia's mother that Mr Johnson "works up north for long stretches". Without asking, Mrs Johnson drops two sugar cubes into her mother's cup. Her mother doesn't take sugar because she's on a diet but Olivia knows that her mother is too polite to say.

The door to the garden is kept locked and there are no rabbits here but Olivia misses Aunty Flo, her horse face and the warm, safe valley of her aproned lap.

Olivia 2

Although Olivia's not supposed to have favourites, Andrew Keating is her star pupil. Andrew writes poetry as though he's playing a violin and twists at his already twisted school tie when he's thinking. He's short-tongued and doesn't get on with his Rs, so he asks other children to read out his poems. Slapping on gold stars like postage stamps, Olivia rewards Andrew's consistently excellent efforts.

"Never thought I'd bag me a teacher with a handful of ologies," Brian says and throws a heavy arm about Olivia's shoulders. She wishes he wouldn't but she doesn't say. Her shoulders grow round beneath his weight.

They have very little furniture; a bed, a fish tank, a bean bag, and for months they have neither a television nor an oven.

They eat raw food, which Brian insists is good for them. People tell them how exciting it is, this starting out, setting up home, but Olivia doesn't feel anything is beginning. Rather, things continue much the same.

At Alexandra Palace, one Sunday, they fly a kite. It is a large, red kite, a Chinese dragon that skates across the blue, white sky. A September wind is blowing hard and Brian says that this fierce wind is both a good and a bad thing.

The kite gets caught in the branches of a tree.

"Bloody kite. I knew this would happen."

Brian paces around the foot of the tree, kicking at the trunk and yanking at the string.

"Why does there need to be so many poxy trees anyway?"

"I like trees," Olivia says and smiles up at the kite. The kite has the guts to do what she can't.

"Stupid thing, stuff it," Brian says and storms off.

The silent bus ride home is mainly uphill. Their small flat rests on a rise, overlooking a wide field of allotments.

After she's finished marking the children's homework, Olivia stacks the exercise books in a tidy pile near her brown briefcase by the front door. She hears the sound of running bathwater, which Brian turns a vivid blue when he adds a capful of Radox.

Brian is quiet after their return from Alexandra Palace, but pokes his head around the bathroom door to ask, "I didn't want to say anything and I know you'll tell me if there's anything to tell. Only I saw the box and I just wondered if . . ."

"Yes. Positive."

Olivia observes Brian's worn and weary appearance suddenly replaced by the shine and sparkle of new coinage. Over the months he writes lengthy lists, ticks numerous boxes and instructs her to do the same.

Olivia loses track of the hours and when the small, wet body falls between her thighs, she slumps back and knows why this and love are called labour. For a long time, Olivia stares at the father and child.

It's a struggle between William or Dan or Jack. Brian suggests Thomas or Tom, but Olivia doesn't like Thomas, Tom or Tommy.

"Does it make you think of a peeping Tom? Bit creepy?" he says, but Olivia doesn't answer.

"I like Dan. It's solid," she says.

"Not too desperate, then?" He laughs.

Brian sterilises the bottles, changes Dan's nappies, treats Dan's cradle cap and tastes Olivia's breast milk. Strolling with Dan in his buggy, Olivia notices that the kite is still there, watching her continue, much the same.

"An only child is a lonely child. They have issues," Brian says. "Not pointing any fingers, Ollie, but it's a known thing."

Olivia can only make love with the lights off; she doesn't like being looked at, or looking, and Dan remains an only child. Olivia has her GCE A-level students at the local comprehensive and she squeezes grades from them good enough to send them on to university. Renting an allotment, Brian grows marrows, tomatoes, radishes and strawberries. The strawberries taste like petrol but Olivia doesn't tell him this, or that there is metal in the air, pollution from the cars.

Brian talks less. Olivia suspects that he thinks she's withholding her eggs. From behind the net curtains she watches father and son plod along in slow rhythm to the allotment, heavy steps, heavy arms, continuing much the same.

Olivia 3

The tears won't come when they bury her mother. They're dammed up inside her head somewhere. Although Olivia's movements are deliberate and slow, she often does things twice over. Speaking in a dry, shrunken voice when she gives the eulogy, Olivia recalls memories she has long forgotten. Memories of their weekly visits to Lindy's launderette and the regular hunter-gathering for shillings, her mother's beehive boxed backwards by the wind, her wild-cat temper and hopeless, long-playing love for Olivia's father.

On the day of the funeral it rains and the sky is dark, but it is the only kind of day on which her mother would have agreed to be buried.

Had it been a warm, sunny day her mother would have been there, sunning herself, kicking off her shoes, sod the grass stains, having a picnic.

Her mother had found fault with Olivia, said she was haunted.

"You think too much, Ollie. That book-reading's doing you no good. It's giving you ideas."

Ideas were dangerous things, could make you take flight and forget yourself.

When she was thirty years old and shortly after Dan's birth, Olivia visited her mother, told her about Uncle Tommy. Uncle Tommy who sits in her life's pocket like keys tearing away at the lining.

"Well, you can hardly call that abuse, can you? I mean, he didn't touch you or nothing."

Her mother spoke without looking at her. When Uncle Tommy died, her mother wept and sent a wreath. Olivia didn't attend the funeral; her limbs weren't working that morning.

"You should have gone, Ollie. Your Aunty Flo thinks the world of you. You read too much into things, always did."

At the funeral, there are faces Olivia doesn't know or hasn't seen for a long time. Strangers shake her hand, nod and offer soft, shuffling words.

A week later, Brian leaves, this time for good. He says that he has had enough of pretending and that Dan is a full-grown man, he'll understand. Olivia is struck by the smallness of the suitcase he's carrying and realises he has somewhere to go, someone who waits for him. Without looking back, Brian walks down the garden path. He leaves the family car and climbs into the waiting minicab.

On Monday, Olivia has the front-door locks changed. Removing the fridge magnets that Brian thought very funny, Olivia feels as though she's thrown off an outgrown girdle.

After Olivia was born her mother invested in a Playtex Cross-Your-Heart bra and girdle and although the girdle crushed her ribs, her mother declared it a lifeline.

The tilted axis that Olivia imagines running through the length of her body can now be straightened. Possibilities flurry and a rush of gladness shifts her thinking. She cancels the subscription to sports television. Next to go is the mattress. Olivia finds herself humming. This is a new kind of breathing, a genuine starting out.

Olivia 4

Olivia allows the staff to bathe her and brush her hair. They marvel at the surprising whiteness of her teeth and the quiet glory of the tight curls she's warred with for much of her life. Among the staff there is Maggie, the Irish cook, and Babsy, the Jamaican staff leader, and a few women from Bulgaria who do the other shifts. Claremont's is very clean; Olivia finds that most homes for the elderly smell of urine. Dan spends a lot of time searching for a home where his mother will be happy. And Olivia is happy. She makes two friends, Henryk and Gwendoline.

Olivia's room is L-shaped, with bay windows that look onto the back garden. Dan pays extra for the view. Olivia has sight of a pear tree that each year is jewelled with pendulous fruit, and a dazzling azalea bush that shocks with gaudy pink blooms, but it is the regular bars of soap placed in her bathroom that delight her.

Like duck eggs of cool, marble beauty they sit neatly on the basin until water spoils their sculpture, purity and perfection.

The staff assume that Olivia dislikes washing, unaware of her love of form, but Henryk understands.

Henryk is Swiss and used to be a professional opera singer. He describes himself as an artist. Olivia notes the bright, lyrical bow ties but ignores his fraying shirt cuffs.

It tickles Olivia when Henryk throws back his head and yodels. He reminds her of Frank Ifield but Henryk hasn't heard of Frank Ifield, nor has anyone else in the home, and Olivia feels very old and foolish for mentioning his name.

"It doesn't matter whether anyone has or hasn't heard of your Frank Ifield, Ollie. He's known to you and that's all that matters," Henryk says. Henryk tidies up Olivia's muddles. He could have added, "Well, that's that, then," and folded his arms or closed a drawer or turned a key or did whatever it was that smug people did when things were sorted and settled, but he doesn't.

Gwendoline steals things from other people's rooms, anything bright, and hides her growing, glittering loot under her bed. Thinking she is eight years old again, she spends many nights calling out for her mother. Sometimes, windows of coherence and clarity suddenly appear and Olivia discovers that Gwendoline was once a journalist, covering war zones. Everybody in the home used to be somebody else.

There are activities: Reminiscence Mondays, bingo on Tuesdays, yoga and stretching on Wednesdays, Cluedo, dominoes and Monopoly on Thursdays and singalongs on Fridays.

The staff find money from the Monopoly bank under Gwendoline's bed, along with a garlic press and nail clippers.

Although the staff can't be certain, it seems that newly arrived Dexter has swallowed a domino; the double six is missing and Dexter has a habit of eating small, inanimate objects. Olivia wins; it's Colonel Mustard in the library with the lead piping. She shines brightly.

Dan visits with his wife, Femi, their infant twins and their eldest daughter, Grace. Olivia sees herself in the curious, moon-faced child. Grace asks her questions like, "Why do you live here? How old are you? Can you swim? Do your wrinkles hurt? What is the best day you've ever had?"

Olivia's best days were those when, as a child, she played with her friend David in the back garden; her wedding day, when she danced until her feet were blistered; and her very best day was the day before yesterday, when Henryk held her and whispered that she was the love of his life.

It's true what people say about life flashing past. Like confetti, memories pour down, sights, sounds, scents, tastes and touch, until Olivia finds herself somewhere near the beginning. Her last memory is of making mud pies, her T-bar shoes boring deep into the black, curdled soil. London's burning, rings on her fingers, bells fastened to her toes. Am. Am. Am.

Reunion

SONYA OLDWIN

F loating.
In the pool. Face down.

Church bells in the distance. Bong, bong, bong, too many to count. Owl hoots.

Wait. Face down? Face down!

Quick, quick, you can't breathe. Turn over. Arms and legs flailing. Nothing. No momentum. No splashing.

You need to get out.

Strange pulling upwards.

Floating.

Above the pool, looking down at the water. The completely calm water.

It's not right. You ought to sit down.

Strange pulling again.

Sitting.

By the poolside, feet in the water. It's not cold, the water. Not warm, either. Or wet. It's there, you can see it. Your feet, dangling back and forth, don't cause a stir.

Your clothes? Not wet.

The water is an illusion?

Wake up. Wake up!

Awake now?

Weird song stuck in head.

Away from the pool, must get away. Away from the dark. It's not that dark. Orange light from cathedral on the other hill. Still. Don't like it. What was I thinking? Can't have been thinking. Did I fall asleep in the pool? Dangerous, night-swimming.

Feel strange. Can't identify strangeness. Quick, quick, run up to the house. Quick now. Get inside, turn on all lights. There should be lights on. There should be windows. There are no windows. Why are there no windows? Where have the windows gone?

Something wrong with my eyes. Lack of oxygen not good for brain, something's happened with my vision. Can't see. Can see some things, can see the grass. The house. The door. It's too far away. No windows. Wood? No, why would there be wood?

Run. Legs have other ideas. They're not doing any running. What are the legs doing? Why is body broken? What happened in the water?

Noise. Owl. Owls are noisy birds.

"Shut up, owls."

Add to list: vocal cords. Also broken.

What else? Why am I not getting closer?

Strange pulling sensation again. I'm at the house. I'm in front of the door. Feet didn't touch grass. Scotty, beam me up. At least to my front door.

Closed.

Can't grab and shake it. Not sure how. It's elusive.

Windows boarded up. With heavy wooden planks. Why? How? Since when? How did I get out of the house? Back door? Back door is for rookies, never use the back door. That's what they expect. Have to have the guts to walk out the front door.

Back door locked, too. Elusive. I have no keys.

I have nothing.

Am all alone. Raspy voice. Crying for help. Who's going to hear it? Nobody home. No light. Everything is dark and I'm – lost.

Lost. In front of my own house.

Why is everything so much louder in the dark? I have goosebumps. It isn't cold.

Hold that thought. Don't know if it is. Can't feel the temperature. List is growing.

What's happening, options: I'm dreaming – nightmaring; I've accepted a dodgy drink; I've been hit over the head and now everything's wrong. Too many explanations. No way of telling. I don't want to be out, alone, in the dark. Not while tripping. Or experiencing head trauma.

I scream. Nothing. If I keep going, I might produce a sound.

Vocal cords protest. Look, we've no idea how to do this any more.

So the broken body parts talk back, is that what this is? Don't need the attitude.

How do I get inside? I'd give my signed Robbie Williams poster to be in my bed.

Scotty again. Inside. My bedroom. I've been taken at my word, and then some. Everything is gone from the Robbie Williams wall. Try to get worked up over it.

Can't. Because it can't be real.

I'm inside. Still dark, but I'm in the house. This place-hopping thing doesn't make sense. Have I learnt the art of teleporting while I wasn't paying attention? So cool.

Room is empty. House is deserted. Feels as if the life I know has gone and I've been left, like unwanted furniture.

Nobody in the house. Having a good look around, searching for clues. Can't find any clues. Absence of clues a clue?

Framed photographs are still here. In the hallways. Along the stairs. In the sitting room. Everywhere visitors can see them. They are all of me, some with Mum and Dad. Most of them, just me when I was little. The little girl I used to be before they abandoned me. No photographs in the bedroom, or any other rooms upstairs. Only where they will be seen.

The furniture is here. Covered by thick fabric covers. I don't see cobwebs. All my nightmares feature cobwebs. Their absence worries me.

A feeling I've forgotten unfolds itself. The big house when I was little. An endless nightmare. I got lost, ended up in rooms nobody used, rooms that smelt of damp and dust and demons. I believed the house was haunted. I told children at school that I lived in the haunted house. They made fun of me.

"Your house is not haunted. It isn't old enough to be a haunted house," they'd say.

"Yes it is. It is older than yours."

Nobody believed me. Parents told me to be reasonable.

Another memory – dinner-party guests; I run down the stairs screaming; Mum has no choice but to play the caring mummy in front of guests because they've seen the photographs. She unleashes her anger on me the following morning. Too late, though. Lesson learnt: guests mean attention. I want that attention.

Where are my parents? I can't keep track, they're always somewhere or other. Always on the move, home for no longer than a month. Because I'm old enough now.

Nobody asks what I think.

Don't care any more.

I'm seventeen, I can take care of myself. I say that, but I am exploring an empty house with no idea what's going on. How I came to wake up in the pool. How I got into the house when it is locked and boarded up.

I need a mirror. What if I've had an accident and spent the last ten years in a coma? What if I'm not here at all? What if some strange thing has happened and I can't remember? I might have blanked it out. I bet I'm disfigured. I bet I look like something out of a haunted house.

Where are the mirrors? None in the bathrooms. Not a single one.

What if I'm a vampire and I've removed them, reminders of my undead state?

That's rubbish. There are no vampires. But why no mirrors here? Furniture still in place, someone could live here now if they wanted. After they located and used the vacuum. The house is covered in a thick coat of dust.

You'd think walking on half an inch of dust would make walking feel different. I don't feel different. I am not sure I can feel my feet. They are there, my feet. But they don't seem to be making any dents in the dust. I turn around. There are no footprints. There should be footprints.

It's like I'm trapped in one of those awful films, or a Stephen King novel. Not that I've ever read one, I'd never sleep again.

If this continues, I will seriously fear for my sleep.

I want it to stop, I want the house to go back to normal.

I want light. There's no power.

I want something to eat.

My heart hammers. If it keeps this up, my ribcage will burst. Or I'll have a heart attack.

When I check for my pulse, there's nothing. Not in my wrists, not in my neck.

What is this? Where am I? Who am I?

I kneel down and write my name in the dust with my index, middle and ring fingers. Broad so I won't miss it. M-A-R-L-E-N-A.

My fingers don't leave a trace.

I am not really here. I'm dreaming. I'm having a nightmare.

The house is not really here. See above.

My eyes are more impeded than I thought. Which would be a nightmare.

Can you make yourself wake up? When you're having a nightmare and you realise what's going on, can you force yourself out? If the answer is yes, how do I do it? I've had enough of this. My body is falling to pieces with every step I take. Nothing is the way it's supposed to be. It is still dark. If anything, it's got worse since I've come to the house.

That was enough for Scotty to beam me out, halfway down the drive. It's the frigging middle of the night. Friends' parents won't be impressed if I show up on their doorstep now, but I don't care. Anything is better than staying here, even parental wrath. Who will it be? The twins? Their mother is too intense even for me. The parents who will be the least annoyed are Vick's. I haven't been to her house for ever. I'm reluctant to go there. Too many memories. Alternative is staying here, alone, not in control of anything. Must overcome reluctance.

All right, Scotty, do your thing.

I close my eyes but when I open them, I'm still in the drive.

I take a step forward. Another one. I don't move. Walking on the spot. There's an invisible barrier I can't cross. The pulling sensation again. I recognise it before it snatches me. I'm back at the pool.

My eyes are getting worse.

The pool in the dark, surrounded by grass that hasn't been cut in months, the stump where the fir should be in the background. Just as I saw it earlier.

The pool in the dark, surrounded by tea lights in jam jars, the fir as I remember it. The night the girls and I made the promise. What a cracker that was.

The pool at dawn, remains of the fir piled next to what is left of the charred trunk. Looks as if something's exploded in the garden. What terrifies me is the pool. The body floating. It looks like mine.

Heart pounding.

Breathe in, breathe out. Breathing is difficult. I open my mouth and it gets worse. Lungs failing? No, no, that's not it. It feels like –

I know this feeling, I've had it before, lungs burning, screaming for oxygen. Is it a memory? Feels real. Why can't I breathe? Why is there water everywhere? In my ears, in my eyes, in my nose, my mouth, my lungs. I'm underwater. Struggling to come up to the surface. Twisting, squirming, fighting. But I can't come up for air because something – someone? – is keeping me under. Someone is keeping me under.

Heart racing now. Is this part of the nightmare? Or has it happened. Is it happening?

I don't know any more. I just want it all to stop. I want this nightmare to stop.

What are the water memories about? They swim at the edge of my consciousness. I can't bring them into focus. Every time I'm close to grasping one, blood rushes faster in my veins, fear clutches me, puts pressure on my throat, my stomach. All my insides are cramped up, trying to get away from whatever danger we're facing. What danger are we facing? More afraid of the memories than of anything that's happened tonight. Are they memories? I am trying to remember but don't quite succeed. A frightening moment that's best forgotten? Why is my brain throwing these memories at me? Brain goes on list of malfunctioning body parts. Bad news. Need my brain to function. I need the whole of my body to function, but above all my brain.

Heart hammers in my chest. I get what they mean about hearts breaking through the chest. That's how it feels.

I hate the dark. Have hated it for as long as I can remember. No particular reason, not as if I'd been sent to my room alone when

I was little. I had all the night lights I wanted, too. They didn't help. Even if they had, they wouldn't help now. There's the cathedral, which is a gigantic night light. None of the light surrounding me helps.

I'm in the dark, alone. All around me, strange things are happening. There's a body in the pool.

I turn and run towards the house, out of instinct. I run and run but never make any progress. I'm shackled to the pool.

"Face it!"

Face it? No way.

Hang on. Where's the voice coming from?

"In a mad world,
only the mad
are sane."
Akira Kurosawa

On the Rocks

ANTONIA REED

The steps from the seafront down to the café are hacked into the bare cliffside, centuries old and probably not legal any more, and the patio furniture is mismatched and shabby. You can't see any part of town from down here. If the cliff crumbled, we would simply disappear. Not that we tell this to the customers as they make their way between us and the world above, nothing but wobbly rope hanging between poles to protect them from a long, chalky plunge.

It's just gone midday in late August, my long summer of going nowhere. In front of me stretches university with its promise of freedom, excitement and enlightenment. But, as much as I'll be relieved to get out of this place, get away from the drab coastline skies and even drabber people, I have no idea how I'm going to manage when I get there. *I don't know why you chose Psychology when you can't stand people.* My mother doesn't realise it's a perfect subject if you're better at studying people than talking to them. After that, who knows. Maybe I'll run away and live under a rock, or work with dolphins; at least they won't expect small talk.

Most of our customers are hiking types, rainproof gear in every shade of unstylish, enjoying a scone, tea and death-defying view at the outer tables. A seagull dive-bombs at their food and one of them screams and nearly falls over the edge. I gasp and then, embarrassed by my own noise, concentrate on wiping the

215

stainless steel. The doors are wide open and the serving hatch opens straight onto the patio, so sticky salt air coats everything in a mist that needs constant wiping off.

My bulbous reflection stares back from a sugar pot. Straight, dark-brown hair, my mother's large blue eyes. The black and white checks of my apron make me look like a policewoman.

Someone comes into view, clambering around the side of the cliff. A woman, taller than average, stylish in a tan trench coat and straight-legged jeans, a peach silk scarf round her neck, slender in a muscular, gym-toned way. Her hands, clutching the gangly ropes, are large and bony, like a model's. She steps down onto our sunken patio, looks over at the hatch and catches me staring. I glare down at the counter and continue my cleaning, feeling my neck go hot.

When I peer up again, she has found a table at the land side of the patio and is studying the menu. There's caution in her eyes when I walk over, but when she notices my apron her shoulders relax and she smiles, swiping a loosened blonde strand behind her ear. She has a slightly hollow, horsey face that makes me think of stables and high tea. She orders with finely painted lips and a deep, rich voice, though her diction seems more forced than natural.

When I carry over her tea and cake, she is gazing out at the ocean, a blue-and-white brochure of some sort opened in front of her. She doesn't seem to be in a hurry to go anywhere. In fact, it's hard to work out where she is going. Looks like she's here alone. *Know the feeling*, I want to say, but think better of it and return to the kitchen.

People come and go; the dishwasher is filled and emptied. And then the scrape of plastic over stainless steel makes me look up at the hatch, where the blonde woman has just returned her tray of crockery.

"Oh. Thanks," I mumble, taken aback. Hardly anyone carries their stuff back.

"You're welcome."

She smiles, then strides around the side of the café and disappears, followed by a series of clomps as she takes the steps up to the toilet block.

*

Stan is unpacking a crate of soft drinks when a family swarms onto the patio, large in number and size. After I've taken their order, I realise that the blonde woman hasn't returned from the toilets.

I don't know why I noticed, but there's a funny, unfamiliar feeling in my belly. I hand my notepad to Stan and push through the stable door at the side of the café.

When I climb the steps, the blonde woman is standing at the top with her back to me. She's swaying in an odd way, and, for an awkward moment, I wonder whether she's praying. And then she turns around, eyes gooey with emotion, and I see the baby held against her shoulder. The cubicles are all empty. A plastic carrycot, smothered in cheap-looking pink-and-white blankets, sits across one of the sinks.

"What the . . . ?"

"I know!" she says. "I just found her in the basket, all cold. No note, no telephone number, nothing."

I lift the blankets individually, check underneath the carrier and peer inside the cubicles. There's nothing to identify the child, other than the colour of the blankets suggesting it's a girl. I'm guessing she's a few months old. The woman gently bobs the child on her arm, patting her back and stroking her cheek with her own. The baby has been dressed in a washed-out red playsuit. She seems content enough, one hand pulled up to her face, the other twining the woman's hair. How the hell did someone carry her here? No comment on the morality of it but ten out of ten for stealth.

I think back through the people who have visited today. Any single women, anyone shifty-looking, anyone who seemed emotional. But there's been nothing special. I look through the open window at the bare cliff face. Patches of grass and wind-blown litter decorate the bleak view. In a way this was the perfect spot: obscure, unobserved and the very last place you'd expect to find a baby. I lean out to look further along the cliff. Only the sound of the sea and wind; and high up, the sliver of bright light between the top of the block and the cliff edge. The world above.

"I'm Karen," the woman says, making me jump.

I swivel to face her. "Sorry. Hannah." I hold out my hand, feeling awkward, but before she can shake it the baby begins to cry and she returns to patting her on the back.

"She's probably hungry," Karen says.

I go through the contents of the store shelves in my mind. Perhaps we have some baby food tucked away.

"I could give her some milk. Mashed potato?"

Karen thinks for a moment. "Milk's probably the safest."

I lead the way down the steps, carrying the baby-basket, then usher Karen through the stable door into the kitchen. Stan gives us a *What the hell?* look.

"Karen, this is Stan, my boss. Stan, this is Karen and . . . something we found in the toilets."

Karen winces when I say "something", but I'm not going to get precious about a baby. It will be reunited with its mother, or given to someone else, hopefully someone better. Neither outcome will involve me, so there's no point getting attached. Unlike Karen, standing in the doorway, the light from outside haloing her like some postmodern Madonna.

"Bloody hell." Stan scratches the bald patch at the back of his head. "I'm a bit out of my depth here."

I rummage around in the back, opting to mix some instant potato into the milk. Stan goes over to Karen. "Who've we got here, then?" he says with unusual softness. "Hello, little fella."

"It's a girl," Karen corrects, while I start the microwave.

Stan coos over the baby until a customer clears his throat theatrically at the counter. I present my concoction to Karen in a little bowl, garnished with a plastic spoon. She tries to look enthusiastic but fails, thanks me, and carries it and the baby outside.

Stan comes to stand next to me. "We should call the police."

I nod, finding it hard to stop looking at the pair outside. The baby's mouth smacks in pleasure and her eyes fix widely on Karen with each mouthful. Suddenly I feel like crying. I swallow it down, though my throat feels painful, and behind me Stan walks over to the telephone.

A coachload of tourists has descended down the cliff to enjoy the area's most exciting cup of tea, and it takes for ever to deal with their requests. Some gush over the baby, asking Karen questions I can't hear. She takes them all, smiling benignly and laughing at someone's joke. The baby is asleep on her shoulder, a dark patch of dribble soaking the serviette she's trapped there. She looks so natural, so in control, like someone who has done this before. I wonder whether she has children, and where they are right now. She looked slightly forlorn earlier, unattached to anyone. Now she's like a different person. If it weren't for the almost impossible chance that the baby was left by mistake, I don't see why she shouldn't just take her. Every child a wanted child and all that.

A uniformed policeman is making his way along the rope path, followed by a woman in a white blouse and navy skirt suit, her dyed-black hair messy from the wind, wearing black stilettos that on principle make me want her to fall over. Karen turns to see where I'm looking and her hands wrap a little more tightly around the baby.

The newcomers give me a nod and, there being no other babies around, make a beeline for Karen. They sit down, one on either side of her, and I feel strangely protective. The three of them talk, though I can't hear what they're saying, and the policeman walks off towards the toilets.

When I go over with some complimentary tea, the woman is rummaging loudly through her handbag. The baby has woken and is playing with Karen's hair. The woman straightens, pen poised over her clipboard. She gives the baby the briefest of smiles, then looks up at Karen. "So . . ."

Karen hesitates, then asks, "Is there any way I could keep her – not for ever, obviously – just while you try to locate the parents?"

"I'm sorry, but that won't be possible. We have to give children to registered carers. You're not a professional foster-parent, are you?"

"No. No, I'm not."

"I'm sorry. I see you've gotten a bit attached . . ."

Karen shakes her head. "I'm just doing what anyone would . . ." She shoots a glance at the policeman, returning from the toilet block. The baby tries to grab her earring and she deftly turns it into a game of pat-a-cake. She looks over at me, but for what? Backup? My fingers fidget with my apron as I go back to the hatch.

And then the questions are over, and the three of them are standing up. The woman pulls the baby-carrier towards her and chirps, "Time to say goodbye," as if she were about to cut a cake.

Karen slowly slides her hand behind the baby's head and leans forward, lowering the girl into the carrier. She begins tucking the blankets around her, but the other woman sweeps it away before she can finish.

"That's great. We'll take it from here."

The little girl howls, arms reaching towards Karen, who says reassuring things while gripping the top of her chair.

The police leave, the woman shaking her head and saying what terrible things people do to children. I look for Karen but she's fleeing in long strides to the toilet block, choking back low-pitched sobs.

Now that the entertainment's over, the tourists start to pack up. Stan busies himself tidying the tables and I load the dishwasher for the last time. Five thirty. When I think Karen's had long enough, I hang up my apron and go out to the toilets.

The light is off, and all I can hear is shaky breathing. I take the liberty of flicking the switch. I brace myself, knowing how stupid the question is. "Karen? Are you all right?"

"Yes, I'm just . . . being silly."

"Don't say that." I knock on her cubicle door. "Can I come in?"

She blows her nose loudly. "I suppose."

The door unlocks and I nudge it open. Karen's legs are so long I can't avoid knocking them. She shifts to make room, balling a load of soggy tissues between her hands.

And then my forced smile freezes on my face. Her make-up has run terribly. The skin around her eyes is raw and puffed, making her look older, and the colour from her lips and cheeks has gone. Where the foundation has been cried away round her mouth, the slight shadow of beard follicles has emerged. She has removed the silk scarf and a small Adam's apple bobs triumphantly as she swallows.

For a moment my sense of balance seems to go, my arms reaching back to steady myself as I step away. I feel a weird mixture of revulsion and fascination, like I've stumbled upon a beautiful but frightening specimen in a museum, only one that lives and breathes and makes me nervous in a way I can't make sense of. And then my brain comes back, and I remember this is the same person as before, who has been polite and kind and perhaps a little alone, and I feel guilty for reacting the way I just did.

"You can't blame them for not trusting me with a baby," Karen mutters, no longer putting an effort into controlling her pitch. Should I still be thinking of her as "Karen"? So glamorous when she, he, whatever, came here. Now she's shaking slightly.

I lean against the cubicle wall, feeling deflated and useless. "Would you like me to . . . call someone?"

Karen sniffles a few more times, then shoves the damp mush of tissues into her coat pocket. "There's not really anyone to call." She glumly tugs her blouse straight across her chest.

Normally I would give up here, accept I'm out of my depth and more likely to make things worse if I say anything, but right now I feel bizarrely inspired.

"Look, I'm not going to pretend I know anything about what you're going through, but why don't you clean yourself up, I'll finish in the kitchen, and we can get out of here?"

Karen's eyebrows rise when I say "we". Have I overstepped a mark? I hold my hands up. "If you want to. I thought you might . . . you know, want cheering up."

Karen is still staring, and panic starts creeping into me. Now I've managed to patronise her as well. Well done. I mumble an apology and open the door.

"No, wait," Karen says, standing up. "I'm sorry, I wasn't expecting . . ." She smiles, a little easier, and I unstiffen slightly. "That's a very sweet offer. What did you have in mind?"

"Er . . ." I hadn't thought this far. "I don't know. The beach? Chippy?"

Karen laughs, genuine and throaty, and in the meeting of our eyes there is something, some understanding that gives me a warm tingle at the base of my spine. It feels clandestine and illicit, the two of us here with her towering over me.

She checks her watch. "Well, my train's not for a few hours. Why not?"

I slip outside to finish tidying the kitchen before Stan locks up. When I'm done, Karen is stepping onto the patio, looking as she did when she first came. Neatly put together, if a little tired. I wish I could have seen her put on her make-up, see the sweep of colour spread over her cheek, the layers coating her face until it is a new one entirely. Sad she has to put on all that stuff just to look normal.

When we reach the promenade at the top of the cliff steps, pink-and-orange sunlight is banding across the front of the shops and cafés, twinkling where it catches a window.

Karen sighs dramatically. "It's like coming out of purgatory."

"Come on, the café's not that bad."

"No, I mean it's so beautiful."

The breeze is lifting her hair around her face, the sun giving her coat a peach glow in front of the dark-blue sea. If I took a picture it would look like a moody fashion shot, all cheekbones and atmosphere. Her shoulders no longer seem taut and guarded; as if her secret was a physical burden she no longer has to carry in my presence. I guess that gives me a strange sort of privilege.

I wonder who she was before she became Karen. A truck driver called Brian with a wife and kids, or a student called Paul who's been living like this for years. Or all manner of other possibilities, full of their own complications and confusion. What life she has left behind and what she's trying to forge now. It hits me that I've never really had to struggle for anything to that extent. I feel grateful – at least in this sense my life has been easy – and also a tiny bit guilty.

We stroll along the seafront until the promenade takes us into the classier part of town, cluttered with bookshops and antique dealers. I try to think of how to get a conversation going. Does she want to talk about the baby? But what use would that be?

I look vaguely ahead. "So . . . what were you here for? Just a day-trip or . . ."

"A conference," Karen replies. "I was presenting a paper, trying to get some funding. It's not easy."

"You're an academic?"

"Clinical psychologist." She catches me staring and smiles. "You weren't expecting that, were you?"

"I wasn't expecting anything."

I do feel confused, though. That someone like Karen could be so successful and not some sad case you read about in the *Sun*. It makes me feel hopeful and inadequate at the same time.

We stop to peer into a bookshop displaying local-history rags and fancy art books.

"What about you?" asks Karen. "What do you do when you're not making a perfect cup of tea?"

"Oh, that's my vocation, can't you tell?"

Karen's reflection smiles, but she stays quiet.

"Actually, I'm starting uni in a few weeks. Psychology." I hold my breath, not wanting her to think I'm ridiculous or sucking up.

"Oh." She turns to me. "Well, if you want a reading list . . ."

I shiver involuntarily. The temperature has dropped and my thin jacket's no use against the damp.

"Do you need to go home?" Karen asks.

"I'm fine," I say, ducking my neck into my collar.

"You're so like my daugh . . ." Karen trails off.

When I look up at her she turns away and clears her throat. I stare uselessly at her long back. God knows what happened there.

"I'm sorry," I say, knowing how pathetic that sounds.

"Not your fault." Karen has turned round again, her face composed. "So, where to?"

I slide my hands into my pockets, considering the options. My fingers find the cool touch of coins, my share from the café tip bowl.

I give Karen a sly smile. "Do you want to experience some local culture?"

It should embarrass me, how little there is to offer in town. But tonight, the rowdy pubs and arcades seem exciting, almost inviting. As the streets get busier, Karen pulls into herself, shoulders raised, eyes fixed on some imaginary world. She doesn't acknowledge the drunken leers, the bottles and glasses being smashed, the occasional smell of piss from an alleyway.

We enter the whirr and red flashing lights of the Grand Arcade, and in its surreal camouflage we both relax. The carpets are filthy and the air hums with alcohol-breath, armpit, unwashed feet and trainers, but Karen doesn't seem to mind, and is refreshingly keen to be frivolous for a couple of hours. We flip a few pinball machines, I show Karen the ultimate 20p tactic on the sliding trays, and I proudly snatch a neon-green parrot from one of the grabbing-claw devices.

Karen snorts as I present the trophy. "You've clearly had a

misspent youth."

"Better than setting fire to bins."

Karen laughs again, and I catch our reflections in the glass. Hers pale and gaunt, mine dark and squat, with the neon splash of the parrot in between.

My stomach growls and when I look at my watch it says nine thirty, way past when I should have been home. I don't want to know how many calls I've missed from Mum, my phone switched to silent the minute I left this morning.

Karen looks at me, and says what I would otherwise have had to. "Time for me to go."

The sky is almost black now, beyond the orange fuzz radiating above the buildings and street lamps. We walk briskly towards the station, not speaking, and I tell myself it's because the air has cooled; but really it's because I hate lingering goodbyes, and this one is going to be especially weird. I would like to see Karen again, know more about her, know she's OK, but there is no reason for her to keep in touch. What can an eighteen-year-old, who hasn't even spent more than a week away from home, offer her?

It's only when the green iron railings and the bridge over the tracks appear further down the hill that I start to slow down, and find myself asking, "You feeling any better?"

Karen takes a moment to answer, and I wonder if that was a stupid thing to ask.

"Actually, I've had a great time. More fun than I've had in ages."

"Really?"

"Really."

We go silent again, my head full of questions I know I can't ask.

Perhaps Karen picks up on my thoughts. "My daughter . . . We don't speak much these days. She finds it difficult, this" – she indicates her body – "situation. It was nice to do something . . . normal with a young person for a change."

The emotion is radiating out of her now, though she remains composed. No wonder the baby affected her so much. Maybe it seemed like a fresh start; or reminded her of what she's missing. I don't want to offer her some platitude like "She'll come around," or "If she can't appreciate you . . ." So I just say, "I hope it gets better."

"Thank you." Karen's face is soft and she touches my arm for a second, and it is such a gentle gesture that I feel myself tearing up. Like her pain and loneliness have flowed into me.

And then we're stepping onto the platform and Karen is checking her ticket against the announcements. Eight minutes.

"Well," she says. "This was a bit of an adventure."

"It was . . . nice to meet you," I say, feeling awkward again. "Even if it wasn't the nicest situation."

Karen flaps a hand. "Can't be helped." Deep breath. Another smile. Softer, her deep-grey eyes holding mine for a moment. "You've been very kind to me," she says. "Kinder than a lot of people."

I shrug, jab my toe at some chewing gum on the floor. "They're clearly arseholes."

Karen laughs and dabs at the corner of her eye. "You're funny."

The loudspeaker announces her train, and in the distance its grey gleam emerges from the night. Karen unzips her bag and extracts a business card. "Here."

I take the card from her long fingers. It's white, with a pink sash behind black letters. *Dr Karen Landsgrove, BA, MD, PsyD*. My stomach feels giddy and my head can't process all the possibilities flying around in it right now. I slide the card deep into my pocket, keeping my hand there to wedge it in place.

"You start studying in a few weeks?"

"Yep. Frontal lobes here I come."

"Good." Her statement is odd. I don't know what she means, but we're out of time. The train is close enough to read the letters on its front. Karen looks at me carefully. "Actually, I'm . . . setting up a home – a retreat for people who are . . . transitioning. If ever you're interested in getting involved – you know, need some work experience, or want to see what you could be doing down the line – or if you just want a chat, just call."

The train doors open and Karen leans down and squeezes me tight for a moment. And before I can react she is gone and the doors are closing and she is waving goodbye, her lips pressed tight and her eyes both sad and happy. My body feels light and heavy at the same time and the train is pulling out and people who have stepped off are pushing into me, but I don't care.

I watch the train disappear, the card nestled against the soft skin of my palm. And then I spin on my heel, imagining my short jacket swinging behind me like Karen's coat, and walk out of the station, thinking about all the things I need to do before term starts.

The Taxi Driver

ANGELA WRAY

Leila slipped through the hole in the fence and looked around. How strange, she thought, that she'd lived in the same house for eight years, her whole life, and never even wondered about next door before. How could this garden be so different from her own? No climbing frame, no swing hanging from the big branch of the apple tree – in fact no apple tree at all, only a gnarled old plum with fruit just beginning to ripen, and a few enormous, untidy rose bushes.

She breathed in the deep, spicy scent of the roses and decided she would pick one on her way out if no one was looking, to add to the concoction in the jar under her bed that she was hoping would one day, by some mysterious process, turn into perfume. The neatly planted roses in her own garden did not have such a powerful scent as these wayward giants, but were controlled and colour-coordinated, with little tags dangling from their necks to remind you of their names: New Dawn, Queen Elizabeth, Canary Bird. Canary Bird was Leila's favourite, not just because of its name, which was almost, but not quite, as nice as having an actual canary in the garden, but also because its little yellow flowers draped round the back door like the entrance to a secret tunnel. It grew up almost to her bedroom window despite her father's efforts to tame it with green twine and lengths of twisted wire.

Today Leila had come home from school and, after making

a cup of tea for her mother, had spent an hour in her bedroom creating patterns with her Spirograph before going downstairs to watch *Blue Peter*. John Noakes had talked about exploring gardens, which, as far as Leila's garden was concerned, was impossible as there was just a big square lawn with flowers round the edge and the apple tree. She knew every inch of it already. That was when she'd had the idea about next door.

She ventured further, tiptoeing through the damp grass that, unlike the lawn in her own garden, was long and wavy. She loved the tickle of the grass as it brushed her bare legs, and reached down, stroking the soft stems with her fingers. A grasshopper leapt up from under her hand, startling her. She stood up straight and looked towards the house. It was exactly the same size and shape as hers, but where hers had fresh white walls with clean net curtains at the windows, here the dull red brick was unpainted, and the grimy windows seemed to stare out at her like an unwashed face. She thought it looked sad because it seemed unloved. She wanted to go into the house and tell it that she for one loved it, especially the garden which was so much more interesting than the neat patch next door that her father tweaked and fussed over every evening and every weekend.

Gosh, I'd love to play here, Leila thought. I would make up stories about elves stealing the plums from the plum tree and eating the eggs from the robins' nests. A man had come into school to tell them about birds and their nests, and since then Leila had spent a lot of time looking for nests in her own garden. Hers didn't seem to be the type of garden where birds wanted to build nests, though, and she was almost sure that this one was.

A cat, sitting at the edge of the path that led to the back door, eyed her with an unblinking stare. Leila approached it, stretching out her hand tentatively. The cat didn't move and Leila realised that it wasn't real. She knelt down to stroke it all the same and thought how lifelike it seemed with its gorgeous thick ginger fur and pretty green eyes. She stroked its eye which was shiny and hard, and then, out of curiosity, tried to stroke her own. A painful mistake, she immediately realised, as her eye reacted by snapping itself shut and watering violently.

"Careful, pet, you'll do yourself a mischief," Leila heard

someone say. She looked up through a blur of tears. A very old man stood at the back door, one hand resting on the frame. He stepped out and reached down a hand to Leila to help her up, before pulling a large white handkerchief from his pocket and offering it to her. She took it and mopped up the tears and the snot that was also dripping down her face. The handkerchief smelt of old people, a bit cabbagey, but it was nice of him all the same and Leila smiled.

"Thank you." She held out the wet handkerchief and the man took it and stuffed it back into his pocket. She looked at him. He had a kind, smiling face with thick white hair and a white moustache a bit like her grandpa's.

"You're Leila from next door, aren't you? I often hear you and your dad out there in the garden. How's your mother these days?"

"She's all right," said Leila.

"Ever get out, does she?" The man seemed to know Leila's family even though she was sure she'd never seen him before.

Leila shook her head. "No," she said. "She stays in bed. The doctor comes sometimes."

"Oh dear, poor thing. Well, give her my regards when you go back. Time for a glass of orange before you go?"

"Yes please." Leila was partial to orange squash. Her father would only buy lime-juice cordial because he said it was better for you, but as he was the only one who drank it it wasn't better for her. The man led the way into the house.

Leila stood in the kitchen and watched as he poured their orange squash into two glasses and produced from the cupboard a packet of custard creams, which he put on a small wooden tray.

"Shall we have it next door?" he said. "My wife's in there."

She followed him through to the living room, where an old woman was sitting asleep in an armchair, her hands and feet neatly crossed, glasses perched on the end of her nose, her hair arranged in an old-fashioned bun. She reminded Leila of a story she'd just been reading about a lady called Mrs Pepperpot.

"Won't your wife want some orange too, when she wakes up?" she whispered to the man. Leila knew about the habits of people who slept a lot – a drink was the first thing her mother asked for, even before the commode.

"No, pet, she won't." The old man put the tray down on a side table and eased himself into the other armchair.

Leila sat on the sofa and took a biscuit from the offered packet, nibbling it all round the edge to save the delicious creamy filling to the end.

"That's just the way I eat them too," said the man, and they nibbled away in silence. Leila liked the old man, she decided, and she was sure she'd like his wife as well when she woke up.

"Where did you get your cat?" she asked, thinking that she would ask her father if they could get one too, since pets, she had been firmly told many times, were out of the question.

"Well, I know this is a funny thought, but he was a real cat once," said the man, smiling. "His name was Binkie. Silly name, I know, but he was named after someone in a book that my wife had just finished reading."

"I don't think it's a silly name," said Leila. She had now separated the two halves of her biscuit and was eating the top section. "But how can he have been a real cat then and now he's just a pretend cat? That doesn't make sense."

"His fur is real. He had the most beautiful fur, and wonderful green eyes, and he was such a lovely cat that we decided to keep him when he died. The eyes are glass, sadly. You can't save the eyes."

"But when something dies it dies, doesn't it? You have to bury it, or something else where you burn it – that's what they did when my granny died." Leila leaned forward, gazing at the old man as she licked the custard filling off the bottom half of the biscuit.

"Cremate, yes. When it's a person you usually bury them or cremate them. But you see, pet, when you have an animal that dies you can have it stuffed by a special person and then you can keep it for ever."

"That's nice," said Leila, looking around the room. "So do you have any other animals like that?" and she explained that she thought her father might let her have a stuffed animal. "He says proper animals are dirty and smelly and need too much looking after and would do their business on the grass."

The man chuckled. "Well, that's true, pet, they would. They haven't learnt to use the toilet like you and me. And your dad must be very busy looking after you and your mother and that garden when he gets home from work."

"I suppose so," agreed Leila, looking longingly towards the biscuit packet. "Thank you," she said as the man passed it over. He took a second one himself, and the nibbling process began again.

"Leila! Leila! Where are you?" Her father's voice sounded anxious. Leila stuffed the biscuit into her mouth and leapt up.

"Better go, pet," said the old man, smiling.

"Yes. Thank you for the orange and the biscuits. And ... um ... can I come again? I like your garden and your cat, and –"

"Leila!"

Leila dashed out of the house and ran down the garden and scrambled through the gap in the fence.

"Hello, Daddy. Just been to see the people next door. They're really nice and they've got a cat called Binkie and –"

"What, old Mr and Mrs Briggs? Haven't seen them for years."

"Yes, and Binkie used to be a real cat but he isn't any more. He got stuffed by someone."

"Oh, of course, now I remember. Old Briggs used to be a taxi driver." At least, that was what Leila thought he said, but by now she was too busy climbing the ladder of her climbing frame to carry on the conversation. "Well, if you go and see them again," continued her father, "just leave a note in the kitchen or tell your mother where you're going so that I don't get home and find you missing, eh? Be a sensible girl."

"All right," said Leila, hanging upside down so that her hair swept the grass.

She often went into Mr Briggs's garden after that, and she and the old man would drink orange juice and eat custard creams together, and sometimes she would sit on his wife's knee and stroke her peaceful, sleeping face.

"I think we ought to read only the kind of books that wound and stab us."

Franz Kafka

The Mining Disaster

ALEX PRESTON

"If one man is fated to be killed by another, it would be interesting to trace the gradual convergence of their paths. At the start they might be miles away from one another – I might be in Pamir picking alpine roses and clicking my camera, while this other man, my death, might be eight thousand miles away, fishing for ruff in a little stream after school. I might be getting ready to go to a concert and he might be at the railway station buying a ticket to go and visit his mother-in-law – and yet eventually we are bound to meet, we can't avoid it . . ."

Vasily Grossman, *Life and Fate*

When the earth began to wrench and roil, we grabbed at solid things: stalagmites, wooden pillars, the heavy trucks that began to buck and rear on the tracks. Some of us lay down on the ground, huddled in tight curls as dust and rock showered from the roof. It was as if we were shipwrecked in a rolling ocean, and everything we reached for betrayed us, revealing itself as shifting and insubstantial. A breathless explosion, a rush of noxious air. Silence. We sniffed, our lips puckering. Firedamp reaching its foul fingers through the darkness towards us. Then a more precipitous shift of the earth and, with a groan and a roar, the coalface began to crumble, the tunnel floor disappearing with it. The trucks clashed and chimed as they toppled, throwing up sparks that threatened to ignite the gassy air. Falling men were visible in the yawning void only by the beams of their headlamps, like hopeless ropes thrown to shore. So many, so many tossed in the dark flood. In that second silence, we looked around. Eighteen lamps, perched on the lip of the abyss. Before, there were fifty of us. Below, now, we could hear running water, the lazy settling of the rocks, a single man calling out. *Mama, oh help me, Mama.* We clung to one another like children.

* * * * *

You don't remember your parents' faces. They are rounded up in the great Vél' d'Hiv' *rafle* of '42. The concierge hides you in the nook of a fireplace, a wardrobe hefted in front of it. You sometimes wonder why you can still remember the grain of the wardrobe's wood on your fingertips, the whirls and whorls that you trace in the darkness, and yet, when you look at the photograph of your parents that Madame Delphy gives you, slightly blurred, your mother in white organdie, your father in shirtsleeves, you can find no bridge that will allow them into your memory.

For the rest of the war the concierge keeps you concealed in her apartment. Madame Delphy has an ear for trouble and, whenever rumours circulate of a *rafle* or a *razzia* (the latter term adopted by Parisian police from the Foreign Legion's colonial adventures), she ushers you into the dark burrow behind the wardrobe. For days you crouch there, afraid to stretch or sniffle, cups of water and crumbling *tartines* passed to you by the kindly, quiet lady. Sometimes, when the light behind her seems blindingly bright after hours in the blackness, you think she's your mother come back to save you.

Madame Delphy is a collector, her rooms on the ground floor act as a glory hole into which flow the abandoned goods of the higher apartments. When someone dies, or, like your parents, disappears, the choicest pieces find themselves squirrelled down to rest in the care of the concierge. There in the dim and dusty half-light, you ride on a child's tricycle – too small for you – with a unicorn's head on its handlebars, squeaking between collections of quartzes and precious stones, Meissen figurines and antique dolls. Stopping to inspect the military paraphernalia, you fix a plumed shako, bobbing, on your head; then you wheel into the room of clocks, whose syncopated tickings accompany your first dance steps. You spend hours with the astrolabe, the barometer with hydrographic chart, the maps of the Ptolemaic constellations.

Most often, though, you sit at your father's roll-top desk, looking into the light well, waiting for the few minutes each day, fewer in winter, when the sun floods the building's shaft with brightness, and all the glittering things in Madame Delphy's collection come alive. Mirrors pass beams of light between them, the quartzes quiver and gleam, the nacreous inlays of pocket watches, jewellery boxes, cigarette cases commence a glowing dance.

Now when you're asked by a journalist, or during the introductory forays of a conference, before you begin to expostulate on horsts and grabens, magmatism and alkali basalts, what was it that brought you to geology, you speak of those few minutes of brightness, of the sun arrowing down into the light well, the shaft suddenly luminous. The regularity of those moments, the expectation and fulfilment, they have given a shape to your mind, a shading – height and depth, light and darkness – which you now find in the rifts and runnels of the earth.

* * * * *

We edged along the narrow ridge – all that was left of the tunnel – imagining ourselves on a mountainside above a roaring cataract, each urging the next not to look down into the blackness where, still, the dying voice of a man, his headlamp swinging from side to side in his agony. We reached the foot of the shaft where the tunnel opened out, allowing us to stand straight, to take stock of the devastation. Timbering and brattice all piled in sulking heaps. Shining our lights upward, we could see that the walls of the shaft had pressed together like two hands in prayer. One of us began to cry, and that was all right, because it drowned out the distant screams of the dying man, the rush of the water which had grown to a galloping torrent in the chasm below. Still the fetid fog in the air, the dust raining from the roof which caught in our beards, silted up our noses and mouths, crusted in the corners of our eyes. We stood there, looking hopelessly upwards, as if suddenly aware of how lost, how alone, how abandoned we were. Down there in the darkness, we could feel the movement of the hurtling earth, the lonely spin of our dying planet. In the silent blackness of the mine we could imagine how it will be when everything is ended, when the sun expires, and where once there were stars there is only an aching and eternal void.

* * * * *

You start school in the spring of 1946, Madame Delphy packing you off with your sandwiches wrapped in greaseproof paper, a cap skew-whiff on your fuzzy brush of hair. In the evenings, she greets you with a kiss and a *goûter* of hot chocolate and *langues de chat*. You sit at the kitchen table in close, happy silence. In 1949, she dies of a subarachnoid haemorrhage, and you win a bursary to the Collège Stanislas. Five lonely years in the scholars' dormitory overlooking the Rue Notre-Dame-des-Champs. The wind picks up speed over the Luxembourg Gardens, meets little resistance in the draughty shuttered windows of the dormitory, and gusts across the beds of the twelve boys. You shiver yourself to sleep. Then it is Jussieu, Paris Diderot, further research at the Sorbonne. You specialise in optical mineralogy and crystal structure, write a well-received paper on isomorphism in clay. You leave the Sorbonne before finishing your doctorate and take up a position at the Société de Peñarroya, swiftly rising to become Chief Mineralogist.

I can see you now, in a suit of grey worsted, your hair's unruly squiggles tamped by a felt fedora. On your face, a certain melancholy distance which means that your colleagues don't ask you to join them for coffee at eleven, wine at five. You return through dusky streets to the apartment you now lease on the third floor of the same block in which you grew up. You put music on the gramophone, lay your crystals on your father's roll-top desk (recovered from an antiques dealer on the Avenue Kléber), and turn them under the light of a green-shaded lawyer's lamp: uvarovite druses, dolomite geodes, pink pyrite vugs in which you place now one finger, now two, running your nails over the reticulated inner surfaces. You sit until the small hours of the morning, looking out into the shadowy light well, and the music plays on.

* * * * *

We knelt and prayed, extending our arms towards the crumbling roof, and soon we were covered in fine dust, like plaster icons. One of the men, Karel, wondered aloud if they would be heard, our prayers, from such a distance, through the strata of compacted rock. We ignored him and raised our voices above the roar of the water. Later, we crawled to the edge of the ravine and stared downwards, stretched out on our stomachs like young tykes spying on sunbathing girls. The black water reflected our torches, we saw occasional islands of coal and rock, soon swallowed by the rising flood. We were all struck by the abysmal horror of it – the depths, the darkness, the water. The river gushed up from the rocks to the western end of the ravine; we could dimly make out the point, off to the east, where it disappeared again under the earth, entering the mouth of a tunnel. The water had swept away the screaming man. There was no sound from above, no drilling or distant voices, only the sense of a whole forgetful world pressing down upon us. *We are lost*, Karel cried out, and no one would comfort him. I, the oldest among us, lifted my hands and began to pray again, sucking the afterdamp into my lungs and pouring out *De profundis clamavi ad te, Domine; Domine, exaudi vocem meam.*

* * * * *

It is in 1976, during a visit to one of the Société's opencast copper mines in Wallis and Futuna, that you feel the first jostlings of the obsession that will come to shape your life. Six miners have been trapped in a cut-and-cover trench, the wood of the support beams worm-rotted and friable. There, cupped in the palm of the mine, in the boiling heat, with the screams of the trapped men in your ears, you are hit with a vision that seems to come into your mind fully formed and thoughtless. You perceive how the surrounding geological stress of the rock might be used to support the tunnel, to free the men. You set a team working with rock bolts and mesh. You feel buoyed up, invincible. As the last stones are lifted away, you step like a god into the mouth of the cave and lead the men out, blinking, newborn, into the brightness.

If this were a film, I would show you first back in Paris, at a workbench, your pen a grey blur as you sketch cross-sections and geomechanical diagrams, early setbacks prompting greater leaps forward. Now, on a turning globe, Air France jetliners ferry you to disasters in Abidjan and Yaoundé, in Linares and Santa Cruz de la Sierra, to Dumas and Plainview. You are there, in khaki, a cowboy hat on the frizzy hair that is now zagged through with silver. The stones are rolled away – employing your patented method – and you step in, smiling, and lead the survivors out. You like to sit with them afterwards as they weep and hug their wives, press their damp cheeks to those of their bright-eyed children, lie with their heads in their mothers' laps. You remember the vision you had of your own mother, come to rescue you from behind the wardrobe as a child, and you want to be here for these moments, when all that was feared lost is recovered, and you can cry with them, press yourself into the soft heat of their love.

* * * * *

Some scenes from Tartarus: three days had passed. We'd finished our drinking water, the hard tack that one of us had kept in a pocket. Then the thirst came, and we looked down into the rising waters of that underground river and almost willed them upwards, even while knowing what would happen when the water crested the lips of the ravine. We all, at the same moment, imagined pressing our mouths into the last few inches of air at the top of the cave, the murky sight of each other underwater, our limbs drifting like weeds in the ghostly green. One of the men went mad. He ran at the mound of rocks and debris at the foot of the shaft, scrabbling at it with his hands, mewling like a cat. We had to tie him up. I drew my knife and cut lengths of rope, bound his feet and hands fast. His name was Branislav. A big, burly boy. When he continued to scream, rolling on the ground like an imbecile, I, as the eldest, took charge. Grabbing him by his bound feet, I dragged him to the edge of the rock face and pitched him off. His screaming didn't change one bit, not until he was under the water and gone. I turned to look at the other men. One of them shrugged. *Pray*, I said. *Branislav didn't pray hard enough.* All seventeen of us, on our knees again, offering up our alleluias and Hail Marys and *Anima Christi*s. I felt, inside me then, a knot of certainty growing. That this was what my life had been leading towards, that this flooding mine was to be the scene of my glory.

* * * * *

You are flown into Čáslav airport in a Breguet 941. Your assistant, Bruno, has radioed ahead with instructions to the site team. You are forty-six, single, wealthy. In the years since you began working at the firm, Société de Peñarroya has been taken over by DAMREC and then reverse-merged into the Imerys conglomerate, but your arm of the business – Mine Safety Solutions, S.A. – has continued its uninterrupted ascent. Now, as Germany slips by beneath, you sift through reams of file notes and technical data until you understand the situation in the collapsed mine down to the most minute detail, and this pleases you. You picture yourself as a surgeon operating on the heart of the earth: instead of scalpels, you have auger bits, instead of stents you have pipe-jacking. You are about to extend the metaphor further in your mind when the plane hits an eddy of turbulence, a delicious lurch where you feel the sudden precariousness of being airborne. Then the plane wheels down, down, like a gull, like a tern, and with three sharp bumps and a squeal of rubber on tarmac, you have arrived.

A car is waiting to hurry you along the *dálnice*. A ribboned functionary of the ČSSR sits beside you, asks you to sign documents ensuring *complete* – he jabs the word with his finger – confidentiality. You have worked with the Russians, you tell him. You know the drill. You smile; he doesn't. You lean back and look out of the window: a brief glimpse of the Elbe, then endless forests of melancholy white birches, drab towns rising like dreams from the flat landscape. A thick mantle of fog lies over the land around the Sokolov mine. You pass between two watchtowers poking up out of the murk. Intimations of the blasted landscape around. Then, as the car – a well-upholstered Dacia – slows, you make out through the fog the usual gaggle of press and politicians, the miners' families who stand in silent, watchful clusters. As you step out into the damp air, they look at you with fretful, fearful hope.

* * * * *

We lost another three men to the river. Two of them, brothers, Serbs I think (they muttered and grunted to each other, barely spoke to us), chanced themselves to the water. They stood on the cusp of the ravine like angels on the rim of a cloud, clasped each other by the hand and jumped. We shone our torches down upon them, but their grip must have slipped, because only one brother was visible, grabbing onto a slab of rock and drinking greedily, his face in the river like a pig in its trough. Then a surge of water and he let go, looking up at us, and we saw him disappear into the mouth of the tunnel. I imagined the two boys, like tongues in the river's throat, sliding onwards, onwards, praying for a break in the rock, then the release of breath, the white choke of the water, and still, even though life had left them, sliding on, deeper, in utter darkness. The third man – Karel – wouldn't pray with us. Now there were thirteen men left, and me. I held my knife in one hand. In the other I waved a cigarette lighter, tracing patterns in the afterdamp as we prayed: green and crimson and sulphurous yellow flames that shifted and glowed. As I wrapped the colours around me, I pictured myself as a bird of some deep paradise, decked in plumage of iridescent light. The men looked to me as their father, reaching up to touch my beard.

* * * * *

The collapse of the shaft proves more difficult than you'd imagined, the rock more porous and granular, the angles of incidence more acute. You install double telescopic jacks, relay bars, a reverse-mounted ram that begins to pump away at the knitted earth, throwing up great joyful clouds of rock and soil. You make a tour of the families, examining the wives in their damp eyes, letting your gloved hand rest on the heads of the children. After three hours, a breach is made in the rock and you oversee the insertion of steel castings. The shaft becomes wider, wide enough for the lift mechanism. You remove the yellow safety helmet and wipe a sleeve across your brow.

* * * * *

You insisted on being the first to descend. This was your indulgence, your *nekyia*: a trip to the land of the dead. The lift machinery clanked and thunked as you passed out of sight of those above ground. Rocks crumbled and shifted, but you were sure of the shaft's integrity, certain of your own calculations. You practised the face you would show to us, the saved – benevolent and wise. There were bottles of water at your feet, flashlights, medical packs. The lift reached the dusty floor of the cave with a rumble. A moment's pause. You could hear the rushing of the water, could see the river that was already slopping over the edge of the cliff; then you turned towards me.

* * * * *

It takes your habitual face a careful moment before it adjusts to the scene. I stand there, have been standing waiting ever since the first distant thuds came to us, five hours earlier. I have been writing your story. The air around me is plumed through with colour, great swirls of light that illuminate my blood-drenched beard. A shimmering green cloud seems to hover above me, brooding. At my feet, thirteen men lie, their severed heads placed carefully on their chests, their helmets still on, torches lit, so it appears that they each have three eyes, all sightless, open and staring endlessly towards you. Your mouth gives a wet little pop as you stare from one to the next and then to me, their father, the prophet of these dark reaches. I hold out my palm towards you, on which is carved a cross, deep-lipped lines peeling back from black blood.

I don't know if the tale I have invented for you is the right one, or if maybe the man now standing on the lift platform before me is instead a Silesian mine owner, a German medic, an English aid worker. But I am pleased with the shape and scope of the story I have given you, and so, when you try to speak, to cry out and reveal your language, I spring forward and press my bleeding palm across your mouth, my knife to your throat. Yours is the last body I heave into the water, the last head, too. I watch all of you go, my children, your bodies sinking, your heads bobbing for a while before the current really takes them, and you are sucked down into the earth's black maw.

I send the lift back up, empty. Then I stand in the heart of the technicolour clouds, running the point of my knife along the cross on my palm, keeping the wound dark and open, and I begin another story, my mind spooling out and up into the world of endless possibilities, the world above ground.

* * * * *

You are born in the military hospital in Prague – your father is an officer, your mother a ballerina at the conservatory, only just seventeen. Within hours of your birth, you are spirited through the snowy night to the Carmelites at the Cloister of the Infant Jesus of Prague. They name you Marek – no, Kazimir – no, Roman. Even as a child, you are drawn to wounded, fragile things. Now you step onto the platform that has appeared in the mouth of the shaft. You stand on the small metal lift and you begin to descend – clunk, clunk, clunk – and as I wait for you, my bloody beard dripping, the waters slopping, my palm held out, I tell your story.

Red Meat

KATE WHITESIDE

Diana is practising not being here. Her hands are pressed together and with her wrists they form a little archway across her stomach. She is still and silent, made of almost nothing, and what there is seems like it may be coming undone. She stands in the large, yawning hallway, looking at the door to Number 17 as if it were a person. She imagines what will happen if she knocks.

The door will not open quickly, as if the person inside has spent several moments with their eye against the peephole, unsure of who it is they see. This person, another woman, more substantial in presence and form, will open the door. Her feet will be bare, her hair perhaps slightly askew, and the expression on her face will say, "I was not expecting company." Music will be playing softly behind her, and a stale, smoky heat will belch out of the flat into the cold hallway.

"Yes?" she might say.

"Janice?"

"Yes?" Concern flexes Janice's brow.

"It's Diana. Diana Luther."

Janice will back up and let Diana into the flat.

Diana supposes the flat will be nice – what she knows of Janice leads her to believe that Janice must be a woman of considerable fortune and considerable vice. There might be trinkets collected from all over the world: things to cause outrage like figures of people copulating carved from rhino horn, or bras made of clam shells draped delicately over the back of chairs as if they're fresh out of the wash and might conceivably be worn, and have been left there by accident. Diana understands that Janice is a beast of a woman, and hairy in a way that rivals most men; there might be a pot of wax heating in the bathroom, or a lady shave on charge. She must hide these things during her sexual conquests, but if she is startled, Diana may glimpse her in her natural habitat. It might appear that Janice, in a flagrant disregard for the rules of femininity, does not often cut her toenails, and Diana will see this when Janice offers her a seat and sits opposite her with her legs crossed.

"So, Diana. It's nice to finally meet you properly. Can I get you a drink?"

Diana thinks that she'll only request a water.

"Cigarette?"

Diana will have to say no, as . . . well, she doesn't smoke.

Diana stares at the gold 17 on Janice's door and traces the number with her eyes as she tries to comprehend what might happen next. Her lips move slightly as she tries to get straight in her head what she might say.

"It's nice to finally meet you properly, too."

No, Diana wouldn't say that. She couldn't. Besides, she's met Janice more than once; only Janice keeps forgetting.

"I hope you don't mind me barging in on you like this. I mean, I hope it's not an imposition. You don't look like you're expecting company." Although Diana isn't brave enough to say this last part.

"No, it's fine!"

Janice is a plump woman, the kind of woman who looks fertile and whole and grounded all the time, vigour pumping around her large frame, emitting an unreasonable amount of warmth.

Diana knows that whatever happens after she knocks on the door, she mustn't cry.

"So how long have you lived here, Janice?"

Janice lights a cigarette, or perhaps she's already lit one and, if so, she rests it on the ashtray. Diana can see beads of sweat forming on Janice's brow. Perhaps, despite the apparent confidence, she knows why Diana is here and she's nervous.

"Days. Months. Or maybe years. I may have been born here."

Diana doesn't know what the answer to this question is.

"It's a lovely flat. It really is."

As Diana says this, she looks at whatever is the centrepiece of the room – a coffee table, a rug, an architectural chair – and she sees Peter sitting on it, nude and flushed with the thought of Janice and her buxom warmth, overflowing with her light and good humour.

"Thanks. I do what I can! I've picked up so much from all over the world, it's a wonder I've anywhere left to put it. It's getting cluttered in here, these days."

"Well, I know you're away a lot. In fact, I met you at the Hastings' a year or two ago. You'd just got back from a trip then. You were telling a story about Chile, or Morocco, or somewhere else exotic. Something about a coconut."

"A coconut? Oh, that must've been Thailand. They don't have coconuts in Chile or Morocco. In fact, if you look at a map of the dispersal of coconuts, you see they only grow on the left- and right-hand side of the world, not down the centre or very far north or south. They only grow on the world's love handles, I always say!"

Diana will laugh, nervously, though the joke she sees Janice making is exactly the same joke she heard her tell at the Hastings' that night a year or two ago.

Janice is aware Diana has finished her water, and after a few more niceties she hurries her out because she has to get ready to entertain in the evening; or because she needs to pack her bags since she's going to a party on the moon and must be at the spaceship no later than six, and wants to pick up some champagne on the way.

In her mind, she knocks again.

"Janice?"

"Yes?"

"Hello. It's Diana Luther. I met you at the Hastings' a year or two ago, and I've met you a few times since then. Can I come in?"

"Diana Luther? Yes, come in."

This time Janice turns her music off. The flat is similarly hot, and has a colourful, worldly aesthetic. Is Janice flushing?

"It gets so warm in here. I keep it warm to encourage other women's husbands to take their clothes off."

Diana and Janice both disappear. Outside the door, Diana thinks again. She imagines knocking once more. Her fingers twitch ever so slightly as she tries to imagine how it might go this time, as if she is playing the conversation on a piano.

"Yes?"

"Hello, Janice. It's Diana Luther. I don't know if you remember me. Can I come in? I'm sorry if it's an imposition."

"No. . . Do come in."

Things are different this time. On the mantelpiece Diana sees a coconut with a straw coming out of it and a pair of sunglasses on the bridge of what would be its nose, alongside all the other artefacts from the big wide world.

"That coconut," Diana begins. "That's very sweet. I always say something about coconuts and love handles, only I can't remember it right now."

"It's OK," Janice offers, "I know what you mean. It's my joke."

"Of course it is."

Diana walks the length of the living room, holding off her impression of Janice until she can think what happens next. Dutifully, Janice stands back, like a dog told to stay.

"Shall we take a seat?" Janice says.

That's it. Taking a seat means Janice can't rush Diana out. If Janice offers her a cigarette this time, she will take it and try to pretend to smoke it.

Sitting at the table, Diana has time. She must use it, she must disguise her shaking hand and her phony cigarette-smoking and she must calculate from second to second what it is that she wants to say.

"I –"

Janice interrupts.

"So, would you like anything to drink?"

"Oh. Yes. Just water, please?"

"Just water? I'll pour myself some wine if you don't mind."

"I don't. May I have a cigarette?"

"I don't smoke," Janice says. "Sorry."

"You don't? I could have sworn you did."

"Oh, just socially, sometimes. Food and drink, those are my vices!" she says, pulling down from the cupboard a bottle of red wine and slapping her thigh. The noise seems to reverberate around the flat, as if she were made of iron underneath that layer of flesh.

"Actually, I'll have wine too. Is it too late?" Diana sees that Janice has water in a glass already. Janice goes to pour it away. "No, wait, don't waste it."

Janice honks with laughter. "Waste it? It's only water, sweetheart. Have some wine."

"OK then. Thanks."

Janice fills the glass to the brim and gives it to her. Diana picks it up, awkwardly.

"Never trust a woman who doesn't drink!" Janice says as she lines up her own glass and pours a substantial amount. "I used to say, never trust a woman who doesn't drink beer, but then I developed a taste for wine. I also used to say, never trust a woman who doesn't eat red meat, but then . . . well, I plumb went right off steak for years."

Diana runs her thumbs over the bowl of the glass. "I don't drink much, really."

"Yep, I used to love steak, but then I was with this little bastard who didn't eat red meat on account of his heart, and so I stopped eating it too. You know how it is."

Diana makes a little noise of recognition.

"So then when I started eating it again, it just didn't taste the same. I mean, I don't care about my heart, but I fucking hate that little fella now, and every time I put a bit of good red steak in my mouth I think about him and his heart. And well, that just ruined it for years."

"You must be sentimental."

Janice swigs her wine. "No, it's not that. Besides, I'm back on steak these days. You can't let some pesky member of the opposite sex do a number on something so good. Ah, wait . . ." Janice pushes her thick body up from the table and snatches up a bag from somewhere else in the room. "I think I might have a cigarette, actually . . ." and after a few moments' fussing, Diana has a sad-looking cigarette in her hand.

"Perhaps I'll smoke it later," she says, and puts it down in front of her. "I don't eat red meat, really. Just fish, and a little chicken."

"Well, that's OK. I bet your heart's in finer shape than mine!"

"Maybe." After a few sips of her wine, she's become meek, quiet and tolerant. Diana knows this is what will happen if she says yes to any wine.

Diana, outside Janice's door, decides not to say yes to any alcohol.

Janice takes another glug of her wine, her throat moving unattractively up and down as it runs down her gullet. Diana sips at her water.

"My Peter likes red meat. Though I guess he eats less of it since we got married."

Janice smiles at her, continues smiling and looks at her glass. "*Your* Peter. Is that right?"

"Yes."

"Well, I live here alone. Nobody's food and drink habits to be worrying about except mine."

"You have a lot of company round, though. Don't you?"

"Oh yes. Plenty!"

Diana can see Janice entertaining a crowd of people and exclaiming, "Wife? Married? What on earth would trouble me about that? Besides, I've not even met the woman, and if you are going to shack up with a cheat then you'd better suppose you've got it coming," and drunkenly shouting, "Chin chin!" to which everybody laughs and tips their drinks down their throats. Diana shrivels when she thinks of her weight on the world versus Janice's. She has so carefully cultivated being pretty and thin that she forgot to be funny and interesting, and she hates Janice for this.

"I guess you have to give them what they want. When they come over." Diana sees Peter again, naked in the middle of the room, drinking as much wine as he wants and eating a bloody post-coital plate of rare steak and bacon.

"Something like that," Janice says. She is looking at Diana intently, which is not a surprise, seeing as whatever happens next is of Diana's making.

"Well." Diana takes a sip of her water and begins to thumb the side of the glass, as if something is stuck on it.

"I bought those glasses in Paris," Janice says.

Diana sees a maker etched on the bottom. It says "Janice's glass".

"I see," Diana says. "You're a big traveller, no?"

"Oh" – Janice waves the recognition away with her hand – "it just fills the time, you know."

"You're not in a relationship?"

"No."

"Don't you ever get lonely?"

Janice smiles at her. "Never. As you said, I have all the company I need."

"You don't have a husband, though."

"I'm not one for marriage."

"Not even a boyfriend?"

Janice continues smiling. "I guess I'm not one for that either." Janice drains her glass. "It's a funny thing, actually." She twists the lid from the top of the wine bottle and begins to pour herself more. "You'd think I'd miss it, or want it, but I don't. But I can see how someone like you might think that."

Diana can feel herself begin to blister from the inside out. She is losing control again and the idea of Janice is too big for her to get a harness onto and rein back in.

"'Someone like me'. Is that what you think of me?"

Janice is still smiling and holding Diana's gaze. "Of course. You got married and got a baby and such. But where is your fun? Who, Diana Luther, actually are you?"

"I never imagined I'd be up against someone like you. Ever."

Janice spreads her hands wide and purses her lips. Her underarms sway regally. "You need to get some more red meat in you."

"Is that your secret?" Diana takes another sip of her water.

Janice drains her glass again and fishes on the counter for the bottle. Her fingers are pudgy and the pads of skin splay out around the bottle as she grips it. Diana looks at her own fingers, so sharp and cold, like the hands of a china doll that no child would want to play with.

"I'm more real than you even when I'm not real." Janice rounds on her and snarls. Diana shouldn't have got Janice drunk.

"Back up a second, please." Outside the flat, Diana holds her temples as she tries to put the pieces back together.

Janice starts to laugh at her, starts to twist from side to side in glee, before, finally, she rears up and swallows her whole.

Diana leans against the door. She rearranges her sleeves, lifts her wrist but doesn't knock. Instead, she presses her hand on the varnished wood and thinks what may have happened this time if she had.

The door opens immediately.

"Yes?"

"Janice?"

"Yes?"

"Janice. It's Diana Luther."

Janice looks concerned. "Luther?"

"Yes. Well, Diana Luther."

"I thought it was Hannah Luther? Peter's wife?" Janice says.

"Hannah?" Diana says. "No . . . not Hannah Luther." Diana hasn't said Hannah's name in a while.

As she goes in, the heat in the flat this time is old, like the hours-old fug of radiators turned on for a set period of time earlier in the day. Perhaps turned on for an hour to heat up the bathroom before a shower. The smell of cigarette smoke is faint, as if somebody smoked just one cigarette a long time ago. The flat is not as grand as the hallway suggests. There is also a plate of food out on the counter. And a coconut on the mantelpiece.

"Oh," Diana says. "That's nice. Like an ornament. Where's it from?"

Janice closes the door quietly behind them. "That? It was a gift," she says, looking at neither Diana nor the coconut.

"Oh. Well. I suppose they're hard to come by. One must go to just the right parts of the world."

"Really?" Janice says. "I don't know where they grow. I can't remember who the hell gave it to me. In fact" – Janice picks up the coconut – "I think I should get rid of it." She thrusts it towards Diana. "Don't you?"

Diana flushes. "I don't know. I thought you said it was a gift?"

"Yes. I did say that." Janice looks down at the coconut in her hand. "Well, what should we do with it, then? Do *you* want it?"

"No, I . . . I've got nothing to carry it back in." Diana imagines herself walking through her own front door with the coconut and setting it on her own mantelpiece.

"Well." Janice rolls the coconut between her hands. "Maybe we should just put it away. So neither of us can see it," and Janice opens a cupboard and puts the coconut inside.

Diana stands in the middle of the room.

"Well," she says, "it seems a shame not to display it, doesn't it?" She opens her handbag and stretches it to test its length and width. "Perhaps I could fit it in here."

"Yeah?" Janice says, and a smile plays with the corner of her lips. "You want it?"

Diana wonders if Janice is making fun of her. "Yes. I'll take it home. Like I say, it would be a shame not to display it."

"Perhaps you're right." Janice is still smiling as she helps Diana fit the coconut into her bag. After they get it in there she struggles to close the clasp, and the whole bag looks bloated as if it has just eaten a large meal.

"Hmmm," Diana says, as she puts the bag on the floor. It's now too awkward to carry on the shoulder, though the coconut is lighter than she expected.

"Take a seat," Janice says.

Diana sits at the kitchen table and smooths her hands along the top. She can feel how rough it is, even through her gloves.

"Would you like some water?" Janice says.

Diana takes a minute to study her. She is slimmer than Diana remembers. Her hair is also pulled back into a bun this time, just like Diana's is.

"Yes," Diana says. "Thanks."

"You can take off your coat."

Diana doesn't want to embarrass Janice by implying that the flat is too cold. She takes off her gloves then wonders where her empathy has come from – why does she not want to embarrass this Janice? Before she has time to think, she has taken off her large coat and gloves and is shivering in the chair. Her expensive coat and gloves look out of place. In this sparse flat, the heavy brown fur commands more presence than most of the pieces of furniture.

Janice puts the glass on the table so that Diana has to reach for it. She takes a seat herself.

"So?" Janice says, waiting.

"So . . . we met a year or two ago, at the Hastings', I believe. You'd just got back from a trip."

"Ha!" Janice snorts. "Yes, I remember the Hastings." She

narrows her eyes at Diana. "I remember you."

"Oh," Diana says. "I didn't think you did. Well, I thought it was impossible."

"Impossible? Impossible how?"

"Well, I'm Peter's wife. That's how."

Janice takes a sip from her own tumbler of water. "Well, that's relatively obvious. Judging by your surname. It makes it so easy to distinguish people's wives." This Janice is so dour. And Diana can't imagine wild parties in this flat. Now Diana just sees some people sitting around talking about what an awful business stealing other people's husbands is. In fact, didn't Diana used to live alone in a place like this?

"I remember you having a good sense of humour. That's all I really remember," Diana says.

"You're the one that doesn't drink, aren't you?"

"Yes. 'Never trust a woman who doesn't drink beer' and all that."

Janice rubs her thumb over her chin, looking for hairs. "I guess people think you're self-righteous."

"Gosh. Do they? Is that what people think when you say you don't drink?"

Janice takes a huge gulp of her water. "Yep. I expect so."

"It's not that at all." Somehow, Diana's eye has turned back toward herself.

"It seems like that. There are so few pleasures in this world, and so little time in it." Her voice rings around the cold, empty flat. "Why deny yourself any of them?"

Diana feels a sting in her chest. She brings more water to her lips. "I'm scared you might be right."

"Do you think this water tastes metallic?" Janice says.

Diana looks at her silvery reflection in the glass. Janice holds hers up to her face so that one eye looks huge and bulbous. Diana takes another little sip. "Maybe," she says.

"I keep meaning to have words with the people who maintain this place. Water tastes dire. I can't be feeding myself that, let alone anyone else."

"Well," Diana says, and pushes the glass away from her, "perhaps I've had enough."

"Sure? Aren't you thirsty? I thought you might be parched, seeing how it seems like you've got something to say."

Janice is trying to rush Diana.

"Well," Diana says, and smooths down her skirt, "I do have something to say."

Janice looks at her expectantly.

"Perhaps I do need a bit more water." But as she reaches for the glass, Janice knocks it over.

"Don't go drinking that. It's poison. Weren't you *listening*, Diana Luther? Are you stupid or something?"

Diana's bottom lip begins to quake and a huge dam of sadness bursts within her.

"Peter . . ." she begins. "He's all I've ever had that's mine."

"That's not true. Now you've got a coconut."

"I shouldn't have come . . ."

Janice points her finger at Diana. She's been getting thinner and thinner this whole conversation. Her face starts to remind Diana of her own. "That's right. You shouldn't have come."

Diana starts to get up. She sees the plate of food on the counter. It is raw meat. "Perhaps I should go. Besides, it looks like you're about to eat."

"Not yet. My mother always swore by letting meat come up to room temperature before we eat."

Diana reels. "We? Peter . . . Is he here?"

Janice laughs. "God, you're funny. I could use your second opinion on the metallic water, you know. You could be my witness, of sorts. Wouldn't it be great to find someone with some money and be able to get out of here? Well, you should know."

"Please," Diana says. "We've got a baby now."

"You took the words right out of my mouth," and a baby's cry streaks out between the thin silence of the two women.

Diana is dizzy. She looks into the peephole and sees herself looking back. She turns without knocking and walks away.

"Like a tropical storm, I, too, may one day become 'better organised'."

Lydia Davis

The Authenticity of Ash Creek

JAMES MITCHELL

I n the end, Burn Day at Ash Creek was everything the brochure promised – that is to say, "an invigorating and authentic reconnection with the raw power of the elements". I did, as money-back-guaranteed, sense my animal spirit kindle at the sight of the flames pouring over the rise towards us, and I did, as I'd imagined, feel the sweat bead under my guest firehood at my throat and trickle down my cleavage in an Amazonian way. And when I looked across at Islington I did, as hoped, see something more than firelight in his eyes as he gathered up the hoses and checked the pressure. Yes indeed, I thought, there was something really real about the two of us together in that moment as we primed the hydrants, listened for the speakers to tell us to start dousing the trees, and struck a pose together for the photos we meant to pick up from the gift shop afterwards.

The things you remember from a moment are so oddly curated. Hot wind, a bird flying for its life, Islington mouthing something that could have been "Ow" or "How" but was probably "Wow". The tallest tree creaking, crying out and toppling; Islington with the grin he had whenever he did anything stupid, the smile he'd worn falling out of a Marylebone bookshop with nothing but a copy of *Oh, The Places You'll Go!* to hide his thing.

And for the longest second, our fingers touching, a pressure through the many foiled layers of the firesuits' gloves, and me wondering what romantic things must have happened in moments like these to people like us, who'd left their fully Venned social circles behind to go on the ultimate authentic journey together.

Islington saying "How now, brown cow," or similar. Me, just about to ask him what.

One Month Earlier, 60°F

The Volvo's radio filled the front seats with Balkan party vibes for a third consecutive hour of pine forest, rusted petrol stations, and wilderness – and I realised I'd made a bit of a breakthrough.

"Hey," I said, "we've heard this one before. Right?"

"Hmm." He lit another Marlboro – or as the bootleg pack stated, "Marlborough" – his first purchase once the men with bootbrush moustaches had thumbed through our passports, stamped them with ornate visas, and admitted us to the Eastern Bloc. "Could be. Check with your phone."

I protested that it was entirely the point of all of this that I specifically *not* check with my phone, and we should sit and wonder, and he nodded. But after another verse of wondering the pressure got too much and I whipped my phone out to look. Crisis averted; we *had* heard it before, and I now had two tags marked "DJ Sven" in my history, instead of one.

"Good to know," he said. "Yeah?"

"Mmh," I said, and focused on the road ahead because every sign looked the same, and if we missed the turn for Новосибирск we'd have to drive for another hour in Siberian dusk.

"It'll be fine. It'll be great!" was his refrain. Like the car, his optimism ran on fumes. He'd hiked across the Andes for a charity, and back for another; he'd studied Zen Buddhism in China when he was twenty; he'd even spent six months in Uganda building schools from clay recovered from the region's river – though they had to be re-rivered to make way for a hospital the next charity project wanted to build. The point is, Islington had stacked up a CV of enriching life experiences next to which Ash Creek must have seemed like just another bungee jump.

I saw the cracked sign that our guidebook said marked the turn to Novosibirsk, and Islington turned our little party bus down it. As he wiggled the car across lanes of honking traffic, I remembered those Russian dash-cam videos people are always sharing, how they always ended with a baseball bat through a windscreen.

We found a little motel just as it was about to close. A converted hospital; its turn-of-the-century architecture had been sterilised after the typhus epidemics, according to the leaflet in reception. The Russian maid bustled us up to the "Presidential Suite": a gilded, heart-shaped bed faced the TV, which blared an overdubbed US comedy into the room. As the maid turned to go, I asked her: "Ash Creek?" She stared at me, blankly. I showed her our brochure. She shook her head and said something like "Shest chaznov": six hours.

As the studio audience whooped at a buffoonish dad falling over, I asked Islington if he was worried. He took a mint from what was surely a kidney dish, and smiled.

"They must have done a hundred Burnings there now. It's all been tested."

Still. A hundred and one is just asking for trouble, surely. Good luck doesn't need pushing.

From day one as a couple, we'd had the misfortune of everything working out exactly according to plan. Both with good enough degrees to get good enough jobs, so that he (IT Infrastructure Solutions) and I (Market Research) could get a good enough flat, and quietly decompose in it. In catalogues, there's always a woman lying on her three-piece suite, laughing with gay abandon. That's what we became, human props in a catalogue. Not on purpose; more the mission creep of a single, innocently purchased object. Buying one coffee table on John Lewis ("Anselm"), and slipping down the vortex of "People who bought this also bought" until we had a furnished apartment.

Life was as frictionless as I could want. We established that recycling was collected on Thursdays, garden waste on alternate Tuesdays. We joined the Neighbourhood Watch. We followed "Ten tips for a perfect Garden Party" (*Observer Monthly*) and enjoyed regular gatherings of cordial murmuring and laughter. Clearing up one morning (a snap thanks to #7: Paper Plates), Islington looked up from fiddling with the Sonos.

"Seen this?"

In the list of WiFi networks on his phone, just after good old SKY82A78, was: Couple In Flat 3 Watch Some Porn Already.

Well.

Islington showed me his favourite sites. Men always have them: you can't clear the cache of the mind.

"I didn't think they could be that long."

He coughed.

"Hmm?"

"WiFi names."

So we took a night class in Sexual Anthropology. Another of our phases, to go with Bikram Yoga, Urban Knitting, Analogue Photography – on ice.

He never knew that I had an almost-lesbian phase – every young modern woman's rite of passage – because one of the mutually understood benefits of baggage is that it can be stuffed, sat on until flat, and locked. But the instructor who greeted us as we finally drove through half an hour of Park Security checkpoints and up to the Ash Creek Visitors' Centre was a study in asexual elevation. If we had a war now – a proper war, not one of those last-item-in-the-news things – and they needed to remake that poster urging women to work in the munitions factories, they would have called Stacey from Ash Creek AuthentiFire to be the model. I'd expected another matronly Russian *gornichnaya*, all rolling pins and Baltic swear words, but Stacey looked like she'd just got back from Venice Beach. Later, we found out she essentially had, "visiting Mom" in Sacramento. A strong chin, hair tied back with a rag, sleeves rolled up to show just a hint of lightly muscled definition. Stacey: ABC1 mid-20s female, body of a gap-yearling; likes: rock-climbing, trucks, freedom. She opened the driver-side door and pulled Islington out.

"The Islington party?" she twanged.

"That's me." Islington gave her a fist bump.

"And I'm Melissa," I said.

Stacey showed us the visitors' training barracks, our yurt, the five-acre grid of wood set aside for our group, and the gift shop: all toy extinguishers and hatchets, and a giant cuddly brown bear in suede. "No actual bears in the reserve, though! We're very safe?" said Stacey. She pointed out the window and across the taiga, at a cruel-looking fence. "Electrified, for your comfort. Let's see the hoses next. That's what the men normally like." Islington gave me a campy game-show smirk, as if to say "Innuendo alert!" Stacey walk-bounded over a ridge, the pistoning of her buns dragging us in their wake.

That night in the barracks we emphatically agreed how nice it was that Stacey hadn't worn her professional veterancy on her sleeve, that despite having clearly gone through the routine so many times before at AuthentiFire she treated our only visit like her first. It was seriously important, we both said, not to let the moss of cynicism choke your life. Hence, Ash Creek. Hence, the training.

After Camp Breakfast, we ten new visitors sat in a semicircle of grey plastic chairs for the briefing. Some were dressed for the occasion, most were not. One had a notebook and a sort-of quill pen with a biro end. I really did try not to assess our fellow campers, but, you know. You can take the girl out of Marketing, but . . .

"I know what you're thinking," said Stacey, giving our briefing the full Camp America treatment. "You're thinking, 'Oh, safety, boring, right? I mean zzzzz and such, like I would actually rather die in the dry heat of a flash fire than listen to this chick for another second.' Right?" She laid her head on her hands like a pillow and did a little joke-snore. The group giggled to acknowledge her routine intro-gag.

"But I promise you," said Stacey, doing a little squat, "that I have trained almost fifty groups since we opened this reserve, and *absolutely nobody*" – she made a fist, her bicep twitched – "has been seriously hurt. Tabitha, why do you think that is, sweetie?"

The sweetie (Tabitha: 6–8 years old; likes: horses; dislikes: boys) looked uncertainly at her mum and dad (cotton, wool, sustainably sourced handmade fibres, probably American, probably rich), who nodded. She mumbled something unintelligible but Stacey clapped her on the shoulder and said, "That's right! Because of *safety*, people. The local laws of Novosibirsk Province and AuthentiFire International prevent me from guaranteeing your safety on a *Literal and Binding level,"* she said, dragging out the italics, "but I assure you that if you listen carefully and practise the drills we've laid down for you, when Burn Day comes and we light up that reserve and your personal forest fire comes rushing towards you, you'll know exactly how to put it out – and what's more, you'll feel more gosh-darn alive than the day you were born, excuse my language."

She rocked back and forth on her booted heels as if she were literally too alive to stand still.

"Any questions?"

A man in business sandals put his hand up.

"Is it sustainable?"

"Sustainable's tough for us, you know? But we carbon offset?"

The first Saturday evening at camp, after equipment maintenance and dinner, we sat in our big group in the communal yurt, swapping our stories and singing the Camp Song we'd been taught. Tabitha's parents were indeed rich, and while she snoozed on her mother's lap the mother told us that what they wanted for her was a taste of the hardships and dangers of a life less fortunate than theirs, an understanding that Mother Nature and Father Time were cruel parents who could take, take, take where previously they might give, give, give without heed of karma, morality or succour, all within a family-fun context.

"Isn't that right, David?" she said, and slapped his phone hand in chastisement.

"I gotta forward this joke to the board, honey."

The woman, Martha (AB1 female; likes: baking, the environment, coffee-table art; dislikes: visible poverty, David), turned to the group for assent. The two gap-year lads, Jack and Mike, were still singing the song –

> *Oh, Ash Creek, we love thee so!*
> *Your mountains high, your valleys low!*
> *We'll never let you go-ooo,*
> *Your liability is void.*

– only now they sang it as a round. Islington had joined in, a vodka-infused echo for each line. He'd spent a lot of time talking to Jack and Mike: they were in the throes of their freedom years, at the height of something that men never quite recover once it's lost. But maybe it's transmittable.

Three Weeks Later, 71°F

With just seven days left until Burn Day our clockwise walks around the perimeter became twice-daily. They weren't as exciting as the brochure made out – three hours of unbroken security fence on the right and spindly trees lined up on the left like overthrown Tsarists waiting for the firing squad. You'd have expected little Tabitha to lag behind, but she led us, gazing up at Stacey in fascination. Just once, after pestering, Stacey let her wear the peaked Marshal's cap. Tabitha had to hold the forest-green thing away from her eyes lest it slip down, but she gave off a commanding air.

"Look at that," said Martha. "David, look."

"Hah!" said David. "Holmberg got passed over for the Partner role. Uh-*gain*. Ow!"

He said "Ow" because Martha had put an elbow into his abdomen.

"Looks like she's found her vocation," said Business Sandals. "How about it, Tabitha?"

Murmurs of encouragement rang round the group. You could see her back straighten, her shoulders pull from her hair like Stacey's did until she snapped a 180 to face us. Her gaze, suitably couraged, made me think of the possible daughter I'd wondered about before. She eyed the wavering treeline, then her charges.

"Troop!" she barked.

We snapped to mock-attention. Islington shouted, "Yes ma'am!" the way he sometimes did to me when he took out the bins.

Stacey watched, the sketch of a smirk twisting her lip. Tabitha scanned her new recruits, marched up to Quill Pen. He was gazing at the trees and writing in his journal, again.

"Trainee! Atten-*shun*!"

He started. He looked actually afraid of this girl, but then Islington and I had privately decided that he was afraid of women in general. Tabitha eyeballed him, then found a lecturing position on a blackened tree stump. Quill muttered something about Man's longing for the denarratived bleakness of the veldt.

Tabitha gave us the Safety Talk we'd heard every day. Not a bad job, really: she misremembered the Safe Standing Distance and Required Water Pressure, and a few other things, but it felt good to notice that she had, because that meant I hadn't.

Unless she hadn't, and I had.

All the way back, I couldn't stop reciting her mangled Stop, Drop, Roll.

Drop, Roll, Stop, she'd said.

I was thinking that if you dropped into a diving roll at a moment's notice, how silly it would look, and how you wouldn't really know where you were rolling. And then once you were doing that, why would you just as suddenly *stop rolling*? What would that achieve, just not rolling any more? If you were to cease rolling in life, without cause, what would you be? Just a person lying on the ground, timbers falling around you and no oxygen left? What would come after Stop?

I wondered.

On the last night – Burnmas Eve, to Islington – Tabitha came into our miniYurt.

"Mom and Dad are fighting," she said. "They sent me here."

Islington seemed to grow an inch taller, his mouth set steely but his eyes smiling. Yes, he would be a good dad, as long as he didn't think about it.

"Tabitha, just in time. We're checking our suits for tomorrow."

Responsibility dried her eyes, and she sat next to us and picked up the foil jacket marked "MELISSA". She made a face.

"Ours are nicer," she said. "No rips."

No doubt. Their maxiYurt had cable TV, too. No overdubbing.

"Well then," I said, "you'll know what a good one should look like."

I passed the silver tape and a pair of scissors over. I assumed we would pay her lip service and let her paw over our gear until she got bored, but Tabitha was meticulous, using every sense to check my suit's integrity. She held the backcloth up to the lamp, watching spots of light appear in the tiny tears and sealing them up with care. She ran her fingers, finer than ours, along the seams inside the sleeves, and gasped whenever she found a rip. When she finished Islington's she made him try it on, "for fit".

"Spin around!" She giggled.

Islington revolved, the light catching his fabric like a disco-ball sacrifice. Tabitha explained that if she had time she'd have tried to nip in the waist a little bit, and we laughed. Islington asked if perhaps she had a business card, if we could send our stuff to New England for alterations. She said she didn't, but she'd make arrangements to have one printed. She gave Islington a hug, and his eyes caught mine, though it's not even like I was angling for them to be caught, I'm almost sure of that.

Tabitha stayed with us long after the curfew gong bonged around the contours of Ash Creek. She said her parents were probably still fighting. So we toasted marshmallows: gummy, injection-moulded product we'd picked up at a service station near Tselinoyarsk.

"Your dad'll be pleased," I said, pointing at the firesuits hanging on the canopy frame. "All brand new like that. We'll be safe as anything."

"Won't know. Never listens to me." Then she said, biting through a chunk of marshmallow-polymer, "He prolly dun know I'm hurr."

Islington flushed, like David was going to march in that second and cuff him, then drag his daughter away. He took out his phone, the way he always does when he wants to avoid conflict. I was opening my mouth to tell him off but he held it up so the repaired firesuits were in the phone camera's frame, whole and complete.

"Tabitha," he said, "what's your dad's email address?"

Burn Day, 572°F

My first thought in that last moment was: It was weird, how all pork was pulled nowadays. When did people start pulling pork, and why? What did "pulling" even mean? It was strange that we had never bothered to find out. The golden tassels on our curtains: what for? Why did self-checkouts say goodbye to you as if you'd take it personally otherwise? Why were we there? All these questions were equally important.

We'd been cut off. I'd been about to ask him what he was saying, when a grizzly bear (likes: fish; dislikes: poorly controlled forest fires) leapt the electrified fence behind us, foaming and raging and licking its burns. In its scrabbling lope it tore the feed line shooting water down our hoses, and the life-giving pressure slackened to a dribble. The nozzles were perfect; we'd checked them at dawn as per Stacey, but we had no control over what happened further up the line. I gripped Islington's hand, all questions suddenly merged into a nameless single "?" and we backed away from the bear, circuitously but inexorably towards the outlier blaze. Towards the fauxthenticity of Ash Creek, which was, in fact, a mountain and was, in fact, covered in spindly and fast-burning pines. I had a flash of the other holidays we could have taken.

The inferno of the taiga was crying. Crying like a TV-family reunion. Or two huge documentary icebergs melting together. Or, well, what else is there to say? The wall of heat screamed of the absolute, a constant roar, replacing all the processes the trees had known – swaying, breathing, growing – with one process, the burn. The fire breathed the wood in and breathed a trunk of smoke out. A chevron of birds broke rank and scattered around the subliming forest, but came together on the other side as if the separation appalled them. The ground at our boots hissed, throwing off the last of the damp from the hoses.

A little girl's cry cut through the sound and behind a security fence, safe but screaming, I saw Tabitha. Her eyes wide, her mouth hanging in terror. Her mum and dad – especially her dad, and I felt relief at that – trying to pull her away but her banging at the fence. I wanted to shout "Don't look, sweetie," but my inhalation curled a plume of black smoke inside my firesuit's hood, bringing me to my knees.

"Remain calm!" Stacey's voice crackled over a loudspeaker. "We have a procedure for this sort of thing!" Then a burst of static, and silence. But maybe we just couldn't hear any more: the flames were almost arching over our heads now, the Safe Standing Distance long broken.

Islington's hand shook. He mouthed, "It's like a . . ." Then trailed off.

I'm sure I was supposed to scream. But that didn't feel right.

Incomparable splendour, the brochure had said. And it was

as we lay there, holding hands and searching for analogies, that the fire took us and we became another line in the world's energy equation, a line that included the dry pines around us, the dying bear in the undergrowth, the cabling and the brochures, the dry hoses and the firesuits' broken promises, the engagement ring in Islington's pocket and the camera in mine all equalsed together into a final value, returned as charcoal, his smile and all my words, my eyes reflected in his, Melisslington, likes: the birds, the trees, the ash, the leaves, the sky, the endless whys, the proteins and protons the family and friends the end the sun the sum.

"Once we believe in ourselves, we can risk curiosity, wonder, spontaneous delight, or any experience that reveals the human spirit."

e. e. cummings

Notes on
Contributors

Talim Arab was born in London and grew up in Queensland, Australia. He studied English Literature and Chinese at the University of Queensland. His poetry was Highly Commended by the 2006 Arts Queensland Thomas Shapcott Award for an Unpublished Manuscript and received third place in the 2001 Arts Queensland Val Vallis Award for Unpublished Poetry; he won the State Library of Queensland Young Writers Award (2006). His short story "Toe Deep in Water" was published in the US magazine *Pif* and recently his poetry was part of the Deep Desires & Broken Dreams exhibition at the Hammersmith Studios, London. He is currently writing a novel about the Indian-Fijian experience: a British Indian-Fijian family planning a memorial dinner set against the looming 1987 Fiji coup. He has a passion for ballet, Bösendorfer pianos, cosmology and zoology.

Julia Bell is a writer and Senior Lecturer at Birkbeck, University of London where she teaches on the Creative Writing MA and is Project Director of the Writers' Hub website. She is the author of three novels – most recently, *The Dark Light*, to be published by Macmillan in May 2015 – and co-editor of *The Creative Writing Coursebook* (Macmillan, 2001) as well as three volumes of short stories, the latest being *The Sea in Birmingham* (Tindal Street Fiction Group, 2013). She also takes photographs; writes poetry, short stories, occasional essays and journalism; and is the co-curator of spoken-word night In Yer Ear.

Mary Bracht is a part-time MA Creative Writing student at Birkbeck. She studied Cultural Anthropology and Psychology at the University of Texas at Austin, and worked as a research assistant in Psychology studying primate bones. Upon moving to London, she rediscovered her love of art, music, theatre and above all, writing. Her first short story, "Tatter'd Weed", was published in Issue 8 of *The Mechanics' Institute Review*, she has been longlisted for the Fish Short Story and Memoir prizes, and has had a thriller, *The Tarot Killer*, published by Eternal Press. "Escaping Time" is an excerpt from her current novel-in-progress. Her website is www.marybracht.com.

Martyn Bryant is from Windsor, UK. He holds two Masters: an MSc in Physics from the University of British Columbia, Canada, which he received in 2007, and an MA in Creative Writing, from Birkbeck, University of London, which he received this year (2014). Since completing the MA he has moved to Montreal, Canada and has had short stories published in *Feathertale* and *Ryga*, and non-fiction (book reviews and interviews) published in *Rover* and the *Montreal Review of Books*. In addition to writing short stories he is working on his first novel, which was partly developed at the Banff Centre four-week Writing Studio under the mentorship of Greg Hollingshead and Josip Novakovich. http://martynbryant.wordpress.com/

Desmond Byrne was born in Dublin but has lived in London since 1986. He is a professional tattooist, has just completed the Birkbeck Creative Writing BA and is currently working on his first novel. A disciple of what he terms "the holy trinity" of Joyce, Beckett and Nabokov, he also sees in his work the possibility of a happy marriage of George V. Higgins and George Eliot.

Paul Flack grew up in Stevenage, Hertfordshire. He has an MA in Creative Writing from University College Chichester and attended a course in novel writing at Birkbeck. He now works in London, writes on trains and sleeps in Surrey. After writing enough short stories to make a collection, he finished his first novel, a dramatic coming-of-age story set on a French Mediterranean island: a restless young Welshman searches for his estranged, yet influential, older brother, as he begins to wonder which of the people in his life he should really be thankful for and which not; a young local woman adds to his dilemmas. The inspiration for the imaginary island was Corsica and its thrilling mix of mountains, beaches and wildlife. When Paul can resist writing more short stories, he's developing a Gothic novel. His work has appeared in Issue 9 of *The Mechanics' Institute Review* and at Liars' League.

Julia Gray is a writer, singer-songwriter and teacher. She has a degree in Classics from UCL and a Post-Graduate Certificate in Children's Literature from Birkbeck, where she is currently completing an MA in Creative Writing. She has written the text for a children's picture book about the endangered Arabian leopard, which will be published by Stacey International in September 2014. Her first solo album, *I Am Not The Night*, was released in 2011 and described by *Word Magazine* as "the sound of a potential realised". Her second album, *Robber Bride*, was released in June 2014. A collaboration with award-winning South African producer Paul Ressel, and recorded with the support of Arts Council England, the album explores how stories can be retold in song. Julia is currently working on a YA novel and is represented by Louise Lamont at LBA Books. She can be found at thisisjuliagray.com.

Melanie Jones is a photographer and English tutor from the south coast who now lives in London. She is currently completing her Creative Writing Master's at Birkbeck. Melanie has been writing short stories for many years and has worked collaboratively with a small group of South London writers. Her work has appeared on the Writers' Hub and she has read at Hubbub. Melanie is now working on her first novel, a mystery set in a Welsh commune.

Walter Jones was born in 1970 and grew up in Johannesburg, South Africa. He moved to London to work as a digital designer in 2000 and has since worked as a freelance writer – writing articles and reviews for various online and offline publications, and publishing work in the 2014 issue of *45 Square*. Walter is currently working on his first collection of poems.

Sara Keene has had a long career in show-business PR, first as a film publicist and more recently as the press representative for a number of actors and directors. She has worked on films as varied as *An American Werewolf in London*, *The Last Emperor*, *The English Patient*, *Hamlet*, *American Beauty*, the Harry Potter series, *The Reader*, *Sherlock Holmes*, *My Week with Marilyn*, *Anna Karenina* and *Skyfall*. She co-founded the entertainment PR agency Corbett and Keene, which morphed into Premier. She is in the second year of a part-time Creative Writing MA at Birkbeck.

Born in London, **Hari Kunzru** is the author of the novels *The Impressionist* (2002), *Transmission* (2004), *My Revolutions* (2007) and *Gods Without Men* (2011) as well as a short-story collection, *Noise* (2006), and a novella, *Memory Palace* (2013). In 2003 *Granta* named him one of its twenty best young British novelists. His short stories and essays have appeared in diverse publications including the *New York Times*, *New Yorker*, *Guardian*, *London Review of Books*, *Granta*, *Book Forum* and *Frieze*. He was a 2008 Cullman Fellow at the New York Public Library and is a 2014 Guggenheim Fellow. He lives in New York City.

Len Lukowski is a transgender writer and performer living in South London. He has had short stories published in *Chroma*, *Aesthetica* and *The Coelacanth Journal*. He is an occasional contributor to the music website Drowned in Sound. Between 2004 and 2009 Len played and co-wrote songs in the queer synth-punk band Jean Genet. In 2011 he formed the band FAGGOT with fellow writer Swithun Cooper and they have been playing together ever since. He is currently in his second year of a Creative Writing MA at Birkbeck and is working on a collection of short stories. He can be contacted at lenlukowski@gmail.com.

Vanessa MacDonald was born in Scotland, but grew up in far northern California. It was from this California background that her story "From Redview" was created. She writes poetry and short stories, and is currently earning her BA in Creative Writing at Birkbeck.

Dave McGowan was born and bred in South-East London and has moved home twenty-seven times in fifty-one years. He's worked nights in a petrol station, been a brickie's labourer, the world's worst painter and decorator, an artist's assistant, a DJ, a cook, a photographer, a baker and once wrote a joke for the telly. He has a grown-up daughter. He likes to explore dark alleys, old buildings and foreign cities. He's been writing for a few years and has a series of short short stories on the Birkbeck Writers' Hub. He is the co-founder and host of In Yer Ear (https://www.facebook.com/InYerEar), a literary evening held on the last Tuesday of the month at the King and Queen in Fitzrovia.

James Mitchell is an advertising strategist and writer of speculative fiction. His work has appeared in *Universe Magazine*, *Kill Screen* and *The Stoneslide Corrective*, as well as the occasional YouTube pre-roll. His writing carries on behind the scenes at saladonions.tumblr.com, and you can tweet him at @jamescmitchell.

Sonya Oldwin used to be an online editor for a travel website. Having a child gave her an excuse to quit – online travel writing sounds much more glamorous than it is. She is currently in her final year of study on the Birkbeck Creative Writing BA. Her short fiction has been published in two anthologies – *100 RPM: One Hundred Short Stories Inspired by Music* and *Scraps: A collection of flash-fictions from National Flash-Fiction Day 2013* – as well as online on FlashFlood. She is currently writing a novel.

Alex Preston was born in 1979. An author and journalist, he lives in London with his wife and two children. His first novel, *This Bleeding City*, was published by Faber and Faber in the UK, and across twelve further territories. It won the Spear's and Edinburgh Festival first book prizes as well as being chosen as one of Waterstones New Voices 2010. His second book, *The Revelations*, was shortlisted for the *Guardian*'s Not the Booker Prize. His third, *In Love and War*, was published by Faber in July 2014. Alex appears regularly on BBC radio and television. He writes for *GQ*, *Harper's Bazaar* and *Town & Country Magazine* as well as for the *Observer*'s *New Review*. He studied English under Tom Paulin at Hertford

College, Oxford, and holds a PhD on Violence in the Modern Novel from UCL. He teaches Creative Writing at the University of Kent and regular *Guardian* Masterclasses. He is @ahmpreston on Twitter.

Josh Raymond graduated from the Birkbeck MA in Creative Writing in 2008 and still meets with The Unwriteables – eleven other graduates of that course – every Friday in term time. His non-fiction piece "The one that got away" was voted one of *Prospect*'s top ten articles of 2010 and nominated for a Foreign Press Association Media Award, and his fiction has appeared in *The Mechanics' Institute Review* and *Tales of the Decongested*. He reviews books for the *TLS* and is working on a novel.

Antonia Reed grew up in England and Southern Germany. She studied English at the University of Cambridge, specialising in medieval literature, both English and Italian. She then completed the Birkbeck Creative Writing MA in 2013, alongside her employment at a London charity. In her writing, encounters with prejudice, loneliness and being "different" – whether in real or supernatural terms – have always been her primary interest. Her work – which includes short stories, articles, poems and a play – has been published online, in anthologies, *emagazine* and other journals; featured by the Short Film Movement; and performed at two theatres. She is halfway through writing her first novel, about a group of young outsiders trying to escape persecution in medieval Europe. Among other projects, she is also working on a contemporary story exploring family loyalty, the complexities of cultural identity, and sexual taboo. For more of her work, visit www.writershub.co.uk, www.antoniareed.wordpress.com or Twitter @_Antonia_Reed_.

Rebecca Rouillard was born in Oxford but grew up in Durban, South Africa. She has just completed a four-year Creative Writing BA at Birkbeck and has been the Managing Editor of the Birkbeck Writers' Hub for the last three years. Rebecca's writing has been published in *Litro*, *Even Birds Are Chained to the Sky & Other Tales*, *Wooing Mr Wickham*, *45 Square* and *46 Square*. Her short stories have also been performed by Word Theatre at the Latitude Festival, at writLOUD, and broadcast on Resonance104.4fm. The first chapter and synopsis of her novel were shortlisted in the Lightship First Chapter Competition in 2011 and she was a runner-up in the 2014 Writers & Artists Historical Fiction Competition.

Angela Shoosmith has a BA in English from the University of Michigan, a Master's of Library and Information Science from Wayne State University and has recently completed her MA in Creative Writing at Birkbeck. She has worked as a children's, adult and digital librarian as well as in communications for local government. Originally from Michigan, she's lived in London for the past eight years with her husband and, now, daughter. Her current focus is on pursuing a career in writing and publishing, with a novel-in-progress about identity loss, the boundaries of marriage and how social media can alter and shape character.

Jacquelyn Shreeves-Lee is currently undertaking an MA in Creative Writing at Birkbeck and feels the course has transformed her understanding of the art of writing. In her stories she tries to unzip human universes and connect with the reader in a way that makes reading an active, visceral experience. When she's not writing, Jacquelyn works as a clinical psychologist and is very fortunate to work with two outstanding community charities, Face Front and Kids Inspire. Currently working on a collection of short stories, Jacquelyn is never more herself than when she's writing. It gets her every time, the way squiggles on a page can cause someone to laugh, shudder or cry; she calls short stories small miracles. Jacquelyn lives with her two sons in North London.

Dave Wakely was raised in South London and Surrey before gaining a BA in English from Loughborough University. Since then, he has worked variously as a musician, a university administrator, a poetry librarian, a web developer and a learning-materials author and editor in locations as disparate as Bucharest, Notting Hill and Milton Keynes. He currently works as a blog writer/editor and journalist and is nearing completion of his part-time Creative Writing MA at Birkbeck, during which he has performed at Hubbub events and as a member of the Birkbeck Poets at the Duke of Wellington. His story "GJ 526.1 A" appeared in Issue 10 of *The Mechanics' Institute Review*. A collector (and player) of stringed instruments and an enthusiastic home cook whose kitchen is his sanctuary, he lives in Buckinghamshire with his civil partner and far too many guitars. http://theverbalist.wordpress.com

Jennifer Whitehead is a third-year student on the Birkbeck Creative Writing BA course. She grew up in Australia and has lived in London since 1995. She works as a freelance journalist and editor and has started writing her first novel. Her influences include Joanna Newsom, Jane Campion and Deborah Treisman. Say hello to her on Twitter @jenniferw.

Kate Whiteside is based in South-East London and divides her time between her creative projects and working for a prominent charity. Currently an MA Creative Writing student at Birkbeck, she produces copious amounts of short fiction and has just completed her first screenplay, an indie feature set in small-town New Jersey. She is currently working on a novel about loneliness and online deception, also featuring aliens. While Kate has an affinity for exploring the disconnected, the disadvantaged and the dysfunctional in everyday life, her style aims to create levity through absurdity.

Angela Wray is originally from rural Essex, and has lived in France, Germany, Durham, London and now Cambridge. She writes novels and short stories, works for a property company selling châteaux in France, and dreams of pedalling off on an adventure. She is very keen on swimming and finds its mindlessness conducive to plotting.